Praise for *Va

"New and extraordinary . . . Go read this!" —David Weber

"Fans of C. S. Forester's Horatio Hornblower will delight in discovering Baker's Sikander North." —*RT Book Reviews* (starred review)

"Baker's military background only serves to raise this adventure above the rest." —*Kirkus Reviews*

"This new series gets a grand start with fine attention to the details of starship engagements and operations, plus plenty of action as well as depth of character." —*Booklist*

"*Valiant Dust* is an excellent example of military SF at its best." —Michael A. Stackpole, bestselling author of *Rogue Squadron*

"Interesting characters, high attention to detail, diverse cast, [and] nuanced politics." —*Sci-Fi Fan Letter*

"In the finest tradition of Honor Harrington, Black Jack Geary, and Nicholas Seafort . . . an exciting new entry that fans of the genre won't want to miss." —Dayton Ward, bestselling author of *24: Trial by Fire*

"Intelligent space opera with lots of vivid action . . . sociological novel which examines the problems (on both sides) of a third-world aristocrat in a first-world navy whose hierarchies are equally rigid." —David Drake, author of the Hammer's Slammers series

"Intensely satisfying. Bravo! I look forward to more exploits of Sikander North!" —Ed Greenwood, creator of Forgotten Realms™

"An excellent mix of military action and political intrigue." —Eric Flint, author of the 1632 series

Tor Books by Richard Baker

BREAKER OF EMPIRES
Valiant Dust
Restless Lightning
Scornful Stars

RICHARD BAKER

SCORNFUL STARS

TOR

A TOM DOHERTY ASSOCIATES BOOK
New York

SCORNFUL STARS

Copyright © 2019 by Richard Baker

A Tor Book
Published by Tom Doherty Associates
120 Broadway
New York, NY 10271

www.tor-forge.com

Tor® is a registered trademark of Macmillan Publishing Group, LLC.

The Library of Congress Cataloging-in-Publication Data
is available upon request.

ISBN 978-0-7653-9079-0 (trade paperback)
ISBN 978-0-7653-9080-6 (ebook)

Our books may be purchased in bulk for promotional, educational, or business use.
Please contact your local bookseller or the Macmillan Corporate and Premium
Sales Department at 1-800-221-7945, extension 5442, or by email at
MacmillanSpecialMarkets@macmillan.com.

First Edition: December 2019

Printed in the United States of America

0 9 8 7 6 5 4 3 2 1

FOR ALEX AND HANNAH

Be fearless, but remember to be kind.
The world needs a little more of both.

A shadow down the sickened wave
  Long since her slayer fled:
But hear their chattering quick-fires rave
  Astern, abeam, ahead!
Panic that shells the drifting spar—
  Loud waste with none to check—
Mad fear that rakes a scornful star
  Or sweeps a consort's deck.

Now, while their silly smoke hangs thick,
  Now ere their wits they find,
Lay in and lance them to the quick—
  Our gallied whales are blind!
Good luck to those that see the end,
  Good-bye to those that drown—
For each his chance as chance shall send—
  And God for all! Shut down!

—Rudyard Kipling, "The Destroyers"

SCORNFUL STARS

PROLOGUE

DS *Carmela Día*, Bursa System

The pirates' third shot cracked *Carmela Día*'s warp ring. That was the moment when Master Pilot Jimena Marron knew that the big freighter wasn't going to get away after all.

"Shit, shit, *shit*!" Captain Varga slammed a meaty fist on the arm of his acceleration couch as alarms wailed all around the bridge. "We lost the warp ring!"

No kidding! Jimena wanted to scream back at the freighter's captain. She hardly needed Varga to tell her what the shrieking alarms and flashing lights meant. The first shot, of course, had been a warning. She'd ignored it, running for the safety of Bursa's inner system and ramming the throttle to the stops to coax a few more g's of acceleration from the straining drive plates. She evaded the second shot with an emergency deceleration, but there was no hope of dodging the third.

"Mayday, Mayday!" Second Officer Molnar had started calling for help the minute they'd spotted the strange ship. "This is the Pegasus-Pavon drive freighter *Carmela Día*, eight point seven AU from Bursa Primary! We are under attack by an unidentified ship and urgently require assistance. Please send help! Mayday, Mayday!"

The pirate vessel—an old drive tug refitted with heavy armor and military-grade kinetic cannons—had been waiting to ambush ships arriving in the outer reaches of the Bursa system. If *Carmela Día* had cut her warp generators just a few seconds early or a few seconds late, she would've unbubbled millions of kilometers farther away from the pirates, and they might have had a chance to outrun them. Instead, Jimena's accurate navigation brought them back into real space less than two light-minutes from the spot where the pirate vessel sat drifting cold and dark, waiting for a potential victim to show up within a potential pursuit envelope. Given the immense size of any star's outer system, she had to imagine that a hundred ships arrived in Bursa for each one that happened to cut their generator in a spot where the pirates had a chance to attack. Today, it seemed, *Carmela Día* was that one ship in a hundred. *Unless they knew our sailing plan, in which case bad luck had nothing to do with it*, she fumed.

Jimena drew a deep breath, fighting the wave of pure panic threatening to freeze her where she sat. She was a professional, after all, and she meant to do her job until the moment it became absolutely, finally clear that there was nothing more she could do. Recharging the warp ring for a microtransit had been their only real chance to escape the attack—there was no way *Carmela Día* was going to outrun anybody with a full load of ore on board. "Think, Jimena, *think!*" she berated herself. "If the warp ring's gone, what's Plan B?"

"Mayday, Mayday!" Molnar repeated, beginning his distress call again.

"Good luck with that," Jimena muttered under her breath. The nearest outpost was forty-five light-minutes away; *Carmela Día* wouldn't receive an answer to Molnar's distress signal for an hour and a half. Even if one of Bursa's patrol cutters was on the right side of the planetary system, it would take thirty or forty hours to reach *Carmela Día*. Whatever was going to happen would be long over by then, which was why Captain Varga had been trying to get the ship into the safety of a warp bubble.

Until, of course, the pirates blew a hole through the freighter's warp ring.

"Helm, come left to course three-four-four, and cut your thrust fifteen percent," Varga ordered, recovering from his frustration. "We need some spare acceleration for evasive maneuvers. They'll be aiming for our drive plates next. Do your best to dodge their fire." He really wasn't a bad captain, not in Jimena's eyes—he'd spent a few years in the Bolívaran navy a long time ago, and he'd been working freight runs since she'd been in diapers. What Emil Varga didn't know about being a merchant spacer wasn't worth knowing; as a rule, Pegasus-Pavon hired good skippers.

"Three-four-four, eighty-five percent thrust," Jimena echoed automatically. She fixed her gaze on the sensor display and let her hands hover above the helm panel, already planning the next move she'd attempt to make the pirates miss. Unfortunately, bulk freighters weren't built for the sort of maneuvers needed to dodge a slug of tungsten alloy moving at a couple of thousand kilometers per second without extreme good luck. And it seemed they'd just used up the last of that.

"They're signaling us, Captain," Molnar reported, his voice shaky.

"Goddamn it." Varga sighed, bowing to the inevitable. "All right, Luis, patch it through. Let's hear what they've got to say."

"*Carmela Día*, this is the ship twenty-five thousand kilometers on your starboard quarter," the pirate said over their comm, addressing them in Jadeed-Arabi. He had a Zerzuran accent and a cold, smug tone that sent a shiver down Jimena's spine. "In case you haven't noticed, I just shot out your warp ring. You aren't going anywhere, so cut your acceleration to zero, stop calling for help, and stand by to be boarded. Do anything stupid, and I'll punch holes in your ship until you're helpless and board you anyway. But that would piss me off, so I don't recommend it. You tell me how you'd like this to go."

Varga activated his comm unit. "This is Captain Emil Varga. Who am I speaking to?"

"You can call me al-Kobra. We're the *Balina*—maybe you've heard of us."

Jimena didn't recognize the ship's name, but her Jadeed-Arabi was good enough to decipher the captain's alias. *The Snake*, she noted. *Of course. What else would a pirate captain be called?*

"We're a bulk freighter hauling a hundred and forty thousand tons of ore," Varga said. "You're hijacking crushed rocks, al-Kobra. Our cargo's not worth your time."

"I know a market where I can get five hundred credits a ton for the refined rare earth ores you're carrying. I'm not real good at math, but let me see . . . that's about seventy million credits of crushed rock. And I'm sure we'll find something else worth our while over there once we have a good look around—spare parts, whatever lithium-c you've got left in your magnetic bottles, maybe someone worth holding for ransom. At least, you'd better hope that we do. Oh, and I'm still waiting for an answer, Captain. How do you want to do this? I have to tell you, I'm not a very patient man."

Varga hesitated.

"Don't do it, Captain," Jimena said, keeping her voice down to avoid being overheard if any of the mics were hot. "You let them on board, they'll gut our engines, empty the bottles, wreck the comms, and leave us adrift and helpless—and that's assuming they don't murder each and every one of us for the pure fun of it."

"We don't have a choice," Luis Molnar shot back. "If we don't put up any more fight, they'll have no reason to kill us. They'll take what they want and go."

"Including any crew members that happen to catch their eye," Jimena said. "Thanks, but no thanks. I say we break out the small arms and fight it out when they try to board us. Let me throw the ship into a three-axis tumble, it'll take them an hour just to get a launch alongside an airlock."

"Help's too far away, Jimena," said the old captain. He punched his armrest one more time, and then shook his head. "They can spend the rest of the day holing each compartment in the ship if they want, and I've got to think about saving lives. Helm, cut acceleration to zero. Luis, secure the distress calls."

Jimena scowled at her helm panel as she zeroed *Carmela Día*'s induction drive. "God, I hope you're right."

"Me, too." Varga tapped the console again. "*Balina*, this is *Carmela Día*. Hold your fire. We're complying with your demands."

"Smart choice, Captain Varga," al-Kobra replied. "Leave your bridge, and assemble your crew and passengers in the mess deck, unarmed—and I mean every single soul on board. If we find that one person stayed at their post or tried to hide, you're all going to pay the price. Do you understand?"

"Assemble in the mess deck, aye. I won't be able to hear your communications there."

"Doesn't matter, Captain. We'll be face-to-face in just a few minutes. And, just in case you've got any funny ideas, remember I've got charged and loaded K-cannons pointed at you. At the first sign of trouble, I open fire, and I won't stop until I'm certain that I've killed every living thing on your ship. Now get moving."

"We're leaving the bridge now," Varga replied. He cut the comm pickup, and shifted to the ship's internal announcing system. "All hands, this is the captain. Report to the mess deck, *everyone*. We can't stop the pirates from boarding us, so we're complying with their demands. We're going to be robbed, but there's no reason to get ourselves killed. Stay calm, do what they say, and we should get through this. Varga, out."

"*Balina* is maneuvering to match course and speed," Jimena reported. "I think they're going to send over a launch instead of docking ship-to-ship."

"No resistance, Jimena," Varga said. He got up from his acceleration couch with a heavy wheeze. "Secure your helm, and clear the bridge. Mess deck, everybody—now."

Jimena locked out the ship's helm, resisting the temptation to throw the freighter into an awkward tumble despite the captain's order. She didn't like their chances, but Varga had made his decision, and it wasn't her place to take that choice away from him and the other twenty people aboard *Carmela Día*. That didn't mean she'd go along with anything the pirates cared to do to her or her shipmates, though. When she left the bridge, she turned to the left and headed for her stateroom instead of going straight back to the mess deck.

"Jimena," said Varga, pausing to look after her.

"Give me a minute to get myself together," she told him. "*Balina* is still twenty-five thousand klicks behind us. If I'm going to spend the rest of the day standing around in a compartment wondering when I'm going to be raped or killed, well . . ."

He winced. "Ten minutes, then. I'm not going to give them any reason to fucking kill us, okay?"

"I know." She hurried back to her room while the other two members of the bridge team headed aft. She could hear other crew members sobbing in panic, shouting in anger, or clattering around their own rooms as they tried to hide their valuables or do whatever it was they thought they had to do before the pirates boarded.

When she reached her quarters, she changed into the dirtiest jumpsuit she had in the laundry bin, rubbed grease into her hair, and threaded her brown ponytail through a battered old ball cap. She didn't think she was any great beauty, but she had a feeling that pirates who spent weeks waiting in empty space might not feel terribly picky about female companionship. Jimena didn't have any special valuables in her stateroom—at least, nothing that would interest a pirate looking for loot—but she rolled up a wad of Bolívaran bills and tucked it into one sock in case she needed a bribe later. Then she slipped a snub-nosed 6.6-millimeter mag pistol into an inner pocket of the shipboard jumpsuit. She'd owned the gun for years and hadn't ever needed it before today, but a woman working in rough-and-tumble spaceports needed to be ready for anything. *I don't care what the captain says*, she told herself. *If it comes down to it, I'm not going down without a fight.*

She heard the thump of a boat at the superstructure airlock just as she reached the mess deck. At a quick glance, all twenty-two crew members appeared to be in the compartment; no one was missing. *Carmela Día*'s hands sat at the mess tables, some silently staring at the bulkheads, some sobbing softly, a handful murmuring prayers. About half were Bolívarans and half were Velarans, with a few Zerzurans and more exotic nationalities mixed in. A couple were new faces Jimena didn't know very well yet and a couple were frankly assholes she wished she didn't know, but overall it was a good crew, responsible and well-seasoned. They'd never had any serious trouble before; the sight of her shipmates scared out of their minds did more to unsettle her than anything else that had happened yet. She took a seat at the end of a table, and jammed her hands under her arms to wait.

"Oh, God," someone whimpered. "What are they gonna to do with us?"

"Steady, there," Varga said. "Keep it together, everybody. We'll get through this."

"They're here," one of the engineers said, and nodded at the starboard-side passageway.

The pirates sauntered into the compartment—eight of them, carrying flechette guns or mag pistols to cover *Carmela Día*'s crew. All of them were men, some young and cocky, a couple old and gray-bearded, and to Jimena's surprise they didn't look all that different from the freighter's crew. They wore battered old spacer's jumpsuits, work boots with magnetic soles, tool belts from which dangled the same sort of hand tools *Carmela Día*'s deckhands often carried, and vac helmets clipped to shoulder straps just like ordinary spacers. *But they've got K-cannons on their ship and they're all carrying guns*, she reminded herself. And there was no mistaking the cold confidence or the predatory grins they wore.

One of the pirates—a tall, fit-looking fellow in his thirties, with dark hair and a short goatee—stepped forward. "Very good," he began. Jimena recognized his voice: al-Kobra, in the flesh. "A smart decision. Which of you is Captain Varga? Stand up and let me have a look at you."

Varga pushed himself to his feet. To his credit, he didn't hesitate a moment. "I'm Varga."

"Have your people line up against the bulkhead, there," al-Kobra said, pointing with the muzzle of his gun. "Face the bulkhead, hands on the bulkhead above your heads. You stay where you are, Captain. No tricks, now."

"You heard him, everyone," Varga said in a weary tone. "Everybody line up."

Silently, the freighter deckhands got up and shuffled over to the bulkhead, finding places to put their hands up. Jimena followed her shipmates, preparing herself for the worst. Several of the pirates hung back, keeping *Carmela Día's* crew covered, while the others holstered or slung their weapons and moved up to begin searching their captives. They weren't gentle about it—wallets, billfolds, jewelry, and the occasional knife or hand stunner clattered to the deck, and at least one of Jimena's female shipmates farther down the line yelped in pain as the outlaw searching her gave her breast a hard squeeze.

"Hah! Look at this one!" one of the pirates gloated. Halfway down the line from where Jimena stood, the big bald-headed man yanked Szonja Hadik—the ship's third engineer, a slender blonde with a pretty face—out of the line and spun her around by the arm to show her off to his fellows. "I think we'll have some fun with her. What do you say, al-Kobra?"

"Not bad," the pirate leader allowed. "Get her out of those overalls, I want a better look."

The big pirate grinned and reached for Szonja's zipper. She screamed in fright and tried to pull away, until he cuffed her with one hard fist. "Stop that nonsense, you little bitch," he snarled.

"What the hell is this?" Captain Varga roared. He wheeled on al-Kobra. "You said you wouldn't hurt anyone if we gave up. Get your hands off her!"

Al-Kobra frowned. "Huh. I don't remember saying anything like that." Then he raised the muzzle of his flechette gun and fired two blasts into Emil Varga's belly at a range of less than a meter. Blood and shredded flesh splattered the deck behind the freighter's captain, who staggered back and collapsed with a horrible groan.

"Son of a *bitch*!" Jimena snarled. She reached for her hidden gun—

—and the rest of the pirates opened fire.

1

Sikander Singh North reined in his roan quarter horse at the top of the ridge and gazed out over the spectacular red-rock mesas of the Kharan Desert. The morning air was cool and clear, but he could feel the first warm stirrings of a breeze that would blur the horizon with orange dust by midafternoon. Over the course of geological ages, that same wind had carved the sandstone hills dotting the rugged landscape into weird spires and fluted curves; he'd spent many long days in the saddle exploring the picturesque rocks as a boy, pretending they were castles or alien ruins. *That was a long time ago,* he reflected. He hadn't visited the North estate at Chittar Creek since the summer he'd turned fourteen, and that was more than twenty years behind him now.

He slid down from the saddle and walked a few steps out onto the rocky overlook, kneading at the small of his back. Horseback riding demanded very different muscles from just about any other exercise he knew, and he hadn't been riding in a long time. Behind him, his brothers Gamand and Manvir rode up and likewise reined in to share the view.

"I always liked this spot," Manvir said, leaning over the pommel of his saddle. Three years younger than Sikander, he favored their mother, with a light frame and an easy smile. "On a good day you can see all the way to the Pir Panjals from up here."

"I remember," Sikander replied. "A little hazy this morning, though. Too bad." He'd visited dozens of worlds during his Navy career, but he'd seen few ranges that could match the Pir Panjals. Like their namesakes on Old Terra, Srinagar's mountains topped six thousand meters and wore a shining coat of snow and ice throughout the year, but the nearest peaks were almost two hundred kilometers from the North family's corner of the Kharan.

"The breeze is picking up early today." Gamand, five years Sikander's senior, took a long drink from his canteen. While Manvir took after Vadiya North, Gamand was the spitting image of their father Nawab Dayan North in his prime, tall and stern and as taciturn as his younger brother was affable. Unlike the younger Norths, Gamand observed *kesh*, wearing a full beard and leaving his thick black hair uncut. He never went out in public without the traditional turban, but in the privacy of the North estate he literally let his hair down a bit, pulling it back into a long ponytail he threaded through a Sangrur Dragons cricket cap. "Time we were heading back, anyway."

"Soon," Sikander said. "I want to soak it in just a little bit longer."

"When do you go back to your ship?" Manvir asked him.

"The end of the week. *Decisive*'s scheduled to finish up her repairs in ten days, and we'll be getting under way for a shakedown patrol soon afterwards. I'll have a lot of work waiting for me."

"Well, that's what you've got a crew for, isn't it? Let them handle the details."

"I try to, but it's customary for the captain to make sure he gets back from leave before the ship goes anywhere. The Admiralty thinks that it sets a good example." Of course, it was more than just setting an example—Sikander *wanted* to get back to *Decisive*, to study every square centimeter from bow to stern and reassure himself that the Neda Naval Shipyard had executed every action item on the repair schedule with the diligence and care he thought his ship deserved. *Decisive* might be an old and well-worn destroyer, but she was Sikander's first command—in fact, the first major combatant of the Aquilan Commonwealth Navy under the command of any Kashmiri—and during the ten months he'd been her captain he'd come to love her with a depth and protectiveness not even his family could easily understand. He suspected that most officers felt the same way about their own first commands.

"I'm just glad you had an opportunity to come home," said Manvir. "Dishu and the children really enjoyed your visit—the kids loved seeing their mythical Uncle Sikay."

"Par and Tani are great kids." Sikander grinned back at his younger brother. Manvir Singh North had gotten married seven years ago, shortly after Sikander's eventful deployment aboard CSS *Hector*. He already had a five-year-old son and a two-year-old daughter. Sikander, on the other hand, had no particular prospects for marriage at the moment, nor did he have the slightest idea about when or if he'd ever have children. Thanks to a career that sent him to distant stars for months or years at a stretch, he'd met his newest nephew and niece only a handful of times. Parsan and Tanuvi were young enough to be delighted by everything around them most of the time and easily comforted when things weren't going their way. "You're truly blessed, Manny."

"Just wait until they're teenagers," Gamand warned. His boys were fifteen and thirteen, respectively. They'd both wanted to join their father and their uncles at Chittar Creek for a couple of days, but they were in the middle of their school terms and had some grades that needed improving, so Gamand and his wife Falina had ordered the boys to keep to their studies. As far as Sikander understood things, some amount of domestic strife had ensued before Gamand and Falina prevailed.

Sikander snorted at the idea of his older brother dealing with teenage rebellion. If there was a rebellious bone in Gamand's body, he'd never seen it. "You know, it's strange," he said after a moment. "When I was a teenager, I didn't really like coming to Chittar Creek. I thought it was boring. I resented leaving my friends in Ishar to spend weeks out of each summer in a hot, windy, orange desert. I wasn't even all that excited about spending a few days of my leave to come here this week. But now that I'm here, I'm surprised by how much I missed it."

"Really? I've always loved this place," said Gamand. "Life's a little simpler out here. The older I get, the more I appreciate that. And with Father's illness, well, we've all been spending more time on Srinagar. The climate's more comfortable for him."

Sikander glanced over to Manvir. "I've been meaning to ask you about that, Manny. How is he doing?"

Manvir doffed his hat—an outbacker with a wide brim—and ran a hand through his hair. "Not as well as I'd like, to be honest," he said. Like Sikander, he was a younger son, and he'd been expected to use the opportunities provided by his family's wealth and education to do something with himself. Sikander had chosen military service; Manvir had studied medicine, becoming a doctor. "Modern genetic therapies can handle most cancers pretty easily, thank goodness. But Father doesn't feel that genetic medicine is in keeping with *amritdhari* beliefs, so he insists on fighting his lymphoma through chemotherapy and radiation treatments. They're better than they were centuries ago, but they take a toll."

"We've tried to persuade him to accept Aquilan genetic therapy, but he's adamant," Gamand added. "As long as he can keep the cancer in check with other types of treatments, he wants to remain observant. In the meantime, I've been doing what I can to lighten his workload."

"Not a day goes by in Ishar without Gam cutting a ribbon on some project or another," said Manvir. "He sleeps with a pair of scissors under his pillow just in case something comes up in the middle of the night. The other day he accidentally opened a library in Kupwara when he missed a turn on his way to lunch."

"I bet." Sikander suspected that Manvir was more worried than he let on; he'd always been one to deflect difficulties with a little humor. "What about Devin? Has he been in touch at all?"

"Devindar and Father still aren't speaking," said Gamand, scowling into the distance. "It hurts Mother quite a lot. She never gets to see Devin's girls anymore, and she misses them terribly."

Sikander frowned. A small dust devil on the valley floor caught his attention; he watched it for a moment. Of all his siblings, he felt closest to Devindar. They were less than two years apart in age, and they were a lot alike in both looks and temperament. Fortunately neither Devindar nor Nawab Dayan had ever tried to make him choose sides in their seemingly irreparable break, but the fact remained that no gathering of the North family these days was complete. Devindar refused to be under the same roof as their father for even the shortest visit, and Nawab Dayan carried on as if his second son had never existed. *Life is too short to be that stubborn,* he reflected. *But neither of them knows how to give any ground, at least not where the other's concerned.*

"Sikay? You with us?" Manvir asked.

"Sorry, just thinking." Sikander brushed the trail dust from his clothes, returned to his patient horse, and swung himself back up into the saddle. "I'm ready to go."

Three more kilometers brought them to the Norths' desert home at Chittar Creek. Sikander enjoyed a rare lazy afternoon at the comfortable lodge, splashing in the pool with Manvir's children, visiting with his parents, and playing cards in the evening after a dinner of grilled vegetable kebobs.

The next morning, Sikander's mother headed back to Jaipur with Manvir and his family, while Sikander joined his father and his older brother on a business visit to the city of Mohali Bay, a thousand-kilometer flight from the Kharan Desert.

Nawab Dayan dozed while Gamand worked, so Sikander entertained himself by gazing out the window; he'd never visited the west coast of Harsha, Srinagar's smaller continent. While the North family owned estates on both of Kashmir's terran-type planets, he thought of Jaipur as his homeworld. Srinagar was a place he visited or vacationed in, an older world of dazzling blue skies and white cities that gleamed in the sun, and it always struck him as arid and mountainous in comparison to Jaipur. Long ago, the Anglo-Sikh colonists who'd settled the Kashmir system had chosen Srinagar as their first home because the planet, while uncomfortably hot and dry in its torrid zone, was immediately habitable. Neighboring Jaipur had required two centuries of terraforming to make its smothering atmosphere comfortable; it remained warm and humid in comparison to most other worlds Sikander had visited.

"What are you looking at?" Nawab Dayan asked.

"The mountains." Sikander had thought his father was asleep. *God, when did he become so thin?* he asked himself. *He's lost twenty kilos since the last time I was home.* Nawab Dayan had always been the very picture of health—tall, strong, sick not a day of his life until his cancer diagnosis. Well-off Kashmiris routinely lived to see their hundred-and-tenth birthday, so Sikander had always assumed he wouldn't have to worry about losing a parent for another thirty or forty years. Now . . . now he was not so sure. He concealed his concern with a small shrug. "I've never been over this part of Harsha."

The nawab peered out the window, getting his bearings. "It looks like we've already crossed over the big peaks. Hmm—I must have been napping."

Sikander glanced back at his father, and found himself remembering another flight they'd shared years ago. *It was when I came home after my transfer off* Adept, he recalled. *Thirteen years ago, right at the end of the Bathinda Strike. We were on our way to Ganderbal.* Summer thunderstorms had marched their way across northern Ishar that day, and the turbulence—

—jars Sikander awake. He glances around, getting his bearings after his catnap, and realizes the other Norths in the cabin—his mother Vadiya, his sister Usha, and of course his father Nawab Dayan—are watching the large vidscreen at the front of the cabin, now tuned to a news channel. It shows a parliamentary building surrounded by grav tanks and soldiers in the uniforms of the Chandigarh Lancers; more soldiers escort civilian prisoners in restraints down the courthouse steps, leading them away. The crawl at the bottom of the screen identifies the scene as the Bathinda State Legislature.

"What's going on?" Sikander asks. "What did I miss?"

"Devindar's been arrested," Usha tells him.

"Arrested?" He comes fully awake at that news. "Why? The strike's over!"

"Yes, but . . ." Usha glances at their parents; Sikander's mother watches the news feed with silent worry, but Nawab Dayan turns away from the screen and picks up his dataslate, ignoring the newscast. Usha sighs, and continues. "A group of armed KLP activists occupied the state legislature building an hour ago. They issued a statement condemning the agreement that resolved the strike, and then surrendered when the Chandigarhi soldiers arrived."

Sikander sits up, watching the screen. Sure enough, the very next activist escorted down the steps is his brother Devindar, holding his head high. The text crawl identifies him for any viewer who doesn't know him by sight: Nawabzada Devindar Singh North of Ishar.

His mother hides her face, but says nothing. "This makes no sense," Sikander says, speaking more to himself than to his family. "Taking over a government building by force? He'll go to prison for certain!"

"That appears to be the point of this exercise in stupidity," Nawab Dayan growls. It seems he is listening, after all.

"Can you do anything, Father?" Usha asks him.

The nawab shakes his head without looking up. "If Devindar chooses this path, then it's not for me to pardon him. I will not intervene."

Sikander begins to protest—Devindar's been married for less than a year, and he and his wife Ashi are expecting their first child. A warning look from his mother stops him before he speaks. Vadiya North can say more with a simple glance than some people convey in a ten-minute speech, and for once Sikander is wise enough to pay attention. What Devindar has done isn't simply a family matter; it's a political question for the nawab, and his father must address it as such. "Damn it, Devin," he growls under his breath. "Why do you have to make everything a fight?"

Nawab Dayan coughed loudly, bringing Sikander back to the present moment. Sikander and Gamand both looked over in alarm, but the nawab cleared his throat and shook off whatever had troubled him. "I am fine," he said with a flicker of annoyance. "Are there mountains on Neda, Sikander? What is it like?"

Sikander relaxed again. "Neda? It's mostly ocean, so its mountains are islands. The naval base lies in the tropics. The beaches are nice, and the fishing is excellent."

"What is Aquila's interest in the place?" Gamand asked.

"Strategic, mostly. Neda's near the border between the Caliphate's Zerzura Sector and the Velar Electorate. It's a good spot for a fleet base on the rimward side of the Caliphate, and it protects important shipping routes. There are a lot of old quarrels in the region—systems that aren't happy with their Caliphate or Velar overlords, independence movements, that sort of thing. The Admiralty believes that an Aquilan presence helps to stabilize the area. Plus, pirates are a problem. I expect we'll spend most of our underway time engaged in antipiracy patrols."

"Pirates?" Gamand snorted. "I've never understood how a ship with a warp generator could let itself be boarded. A few seconds in a warp bubble should be enough for even the slowest freighter to escape."

"Charging a warp ring takes time, Gamand. On *Decisive* it usually takes us an hour or more. Freighters are bigger than destroyers, so they need larger rings, more time, and more charging matter—which is quite expensive, I might add. Commercial vessels don't like wasting a charged ring. Anyway, a freighter threatened by attack may need several hours before it's ready to establish its warp bubble. That's the window during which a pirate can make his approach, and the first thing he does is fire on the freighter's warp ring to make sure it doesn't bubble up."

"Fine, then. So why don't the powers in the region hunt down the pirates?"

"They lack resources," said Sikander. The Terran Caliphate stood in the very heart of human-controlled space, but it hadn't been a significant military power in a hundred years; its entire fleet would barely make a single squadron in the navy of a major power like Aquila or Dremark. The neighboring Velar Electorate was in little better shape. "They don't have the ships they need to secure their systems, but Aquilan shipping lines expect someone to do something to keep the starlanes safe. The Commonwealth Navy seems to be that someone."

"One might question whether a two-year assignment to a demonstration of resolve in a distant frontier is worth your time," Nawab Dayan observed. "There are things here in Kashmir that I could use your help with. I never meant for you to spend the rest of your life in the Aquilan navy, Sikander."

That's new, Sikander realized. Each time he visited home during his fourteen years of active duty, his father asked how his career was going or what assignments he looked forward to, but they'd never spoken about what he might do when he was finished with his service in the Aquilan navy. If he were to be perfectly honest with himself, he felt intimidated by the prospect of walking away from the only career he knew. *What would I do here?* he wondered. *Spend my days cutting ribbons and giving speeches like poor Gamand?*

The flyer's pilot saved him from the necessity of deciding on a reply. "Your Highness, we're beginning our final approach to Mohali Qila," he announced over the cabin circuit. "Please secure your safety belt. We'll be on the ground shortly."

Seventy minutes after leaving Chittar Creek, the nawab's transport overflew the city of Mohali Bay, favored with the usual priority traffic routing a ruling nawab and his escorts enjoyed. Colorful sails dotted the turquoise water below, but they continued past the white beaches of the bayfront to the harbor district on the other side of the city's crescent-shaped peninsula. Sikander caught a glimpse of a steep island with concrete dry docks in the middle of the harbor before the flyer banked in that direction and he lost the view. A moment later, the flyer flared gently and set down on a large landing pad in front of a boarded-up administration building. No one else was in sight—Mohali Qila was a mothballed military facility that had been out of service for decades.

Sikander waited while the cabin steward opened the flyer's door and secured the short set of steps to the ground, then followed his father and Gamand outside, blinking in the bright glare of the Srinagaran sun. The smell of the salt air and the distant cries of seabirds struck him at once; they were no longer in the Kharan, that was for certain. Around them, the escort flyers alighted to disembark a dozen Jaipur Dragoons in their resplendent uniforms. Nawab Dayan went nowhere without an armed escort—something else that had changed for the worse in the years that Sikander had been away from home. Kashmir's politics had always been unsettled at best, but it seemed that the situation grew more troubled every year.

"The base looks like it's in good shape," Gamand observed. "And I like the fact that it's on an island with a bit of distance from the city proper. That should help with security concerns."

"Or limit the collateral damage from enemy strikes, if it ever came to that," said Nawab Dayan. He looked to Sikander. "Where should we begin?"

Sikander studied their surroundings before replying. This was the reason his father had suggested he accompany them on this side trip: Sikander's professional experience made him the North best able to assess Mohali Qila's potential value. "I'm not an expert in construction techniques or facilities," he began. "I've spent my career driving ships, not building them. That said, I'd like to start by looking over the yard's power station and the machine sheds. You can rebuild or replace administration buildings in a matter of weeks, but it could take years to order in heavy machine tools or build new fusion generators if those are in bad shape. Down this way, I think."

They set off down an access road that sloped gently down toward the large buildings by the island's concrete wharf. Along the way they passed several large dry docks, now standing open to the water. Sikander decided that they probably needed work after years of disuse, and paused to point them out. "Better have the technicians check the dry docks' pump systems and the gate mechanisms, too. That sort of machinery might be hard to find in Kashmir."

"Do we need the dry docks?" Gamand asked. "Starships can land, after all."

"If you want to work on anything bigger than a corvette, yes. Large ships are too heavy to rest on a planet-surface docking cradle without damage, but they can sit in water just fine." Sikander eyed the Mohali docks, trying to gauge their actual size—three hundred meters or so, he guessed. That was certainly more than any Kashmiri construction effort would need for a long time. While the induction drives of a modern starship could easily handle powered flight in a planetary atmosphere, that didn't mean it was easy to find a place to *park* a couple of hundred thousand tons of steel. For that reason the largest ships generally remained in space, making use of the orbital transportation infrastructure . . . if, that is, a planet had any. Srinagar and Jaipur were still in the process of industrializing their orbital space, so surface shipyards would likely remain useful for years to come. "You might want to have your technicians look into subdividing the docks so that work can proceed on more than three hulls at a time, if they're small enough to fit."

Nawab Dayan nodded to his personal secretary, a lean young man in an Aquilan-style business suit. "Omvir, make a note of that, will you?"

"Yes, Nawab." Omvir Bhind quickly jotted something down on his dataslate as they continued on their way.

They continued to the machine sheds, where Sikander found that most of the yard's heavy machinery was still in place—in all likelihood it had simply been too expensive to move when Mohali Qila had been shut down. The power plant, on the other hand, was a disappointment. Only bare concrete floors and disconnected power conduits remained to show where the original generators had once stood. "I think you'll need to order a new fusion plant," Sikander observed. "Altair United or Reed-Nagra make good ones, but I couldn't tell you what it will cost or how long it will take."

"I believe the answers are 'too much,' and 'too long,'" Gamand said. He shook his head. "I've been looking into generators for some other investments. It turns out that fusion plants are a bottleneck for many industrial concerns. The waiting list is years long."

"Perhaps it was too much to hope that Harsha Pransa had left the place ready for immediate reactivation," Nawab Dayan said. Mohali Qila had formerly served as a shipyard and naval base for Harsha's seagoing navy in the days when Harsha had been an independent nation, before Aquila had forcibly united Kashmir under the Khanate. Similar mothballed military facilities could be found in Ishar and most of the other former nawab states. "Ah, well. Omvir, add one industrial fusion plant to the project requirements, if you please. If it's a long wait, we might as well put our names on the list as soon as we can." He looked at the empty power station one last time, then headed for the door.

Outside, they found a long-disused lunch area with plain concrete benches beneath the shade of overgrown trees. It overlooked Mohali Harbor and the city skyline, a few kilometers away. Nawab Dayan took a seat, slowly lowering himself into place while Gamand stood close by, unobtrusively ready to help. "Too much walking for me, I'm afraid," Nawab Dayan said, breathing heavily. "My doctors keep telling me to rest more, but it is easy to forget myself in such fine weather."

"Shall I have your flyer brought down closer, Nawab?" Omvir Bhind asked.

Nawab Dayan nodded. "That might be best." The secretary hurried off, speaking into his comm device; the older man gazed out over the bay and the colorful sailboats in the distance. Then he looked to Sikander. "What do you think? Can we use this place?"

Sikander considered the question carefully. "Assuming you can replace the power plant, I see no reason why the shipyard couldn't be brought back into service. You'll be limited to small or medium-sized hulls, so you shouldn't plan on building interstellar bulk carriers here. But I couldn't tell you whether it's a sound investment or not."

"It isn't," Gamand said, grimacing. "We'll lose tens of millions."

"Then I guess I don't understand why you're interested in it, Father. Foreign builders with mass-production techniques are going to undercut your prices; you'll sell any ship you build here at a loss. For that matter, the Aquilan-owned asteroid yards at Nun Kun or Sadhna are already capable of turning out bigger and more competitively priced ships than you'll be able to build in Mohali for ten years or more. Buy a stake in one of the existing yards if you want to diversify the family industrial holdings."

"Call it an investment in the future," Nawab Dayan replied. He waved a hand to indicate the city across the bay. "A shipyard here would employ thousands of Mohalis. Those Mohalis will learn to build ships—yes, ordinary lighters and tugs and workboats for now, but someday they'll build ships with warp rings that can go to other stars. We're not just investing in a shipyard. We're investing in *shipbuilders.*"

Mohalis? Or does Father have someone else in mind? Sikander gave the nawab a sharp look, thinking about their conversation during the flight. Dayan Singh North had a hundred military or industrial experts in his employ who could tell him more about what was involved in launching a shipbuilding business than he could. *Today's visit isn't about finding out what I think about a family investment in Mohali Qila. It's about showing me something I could do at home.* He had to admit that the idea held a certain attraction. Kashmir wouldn't be building its own battle fleets any time soon, but laying the groundwork for an independent, domestic shipbuilding capability . . . that would be a worthy challenge. *And while we'll never build battleships at Mohali Qila, we might someday build fine torpedo boats for the Khanate Navy. Wouldn't that be something?*

The nawab's transport appeared through the trees, its drive plates crackling in the humid air, and settled down lightly on the wide concrete wharf. Omvir Bhind returned, and bowed to Sikander's father. "Nawab, we're due back in Sangrur in five hours," he said. "Shall I reschedule your evening events?"

"No need, Omvir. I believe that we've seen what we needed to see here." The nawab got to his feet, and gave Sikander and Gamand a quick smile. "Come on, you two. Your mother will have my head if we're late for dinner."

2

Jaipur, Kashmir System

High summer in Srinagar's southern hemisphere turned into a beautiful spring day on neighboring Jaipur after a short hop across the Kashmir system. Jasmine and frangipani in full bloom adorned the vast lawn of the Norths' Long Lake estate. Luxurious power yachts rested alongside the long wooden dock or lay at anchor just offshore, while others serenely cruised past the estate. Hundreds of guests wandered the grounds, chatting with each other in small groups or partaking of the expansive buffet set out by the estate staff. Sikander lounged on a low fieldstone wall that divided the house's patio from the lawn, gazing out over the colorful assembly and nursing a glass of iced tea. Opening Day of boating season was an excuse for the Norths to throw a lavish party at Long Lake, and this was the first time in ten years or more that he'd been home for the occasion.

An especially lavish yacht rumbled by on the lake. *The Reel family boat?* he wondered. *Or does that one belong to the Kings?* If there were two Jaipuran families wealthier than the Norths, the Reels and the Kings might be them; the boat had to be thirty meters, or close to it. It struck him as a little over the top, but it certainly was a handsome vessel. *We could build those at Mohali Qila. Hull fabrication, system design, and generators are much the*

*same between modern spacecraft and watercraft. A luxury product
line might help the yard get to the break-even point faster. But how
do you go about convincing the people who can afford that sort of
toy that you've got a premium product to offer? Find a prestige client
to begin with, I suppose. . . .*

"Good God. I'm actually thinking about it," Sikander muttered. He had a ship to get back to at Neda and a career to continue in the Commonwealth Navy—important duty, honorable
and prestigious if not quite so prominently in the public eye as a
prince's duties often were. More to the point, he was *good* at it; his
military service was not just a job, but a calling. Perhaps his father
was slowing down a little, but the family's affairs were in good
hands under Gamand, and there were plenty of other Norths—
Manvir, Usha, his cousins Amarleen and Dilan—ready to look
after things in Kashmir. *Then again, serving closer to home someday would be just as honorable, and perhaps just as important.*

"Ah! There you are, Sikander." Begum Vadiya North glided up
to join him, dressed in an elegant blue kameez with a matching
scarf. "Hiding from our guests?"

"Not at all. Simply enjoying the afternoon and taking it all in."

"It would be nice if you mingled a little bit. You're away so
much that our friends and neighbors never have the chance to
see you."

"I am mingling!" he protested.

"By yourself, it seems. I don't think that is how it's done." His
mother nodded in the direction of the party below. "Our friends
ask after you when you're gone, you know. They're very curious
about where you're serving and which planets you've visited and
whether I think you'll come home soon. But if they see you up
here brooding all by yourself they assume you wish to be left
alone. Go be sociable!"

Sikander bowed in mock surrender. "Fine. I suppose I wasn't

mingling, Mother. But in all honesty I don't recognize many of the people here. It's been a long time since I was home for one of these."

"All the more reason to make an effort to meet our guests today," Vadiya said. "Come with me. My son is home for a few days, and I intend to show him off while I can."

"If it makes you happy."

"It does," she replied. Begum Vadiya led him down from the patio to the party on the lower lawn, and before Sikander could catch his breath, they were surrounded by partygoers. This was his mother's world: Nawab Dayan engaged in Jaipur's social calendar grudgingly, but Begum Vadiya was born for this stage. She greeted scores of people Sikander had never even heard of by name, offering a different expression of welcome or a polite inquiry about one person's health or the college interests of another's children without a moment's hesitation. It never failed to amaze Sikander—Vadiya North had demonstrated again and again that graciousness and leadership in these circles was just as much a part of governing effectively as anything his father did as Nawab of Ishar. He found that he remembered more people than he thought he would. Some of his parents' friends seemed older than he recalled, but then again he'd spent little time on Jaipur since leaving for High Albion at eighteen. Naturally, he also found that a few of his own childhood friends and schoolmates now had families and careers. *It turns out that Jaipur doesn't remain frozen in time when I'm away,* he realized.

"Sikander, you remember Mrs. Lawton and her daughter Jaya?" Begum Vadiya said, making yet another introduction as they drifted into an open-sided pavilion close by the lakeshore.

"Of course," he answered. "A pleasure to see you again, Mrs. Lawton. And you, too, Jaya." Nira Lawton, the wife of a wealthy sirdar and longtime North ally, looked much the same; as long as

Sikander could remember, she'd been a rather plump and motherly sort. Jaya, on the other hand, had been a few years behind Sikander in school. He remembered her as a skinny teenager, but now she stood ten centimeters taller than her mother and looked absolutely stunning in a flowing green kameez.

"Sikander!" Mrs. Lawton embraced him as if he were one of her own children. "How good to see you home! Where are you stationed now? Will you be staying long?"

Jaya simply smiled. "Hello, Sikay. Nice to see you."

"Nira, you're smothering my son," Begum Vadiya said with a laugh. "You know, I'm glad we ran into you. I've been meaning to ask you about the Lake Days charity auction. Do you mind mixing a little association business with pleasure?"

"Oh, certainly!" The two older women drifted away, chattering about the next event on the calendar.

Sikander found himself standing beside Jaya, the two of them momentarily alone in the pavilion. Jaya watched their mothers move off, and gave a small snort. "Well, that's certainly a little suspicious," she observed. "I know for a fact that there's nothing about that auction that hasn't been hashed out any time in the last twenty years or so they've been holding it."

Sikander gave her a sympathetic look. "You don't think—?"

"My mother's been throwing me in front of every eligible bachelor in Ishar since I graduated, and that was nine years ago. But I have to admit I thought your mother was above that sort of thing."

"Normally, she is. In fact, she hasn't ever said a word to me about 'finding someone' or 'settling down.' It's just a look she gives me from time to time." Sikander shook his head. His mother was rarely so transparent. Was it possible that she and Nira Lawton had hit upon the ploy of allowing him and Jaya to discover they shared a similar predicament, and see whether that sparked anything? *Oh, that's devious*, he decided. Well, two could play at that game. "I suggest that we foil our mothers' efforts by doing exactly what they hope we will, and sticking close by each other for the rest of the afternoon. That should stop them from trying to arrange any more unexpected introductions for either of us, and in all honesty, I'd enjoy catching up a bit."

Jaya raised her glass in salute. "You're smarter than you look—that would certainly serve them right. Count me in."

"Great. Let's get something to eat, then."

They made their way over to the buffet pavilion; Jaya took Sikander's arm, staying close beside him. He had to admit that wasn't an unwelcome development; she had beautiful hazel eyes, long black hair, and an easy laugh. As teenagers, he and his brother Devindar had both been smitten with Jaya's older sister Hamsi—in fact, they'd once stolen the family yacht to go over to the Lawton estate in a ridiculous effort to impress her. Jaya used to be the tag-along little sister they'd had to put up with in order to get close to Hamsi. *Not so little now,* Sikander realized—thirty or so, if his math was right.

"I hear you're the captain of a starship," Jaya said once they'd filled their plates and retreated to a pair of wooden deck chairs by the water. "What's that like?"

"Not quite as romantic as it sounds. The Commonwealth Navy likes its paperwork, that's for certain. But I've got a good crew, and my ship's just finishing up a refit—I'm looking forward to putting her through her paces." He dunked a carrot stick into some dip. "How about yourself? What do you do?"

"Fashion designer, believe it or not. I've got my own company, and we're doing well. You can find my dresses in high-end stores throughout the system." Jaya grinned. "In fact, your mother's wearing one of my designs today. And she looks great in it."

"Really? I had no idea!" Sikander nodded at Jaya's flowing tunic. "Is that one of yours, too?"

"No, this is a Patel I bought last week. I feel that it's a little, well, immodest to wear my own designs."

"Did you study design in school?"

"A little, but my real interest was business. Dresses are only the visible part of what I do—building a global brand, that's the real challenge. I was fortunate to begin with the family money, of course, but I paid back every credit of that five years ago. Mostly I worked hard and studied the market to figure out the best places where I could carve out a little space of my own. I wanted to earn any success that came my way."

"So you're a captain of industry, so to speak. What's that like?"

"Not as romantic as it sounds!" Jaya laughed. "I mean that in both senses of the word. I don't get to spend very much time on the design work anymore because managing the business demands most of my attention. And my mother worries about my prospects because I'm really too busy to date."

"Then we'd be great together," said Sikander. "As it turns out, I'm never around."

He timed it perfectly; Jaya had a mouthful of champagne she half snorted through her nose. "Oh, damn it! You did that on purpose!" she said after she recovered.

"Like you said, I'm smarter than I look." He grinned and got up. "Stay right there. I'll get you another."

Sikander wound up enjoying the Opening Day party more than he'd thought he would. Jaya Lawton was good company, and their plan seemed to work: As long as they were together, Nira Lawton and Vadiya North avoided bringing any other well-pedigreed single people around for them to meet. He learned that the business of Kashmiri high fashion was more serious than he would have ever guessed, and in turn Jaya questioned him for an hour or more about his experiences on far-off worlds; she hadn't ever traveled outside Kashmir. She was especially curious about his tour of duty in the Tzoru Dominion, and somewhat disappointed by how little attention he'd paid to Tzoru clothing and design motifs—"I'm always looking for unusual inspirations," as she explained it. When evening came and the party began to wind down, he was tempted to see whether her interest extended as far as he thought it might, but he settled for a chaste kiss on the cheek; he would be on his way again in just a few days, after all. That might have been the ideal situation for something casual, but given how close their families were, Sikander decided it might be wiser not to ask for trouble.

The day before Sikander was scheduled to depart for Neda, he took one of the nawab's flyers to visit his brother Devindar. Devindar spent much of his time in Taraghara on Srinagar, home of the Khanate Sabha, but when the Sabha wasn't in session he lived and worked from a fine town house in the university town of Ganderbal. He and his family met Sikander on their rooftop landing pad; when Sikander climbed out of the flyer, Devindar stepped forward to embrace Sikander in a crushing hug. "Sikay! It's good to see you!" he said with a laugh.

"Devin! It's been too long." Sikander returned his brother's embrace, and thumped him on the back for good measure.

"Hello, Sikander," said Ashi, Devindar's wife. "Girls, you remember your uncle Sikander?"

Rida and Ruhi North—age ten and seven, respectively—rushed up to join the embrace. "Uncle Sikay! You're back! Is your ship here? Did you bring us anything from another planet?"

"Two of my four favorite nieces," Sikander replied—four, of course, being the number of nieces he currently had—and grinned at them. "I might have a little something for each of you in my bag, if I remembered to pack it. Ashi, what are you feeding them? They're getting so tall!"

"You haven't seen them in a year and a half." Ashi smiled warmly; she was surprisingly soft-spoken for someone married to a firebrand such as Devindar, but she'd always liked Sikander. "They grow like weeds at this age. Come on downstairs—dinner's almost ready."

Dinner turned out to be tandoori-style chicken, with lentil stew served over rice; Ashi liked to cook for special occasions, and she'd sent the small domestic staff home for the evening. Rida and Ruhi naturally peppered him with all sorts of questions about places he'd been and aliens he'd met—they were both beginning to study the stellar geography of human space and the neighboring non-human species, although Rida was naturally much farther along. Both were fascinated to learn that he'd actually spoken with Nyeirans on a few occasions. If there was something as unsettling to the typical human as hundred-kilo tentacled monsters in chitin carapaces, Sikander would be hard-pressed to name it. "But the Nyeirans are very polite!" he told the girls, which struck little Ruhi as so unlikely she spent the rest of the meal giggling between bites.

After the meal—and a few small knickknacks for the girls Sikander had picked up in his travels—Ashi ushered her daughters up to their rooms to begin the nightly routine of baths and bedtime. Devindar and Sikander had kitchen duty, which they accepted with shrugs of resignation. Any member of the extended North family had more than enough money to have someone else do the cooking and cleaning up, but their parents had insisted that Sikander and his siblings spend some time on domestic chores so that they'd be able to look after themselves as adults if they ever needed to. It pleased Sikander to see that even after years of estrangement from Nawab Dayan, Devindar thought enough of the family tradition to stick to it even when he didn't have to. Sikander didn't mind helping; while his valet Darvesh usually attended to the menial duties when he was away from Kashmir, Darvesh was off enjoying some rarely used vacation time of his own as long as they were home.

"You'll never believe who I ran into the other day," Sikander said as they finished up the dishes. "Jaya Lawton. I spent most of the Opening Day party catching up with her. Did you know she's a very successful designer now?"

"Just about everybody on the planet knows that, Sikay—it's hard to miss the Hasa logo. I gave Ashi one of Jaya's purses for her birthday last week."

"I suppose that's what I get for spending so much time away from home."

"Don't feel too bad. I didn't make the connection between Jaya and Hasa purses until Ashi educated me on the topic." Devindar wiped off his hands on a kitchen towel and tossed it to Sikander. "Remember taking the family boat to go see her and Hamsi?"

"Every time I visit Long Lake. Speaking of Hamsi, Jaya told me she has three children now. Can you believe that?"

"And another on the way, from what I hear." Devindar nodded at the refrigerator. "Care for a beer?"

"Yes, please." Most observant Kashmiris didn't drink, which meant Nawab Dayan's cellar was poorly stocked at the best of times. Sikander, on the other hand, enjoyed a cold lager on a warm day or after a job well done, and he judged the kitchen clean enough to merit a small reward. He watched his brother study the selection in the refrigerator and choose two bottles. "I saw you on the news the other night—*The Daily Question*. They seem to think you might get an important post in the next government if the KLP wins enough seats in the election."

"Oh, you watched that, did you?" Devindar opened one bottle

and handed it to Sikander, then opened the second for himself. "I hope you didn't pay any attention to that 'Tiger of Ishar' nonsense. Newscasters are in the business of stirring up a bit of sensation if they're looking for a bump in the ratings."

"Do you think you'll win?"

"If the governor-general allows the election to go forward, then yes, I think we will."

Sikander raised an eyebrow. "The Aquilans can't suspend the election just because they don't like the way the polling looks. Good God! Ten billion people would be out in the streets the next day."

"They can't very well let a pro-independence party with so-called terrorist roots take over the government, either. They know that we'll pass a resolution abrogating the Treaty of Taraghara on the first day we're in office."

"Which the governor-general won't sign into law. So why even bother?"

"Because I want to put that bill on her desk and make her veto it. Let everybody see exactly how much self-rule the Aquilan government is really willing to extend to Kashmir." Devindar took a long pull from his beer. "For years we've continued this polite fiction that the Khanate government uniformly supports continuing our special relationship with Aquila. The Sabha's never passed a resolution of independence, so the voters assume that the Aquilans simply haven't been asked to move out yet. And they assume that we haven't asked because we don't feel that we're ready. Well, I think it's time we asked. And I mean to make the Aquilan government say out loud what we all know to be true: They never intend to let us go."

"And you think the Aquilans will suspend an election to avoid saying that." Sikander found that unlikely. Yes, the Kashmiri Liberation Party advocated for ending the Commonwealth's role in overseeing what should be Kashmir's own affairs, and millions of people—well, billions, if the *Daily Question* piece was any indication—were ready to cut Kashmir's ties to Aquila and go their own way, regardless of the consequences. But moderate parties such as the pro-business Federalists or the United Democrats were in no hurry to separate their constituencies from Aquilan subsidies and favorable trade status. For that matter, Sikander didn't like the idea of sending away the Aquilan navy; he'd seen what happened to isolated systems and minor powers left to the mercy of aggressive states with bigger fleets. No, it seemed to him that the governor-general's office might be happy to stand aside and allow the KLP to frighten all the moderates by passing a radical bill of separation, counting on the centrists to rebound and throw a little cold water on the more heated rhetoric.

"The only question is what pretext they'll use to shut us down." Devindar shrugged. "From my point of view, it doesn't matter how they do it—a veto is a veto. The voters will see through it, and they'll demand to be heard."

"You know, the Aquilans might surprise you," Sikander told him. The idea of suppressing a free and fair election in Kashmir wouldn't go over well with the Aquilan opposition parties or media—something that Devindar and his KLP colleagues might not fully appreciate. Serving in the Commonwealth Navy, Sikander had reason to pay more attention to Aquila's domestic politics than most Kashmiris. "Aquilan foreign policy generally supports the right of self-determination throughout Coalition space. They won't lightly abandon that principle."

"That sounds like your hostage syndrome speaking," said Devindar. "It's not your fault. Father sentenced you to it when he sent you into the Aquilan navy as an impressionable teenager. Anybody would have been compromised in your situation."

"Hostage syndrome?" Sikander scowled. "That's pretty smug,

isn't it? You're giving yourself permission to disregard my views by telling yourself that I'm damaged in some way."

"What else am I supposed to make of the situation, Sikay? You've put on a spotless Aquilan uniform every day for the last fifteen years, give or take, and you seem perfectly happy to keep on doing so. If your navy ordered your ship to Kashmir and told you to, I don't know, arrest the leadership of the Liberation Party on charges of sedition, I worry that you might actually do it."

"That wouldn't happen, but no, I would not. Free speech and political activity are protected under the Commonwealth constitution as well as our own. I'm sworn to defend them both, which means I'm expected to refuse unconstitutional orders."

"Would another Aquilan officer refuse that same order?"

"I know many who would, for the reason I just gave you."

"And some who wouldn't, I suspect." Devindar pointed the neck of his beer bottle at Sikander for emphasis. "Because you serve Aquila in some other star system, *those* officers are available to serve here, Sikay. When you put on that uniform and salute that flag, you participate in everything that's done in its name."

"Which, on the whole, preserves peace and stability throughout human space. Yes, it's not perfect—I find it just as obnoxious as you do that an Aquilan governor enacts or vetoes our laws, or that our military forces are limited to planetary defense only, or that we can't trade with whomever we please without going through the Commonwealth first. But you forget, Devin, that I've seen what happens when people fail to preserve the peace. If it wasn't for the Commonwealth Navy, the Gadira incident would have led to a war that could have left a hundred worlds in ruin, and a dozen great powers would now be fighting to carve up the Tzoru Dominion into spheres of influence. Aquila works hard to check the excesses of more aggressively imperial powers and stabilize international relations. That's *important*."

"No, Sikay, that's *convenient.* Aquila protects your international order because right now they're on top, and frankly they like things the way they are."

"God help me, you haven't changed a bit. Sometimes I think you argue for the sheer sake of arguing!" Sikander waved his free hand in frustration. "Has it ever occurred to you that other people have valid viewpoints, too?"

"I'm a lawyer and a politician, Sikay. I'd better be able to argue." Devindar smirked at Sikander, amused by his younger brother's irritation. "Besides, I'm not wrong about this, and you know it. Don't you think it's time you paid a little more attention to what your Aquilan service says to people back home?"

And don't you think it's time you paid attention to what your politics stand for? Sikander wanted to retort, but he stopped himself from saying so—he saw Devindar only once every year or two, and he had no intention of letting his older brother's needling sour the occasion. Instead, he took a long swig from his beer before he spoke again. "Enough, Devin. I don't want to fight. Change the topic."

"You brought up the election," Devindar said with a small frown. Evidently he was just getting warmed up, and he wasn't ready to let the argument rest. He studied Sikander for a long moment, and then shrugged awkwardly. "All right, then—no more politics for tonight. Get yourself another beer, and tell me all about your starship."

When Sikander flew back to the Sangrur palace early the next day, he found that Darvesh Reza had already returned and was busy packing for him. The tall valet set out Sikander's dress whites, and busied himself buffing out some microscopic scuff in one of Sikander's shoes. "Welcome back, Nawabzada," he said. "How was your visit with Nawabzada Devindar?"

"Good," Sikander replied. If he hesitated for half a moment before answering, Darvesh did not seem to notice. "We stayed up talking for half the night, and his daughters are frighteningly smart for their ages. If they follow Devin into politics I think they'll be running Kashmir before we know it."

"I am pleased to hear that, sir."

"How about your leave? Did you have enough time to visit with your family?"

"I did, sir. I admit that I have missed home cooking during your deployments. Aquilan fare is fine in its own way, but it's so bland."

"I won't argue with that," Sikander said. Most Kashmiris would agree, although Darvesh relished truly fiery seasonings. How he could taste anything at all after a lifetime of eating the sorts of spices he favored mystified Sikander. "It's been a good visit. I'm up to my elbows in nieces and nephews these days—I almost wish I didn't have to go."

"A man never truly appreciates his family until he spends some time away from them. Perhaps it is the brevity of your visits that makes them special to you."

"In other words, leave before I remember the different ways they can annoy me?" Sikander chuckled softly, and began to dress himself for their trip. Darvesh silently held up his tunic, offering a sleeve; Sikander considered what he'd said, until a new thought struck him. "You know, Darvesh, I've kept you away from Kashmir for a long time now. I know you have family you miss as much as I miss mine. If you want to stay, I'll understand. We can arrange for someone else to travel with me."

"I thank you for your concern, sir, but I fear I would not be so easily replaced. A certain attention to detail is required in this position."

"I'm serious. You don't have to miss your home and family on my account."

Darvesh inclined his head, and covered his heart with one hand. "I carry them with me wherever I go, Nawabzada. Please be reassured that I am content in my duties. Now, you must finish dressing and say your farewells. Our shuttle departs soon."

Sikander set a hand on the older man's shoulder. "Very well, Darvesh. If you say so."

He finished getting dressed, and collected a few small things he'd picked up during his visit that he wanted to take back to *Decisive*. Then he left Darvesh to see to the packing, and went to go find his father and mother. He'd already said his good-byes to Gamand, Usha, Manvir, and their families before his trip to Ganderbal; the Norths were scattered all over Ishar, and maintained busy schedules. He found Nawab Dayan and Begum Vadiya taking a late-morning tea break on the south veranda, enjoying the palace's view over the White River valley and the green hills beyond.

"Mother, Father, I'm afraid that it's about time for me to catch the orbital shuttle," he said as he joined them. "I don't want to miss the liner."

Begum Vadiya stood and embraced him. "I've been dreading this moment since the day you arrived," she said. "Come back as soon as you can. We miss you when you're away."

"I will, Mother," Sikander promised. "I admit that it's getting harder and harder to leave each time I visit."

"Have a safe journey," Nawab Dayan said, getting to his feet a little more slowly to shake Sikander's hand. He wore the uniform of a colonel in the Jaipur Dragoons, his customary working clothes. When Sikander had been younger he'd found it somewhat in-timidating, especially since his father had towered over him. Now

Dayan North's once-immense height turned out to be a mere three or four centimeters more than Sikander's own hundred and seventy, and the uniform hung loosely on his thinning frame. It struck Sikander that the uniform was something the two of them shared, even if he wore Aquilan dress whites and his father wore Jaipuran service khakis. Most North men spent at least a little time in military service, but in his immediate family only his father and he had worn a uniform for anything more than cadet's training and ceremonial functions.

Nawab Dayan must have sensed it too, because he unexpectedly pulled him into an embrace. "I am proud of you, Sikander," he said. "Command suits you well."

"Thank you, Father." Sikander hugged him back, trying not to think about the gauntness he felt through his father's khaki jacket. "It's been a good visit. I don't think I realized how much I needed this."

"Whatever seed that is sown, a plant of that kind comes forth," Sikander's father quoted. He released Sikander. "Remember that—it's good advice for any who carry the burden of leadership."

"I'll remember."

"Oh, and don't forget to write your mother. It makes her day when she gets a message from you."

Sikander smiled. "I'll remember that, too," he promised.

He embraced his mother once again, and then left to catch his shuttle.

3

Otto Bleindel studied the sitting room's aquarium, admiring the colorful collection of tropical fish circling their small glass world. He wasn't sure, but he thought he recognized half a dozen Terran species in the tank, which spoke volumes about the wealth and tastes of the man he was about to meet. Almost three hundred light-years separated the fish in the aquarium from the seas of Earth; someone centuries ago had made the extraordinary calculation that pretty little living ornaments needed to be transported across unthinkable distances between the stars so that well-appointed rooms on an entirely new planet could be properly decorated. Considering the time and trouble it must have taken to bring the correct mix of species, the proper sort of minerals to make Earthlike salt water, fish food, and the various filters and pumps—and glass, of course—needed to provide the fish with their own little Earth on a planet orbiting a star one couldn't even see with the naked eye from humanity's home planet, the aquarium represented a meticulous commitment to perfection . . . and an impressive display of power.

"You like fish?" Hanne Vogt asked, watching him study the tank. A long-legged, athletic woman of forty, she wore a skirt that showed just enough knee to be mildly scandalous in some quarters of the Zerzura Sector. Only the most reclusive Caliphate worlds imposed any kind of body-covering garments on women; Dahar, as the capital world of the sector, tolerated the normal business attire found throughout the nations that made up the Coalition of Humanity without complaint. On the other hand, Hanne Vogt had the poise and confidence to make even a fairly modest skirt and jacket seem like it pushed cultural boundaries. She also possessed a first-rate brain and a keen eye for opportunity, which made her perfect for her role as one of the Imperial Foreign Office's leading troubleshooters. "I wouldn't have taken you for the type."

"I hardly noticed the fish," Bleindel told her. "Yes, they're pretty enough, but I was thinking about systems and power. Someone went to a great deal of trouble to find just the right conditions and the best mix of species to make this aquarium work. If you walked away and ignored it for just a few days, well, all these little fish would be floating at the top of the tank when you came back. It strikes me as something of a metaphor."

"In this metaphor, we're the tank keepers?"

"Exactly." Bleindel turned away from the aquarium and joined Vogt on the comfortable couch. He dressed more conservatively than she did, wearing a plain gray business suit and a steel-blue tie that matched the pale color of his eyes. Where Hanne Vogt's pose radiated confidence and allure, his posture hinted at discipline and control. Not a particularly imposing figure, Bleindel was a little on the short side and lightly built, although he was more athletic than he looked. But every movement he made was a study in precision and efficiency; he had to make a conscious effort to adopt the relaxed body language or casual ease most people wore throughout their day as a matter of course. "We have a specific set of conditions we're attempting to create so that the fish that interest us will flourish. Most of our work takes place out of sight and out of mind. If we do it well, the casual observer would never even guess that the work had been done at all."

"And if we fail to maintain our investment, a lot of expensive fish die, and the tank starts to stink. I suppose it's not terrible as far as metaphors go, but I've never had much patience for them. Analogies can only get you so far."

A stern-looking woman wearing a modest Daharan-style dress approached the sitting area where Vogt and Bleindel waited, her low heels clicking on the marble floor. "Ms. Vogt, Mr. Bleindel, I am Nenet Fakhoury, appointment secretary to Marid Pasha," she announced in Jadeed-Arabi. Bleindel had studied enough to be comfortable in the language, while Vogt was quite fluent—any diplomat who spent time in the Caliphate worlds had to be, since few Caliphate officials deigned to conduct their business in any other language. "His Excellency will see you now. This way, please."

"Of course," Vogt replied with a warmth that didn't fool Bleindel at all. After months of working closely with Hanne Vogt, he'd learned that she didn't waste much sincerity on underlings. The two of them rose and followed the secretary along one of the palace's grand halls, a beautiful space with five-meter windows lining the left-hand wall to offer a sweeping view of Mersin's mountaintop towers and the undulating wisps of cloud tops a kilometer or two below. Much of Dahar's atmosphere was too dense and toxic for humans, but at an elevation of three thousand meters above sea level the air was perfectly breathable and free of the dense low-level clouds that made the true surface a gloomy orange underworld. Fortunately, vast areas of Dahar's rugged surface consisted of uplands that rose clear of the choking murk, providing plenty of room for a planetary population approaching a billion people to build cities and till farmland in the open air. Bleindel had read that pressurized greenhouses and semisealed habitats extended downslope to within a kilometer or so of the bottomlands—and Dahar's entirely alien native ecosystem—but no one lived at those elevations by choice, not when the highlands were so near to human ideal. Mersin was a city of islands, but its islands were mountaintops and its canals gorges filled with orange mist. *A striking site for a planetary capital but not terribly practical,* he decided as he admired the view. Among other things, a lack of level ground in Dahar's big cities limited spaceport construction.

At the end of the hall, the secretary showed them into a splendid library that evidently served as a working office. Two palace guards in spotless uniforms kept watch beside the door. Near the floor-to-ceiling windows on the room's opposite side stood a tall, broad-shouldered man in a dark mandarin-style jacket and military trousers, which he wore bloused into well-shined boots. He wore a flat round cap adorned with gold braid, and silver streaked his close-cropped beard. "Marid Pasha, the representatives from the Empire of Dremark," Fakhoury announced. "Special Envoy Ms. Hanne Vogt, and attaché Mr. Otto Bleindel. Ms. Vogt and Mr. Bleindel, may I present Pasha Marid al-Zahabi, governor of Zerzura Sector?"

"Thank you, Nenet." Marid Pasha came forward to shake Vogt's hand and then Bleindel's, while the secretary retreated to a desk by the door. "Welcome to Dahar, Ms. Vogt, Mr. Bleindel. I trust your journey was comfortable?"

"It was, thank you," Vogt replied. "A little long, but the warm welcome your government has extended to our mission certainly makes the trip worthwhile." The home systems of the Empire of Dremark lay almost five hundred light-years away in the neighborhood of the Coalsack Nebula, on the opposite side of the Terran Caliphate from the Zerzura Sector. Even the swiftest courier ships required more than a month for the journey.

"Think nothing of it. Dremish investment in Zerzura is very important to our development. Your businesses are revitalizing the sector economy after decades of stagnation."

"That's one of the reasons I'm here today, Pasha. My government believes in following up on success; when something is off to a promising start, that's the best time to double down on your investment. We're pleased by the results we've seen so far, and we have some ideas about expanding our efforts in Zerzura."

"I'm anxious to hear more about what you've got in mind. Why don't we have a seat, and perhaps some coffee? Given our unique soil chemistry, Dahar grows some of the best you can find anywhere." Pasha Marid gestured toward a sitting area by the room's broad windows. The office faced away from the city proper, and a vast unbroken skyscape stretched away for a hundred kilometers outside.

"That would be wonderful," Vogt replied, following Marid and taking one of the seats; Bleindel chose the one beside hers, while the pasha sat opposite them. A palace steward appeared with a coffee service and set it on the low table between them, pouring three small cups.

"Try it black first before you add anything," the pasha advised, choosing one of the cups. "You might like a little sugar, but it really doesn't need much help."

Bleindel helped himself to a cup, and took a cautious sip—he'd traveled enough to be wary of local delicacies. To his surprise, the coffee was as good as the pasha claimed. He'd become a connoisseur of Arabian-style coffee during his assignment on the distant planet of Gadira years ago, and time had only sharpened his appreciation. "This is excellent," he remarked.

Marid Pasha beamed. "It is, isn't it? I discovered it soon after I was appointed to this sector." He sipped his own coffee, savoring the taste for a moment before setting down the cup and fixing the two Dremish with a measuring gaze. "While I'm naturally interested in any opportunities to increase international investment in Zerzura, I confess I am curious why routine economic development requires the attention of a special envoy from your empire's Foreign Office, especially one with such a mysterious record as you, Ms. Vogt. Your consular offices usually handle this sort of contact."

"For routine matters, yes, that's true. However, we see the opportunities presented by Zerzura as anything but routine." Vogt sipped at her coffee and nodded in appreciation before quietly reaching for the sugar. "And, to be frank, we do have a specific concern about the security of increasing investments in this sector—your piracy problem. My superiors sent me to personally assess the situation and discuss steps that could be taken to abate this menace."

"I see." Marid Pasha gave a small shrug. "No one knows better than I do the challenge posed by piracy in my sector. Our intersystem carriers in Zerzura are losing millions to insurance costs even if they manage to avoid attacks on their ships, and some foreign traders are detouring around us altogether. Unfortunately, we're a long way from Terra, and the Caliphate simply doesn't have the interest—or the military resources—to sustain an antipiracy campaign in this part of space. My complaints fall on deaf ears."

Bleindel sipped at his coffee, studying the pasha's expression. On paper, the Terran Caliphate was one of the largest powers in the Coalition of Humanity, home to dozens of long-settled worlds that had been colonized by humans during the First Expansion from Sol—and, of course, Terra itself. In fact, though, the Caliphate was a power in decline, eclipsed centuries ago by Second Expansion star nations founded outside its stifling and reactionary culture. The Caliphate had never developed the sinews of a modern multistellar state, and was better understood as a collection of poorly organized sectors and virtually independent worlds than a cohesive nation. The only reasons the more advanced states ringing the Caliphate—say, the Aquilan Commonwealth, the Republic of Montréal, or the Empire of Dremark—hadn't already started to carve away the outlying portions of the decrepit Caliphate were the fears that some other power might come away with more of the spoils once the looting began, and that squabbles over choice territory could spark a major war. For the moment, everybody seemed happy to maintain the polite fiction that what Earth said mattered.

"I can imagine," Vogt said to Marid. "The Caliphate is huge, and Zerzura is only one sector. Given the difficulty in securing more action from Terra, we'd like to provide direct assistance to Zerzura and help you deal with the piracy problem yourself."

"What sort of help do you have in mind?" said Marid.

Vogt glanced at Bleindel; he recognized his cue. "You need warships, Pasha," he said. "The only thing that will deter pirates is a fleet based in the area to escort trade vessels through dangerous systems and suppress pirate activity with vigorous patrolling."

"That may be true, but turning my sector over to the Dremish Navy is the sort of thing that will bring me the Caliphate's attention in a hurry," Marid Pasha said in a dry tone. "Trade and economic development are one thing, Mr. Bleindel. Basing rights are another thing altogether."

"We're not interested in basing rights, Pasha," said Bleindel. "We're talking about providing the Zerzura Sector Fleet with Dremish-built warships. They're hand-me-downs, of course— ships that we're replacing in our own fleet—but they have been meticulously maintained. We Dremish enjoy something of a reputation for superior workmanship, you know. And any fighting ship, even one with a few years on it, is nothing a pirate would want to tangle with. You find the crews, and we'll provide the hulls and refurbish them for service at a nominal cost."

"That strikes me as very generous. What are you going to want in return?"

Hanne Vogt answered. "Not as much as you might think. We see this as a way to protect our investments in Zerzura, and perhaps create the conditions for more cooperation in the future. A friendly fleet in Zerzura would relieve some of our concerns about potential troubles in the Velar Electorate or the Principality of Bolívar, after all. Like you, we're becoming frustrated with Terra's inattention to the problems in this region of space." She shrugged her graceful shoulders. "We see no reason for our investments here to suffer from Terran apathy if there's a responsible local partner who can address the security questions."

"I doubt that Terra will approve my purchase of a Zerzuran fleet at any price."

"Then why get Terra involved?" Vogt replied. "You have a reputation as an independent thinker, Marid Pasha. Five major worlds and a dozen smaller outposts represent enough of tax base to support a modest fleet. If you need one and Terra isn't able or willing to provide it, I'd say you're within your rights to look after your sector's security needs by other means."

"That is an interesting proposition." The pasha stood up and paced over toward the window, gazing out over the colorful clouds below with his hands clasped behind his back. "I should probably tell you that I've had similar conversations with other parties who are also concerned with Zerzura's security. It seems that my troubles are worrisome to quite a lot of foreigners these days . . . although I must admit that nobody has yet offered me a navy of my own."

"Sometimes the simplest solutions are best. You need a fleet. We have some ships we can spare, and we'd like to help out a friend."

The pasha allowed himself a single bark of laughter, and

turned back to face his guests. "I'm just an old soldier, Ms. Vogt, but I know that nothing is quite that simple."

Nenet, the pasha's secretary, chose that moment to break in on the conversation. "Marid Pasha, the Velaran consul and the commander of the *Vashaoth Teh* are here. You are scheduled to meet with them at the top of the hour."

"So I am. Well, we probably shouldn't keep them waiting. Velarans are prickly about that sort of thing." Marid offered the Dremish envoys an apologetic smile. "I hope you understand."

"I'm familiar with Velaran manners," Vogt said. She rose to her feet, and Bleindel followed her lead. "By all means, you shouldn't make them wait. I've enjoyed our conversation and the excellent coffee, Marid Pasha, and I look forward to our next meeting."

"As do I, Ms. Vogt. You've given me a lot to think about this afternoon. You may transmit your proposal with all the details and fine print to my secretary's office, and I'll have my people study it carefully." The pasha walked them to the door. "Will you be in Dahar for a while?"

"I mean to speak to some of our Zerzuran business contacts and local sources about their views on the piracy problem, but I am otherwise at your disposal. We're staying aboard the *Polarstern*."

"We'll be in touch. Ms. Vogt, Mr. Bleindel, enjoy your stay in Dahar." The pasha shook their hands, and nodded to one of the soldiers by the door. "Major Terzi can show you back to your flyer. Major?"

"Yes, Excellency," said Terzi—a compact, battle-scarred veteran with cold, hard eyes. "This way, if you please."

Bleindel and Vogt shared a look, but said nothing as they followed the silent officer to the landing pad where *Polarstern*'s orbital shuttle waited. The day was colder than it looked from inside the palace with its bright sunlit windows, and Bleindel thought he detected a slight hint of something sharp and cinnamon-like in the air—a whiff of the exotic cloudstuff from lower down on the mountainside. *It's toxic,* he reminded himself. The palace might be situated in a picturesque spot, but the planet of Dahar was not what it seemed to be from Marid Pasha's elevation. *And there's another metaphor if I ever heard one!*

Terzi gave them a shallow nod as a farewell, and returned inside. Bleindel waited until the orbiter's crew sealed the cabin hatch behind them before speaking again. "Well, that was not as productive as I'd hoped," he observed as they climbed up and away from the palace and its mountaintop city. "'We'll be in touch,' really? Most people are more impressed when you offer them a fleet."

"Diplomacy has its own rules," Hanne Vogt told him. "You're a spy, Otto. In your line of work, you set objectives and execute missions. My job, on the other hand, is all about the process. Our first meeting with Marid al-Zahabi went more or less as I expected, including the next appointment providing a simple and polite reason to finish up with us for the day."

"If you say so." He glanced out the window to admire the striking scenery, the orbiter's thrust gently pushing him back into his luxurious seat despite the inertial compensation—without it, he'd be struggling to remain conscious under ten g or more of acceleration. "What do you think the pasha meant with that remark about conversations with other parties?"

"He wanted to make sure we understood that we'd better bring him a competitive offer if we want to secure his loyalties. Otherwise, he just might choose to align himself with another power that outbids us."

"The Velarans?"

"Not likely. They have no interest in bringing any more human worlds under their control when they've already got serious problems with human separatist movements. And I doubt that they have the money or resources to get involved in a bidding war for the Zerzura Sector even if they did want it."

"There's a Velaran cruiser in orbit right now," Bleindel observed. He glanced out the window, looking to see if *Vashaoth Teh* happened to be in sight now that they'd climbed above most of the atmosphere. Dozens of large freighters and transports glittered brightly in low orbits above the shuttle, but he couldn't tell if one of the distant lights in the blackness ahead of them was the Velaran ship. "It's the biggest warship in the sector at the moment, last I looked."

"And it's here to remind the Terran Caliphate in general—and Marid Pasha in particular—to keep any separatist sympathies to themselves." Vogt didn't bother to look out the window; instead, she opened her dataslate and started jotting down notes to herself as she talked. "The Velar Electorate might not have much of a fleet compared to our own, but it's light-years ahead of anything the Caliphate could deploy this far from Earth."

"That would change if Marid Pasha had a squadron or two of Dremish-built cruisers under his command," said Bleindel. He glanced back to Vogt. "So the Aquilans, then?"

"Or maybe the Montréalais, although my money's on the Commonwealth. The Aquilans are in a better position to buy the pasha, and their base at Neda means they have something of a foothold in Zerzura already." Vogt tapped the stylus of her dataslate against her chin. "I wish I knew what they're offering. I think that their domestic politics would make it difficult for Aquila to offer direct military assistance such as bargain-basement warships, but they're not going to sit on their hands once our interest in Zerzura comes out into the open."

Bleindel grimaced in distaste. He had firsthand experience with Aquilan interference; eight years ago, the presence of a sin-

gle Commonwealth Navy cruiser at Gadira had completely un-
raveled months of hard work he'd put into laying the groundwork
for the Dremish takeover of that world. He'd barely escaped the
disaster with his life, and it had taken him years of hard work to
repair the damage done to his career and reputation in the security bureau. "I can put my team to work on that," he told Vogt.
"Establishing surveillance of the Aquilan consulate or securing a
source or two within the pasha's government shouldn't be all that
difficult. Dahar is enough of a backwater that we have quite a lot
of room for discreet operations of that sort."

"Do it. I want to be a few steps ahead of the competition if
Marid Pasha's ambitions begin to attract more serious attention
from the other powers."

Bleindel noted that Vogt hadn't bothered to add *and don't
get caught*, which he rather appreciated. Most people unfamiliar with the sort of work the KBS did seemed compelled to tell
the Empire's spies to perform their jobs competently. Of *course*
the experts under his command would do everything they could
to minimize the risks of any operation—it went without saying,
didn't it? "I'll have some proposals for you by the end of the day."

"Fifteen minutes to rendezvous, ma'am," the orbiter's pilot announced over the cabin's intercom. "Dahar Control is routing us
around a bit of orbital traffic."

"Thank you, Lieutenant," Vogt replied. She returned her attention to her dataslate.

Bleindel sighed in irritation; now that he had something to do,
he was anxious to get back to their ship and get to work on it.
He glanced out the window again, looking for the traffic interfer-
ing with their flight path. Scores of small shuttles, workboats, and
cargo lighters lingered in the space above Mersin, the typical collection of light traffic one expected to see around any good-sized

planet . . . and, just coming into view, the teardrop-shaped hull of the Velaran cruiser. *Vashaoth Teh,* he remembered. He admired its striking maroon-and-silver paint scheme, watching as its orbit brought it steadily closer.

An idea struck him.

He considered it carefully for several minutes, studying the Velaran cruiser through the window until it once again disappeared out of sight. Then he turned and addressed Vogt. "If you're concerned about Marid Pasha playing us off against the Aquilans, it occurs to me that we could do something to provide him with a sense of urgency," he said. "For example, if tensions with the Velar Electorate suddenly became more serious, he might favor the offer that includes a battleworthy fleet."

It didn't take her long to discern the direction of his thoughts. "You're thinking about provoking the Velarans?"

"I have something in mind, yes."

"The last thing we want to do is start a war between the Electorate and the Caliphate. The Velarans are our allies—sort of, anyway—and the Caliphate is turning into a good place for the Empire to do business."

"I know. I was thinking in terms of third-party actions," Bleindel said. "Someone who doesn't represent Marid Pasha's sector government or the Terran Caliphate; as you say, we don't want to start a war, so we don't want the Velarans to see it as a direct attack. But if our agents provocateurs represented a problem that the Velarans expected the governor of Zerzura to do something about—"

"—we could count on those prickly Velaran sensibilities to kick in," she said, finishing his thought. "And some Velaran bluster might remind Marid Pasha how far Zerzura is from any Terran help."

"Exactly." Bleindel nodded. "Sometimes your process involves turning up the temperature, right?"

"Okay, Otto, you've got my attention." Vogt put away her dataslate, and fixed her attention on him. "Tell me what you've got in mind."

4

Tawahi Island, Neda III

Sikander climbed out of the flyer's roomy rear seat, taking in the warm air and brilliant blue waters of the Tawahi Island base. One of the things that he disliked about his job was the fact that he spent so much time inside windowless hulls; vidscreens slaved to exterior cams provided the illusion of daylight, but there was nothing like the smell of fresh air or the sound of the breeze rustling in the palms. No naval base was really pretty, of course—too much concrete and steel, not enough natural scenery—but he found the Commonwealth Navy's base on Neda III more pleasant than most.

Decisive rested alongside the pier, her hull gleaming with a fresh coat of the nanopolymer that served as a warship's paint: clean white hull, buff-colored turrets and upperworks, bold red piping around her bow and drive plates. *On the other hand, it could be that I like Tawahi because this is where my ship is,* he reflected. He'd never met a captain who didn't think his command was the most beautiful thing in the universe, with the possible exception of his spouse or children.

"Looks like we're home," he said to Darvesh, who unloaded their small collection of suitcases and settled the tab with the flyer's pilot. "And the ship's in one piece, too."

"I am relieved to see it, sir," Darvesh replied. "I know you were concerned."

She definitely looks better than the last time I saw her, Sikander decided. When he'd departed for leave, *Decisive* had been encased in the scaffolding of an orbital shipyard, her engineering spaces open to vacuum to facilitate the overhaul of her fusion generators. With twenty-five years of service behind her, *Decisive* had accumulated quite a bit of wear and tear. Some experts in the Office of Construction and Repair had suggested mothballing her rather than paying for the refit, considering her something of a white elephant with little value in the modern battle fleet. *Decisive* was big and roomy as destroyers went, almost the size of a light cruiser, but she'd been built around what was most likely a flawed tactical concept—a long-range "gunfighter" with a minimal torpedo battery. *Decisive* mounted eight kinetic cannons in her rounded turrets, as compared to the four or five most destroyers carried, but she had only four tubes for her warp torpedoes, and a paltry one reload for each. Most destroyers were built for torpedo attack; *Decisive's* designers had regarded it as an afterthought.

Sikander didn't care; he loved her anyway. The big hull gave *Decisive* plenty of endurance for extended cruises, and serving in a strategic backwater like Neda meant that her unsuitability for the usual squadron operations didn't matter. There were no enemy battleships in the Zerzura Sector to make him wish he had the torpedo battery a destroyer should have carried—*Decisive* more than outgunned any pirate they might run across.

Eager to get started, he picked up one of the bags despite Darvesh's look of disapproval and headed from the landing pad to the pier. Major fleet bases tended to be orbital cities like the one at New Perth, but Neda lacked that sort of system infrastructure, so the Commonwealth Navy's Pleiades Squadron moored in the waters of Tawahi Roads instead. He strode up the brow to the large hatch at *Decisive's* boat deck, pausing to salute the Aquilan flag displayed on the quarterdeck.

The officer of the deck came to attention and returned his salute, while the petty officer of the watch keyed the ship's intercom and struck the four bells naval tradition required for a commander of Sikander's seniority. "CSS *Decisive*, arriving!" she announced.

"Welcome back, Captain! And you too, Chief Reza." Lieutenant Commander Amelia Fraser, *Decisive's* executive officer, met Sikander and Darvesh on the ship's quarterdeck with a crisp salute, then broke into a wide smile and stepped forward to shake Sikander's hand. "How was your leave?"

"Good, XO, good. I saw most of my family, spent some time with the younger nieces and nephews, and even managed to go horseback riding for the first time in ten years or so." Sikander knew he'd gotten lucky in his executive officer; she was tireless without falling into the martinet-like caricature XOs in the fleet often adopted. Too many officers in her position acted like volcanoes waiting to erupt, but he'd never seen her lose her temper. No, when Amelia Fraser needed to set someone straight, she did it with an I'm-not-mad-I'm-just-disappointed routine that left even the greenest ensigns or most careless deckhands feeling about a centimeter high. Sikander made a show of looking around the ship's boat bay with an expression of surprise. "I see that nothing's on fire and there's a fresh coat of paint on everything. You must have been expecting me."

"Chief Reza's doing, sir," Fraser said. "He warned us you were on your way over when the orbiter touched down at the shuttle field."

"How am I ever going to catch someone napping if you do that, Darvesh?" Sikander said to his valet. "Sometimes I wonder whose side you're on."

"It's important to see to the formalities, sir," Darvesh replied.

"If you say so." Sikander returned his attention to his executive officer. "How's the ship? Did the shipyard complete all the work orders, or do we still have some action items to get to?"

"They missed a few things, sir, but nothing major. Just a matter of making sure we dot the i's and cross the t's, really. We could get under way in ten minutes if you wanted."

"That isn't necessary, but it's good to know. Give me an hour to get settled, and then let's get the department heads together. I'm sure everything is in fine shape, but I've been gone awhile and I feel like I want to start catching up."

"It's already in the plan of the day, Captain," Fraser said. "Is 1100 soon enough?"

"Perfect, thank you." Sikander grinned—it felt good to be back. "Fill me in while we walk."

They left the quarterdeck and headed forward toward the ship's berthing areas and command decks, Fraser quickly summarizing the major events of the last three weeks. The only thing of note that Sikander had missed was the ship's undocking from the re-pair facility and its landing at Tawahi, but he'd expected the shipyard to finish up with *Decisive* while he was away and he'd been happy to allow his second-in-command to oversee the brief flight from the orbital dock down to the ship's customary mooring spot in the squadron's planetside base. Not every captain would have willingly missed any ship's movement, no matter how small, but Amelia Fraser enjoyed his complete confidence, and trying to get back early enough to see to it himself would have made it pointless to make the trip back home.

Sikander found a file full of correspondence waiting for his attention in his cabin, and spent the rest of his "settling-in" time skimming the messages to see if anything required an immediate reply. An hour before noon, he changed into the buff-colored jumpsuit that served as shipboard working dress, then headed down to the wardroom. Many commanders preferred to meet with their department heads in the more private and intimate setting of their own cabins, but Sikander felt that he spent more than enough time cooped up in his own quarters. On his ship, the officers' mess doubled as the ship's executive conference room. It also had the added advantage of a fully equipped galley and a well-stocked refrigerator right next door.

Amelia Fraser waited for him at the long table with six other officers: Lieutenant Michael Girard, operations officer; Lieutenant Commander Jaime Herrera, gunnery officer; Sublieutenant Zoe Worth, ship's flight and deck officer; Lieutenant Commander Grant Edwards, supply officer; Lieutenant Carla Ruiz, medical officer; and Sublieutenant Reed Hollister, power plant officer. Girard was an old shipmate of his from CSS *Hector*, a fellow survivor of the furious battle at Gadira; Worth had served with him aboard *Normandy* as a brand-new ensign when he was the assault transport's XO. Herrera, Edwards, and Ruiz were all new shipmates, but during his time aboard *Decisive* Sikander had learned that he could rely on them to run their departments efficiently and generally count on their judgment. Hollister he didn't know quite as well, but that was because he was the senior division officer in the Engineering Department and not the actual department head. Chief Engineer Victoria Walsh had rotated out just before Sikander departed for his leave, so Hollister had stepped up to serve as the acting chief engineer until Walsh's replacement reported aboard.

A good team, Sikander reflected. *Decisive* might not have been a frontline fleet destroyer, but she'd certainly collected a first-rate crew.

"Attention on deck," Fraser announced. The assembled group stood and faced the door.

"Carry on," Sikander replied; his officers returned to their seats. "It's good to see everybody. What did I miss?"

"We took her out for a spin while you were gone, Captain," Herrera quipped. A strapping New Caledonian with a weightlifter's sculpted physique, he concealed a very unserious personality behind his fierce appearance; he let no meeting pass without some attempt at humor. "She's fast off the starting line but fishtails on the corners if you don't watch yourself. Might be missing some paint on the rear quarter panel, sorry."

"So I shouldn't look too closely at the odometer?"

"Oh, we rolled it back, sir," Worth said. She was positively tiny beside the hulking gunnery officer, dark-haired and so young-looking she probably could have passed for a student if she dressed for the part. She was responsible for the ship's deckhands and flight operations. "You'll find that it shows a kilometer less than when you left."

"I expected no less from you," Sikander said, and took his seat at the head of the table. "Okay, let's get to work. XO, walk me through our job list from the refit, and tell me what we missed."

"I've got it right here, Captain," Fraser answered. She pointed a remote at the wardroom's big vidscreen, and pulled up a file Sikander had studied for hours before going on leave: the list of repairs, special maintenance, refits, upgrades, and replacements that *Decisive* had accumulated over the two and a half years since her previous visit to the shipyard. When he'd left, half the items had been highlighted in yellow for "work under way, not complete"; now the vast majority of the list was a very reassuring green. Clearly the Neda Naval Shipyard had been hard at work while he was off in Kashmir, and that meant his officers and crew had been busy as well.

One by one, his department heads took turns explaining the

items on their portions of the list that remained incomplete—an old power conduit no longer in use that was too much trouble to remove, a food-storage freezer that slowly lost refrigerant but wasn't worth replacing, pocking and pitting on the ship's bow armor that didn't quite meet the requirement for patching but had been close enough that Sikander had wanted it added to the list, and a dozen more mostly cosmetic issues. The Commonwealth Navy had its budget constraints, but Sikander wanted to make sure he understood exactly what hadn't been done and why it had been skipped. No captain liked the idea of leaving the shipyard with parts of the to-do list unchecked, no matter how small. Fortunately, it seemed that Neda had taken care of the major issues; Sikander really had no cause to complain.

"Very good," he said when his department heads finished their reports. "*Decisive* didn't get ten years younger while I was away, but she certainly has that new-flyer smell. I'm looking forward to shaking her down. So, Mr. Girard, why don't you tell us about when and where we're going?"

"Aye, Captain," Michael Girard replied. As *Decisive*'s operations officer, Girard was primarily responsible for mission planning and analysis. When Sikander had first met him eight years ago aboard CSS *Hector*, Girard had been a young ensign terrified by anyone with more than one stripe on their sleeve. He remained a little bookish and thoughtful, but he'd grown more comfortable in his own skin over the years, and he was quite possibly the smartest officer Sikander had ever served with. "The squadron's assigned us to a four-system patrol in the Zerzura region: Tejat Minor, Bursa, Dahar, and Meliya. We're to get under way at 0800 on the twenty-first, and accelerate for a transit to Tejat Minor at 1930 hours. It's a four-day transit, after which we'll be on station for twelve days before continuing on to Dahar. The op plan calls for routine propulsion tests and casualty drills—"

"Checking the shipyard's work, I suppose," Sikander observed.

"Exactly, sir," Girard continued. "I expect we'll finish up the shakedown tests within the first few days of our arrival. The rest of our deployment is devoted to antipiracy patrols: six days on station in Bursa, followed by twelve more days in Dahar before returning to Neda by way of Meliya."

"Meliya?" Worth asked. "That's not a Caliphate system."

"No, it's Velaran," said Girard. "But it's nearby, and they've got trouble with piracy, too. In the spirit of cooperation, the Velarans are allowing our squadron to add Meliya to our regional patrols."

"Do we have any specific assigned stops or patrol routes within each system?" Sikander asked his operations officer.

"No, sir. The squadron's given us a good deal of operational discretion in that regard."

"In other words, 'See if you can think of a way to get pirates to show themselves while you're around,'" said Herrera. "Not that any will."

"There's a first time for everything, Guns," Amelia Fraser pointed out. "But even if the pirates aren't stupid enough to put in an appearance while we're in the system, the fact that we're keeping them away means that the shipping lanes will be safe, and that's the whole point."

"Sure, XO," Herrera acknowledged. "But I'd really like to *catch* some pirates someday."

Sikander didn't disagree with his gunnery officer. It was disheartening to spend cruise after cruise sailing through seemingly peaceful systems, only to discover later that the region's pirates had launched a raid or attacked a merchant ship after *Decisive* had left the area. All the other Aquilan warships in Pleiades Squadron shared similar tales of disappointment. The problem was simple: planetary systems were *big*, and a criminal who had a little patience could simply go to ground somewhere out of sight—say, a

worthless rock of a moon or an asteroid with an eccentric orbit—
and wait out the patrolling ship. During his previous deployments in Zerzura's systems Sikander had tried searching likely
hiding spots instead of just standing guard, but it turned out that
planets (and moons, and asteroid belts) were big, too, and a single
ship couldn't hope to make any kind of thorough search without
months of effort. *And even if we did find an unidentified ship hiding in some crater, who's to say it's a pirate if we don't find it engaged
in piracy?* he reflected. "Tell us about Tejat Minor, Mr. Girard,"
he said, refocusing the discussion. "As I recall, it's been a while
since *Decisive* dropped by."

"Yes, sir." Girard picked up the remote on the table and pointed
it at the nearest vidscreen, bringing up a system map with planetary orbits marked in bright circles around the central star. "It's
a multiple-star system whose primary component is the red giant
Tejat, here. Tejat Minor is a distant red dwarf companion with
five planets of its own. The second of those is a semi-terran world
settled back during the First Expansion. It's the system's only inhabited planet, so naturally that's where the commercial traffic
concentrates."

"What's the recent pirate activity look like?" said Grant Edwards. He was a laconic New Andalusian who pressed his shipboard uniform into perfect creases and preferred smart spectacles
in place of the corrective eye surgery most other nearsighted
Aquilans chose.

"Five incidents so far this year," Girard answered. "The most
recent was two months ago. An inbound Bolívaran container ship
with a mixed cargo was intercepted about forty light-minutes out
by this ship, here." He switched the display to an image of a black-
painted light freighter that had been refitted with kinetic cannons
in open-space mounts. "The pirates put a shot through a drive
plate to show they meant business, boarded, and held the crew at

gunpoint while they removed several cargo containers with valuable consumer goods."

"The Caliphate authorities just sat on their hands and watched all this happen?" Edwards asked.

"Their local defense force consists of three system cutters, the newest seventy years old," Girard replied. "It would have taken them days to just reach the scene of the attack."

"Which is why the Admiralty's sending us," Sikander said. He glanced at the time display in the corner of the vidscreen; they'd run past noon, which meant that there were probably some hungry and annoyed junior officers lurking outside the wardroom while they waited for the department heads to finish their meeting and move on to lunch. "Mr. Girard, I assume you've got that summary of pirate activity in a convenient format?"

"Of course, Captain. It's already in your inbox."

"Copy it to all the department heads, please. On that note, let's adjourn. I know everyone has a hundred things to do to get ready for departure next week." Sikander looked around the table at his officers, and smiled broadly. "And let me say again: It's good to be back."

After lunch, Sikander spent several hours catching up on the mountains of paperwork—well, the digital version thereof—that required his personal attention after a three-week absence. The daunting backlog almost made him regret coming back, but he powered through the chore; he'd learned through hard experience that putting it off would only make the final reckoning worse. He did find time to study Michael Girard's analysis of pirate activity, which at least made for interesting reading. While no one had been hurt in the July incident, the one before that had left a crew of sixteen aboard a tanker dead, and back at the beginning of the year, eleven passengers—young men and women, evidently selected for their looks—had been abducted from a liner.

Most likely, they'd been sold into the sex trade, shipped to some distant world or outpost with no identities except those provided by their captors and little hope for help from local authorities who were either apathetic or complicit. After finishing the summary, Sikander decided that "interesting" was no longer the right word to describe the pirates' depredations. There was nothing remotely amusing about what had been going on in the Zerzura Sector.

The next day, *Decisive*'s new chief engineer reported aboard. Sikander was reading through the morning's message traffic when a knock came at his cabin door. "Come in," he called.

A lanky, good-looking officer in Aquilan dress whites entered the room, his cap tucked under one arm. Like Sikander, he wore a green sash with his Aquilan uniform, signifying dual service in the Commonwealth Navy and the Royal Kashmiri Navy. He marched up to Sikander and saluted crisply. "Lieutenant Amar Singh Shah, reporting for duty," he announced. "I'm your new engineering officer, sir."

"Commander Sikander Singh North, commanding officer." Sikander returned Shah's salute, and accepted the datastick Shah presented—the customary orders and personnel file. "Welcome aboard *Decisive*, Mr. Shah. I wasn't expecting to see you until tomorrow. You're early."

Shah grinned easily. "I'm anxious to get started, Captain."

"I certainly don't object to that." Sikander stood and nodded toward the small conference table by the large vidscreen in his suite. "Have a seat, Mr. Shah. Can I get you some tea or coffee?"

"Tea, please." Shah set his cap on the table and sat down.

"A traditionalist, I see. I'm afraid I've fallen prey to the vile Aquilan preference for the bean instead of the leaf." Sikander wasn't surprised; many Kashmiris preferred tea to coffee, and Jaipur's plantations produced some of the best to be found anywhere in human space. He busied himself with the hot water, brewing a cup of coffee for himself. He found himself remembering the day he'd reported aboard CSS *Hector* eight years ago, and Captain Elise Markham performing the same time-honored ritual on his behalf. *Strange to find myself on the other side of the table,* he reflected. Elise Markham had been a natural at this part of the job, supremely comfortable in her place, calm and reassuring in those first anxious moments of introduction. He couldn't go wrong by emulating her example. "How was your journey?"

"Swift and uneventful," Shah said. "I came straight from Laguna."

"No leave after Department Head School?"

"I had five weeks back home before I started the course, sir. And, as I said—"

"You're anxious to get started." Sikander dropped a teabag into the cup of steaming water and poured himself a mug of coffee, then brought them over to the table. "Welcome aboard, Mr. Shah. It's a pleasure to meet you."

"Actually, this is not the first time we've met," said Shah, reaching for his tea.

"It's not?"

"When you were a sublieutenant, you attended a wedding banquet at my uncle Niyam's villa near Sangrur. I was only fifteen then and short for my age, so there's no reason you should be expected to remember me. I grew into my height a little later."

Sikander studied Shah closely, searching his memory. He remembered the wedding celebration at the King estate and he recalled meeting some of the younger members of the King family, but he didn't remember any Shahs . . . "You're Amar King!" he said suddenly.

Like the Norths, the Kings ruled as nawabs over a major region of Kashmir—in their case, the continent of Chandigarh on Srinagar—and they owned estates throughout Kashmir, including one on Long Lake even grander than the North manor there. Before the Aquilan conquest of the system, the Kings and the Norths had often been rivals or even enemies, caught up in the great game of the families vying for control over Kashmir's worlds. Even today, more than a hundred years after the Aquilan admiral Alberto Reyes had smashed the last independent Kashmiri fleets, the traditional divisions lingered . . . and the Aquilan governors-general sometimes exploited them. *Like the King soldiers at Bathinda,* Sikander remembered. The Chandigarh Lancers—

—march swiftly from the stern gates of the transports, carrying their heavy mag rifles at port arms. Instead of their scarlet parade uniforms, they wear mottled brown combat armor and battle helmets. This is a combat operation, not a mere show of force, and it's breaking news all across Kashmir.

Sikander watches the live feed on an entertainment system in the Sangrur palace's family residence. He's stunned by developments in Bathinda. "They can't do that!" he snarls at the vidscreen.

"It seems that the governor-general thinks that he can," his older brother Devindar says in a bitter tone, watching the report beside Sikander.

"This is Jaipur!" Sikander says, waving a hand at the screen. "We're a sovereign state! If the situation requires troops, it's a job for our dragoons, not King lancers from Srinagar. They have no jurisdiction here!"

"The classic tactic of the imperialist power," Devindar observes. "Send troops from one part of the empire to quell troubles in another. Are you really so surprised?"

Sikander doesn't answer. In fact, he is surprised. Aquilan soldiers—well, Chandigarhi soldiers led by Aquilan officers, which are more or less the same thing as Aquilan soldiers—haven't entered his father's domain without invitation since before he was born. For generations, the Aquilans have exercised control over Kashmir by permitting the system's nawabs to govern their own states with varying degrees of autonomy. Does Governor-General Braxton think we can't trust our own troops to suppress the strike? *he fumes.* Or does he think that the Norths are the ones who can't be trusted?

"*I wonder if Father knew about this,*" Devindar muses. "*For that matter, did he ask for the governor-general to intervene? He's been looking for a chance to crack down on the liberation movement. This way he can keep his hands clean while someone else handles the KLP.*"

"*Keep your conspiracy theories to yourself, Devin,*" Sikander snaps. "*I don't want to hear them.*"

"*No, I guess you don't. But that doesn't mean they aren't right.*" Devindar watches the screen a moment longer, then suddenly turns on his heel and hurries away.

"*Where are you going?*" Sikander calls after him, worried that his brother is about to go confront Nawab Dayan. Today is not the day to test their father's patience.

"*Bathinda,*" Devindar says over his shoulder. "*That's where the struggle is, and I need to be there. See you around, Sikay.*"

"I see that you remember me after all," said Shah, bringing Sikander back to the present.

"You peppered me with questions about the naval service." Sikander shook his head, brushing away the memory of Chandigarh Lancers landing in Bathinda and his old argument with Devindar. "If you're here, I suppose you were satisfied with the answers I gave you."

"I was. I knew it would be hard at the Academy—you made that much clear—but I wanted to test myself, and your example inspired me to apply. I was one of eleven Kashmiris admitted to the class of '03, thanks to you."

"It was long past time for the Commonwealth to make room for more Kashmiri officers in the service." Sikander had never considered the idea that others might follow in his footsteps. In fact, he was a little uncomfortable with it; the only reason he'd been admitted to the Academy was that his father had pulled strings and called in favors in order to send him to High Albion. He wondered how many Kashmiris were in this year's Academy class, and resolved to find out. "I should have recognized you from your service jacket. I'm afraid the name threw me off."

"When I entered the Academy, I decided that I preferred the sound of it in High Panjabi, not Standard Anglic. Many of the Kings in my generation choose to go by Shah instead."

"I see." Sikander wondered what the older Kings made of that. It had never come up in his own family; they were happy to be known as Norths, not Utaras. He'd heard of other Kashmiris dropping Anglic family names or place names, but he'd never really seen the point of it. Kashmir had been originally settled by people descended from the Sikh diaspora on ancient Earth, many in blended families. They were English and Canadian and Indian and American as well as Punjabi, united by a common faith. To Sikander, recognizing the fullness of that heritage didn't make one less of a Kashmiri or imply undue sympathy for the Anglic-descended peoples who made up most of the Commonwealth of Aquila. Certainly he'd never heard Devindar or any of his friends come out and say that Kashmir's Anglic names had to go, and Devindar's anticolonialism lagged behind nobody's.

It's none of my business, he reminded himself. People had the right to be called what they wanted to be called, and if he detected an implicit criticism in the younger Kashmiri's choice, that was his problem, not his new chief engineer's. "Shah it is, then. You're joining us at a good time; we get under way next week to perform in-service trials after our recent yard time. Have you given any thought to how you'd like to get started with your department?"

"I have, sir. I plan to conduct a rigorous inspection of all the repairs and installations completed during the ship's refit. It's as good a way as any to familiarize myself with the engineering plant and the mechanical systems, and it never hurts to check up on the work that's been done."

"We've been doing a lot of that already," Sikander said. "But some extra thoroughness doesn't hurt, and a chief engineer shouldn't be afraid to get dirty. Go on."

"I believe I'll have my division officers and their chief petty officers walk me through what's been done in each of their spaces. That should give me plenty of opportunity to see what my junior officers know, as well as showing them something about what I expect from them."

"I approve. I think you'll find that you're inheriting a good team. If Lieutenant Walsh—your predecessor—had a weakness, it was her tendency to rely on senior people to fix things instead of allowing more junior hands to make a few mistakes while learning what needed to be done. That made sense when we were trying to keep some problems in check until the yard could get at them for a proper repair job, but now that we're done with our refit, I think it's time to invest in our people again."

"That seems sound to me, sir. I'll keep an eye open for that sort of top-heavy thinking as I get to know my team."

"Good." Sikander drained the last of his coffee, and stood. "Well, Mr. Shah, I'm pleased to see that you found something useful in whatever it was I said to you ten years ago. Make sure you introduce yourself to the XO—she's sharp as a tack, and she knows your department well. She can be a great resource for you. And, of course, my door is always open."

"Thank you, sir."

"Great to have you aboard—welcome to *Decisive*." Sikander shook Shah's hand firmly, and walked him to the cabin door.

Shah certainly seems confident, he decided as he returned to his desk. *Perhaps too confident?* Back when Sikander had started his own first department-head tour aboard CSS *Hector*, he'd adopted more of a watch-and-wait attitude, avoiding big changes until he had a sense of how his subordinates worked. Shah seemed eager to dive in—not unusual in new department heads, but likely to lead to turmoil as everyone adjusted to the new boss's leadership style. And, even though Sikander didn't like to dwell on it, the Aquilan officers and enlisted hands who made up the great majority of *Decisive*'s Engineering Department might not react well to a Kashmiri department head suddenly questioning how things were done. He hoped that after a year of command he'd more than proven to *Decisive*'s crew that Kashmiris could do the job, but he'd also chosen to tread softly and show a certain amount of open-mindedness in his leadership style.

That also means allowing my department heads the chance to show me that they can do things their own way, he reminded himself. *If I wouldn't advise an Aquilan officer to go lightly, I shouldn't treat Shah any differently just because he's a Kashmiri.*

Later in the afternoon, Sikander and Darvesh left the ship to run a few errands ashore. First they took a hired flyer over to Sikander's bungalow in Tawahi City to drop off their extra bags from the extended stay in Kashmir. The nonmilitary portion of Tawahi was a thoroughly Aquilan bubble on a world that otherwise hadn't changed much in the centuries since it had been a Caliphate colony; decent rental houses cost a small fortune, but Sikander hadn't ever had to worry much about whether he could afford something. The spaciousness of captain's quarters notwithstanding, it was healthy to be able to leave the ship in the evenings and on weekends simply to avoid the temptation to work all the time. He often brought paperwork home with him, but reading reports in shorts on his own back patio at least offered a change of scenery. He also enjoyed having a place where he could entertain *Decisive*'s officers or his colleagues from other ships in the squadron.

The house seemed fine, so Sikander left Darvesh to restock the groceries while he retrieved his personal flyer—a sporty performance sedan—from the garage, heading back to the naval base. He parked on a landing pad near the squadron headquarters building, smoothed the front of his uniform, and went on inside. Like Helix Squadron on the Tzoru frontier, Pleiades Squadron served as a standing force assigned to a distant station; ships occasionally rotated in or out, but at any given time an odd mix of half a dozen or so Aquilan destroyers and corvettes operated from the base at Neda. It was a less exotic posting than the remote Tzoru Dominion, but still a long way from the Commonwealth's home territory. Some officers regarded it as a sleepy assignment unlikely to do much to advance a career or provide the same opportunities for building patronage networks that a main-battle-fleet billet offered, but Sikander had never looked at it that way. He preferred the freedom and independence of serving at a small outpost a long way from the Admiralty's bureaucratic eye.

"Commander North to see Captain Broward," he told the admin specialist at the squadron's reception desk. "I believe he's expecting me?"

The admin checked his dataslate. "Yes, sir. Go on in."

Sikander nodded his thanks, and headed into the squadron CO's office, pausing to knock once at the door. "Captain Broward?" he called.

Wilson Broward, commanding officer of Pleiades Squadron and the sitting Senator St. John, looked up from a row of colorful windowsill plants he tended and set down his watering can. "Commander North! I see that you've returned. Come on in."

"Thank you, sir. It's good to be back." Sikander walked in and offered an easy salute, which Broward returned with an absent wave of his hand; he didn't really stand on the formalities. Short in stature and rather thick-waisted for a serving officer, Broward had passed the customary retirement age for officers who failed to screen for flag rank years ago. Most who reached the rank of captain and missed out on a commodore's star chose to retire at fifty-five or sixty, but Wilson Broward had simply shrugged it off and kept on going, bouncing around various shore commands and the sort of postings more ambitious officers avoided as career suicide. How he'd managed to even reach a captain's rank in the first place Sikander couldn't say, but then again, a senator's seat went a long way in the Commonwealth Navy.

"How was your leave?" Broward asked.

"Very good, thank you. I had a nice long visit with my family. But I admit I missed *Decisive*."

"There's nothing quite like your first command," Broward agreed. "I kept an eye on your XO in case she ran into any headaches with the shipyard, but as it turned out she didn't need my help."

"She doesn't really need mine, either," Sikander admitted.

Broward laughed out loud. He had a pleasant laugh, rich and rolling, and he seemed to use it a lot. No doubt his amiable nature had helped him along the way just as much as his lofty pedigree; Sikander honestly liked the man even when he wondered whether he was any good at what he did. "Half the job is recognizing when our people just need us to stay out of their way. Speaking of which, I'm sure you're anxious to take *Decisive* out and give her a good shakedown cruise."

"I am, sir. We're scheduled to provision and fuel the ship first thing next week, and get under way Thursday morning."

"Good. She's a handsome ship, but she'd look better in space."

"I agree. Anything you'd like to add to the op orders, sir?"

"Not especially. After you see to your shakedown exercises, it's a standard antipiracy patrol. Escort any merchant ships that request protection, stop and investigate suspicious vessels, show the flag—just like your last two patrols. I imagine that any pirate in your neighborhood will go to ground when he sees *Decisive* on the beat, but at least you'll make them keep their heads down."

"Until we move on to the next system, anyway."

"Well, we can't be everywhere at once, and extended patrols are better than nothing. You're in a rotation with Giselle Dacey's *Harrier* and Davis Newcomb's *Vigilant*, so any troublemakers in the systems you visit can't be sure when another one of our destroyers might pop up."

"Very good, sir." Sikander hoped it worked out that way, but as Broward said, it was better than nothing.

"I suppose the only thing I'd add is a note of concern from the Foreign Ministry," said Broward. "They're worried that the Caliphate's sector governor—a fellow known as Marid Pasha—might be thinking of going his own way. The sector government quietly put out some feelers to the neighboring powers, and our diplomats got wind of the pasha's dissatisfaction with the state of affairs in his corner of the Caliphate. Zerzura is independent in all but name anyway, and Terra probably couldn't do anything to stop him if Marid Pasha did declare himself king."

"I haven't met the man, but I'm familiar with his reputation," Sikander said. "What does that mean for us?"

"No one's really sure. The most pessimistic estimates suggest that Marid Pasha could precipitate a general fracturing of the

Caliphate by inspiring other sectors to follow Zerzura's lead. Some others think that he might instead have ideas of forming his own Terran union by convincing his fellow pashas to support him." Broward inspected one of the small plants on his windowsill, and applied a little more water. "We've got a special envoy on Dahar now, trying to sort things out. God knows the Caliphate could use some new blood at the top, but the Foreign Ministry's worried that Dremark or Montréal or Velar might see this as an opportunity to rearrange this whole region more to their liking, and of course we wouldn't want that."

"The sick old man of the Coalition." Sikander had certainly read plenty of speculation over the years about whether the Terran Caliphate could survive in its current form, and what it would mean for the great powers that made up the rest of the Coalition of Humanity if it collapsed. "Sir, I have to admit that I'm not sure how that impacts our antipiracy patrols. Am I supposed to avoid stepping on Zerzuran toes? Cooperate with other powers, or keep my distance if I run into any of their ships?"

"Carry on as you normally would, I suppose," said Broward with a shrug. "Our best course of action is to show this Marid Pasha that Aquila can be a valuable friend, so do what you can to catch pirates. Good hunting, Commander."

5

hrieking sirens from his cabin's alarm panel woke Sikander an hour before reveille on *Decisive*'s third day of propulsion tests in Tejat Minor. He flew out of his bunk in his sleeping shorts, dimly recognizing the unique warble of a power plant failure alert, and punched the ship's command circuit. "This is the captain!" he barked. "Main Control, report!"

No one replied for a moment, although Sikander heard shouts and alarms wailing in the engineering spaces over the live audio feed. He was about to repeat his order when he finally got an answer: "This is Sublieutenant Hollister, sir, engineering officer of the watch. Catastrophic failure of magnetic containment in generator two. The thermal failsafes kicked in and vented the reaction chamber to space. We did not, I repeat we did *not*, suffer a containment breach—it looks like the system caught it in time. We're bringing generator three online now to pick up the load."

Sikander shook his head, not sure he'd heard the report correctly. The ship's fusion generators—*Decisive* carried four of them, two each in the two generator rooms—were about the safest and most reliable system in the whole engineering plant. Theoretically, a sudden failure of the magnetic fields that contained the fusion reaction could result in star-hot plasma breaching the generator chamber and slagging the surrounding compartment, but fusion plants were designed to shut down automatically long before that sort of disaster could unfold. If the fusion generator had dumped its incandescent fuel mix out into space instead of quietly shutting down, something had gone very wrong indeed.

"Captain, Bridge," his command circuit announced. "Sublieutenant Worth, officer of the deck. Sir, we've had a serious casualty in engineering. We just lost generator two, but it appears there is no other damage—I'm trying to get more details now. Shall I set general quarters?"

"I'm already on the line with main control, Ms. Worth," Sikander told her. He briefly considered whether to send the ship to battle stations; it would provide *Decisive* with the most extensive and redundant level of system settings and compartmentalization, providing some extra protection against cascading damage. But it would also distract the team currently working on the problem in the engineering spaces, and wake up the whole crew for a situation that seemed to have already run its course. "No, don't sound GQ. Secure from maneuvering and leave all power settings and machinery configurations as they are unless main control tells you otherwise."

"Secure from maneuvering, don't change any power or machinery configurations, aye, Captain. We'll just coast until we hear otherwise. Bridge, out."

"Main Control, captain speaking," Sikander said. "I'm on my way down."

"Aye, Captain," Hollister replied. "Um, Mr. Shah just got here."

"Very well. Carry on." Sikander cut the comms, and checked the damage-control circuits and status displays by his desk—a captain's stateroom included repeaters for most of the ship's alarm systems. Several indicators in the engineering plant flashed orange, but nothing else seemed to be in imminent danger. Until this moment, the shakedown cruise had been going well—they'd gotten under way on time, they'd executed a seamless transit from Neda to Tejat Minor, and for the last three days his engineers had worked the ship's propulsion plant from one end to the other without finding anything more serious than scuff marks and misplaced tools after the stint in the shipyard. Losing a major system like one of the ship's four generators was *not* supposed to happen just weeks after a refit.

It must have been a faulty installation, he thought as he pulled on his uniform and ran a comb through his hair. *Thank God the reaction vented safely!*

He left his cabin and hurried aft. *Decisive's* main engineering plant consisted of two generator rooms, two engine rooms housing the ship's induction drives for propulsion in normal space, the drive room with its warp generator and exotic-matter storage system, and various auxiliary spaces for the ship's life-support and artificial-gravity systems; the five large machinery rooms formed the core of the ship. The main control station was located between the alternating engine and generator rooms, eighty meters aft and three decks down from Sikander's cabin. He refrained from sprinting, since it was important for the commanding officer to avoid an appearance of panic, but he did make the trip in less than a minute.

He found Amelia Fraser only half a step behind him when he reached the last hatch. "Good morning, Captain," she said. "Not the way we expected to start the day, is it?" Her only concession to the unexpected hour was a simple ponytail instead of the more carefully arranged bun she usually favored for her shoulder-length hair.

"Not quite," Sikander admitted. Naturally, his XO had responded just as quickly as he had; the ship's info assistant repeated the same alarms he received in her cabin, too. "Well, let's see what the trouble is."

He opened the hatch and headed inside. Main control was about half the size of *Decisive*'s bridge, a long and narrow room that ran athwart the ship with armored windows looking out on the drive room to one side and the first engine room to the other. Between the windows stood large consoles that controlled virtually every system in the engineering plant—hence the name of the compartment. In addition to the normal watch team, half a dozen senior personnel from the Engineering Department crowded into the control room, including Amar Shah, main propulsion assistant Olivia Haynes, Chief Petty Officer Nicole Ryan, and Generator Tech First Class Eduardo Cruz of P Division. Everyone in the compartment seemed to be talking at once.

"Captain's in main control," Chief Ryan announced loudly, cutting through the chatter.

"Carry on," Sikander told the assembled engineers. "Mr. Hollister, you've got the watch. What's the status of the power plant?"

Reed Hollister glanced around uncertainly; sweat gleamed on his forehead, and his eyes seemed as wide as saucers. "Um, Mr. Shah has relieved me, sir. But we secured generator two and we brought generator three online. Generator one was unaffected by the, er, problem, and it's fine. No outages or interruptions in supply as far as we can tell."

"Very well," Sikander replied. He wasn't sure that he approved of Shah relieving Hollister—if nothing else, it could be seen as a very public expression of no confidence in his subordinate—but he'd bring that up with Shah later. By regulation the chief engineer of an Aquilan warship had the right and duty to assume the engineering watch whenever he saw the need, and as far as Sikander knew Shah was correct in doing so. "Thank you, Mr. Hollister. Mr. Shah, can we resume our previous acceleration?"

"Yes, Captain," Shah replied. "Our power-plant configuration is now stable and no other systems are affected."

"XO, please advise the bridge to resume course," Sikander told Fraser. *Decisive* was millions of kilometers from any possible collision danger or need to maneuver, but they had a patrol plan—he saw no reason not to continue it. Fraser moved over to the ship's intercom and called the bridge, while Sikander turned his attention to the displays in the control room. Other than the icon for generator two blinking red, everything else seemed normal enough. "Okay, Mr. Shah. I see that the generator's magnetic bottle failed and the normal shutdown routine didn't kick in, so the thermals blew out and vented the chamber to space. Can we tell *why* that happened?"

"No, sir, not yet," Shah replied. "The watch was engaged in conducting some routine capacity checks on the generators when it happened, so I imagine that's the immediate cause of the failure. But as far as I can tell on a quick inspection, nothing exceeded normal operating parameters. It will take a little investigation to determine exactly how the capacity checks blew the bottle."

"And shorted out the shutdown routine," Chief Ryan added. "We've got two faults here, Captain, not just one."

Sikander nodded—he'd already noticed that much. He didn't have the specialized training of an engineer, but any Aquilan officer who aspired to command needed to learn the fundamentals of operating the ship's engines and power systems. He'd qualified as an engineering officer of the watch back in his second division-officer tour, and Command School had included a strong focus on ship systems as a refresher for officers who hadn't spent much time in engineering billets. "How bad is the damage to generator two? Can we make repairs under way, or do we need to return to a repair facility?"

Petty Officer Cruz spoke up; as the leading technician in the power plant team, he was the ship's resident expert on the fusion generator. "Sir, at a minimum we'll have to replace the thermal-fail panels and the injector nozzles. We carry spares for those, and it's not too bad a job. But I'm worried about the control circuitry—something clearly failed there to short out the magnetic bottle, and we won't know what until we crack open the console and trace it out. I'll know more in a few hours."

"Then I'll get out of your way and let you tear it down," Sikander replied. No one would work any better with the commanding officer hovering over their shoulder; time to let his people do their jobs. "Mr. Shah, keep me posted."

"Aye, Captain," Shah replied.

Sikander took one last look at the display, and left the compartment. Fraser followed him out and closed the hatch behind them; they paused in the passageway just outside main control. "What do you make of it?" he asked her.

"Bad installation from the shipyard," she replied. "It must be. The generator itself is original machinery, but the control units were all replaced during the refit. What else could it be?"

"If we can't repair the control unit, we'll be short a generator," Sikander said. *Decisive* could run on the output of a single generator in an emergency, but normal operation called for two generators online and two offline at any given time, and of course all four generators were expected to be in service during any kind of combat or emergency maneuvering. "Our standing orders would require us to cut short the patrol and return for repair."

"Damn. It feels like we just got here. I'd hate to turn around and head for home."

"Me too. I came here to look for pirates, not to break down and return to base." Sikander sighed. "Well, I'm up now. I might as well have some breakfast and start the day."

Three hours later, Amar Shah came to see him, with Supply Officer Grant Edwards in tow. The engineer's jumpsuit had picked up some soot marks, but he otherwise seemed as fresh and alert as when Sikander had seen him first thing in the morning. "I have some news, Captain," Shah began. "We're still working to determine how exactly the fault occurred, but we believe the generator is not seriously damaged. We'll have to replace some circuitry in the control unit, and then we can bring generator two back online. As a precaution, I have ordered that we avoid running any of the generators in the test mode number two was in until we finish our investigation into the cause."

"Very good," Sikander replied—it was certainly better news than he'd expected to hear. "I believe I hear a 'but' coming?"

"You do, sir," said Edwards. "Replacing the control circuitry will deplete the ship's spare-part stock. It's a mission-critical stock and we're supposed to seek immediate resupply when we fall under the minimum level."

"Plus, we just experienced one failure," Shah pointed out. "If we have another—"

"We won't be able to fix it," Sikander finished for him. "Damn. So it's back to base."

"Maybe, sir," Edwards said. "I've been looking into local sources to see if we can restock without heading back to Neda. There's nothing here in Tejat Minor, but there's a local logistics facility in Bursa that should have the spare boards we need. It would probably cost less than a thousand credits out of our operating budget."

"Bursa, you say?" Sikander ran a hand through his hair, thinking. It was the next system on their patrol route, and technically closer than Neda. While Captain Broward certainly wouldn't

fault him for bringing *Decisive* back to base, it would throw off
the rotation Pleiades Squadron had arranged to patrol the Zerzura Sector. Using a little initiative to make repairs and stay on
station was well within Sikander's discretion. "All right. Mr. Shah,
proceed with the repairs. Mr. Edwards, prepare your shopping
list. We'll cut short our stay here in Tejat and restock our spares
in Bursa as regulations require. I'll have Mr. Girard work out the
schedule change."

Decisive departed Tejat Minor the following day after a nine-hour
acceleration. The trip to Bursa was a bit shorter than the first leg
of their patrol from Neda to Tejat, a warp transit of just under four
days. Most of the ship's company quickly fell into their transit routines of watchstanding, professional study, and working out, but
the engineers pored over the power-system diagnostics and fault-
testing around the clock, while the Ops Department adjusted
the ship's patrol plans and prepared an arrival briefing for Bursa.
Michael Girard presented it to all the officers not on watch—or
busy overseeing the generator repairs—halfway through the trip,
assembling *Decisive*'s department heads and division officers in
the wardroom just before supper.

"Attention on deck!" Amelia Fraser called as Sikander entered
the room.

"Carry on, everybody," Sikander replied, taking his usual seat
at the head of the table. "Mr. Girard, you have the floor."

"Thank you, Captain." The very idea of addressing twenty
fellow officers and the ship's captain would have sent the young
Ensign Girard into a panic attack, but he'd gained a little self-
confidence since Sikander had first met him. He began by calling up a cluttered system map on the wardroom's large vidscreen.
"This is the Bursa system, named for its primary inhabited world.

We're scheduled to terminate our transit at 1423 hours the day after tomorrow, which should return us to normal space about here. As you can see, that's a remote arrival point. The Bursa system is home to three significant asteroid belts, and we need to make sure we err on the side of safety. Most inbound shipping arrives at least seven AU out."

"No reason to show off with precision navigation," Sikander observed. Or scour the locals with hard radiation if *Decisive* missed its arrival point by a little bit, for that matter—starships dumped vast amounts of energy in arrival cascades when the time came to cut off their warp bubbles, so it was important to make sure you didn't make your arrival too close to anything you cared about. And, since ships returned to normal space with the same velocity they'd built up during their transit acceleration, it was a good idea to make sure there was plenty of open space around the intended arrival point. Colliding with an asteroid or an ore freighter when you returned to normal space at eight or ten percent of the speed of light would be spectacular, to say the least. "Continue."

"Bursa itself is a semi-terran moon of the fourth planet, which is a superjovian that helped to make all those asteroids. No other moons or planets in the system are remotely habitable, but the asteroid belts are rich and they're the center of an impressive extraction industry."

"Lots of places to hide," Zoe Worth observed. "And lots of local traffic for a pirate to blend in with."

Girard nodded. "Bursa has suffered more pirate incidents than any other system in the Zerzura Sector. It's probably our best chance to actually catch someone in the act."

"Is there any pattern to the attacks?" Sikander asked.

"They're pretty random, sir." Girard continued on to an overview of the recent attacks in the Bursa system: a dozen attacks over the last year, including two superfreighters plundered of cargo worth millions. If there was a pattern to them, Sikander couldn't see it. *You'd think at least some of these pirates would be rich enough to retire by now,* he thought glumly. *God knows they seem to be doing all right for themselves!*

His officers seemed as stumped as he was. "How do we catch them?" Carla Ruiz asked. "The only rule of thumb I see here is that acts of piracy stop whenever the Navy's around. The cockroaches don't show themselves when we're in the kitchen, and we can't be everywhere at once."

"Sooner or later someone is going to make a mistake," Sikander replied, speaking as much for his own reassurance as the medical officer's. "All we can do is be ready to act when our opportunity comes. Have a little faith, Doctor."

The day before their arrival, Amar Shah notified Sikander that he'd completed his initial investigation into the generator two failure. He came to Sikander's cabin to present his report; Amelia Fraser joined them. Darvesh Reza quietly set out coffee, tea, and small pastries for their discussion before disappearing into the tiny galley that adjoined Sikander's cabin. Sikander and his XO studied their dataslates for a long time, reading over the summary. When they finished, Sikander set down the report, frowning. "So it comes down to a bad installation, as we suspected," he said.

"Yes, sir," Shah said. "Two of them, just as Chief Ryan predicted. The control unit had a bad board, which failed when a minor power fluctuation shorted out a vulnerable component. The control unit should stand up to that sort of thing, but our generators are no longer new models and the available parts have been sitting in storage for twenty years in some cases. Anyway, the board's failure caused a cascading failure in the control program—"

"—which collapsed the magnetic bottle," Fraser said, finishing Shah's thought. She'd spent more time in engineering billets than Sikander had; she had a better grasp of the power systems than he did.

"As you say, ma'am," Shah replied. "That failure I can forgive. Nothing would have showed up in the routine testing performed after the installation. The second fault is the one I'm angry about: The magnetic flux sensor was improperly installed. There was a bad weld which created a gap in the sensor's thermal protection. When the bottle started to fail, the reaction chamber's rising temperature melted the sensor before it triggered fuel-injection shutdown. As a result, the bottle collapsed completely and the thermal panels—our last line of defense against a containment breach—vented as designed." The Kashmiri engineer shook his head in disgust. "Thank God those at least were properly installed. Otherwise we likely would have lost the entire generator room."

Sikander frowned. He hadn't realized just how close they'd come to disaster. In retrospect, returning to Neda might have been a better decision than making the repairs and continuing their deployment. "All right, Mr. Shah. Make sure you've got your investigation fully documented, and I'll forward your report to the squadron and the shipyard. Clearly we need to hold the yard to a higher standard."

"Yes, sir. I have already prepared the report." Shah made a few notes on his dataslate, then pulled up a new document. "In addition, I have drafted a letter of reprimand for Sublieutenant Hollister for you to attach to the report."

"A letter of reprimand?" Sikander asked sharply. That was a very serious step—few careers survived a formal reprimand. "On what grounds?"

"Mr. Hollister signed off on the flux-sensor installation, Captain." Shah showed Sikander the digital form on his dataslate. "Here. You can see he specifically checked approval for the weld-test inspection last month. The shipyard made a mistake, yes, but so did he when he accepted substandard work. His oversight could easily have led to very serious damage to the ship, or even loss of life."

"He was acting chief engineer at the time," Fraser pointed out. "He must have signed fifty acceptance certifications a day toward the end of our yard time."

"Which does not relieve him of the obligation to confirm that the work he certifies was actually accomplished," Shah replied. He looked back to Sikander, his expression unflinching. "I believe that someone must be held accountable, sir."

Sikander hesitated. In theory, yes, an officer was responsible for anything he signed. But in practice, the Navy expected that a division officer would delegate a job like verifying a weld test to an enlisted technician with expertise in that sort of work, then rely on his subordinate's report. He could easily imagine that the weld had looked okay to a visual inspection, or that a busy generator technician had spot-checked some welds without checking each and every one. A formal reprimand would have been appropriate if Hollister had *known* it hadn't been checked and signed off anyway . . . but if he'd been *told* that it had been done by a shipyard worker or a *Decisive* crewhand and had no reason to suspect otherwise, then it was an honest mistake in Sikander's book. *For that matter, it might have been an honest mistake from the start,* he thought. *A misread instrument, simply forgetting to check one part of the job, a distraction at the wrong moment. We're all human, after all.*

"Let me think on the question of a reprimand," he told Shah. "It's not a step that should be taken lightly. But go ahead and transmit the rest of the report when we arrive in Bursa. I will add my endorsement of your findings."

"Sir—" Shah started to object, then stopped himself with a small scowl when he saw that Sikander had made his decision. After a moment, he nodded. "Yes, Captain. I will await your decision."

"Thank you, Mr. Shah. And please convey my appreciation to your team, as well." Sikander tapped his finger on the report on his dataslate. "This represents a lot of hard work in a short amount of time. Carry on."

Sikander took his place on the bridge a few minutes before the end of the ship's transit, making a show of reading through old message traffic on his dataslate while he quietly observed his crew at work. Like the command decks of most Aquilan warships, *Decisive*'s bridge was located in the center of the hull in the forward third of the ship for protection against enemy fire, although no destroyer was designed to stand up to heavy damage—agility served as *Decisive*'s best defense. A series of deck-to-overhead vidscreens arranged in an arrowhead shape provided a nearly 360-degree view from the ship's exterior hull cams, over which the tactical sensors displayed augmented icons and informational tags describing anything the bridge team needed to know about. In routine operation that meant the locations and orbits of celestial bodies and the course and speed of system traffic, but in combat the displays included targeting data, threat analyses, damage reports, and more. At the moment, however, nothing more than a scenic starfield and a large countdown ticking down the time remaining in the ship's transit occupied the bridge's displays. Ships in a warp bubble couldn't see anything of the universe outside their own warp field, so the ship's systems projected a best-guess image of what they'd see if they were in normal space. Sikander had always rather liked the view, even if it was only a simulation.

"One minute to arrival, Captain," Lieutenant Girard told him.

He served as the ship's officer of the deck during transit initiation and termination. "All stations report manned and ready."

"Very well," Sikander replied. Aquilan warships normally assumed battle stations for arrival, not that anyone expected to come under immediate attack—after all, the idea was to arrive with a safety cushion of millions of kilometers of empty space. However, if some catastrophic error in navigation left the ship in immediate peril upon its return to normal space, setting general quarters meant that the ship was as ready as possible to deal with sudden damage or emergency maneuvers. He keyed the ship's general announcing system from his command seat. "Attention, all hands: This is the captain. Make ready for imminent system arrival."

He returned his attention to the countdown timer. Precisely at 0:00:00, the ship's warp generator cut off, and *Decisive* returned to normal space in the Bursa system. Some people claimed that they could tell when a ship dropped its warp bubble, but Sikander doubted it: No one had ever proved that the pocket of space surrounding a ship inside a warp bubble differed in any way from the rest of the universe outside of it, or demonstrated any physiological effects to warp travel. The only cue that anything had changed was a sudden flicker in the bridge displays as the ship's computers replaced the simulated projection with live sensor feed.

"Clear arrival, sir!" Ensign Grace Carter reported from her post. A bright and almost painfully eager young Caledonian, she served as *Decisive*'s sensor officer. During battle stations, she manned the bridge's sensor post and supervised the ship's sensor techs. "We have a little traffic at nine million kilometers bearing zero-five-zero up thirty, but our courses are diverging."

"Very well," Girard replied to the report. He studied his own displays at the tactical officer's position, then looked up at Sikander. "We're about fifteen light-seconds off target, Captain—we cut the warp generator a bit late."

"Close enough, Mr. Girard." In fact, it was pretty good—once or twice Sikander had seen ships miss their navigational targets by dozens of light-minutes, a rather unsettling lack of accuracy. Tiny deviations in course or timing ensured that no one ever hit the exact point they were aiming for, another reason that ships initiating a warp transit made sure to navigate toward safely empty patches of space at their destinations. "Send our arrival notification to the local authorities, depower and retract the warp ring, and secure from transit stations. Set course for Bursa."

"Aye, sir," Girard replied. Somewhere aft of the bridge, the motors controlling the ship's warp ring hummed briefly, folding the structure back into its hull fairings. "Looks like about nine . . . make that eight hours and forty minutes at standard acceleration to kill our velocity and reach orbit."

"Very good." Sikander returned his attention to his reading as the bridge team settled into their normal-space underway routine. *Decisive* spun around to point her powerful drive plates in the direction her intrinsic velocity carried her, and began applying thrust to decelerate and begin bending her course toward Bursa's inner system. While Sikander had no special obligation to remain, he'd always felt that it was good for the commanding officer to see and be seen by the crew, and he enjoyed the comfortable buzz of activity on the bridge. Some captains allowed the administrative burden of the job to trap them in their cabins, but he'd never felt the need to seek isolation in order to concentrate, and preferred to work on a busy bridge whenever he could.

He lost himself in his electronic paperwork for an hour or more, approving a number of routine reports and evaluations. Then Michael Girard called for his attention. "Captain? We've got something unusual here."

Sikander looked up and put away his dataslate. "What's that, Mr. Girard?"

Girard pointed toward the display screen. "Unknown vessel, bearing three-two-five, distance thirty million kilometers. Zero acceleration, no transponder, no response to our comms."

"That's suspicious," Sikander observed. He stood up and joined Girard by the display. They were still quite a way from the busier parts of the Bursa system—any ship they ran into out here should have been under acceleration and going somewhere more interesting. *And of course no honest captain turns off the ship's transponder,* he told himself. "Very suspicious, in fact. If you were a pirate looking for an opportunity to ambush an arriving ship . . ."

"Then you might go dark and coast along in the system's outer reaches," Girard said. "She has to know we're here, Captain. We're not exactly hiding and we just pinged her with radar."

Sikander nodded. A ship might hope to avoid attracting attention by reducing power and avoiding electronic emissions, but in general open space was a terrible place to hide—simple thermodynamics made it impossible. Maybe a freighter with civilian-grade sensors might not notice a powered-down pirate at long range, but anyone paying attention to their surroundings couldn't miss the thermal signature. If Girard's drifting vessel was a pirate, he appeared to have a great deal of misplaced confidence in his ability to avoid detection. "Class and type?" he asked.

"Messina-class medium bulk carrier. We can't quite read the registration number off the hull yet, so that's all we have for the moment."

"Bulk carrier?" That seemed an unlikely type for use as a pirate, but it was possible that *Decisive* had detected a ship under attack—another vessel might be close alongside the target, hiding in her sensor shadow. "Change course, Mr. Girard. Give me the fastest interception we can manage at full military acceleration."

"Aye, sir. Helm, come left to new course two-seven-seven. All engines ahead full." Girard studied his tactical display for a moment. "Thirty-five minutes to firing range, Captain. Eighty minutes for a zero-zero intercept."

"Very well." Sikander made himself return to his battle couch, settling in for the wait. *Could we really catch a pirate by pure dumb luck?* he wondered. The odds of ending their warp transit in the neighborhood of a pirate hoping to ambush incoming traffic seemed literally astronomical, but then again, if their quarry was indeed lurking near likely arrival spots, maybe it wasn't so unlikely after all. . . . He tapped his seat's comm panel. "XO, could you come on up to the bridge? We might have something interesting here."

"On my way, sir," Fraser replied. She appeared less than a minute later—like Sikander, she had a cabin that was located very close to the bridge. "What's up, Captain?"

"Unidentified ship, no transponder," Sikander told her. "We're heading over to have a look."

"That seems a little shady," Fraser observed.

"My thoughts exactly."

"Sir, we've got a registration for the target," Girard reported. "Her hull number indicates that she's the *Carmela Día*, sailing under the Pegasus-Pavon line. Bursa Traffic Control lists her as overdue—she was supposed to arrive eighteen days ago."

"That doesn't sound like a pirate vessel to me," Fraser said to Sikander.

"No, that sounds like a victim," Sikander agreed. "Anyone hiding in her sensor shadow, Mr. Girard?"

"No, sir, I don't believe so. It's just *Carmela Día*."

"Very well." Sikander sat back in his seat with a grimace of disappointment; he'd allowed himself to hope that maybe they'd actually caught one of the bad guys this time. Regardless, they had an obligation to investigate and to do what they could for any survivors. "Mr. Girard, make for a zero-zero intercept, and have the rescue and assistance team stand by. Someone over there may need our help."

6

Mersin, Dahar II

"Marid Pasha certainly knows how to throw a party," Omar Morillo observed. The handsome Bolívaran wore a striking plum-colored dinner jacket and a rich yellow bow tie with tight-fitting gray pants; his wavy russet hair was swept up in a spectacular pompadour that had earned the admiration of more than a few of the unattached women attending the governor's Founding Day banquet. "Now, if only he'd be so good as to serve a nice malbec or perhaps a tempranillo with the buffet spread, I might almost consider it worth attending."

"We're in Caliphate territory," Elena Pavon replied to her executive assistant. "What did you expect?" Most Zerzurans looked the other way when it came to serving alcohol in private, but not even Marid Pasha could ignore the social convention for such a high-profile public occasion. Omar would have to content himself with sparkling cider or fruit punch—and so would she, for that matter. *Just as well,* she decided. She wasn't at the Founding Day gala to celebrate; she was here to *work,* to make connections and see and be seen, and she didn't need the temptation of a glass or two of wine to get in the way of business. Likewise, she'd brought Omar along as her date for the evening to deflect the attentions of any handsome Zerzurans who might otherwise have been drawn by her daring gold evening gown and beautifully coiffed hair, so dark it was almost blue-black. Men who knew nothing about her family's wealth often found her looks sufficient to try their luck, and while that could be flattering in its own way—and perhaps a very interesting diversion, in the right time and place—Elena wanted to avoid that sort of complication for the evening. Keeping Omar close at hand would deter most of the would-be lovers. Best of all, Omar's romantic interests ran toward men, not women. He was quite immune to her charms and wouldn't mistake her intentions. *Sorry, ladies,* she silently told the women stealing glances in Omar's direction. *He's just not that into you.*

"Oh, I'm not surprised," Omar said. "But that doesn't mean I'm not a little disappointed. When the boss is picking up dinner, I feel obligated to run up the tab."

"You'd better not let her find out." Elena put on a dazzling smile and slipped her arm through Omar's as they descended the wide, sweeping staircase to the lovely open-air terrace that served as the banquet venue. The cliff-edge gardens of Mersin's swankiest hotel offered a sweeping view of the city, crowned by the pasha's spectacular mountaintop palace only a kilometer away. Hundreds of beautifully dressed women and men in a mix of elegant evening wear and splendid uniforms chattered and laughed below as a string quartet played softly in the dusk. Most of the women in attendance wore gowns cut slightly more conservatively than hers, and many added sheer headscarves for modesty. Only the most stringent Caliphate worlds insisted on the traditional hijab, but even in a culturally mixed frontier such as Zerzura the old fashions lingered on. No one was on the dance floor yet, not that there would be much dancing for couples anyway; in Elena's experience with similar occasions on other Caliphate worlds, there might be some sex-segregated traditional dances later on, or possibly some chaste line dances if people really decided to let their hair down.

She and Omar paused at a few steps above the floor, and she handed her invitation to the majordomo who stood ready to announce her arrival. "Ms. Elena Trinu Rhodanthe Pavon of Meliya and Nuevo León," the attendant read loudly. Elena noticed that at least a few heads turned in her direction; she might not be particularly well known in Dahar, but the Pavon name certainly was. She lingered a moment longer on the steps, and then she and Omar ventured down into the party.

She found herself engaged in the familiar routine of the receiving line, meeting a dozen or more of Dahar's prominent citizens in a quick swirl of activity. Governor Marid al-Zahabi did not seem to be in attendance—not unusual, since the pasha rarely attended his own parties—but many other high-ranking planetary and sector officials were. In rapid succession she met the mayor of Mersin and his wife, a tea magnate who was helping to sponsor the event and the locally famous vid starlet who was his companion, the regent of the planetary university and her husband, and the stern-looking woman who served as the financial secretary of Zerzura Sector. Then the line brought her face-to-face with a plump middle-aged businessman in an expensive jacket, a Caliphate admiral in dinner-dress uniform with loops of gold braid at the shoulder, and a younger man in civilian clothing who eyed Elena with a small smile.

"Admiral Torgut al-Kassar, commander-in-chief of the Zerzura Sector Fleet," the hotel's automated info assistant whispered in her native Español through the hidden comm device behind Elena's ear. "Mr. Hidir al-Kassar, president of Suvar United Shipping. Mr. Gadi al-Kassar, his assistant." At the same time, the automated system provided Elena's own name and position to the al-Kassars. Elena didn't need the introduction to see that the three men were closely related. The admiral was a little taller and in better shape than the older businessman, but they had the same receding hairline and the same frown lines, although Hidir tried to conceal his with a generous mustache. Gadi, on the other hand, was a leaner, thirtyish version of the older al-Kassars who wore a neatly trimmed beard.

"Ms. Pavon, a pleasure," Hidir al-Kassar said in Jadeed-Arabi; Elena spoke it well, since it served as the language of government and business in the worlds of the Terran Caliphate and many of the neighboring systems. He extended his hand. "It's good to meet a colleague, so to speak."

"Or a competitor, Mr. al-Kassar." Elena shook his hand. Pegasus-Pavon was an international shipping line spanning thirty systems, but Suvar United did quite well for itself in Zerzura's five major worlds. "I understand that you've just ordered two new container ships—business must be good. My congratulations."

Hidir al-Kassar gave a small shrug. "Ah, well, we have been lucky. Zerzura's economy is expanding; there are many opportunities for growth in this sector, as I am sure you know."

"I agree—there's plenty of room in this sector for a number of carriers. We hope to expand our own capacity in this region, too . . . just as soon as the security conditions improve." Elena gave a shrug of her bare shoulders and sighed, but she kept her eyes fixed on the Suvar executive. It hadn't escaped her attention that Suvar United's business in Zerzura seemed to be thriving while Pegasus-Pavon was targeted every few months by cargo hijackings or ransom demands. "In fact, we now have a ship overdue at Bursa and presumed lost: *Carmela Día*, a bulk freighter. It seems like another act of piracy."

"Not again!" Hidir grimaced in sympathy. "Some days it seems that Zerzura takes two steps back for every step forward. Suvar

United has lost ships to piracy, too, although none as large as *Carmela Día*."

"Another one?" said Gadi, although he seemed more interested in Elena's bold evening gown than in expressing his condolences. "That is awful. Have you notified my uncle's department about the situation?"

"Yes, Gadi, she has," Torgut al-Kassar answered for Elena. The admiral offered his hand to her; she hesitated a moment before she took it. "Ms. Pavon, a pleasure to see you in a social setting. Let me take this opportunity to reassure you that the fleet is doing everything in its power to locate your missing freighter."

"Then you've dispatched additional search assets to Bursa?" Elena asked. "And Tunis? She might have been attacked before she began her transit."

"We will as soon as those assets become available," the admiral said easily. "You must understand, Ms. Pavon, that planetary systems are unimaginably vast areas, and thorough searches take a great deal of time. I am afraid that you will have to be patient—I promise you that we are doing all that we can."

Elena took a long and deliberate look around the Founding Day celebration, making a show of studying the handsome uniforms and lavish setting. "I am sure that you are, Admiral," she said, smiling sweetly to twist the dagger. "I would never want to suggest that you are doing less than your very best."

Torgut al-Kassar's smile froze on his face. *Oh, so you noticed that, did you?* Elena told herself. *Good, maybe you'll turn some of that anger on your subordinates and do something for once.* She tilted her head in the slightest of nods, and allowed the arriving guests behind her and Omar to move the two of them on down the receiving line. Gadi al-Kassar stared after her in a rather predatory manner; Elena pretended not to notice, and refused to look back at him.

"You know, you're not going to make many friends that way," Omar murmured as they moved to the next official in line. "Admirals aren't used to that sort of treatment."

"Then he shouldn't have patted me on the head and told me to be patient," Elena replied. "I am *through* with being patient. We've lost two ships now in Zerzura within the last two years. That's a couple of hundred million credits in hulls, let alone the lost cargo and the lives of our employees. And how many times have we lost partial cargoes or been forced to pay ransoms?"

"Six, if you count that New Kibris kidnapping."

"I do." Technically it wasn't piracy, since *Safira Vega*'s master had been abducted while the ship was in port, but Elena had signed the ransom check, and the payment arrangements had been the same as in other incidents. "Our insurance rates are astronomical already—and if we have to write off one more cargo or make one more ransom payment, Orion Starways will drop us for sure. Exactly how much more patient are we supposed to be?"

"You don't have to convince me. I see the same P&L statements you do." Omar steered her past the end of the receiving line and out onto the terrace. The night was warm, despite Mersin's elevation; the faint cinnamon scent of Dahar's atmosphere grew stronger as they moved closer to the balustrade.

"I know." Elena drifted over to the rail and gazed out at the cityscape. She wasn't proud of taking out her frustration on her executive assistant, but Omar understood the pressures she faced. While many people in Elena's social circle imagined that someone with her wealth and pedigree wouldn't trouble herself with something as mundane as watching a bottom line, the Pavon family believed in hands-on management of their business empire. Not only was Elena the heiress to the Pavon fortune, she was the director of the Meliyan-Zerzuran region for the Pegasus-Pavon line, responsible for the company's business operations from its headquarters at Nuevo León in the Principality of Bolívar to its bridgehead at Meliya in the Velar Electorate. The shipping routes Elena oversaw in Zerzura accounted for nearly a third of the company's total revenue, but if Pegasus-Pavon couldn't get affordable insurance rates for its operations, her father would have to shut down the company's Meliyan-Zerzuran region altogether. Tadeo Pavon might not hold Elena responsible for the necessity of closing down her part of the shipping empire, but *she'd* certainly hold herself responsible. *And I'll be damned if I give up my region without a fight,* she silently fumed.

She turned back to the banquet. "I don't even know why I'm here," she said to Omar. "This is a waste of time. Maybe we'll have better luck with the system authorities in Bursa. Shit, maybe we'll be able to *pay* them to go find our ship."

"Bursa is the one place we know our ship *isn't,* since it never made port. Most likely, the pirates took *Carmela Día* to some empty star system and stripped her in the middle of nowhere. But if someone stumbles across her wreck, the news will eventually make its way to Dahar, and Dahar is where you need to be to apply some pressure—some *subtle* pressure, mind you—on Marid Pasha to invest in more antipiracy measures." Omar gave her a stern look. "Then again, keep on embarrassing Caliphate officials by reminding them they're weaker than they'd like to think, and they'll ignore you wherever you decide to go."

"I suppose you're right," Elena admitted. Doing something, anything, seemed like it would be better than waiting around in Dahar for news that might never come and pestering the Zerzuran authorities to do jobs they should have been doing without any prodding from her, but Omar was ten times the diplomat that she was. Her natural inclination was to demand results, but he generally managed to channel her impatience into constructive action. It made them a very effective team: Elena had energy and drive in abundance, while Omar provided the tact and perspective she rarely had the patience to practice.

"Do you want to leave?" Omar asked. "If the pasha isn't likely to make an appearance, then there's no particular reason to extend the evening."

"No, we need to stay a little longer. There are a couple of people I'd like to run into. And I'm actually a little hungry—that spread did look good."

"Then let's get something to eat," Omar said.

They made their way to the buffet table and helped themselves to a fine selection of delicacies from half a dozen different worlds. Elena decided that Omar was right; a glass of wine would have gone down well with the meal. After they ate, she turned her attention to the party, searching for familiar faces. Dozens of Dahar's business leaders and government officials were in attendance, and of course Pegasus-Pavon wanted to be seen as a good corporate citizen in the region. Many of the party guests did quite a lot of business with her family, and it was important for Elena to visit with each and exchange a few pleasantries—personal connections went a long way toward smoothing the road when it came time to discuss carrying contracts worth millions or persuading officials to streamline regulations. Likewise, more than a few guests had come to the gala with the idea of meeting *her*, and sought out the opportunity to introduce themselves. Some offered potentially valuable proposals for her to consider, some hoped to secure Pavon patronage for various charitable projects, and some were frankly nuisances that Omar Morillo smoothly interrupted and directed away from Elena when he had to. Once or twice she met interesting people that she didn't need anything from and who didn't need anything from her; she found the Dremish special envoy Hanne Vogt to be a powerfully confident and attractive woman whose gown was even more daring than Elena's, and later on she chatted with Dahar's Aquilan consul, too. But throughout the socializing, the problem of *Carmela Día*'s disappearance and the powerlessness of the Zerzuran authorities never strayed far from her mind.

Later in the evening, Elena disentangled herself from a Caliphate general named Karacan—who seemed to think he could impress her by loudly telling stories of his own adventures—and retreated to the edge of the terrace again, enjoying a few moments of comparative solitude. Her eye fell on a woman standing a few meters away, wearing the burgundy dress uniform of the Velar Electorate Navy with gold sunbursts on her silver shoulder boards. *Captain Szas of that Velaran cruiser*, she reminded herself. She'd seen the woman on a newscast earlier in the week. Beside the Velaran captain stood a Paom'ii in the kilt and jeweled harness his people preferred to human-style clothing; the tawny fur of their pelts was all the covering they really needed, but Paom'ii took great pride in their personal appearance and required some amount of clothing to properly display the lavish ornamentation they favored.

Perhaps I've been talking to the wrong navy, Elena realized. If the Caliphate was stretched thin in Zerzura, one of the neighboring powers might be able to provide some more assistance. She made her way over to the Velarans, who stood chatting with a mixed group of humans and Paom'ii at the far end of the terrace. Elena waited for a break in the conversation before she stepped forward and extended her hand to the woman in uniform. "Captain? I'm Elena Pavon. Might I have a few minutes of your time?"

"Ms. Pavon, how do you do?" Szas replied. Her Jadeed-Arabi was almost as good as Elena's, which was impressive considering that it was probably her third or fourth language. She was tall and sturdy, with a broad face and a practical bob haircut. "Dame Hedi Szas, at your service. Would that be the Pavons of Pegasus-Pavon line?"

"Yes, in fact. Tadeo Pavon is my father; I serve as the company's regional director in Meliya."

"I see your freighters all the time." Szas nodded to the Paom'ii who stood beside her; Elena noticed that the alien's kilt and harness matched the burgundy of Szas's uniform, and had a distinctly martial look. "This is my second-in-command, Meritor Pokk Skirriseh."

"I am pleased to meet you, Ms. Pavon," the Paom'ii said, extending his three-fingered hand. He spoke in a buzzing, resonant voice in his native tongue, which included elements that were simply outside the normal range of human hearing; a translator device on his collar repeated his speech in formal-sounding Jadeed-Arabi. Close up, the alien towered over Elena, standing almost two full meters in height despite the naturally hunched posture of his species. She'd heard Paom'ii described as something between an orangutan, a lion, and an owl, and while she had only the vaguest idea of what an orangutan must have been like, she'd always found the description apt: Meritor Pokk had a long, thin torso covered in fine golden fur, short legs with wide three-toed feet, long arms, and a face with large, dark, close-set eyes above a stiff beak-like mouth. Like most of his kind, he wore his dark mane in carefully arranged curls, and dyed the natural stipple patterns of his fur to make them stand out more. Elena found his huge hand warm and rough, but he was careful not to squeeze too hard.

"Likewise, Meritor," Elena told him. She was no stranger to Paom'ii; the demands of her family's business meant that she spent close to half her time on Meliya, an Electorate world jointly ruled by humans and aliens. They could be trying at times, since they missed many human social cues and generally didn't care about business matters, but Paom'ii in positions that required them to work closely with humans—say, serving aboard a warship with a mixed-species crew—generally adapted well to human interactions and socialization.

"What can we do for you, Ms. Pavon?" Szas asked.

"I hope you'll forgive me for bringing up work, but one of our ships on the Nuevo León–Meliya route has gone missing near Bursa. *Carmela Día* is now nearly a month overdue. I reported the disappearance to the Zerzuran authorities, but they tell me they don't have the resources to conduct a search. I was hoping that you could look into the situation as long as *Vashaoth Teh* is visiting in Zerzura."

Szas exchanged a long look with her alien colleague. Although the Electorate's human citizens were in theory coequal with their Paom'ii comrades and there was no reason a human commander couldn't exercise the authority normally expected in a ship's captain, in practice humans and Paom'ii serving together shared decision-making in a sort of dual command. Of all the great powers that participated in the Coalition of Humanity (or partially participated, in the case of the Velarans), only the Electorate represented two allied species. The alien Paom'ii held many of the Electorate's high military posts and executive government positions, which meant that human commanders such as Captain Szas had to consider Paom'ii interests alongside their own in any major decision. However, the Electorate's humans outnumbered their Paom'ii allies and drove most of the nation's industrial and financial activity. Meritor Pokk gave a small side-to-side waggle of his head, which Elena took as a sign of ambivalence . . . although she was not entirely sure.

"We are sorry to hear that," Szas said after giving the meritor a chance to speak if he had anything to say. "However, I regret that our itinerary is already set: We're scheduled to return to Meliya at the end of the week. Diverting to Bursa is just not something we can do."

"Pegasus-Pavon is a Velaran corporation," said Elena. Well, half-Velaran, anyway; her family's shipping line enjoyed dual corporate citizenship in the Principality of Bolívar. "And many of *Carmela Día*'s crew are Velarans, too—these are your citizens who have gone missing. Surely a small change to your itinerary would be understandable in these circumstances."

"It is our duty to protect Velaran trade and render assistance to Velaran citizens in danger whenever we can," Meritor Pokk acknowledged. "But your account makes it clear that *Carmela Día* is missing in the Terran Caliphate's territory, not our own."

"Which means that we're outside our jurisdiction," Szas added.

"So? Other nations operate in Zerzura without restriction: Dremark, Aquila, or Montréal, for instance. Pirates are enemies to all nations."

"I can't speak to the diplomatic agreements in place between other powers, Ms. Pavon," said the captain. "All I can tell you is that Electorate warships visit Caliphate space under very specific conditions. Unless we receive a distress call or actually observe a vessel under attack, our hands are tied."

They can't very well send a distress call if they're missing! Elena wanted to point out. Instead she replied with a small frown of disappointment, and tried a different approach. "Oh. That's unfortunate, but I understand. Since you can't look into *Carmela Día*'s disappearance directly, could you ask the Zerzuran fleet what they're doing to find our ship? I have to imagine that if you let Marid Pasha's commanders know that *you* know about the situation and that the Electorate is concerned about what happens to its citizens in this part of space, they might allocate more resources to the search." *And a pointed question or two from a Ve-*

laran captain might remind the Zerzurans that someone else might see the need to step in and straighten up the mess in their sector, she added to herself.

"We are not empowered to present any new diplomatic initiatives," said Meritor Pokk. "Perhaps you should address your concern to the Electorate consul in this system?"

"I'm not asking you to negotiate a new treaty. I merely thought you might say a word or two to your counterparts in the Caliphate's Zerzuran fleet to let them know you're paying attention."

The Paom'ii officer straightened up, drawing his shoulders back and clacking his bill sharply at Elena. "Do you mean to imply that we are not taking this matter seriously?" he said in a flat tone.

Szas shot Elena a look, and set a hand on the Paom'ii's shoulder. "I think, Meritor, that Ms. Pavon simply does not appreciate the limits of our authority in Zerzura and assumes we can do more than we are already doing. A simple misunderstanding."

"A simple misunderstanding, of course," said Omar Morillo, rejoining the conversation. He stepped in front of Elena, and pointed over toward the terrace's entranceway. "I hope you'll forgive me for interrupting, but Mr. Smith and his wife are saying their good-nights, and I know you wanted to see them before they left."

Brilliant, Elena, she told herself. She knew very well that Paom'ii took *everything* personally, but she'd allowed her frustration to show. Meritor Pokk probably wouldn't physically confront her over one sharp remark, but he'd remember the offense and he might hold it against her—or her family—in the future. She was lucky that Szas and Omar were on hand to deflect Pokk's ire. "Oh, yes, I did need to talk to him," she said to Omar, taking advantage of her assistant's little ploy. "Please excuse me, Captain, Meritor."

The Paom'ii studied her coldly for a moment, and then finally nodded. "We understand. Good night, Ms. Pavon."

"Good night, Ms. Pavon," Captain Szas added. "When we find the right opportunity to raise your concerns with the pasha's government, we will. You have my word."

Smiling, Omar took Elena's arm and led her away from the Velarans. He made sure they were a good twenty meters distant before he said anything—Paom'ii had very keen ears. "Were you seriously about to get into an argument with the Paom'ii?" he whispered. "You are aware of how that turns out, aren't you?"

"I didn't say anything that bad. He was the one reading too much into it."

"That's what they *do*, Elena. You'll have to watch your step around that one now."

"I know, I know." She shook her head in disgust. "I'm done here. Let's go."

They left the party without any good-byes, slipping out through an interior hallway that led to the hotel's elevator bank and then to a spacious landing pad on the other side of the building. Omar summoned Elena's luxury flyer, and joined her in the rear seat when the vehicle alighted before them. "Home, please," he told the pilot.

"Right away, Mr. Morillo," the pilot replied. He lifted off and set a course for Elena's penthouse apartment on the other side of Mersin; while she spent only a few weeks a year in Dahar, she maintained a full-time residence and household in Zerzura's capital system.

Elena stared out the window at the pasha's palace, brightly illuminated by colorful spotlights above the striking cliffs of its mountaintop. The Founding Day gala left a bad taste in her mouth, even though she'd attended hundreds of events just like it across a dozen worlds in her thirty years.

"Care to talk about it?" Omar asked her after a moment.

"We're going about this all wrong," Elena said, waving a hand in the general direction of the pasha's palace. "The Zerzurans are fucking useless, and so are the Velarans. No one within fifty light-years has got half an idea of what to do about what's been going on in this sector, and it's going to put us out of business. What do the pasha's admirals think is going to happen to Zerzura's economy if Pegasus-Pavon stops carrying their trade? I tell you, I'm not writing one more ransom check. It's time to take matters into our own hands."

"I see," said Omar, his tone guarded. "What exactly did you have in mind?"

"Whoever stole our freighter has a hundred thousand tons of enriched rare earths on their hands. The ship's valuable, but so is the cargo—if they can find a buyer. So let's figure out where they intend to sell the freight." Elena nodded to herself, seeing the idea take shape as she talked. "We'll put our people into the commodities markets in all major systems nearby, and we'll watch for ores that match *Carmela Día's* load. Then we'll hire private investigators—or just *pay* the damned system police if that's what it takes—to identify the sellers, find out who they got the ore from, and find out who *those* people got the ore from, all the way back down the chain until we find whoever it was who seized our ship."

"If the criminals are smart, they'll break the load into smaller lots—it would look suspicious if a *Carmela*-sized lot suddenly appeared all at once on an exchange."

"Which means that we'll have a better chance to catch at least one of them in the act of turning our cargo into cash," Elena said.

"That's going to be expensive," Omar warned. "Especially if we have to pay off officials to get access to exchange records."

"Paying insurance and ransom is already ruining us. I'd rather spend that money to solve the problem by identifying the bastards who are behind this and shutting them down. It's going to be cheaper, a lot cheaper, in the long run."

"What do we do if we develop some actionable intelligence from all this?"

"We lead the pasha's agents to the bad guys if we have to drag them there kicking and screaming," Elena said grimly. "And if that doesn't work, we'll find someone else who can deal with the problem, or we'll outfit our own privateers and see to it ourselves."

"'Millions for defense, but not one cent for tribute,'" Omar observed. "I have a feeling it's going to be more complicated than you think it will be."

"We won't know until we try," she told him. Then she pulled out her dataslate and started making notes about what she would need and how she'd pay for it all.

7

CSS *Decisive*, Bursa System

No one aboard *Carmela Día* needed Sikander's assistance—the pirates had left no one alive.

"God is Truth," Sikander murmured aloud, staring at the vid feeds from *Decisive*'s boarding team in sickened horror. One whole bulkhead of the destroyer's bridge displays had been repurposed to show him the helmet-cam imagery from the teams searching the derelict, drifting dark and cold ten kilometers away. "What sort of monsters are we dealing with?"

Amelia Fraser did not respond to his rhetorical question. She stood beside him, her face fixed in an expression he'd never seen on her before: eyes narrowed, jaw clenched, cold fury radiating from every pore. She tapped the comm device on the arm of the tactical station. "Boarding team, XO. Where are you, Mr. Herrera?"

"The mess deck, ma'am," Jaime Herrera replied. His voice was muffled somewhat inside the helmet of his vacuum armor, but Sikander could hear the flat anger in the gunnery officer's tone. "It looks like they rounded up most of the crew here before they . . . did what they did." In the vid window that represented Herrera's personal cam, Sikander saw a gloved hand with a flashlight come into view. The harsh beam struck tiny frozen sparkles from bits of dust and debris drifting in the airless room, illuminating a night-marish scene.

At least a dozen bodies floated in the compartment, spinning slowly or snagged in place by a table or some small fitting on a wall. Men and women, young and old, each dressed in a working spacer's shipboard jumpsuit and staring sightlessly at the Aquilan boarding party who'd discovered the scene of their murder. Bullet holes surrounded by dark rings of frozen gore marked most of them; blood splatters on the bulkhead at the aft end of the compartment hinted at where they'd been shot.

"It looks like someone made a fight of it," Herrera added a moment later. He pointed his flashlight at the body of a dark-haired woman whose jumpsuit was marked by at least four or five gunshot wounds; she still clutched a small mag pistol in one pale hand. "I hope she got one of the bastards."

"Secure any bodies that are at risk of drifting away and continue to the bridge," Fraser said to Herrera. "We might find logs or manifests that will be helpful in identifying the victims." Sikander noted that his exec hadn't bothered to suggest that the boarding party might discover survivors. All the airlocks and interior hatches stood open to vacuum; a random assortment of clutter and discarded tools that hadn't quite been carried out into space when the ship's atmosphere had vented still drifted in the silent passageways.

He looked away from the awful scene the first boarding team had discovered to a view that showed the drifting wreck with *Decisive*'s launch alongside. At this range the destroyer's hull cams couldn't miss the damage scarring the freighter's warp ring and drive plates—*Carmela Día* had been crippled by K-cannon fire before she'd been boarded. "How many, Mr. Girard?" he asked quietly.

"Twenty-two, sir," Michael Girard replied. The youthful lieutenant looked like he was about to be sick. Eight years ago, he'd faced the terror and panic of a pitched space battle beside Sikander on the bridge of the cruiser *Hector,* and come through hell with the right to hold his head high; it took a lot to shake him. "That's the registered complement, though. It's possible they might have been a little shorthanded for this run, or they might have been carrying a handful of passengers. We won't know for sure unless we find the log."

"Accounting for them all won't be easy," said Fraser. "If they were blown out an airlock at ten or fifteen meters per second a couple of weeks ago, the bodies could be scattered over thirty or forty thousand kilometers by now."

"I know, but we're going to recover as many as we can," said Sikander. "We'll find some of them, at least, and I have to imagine that it would be better for the families to know for sure what happened to their loved ones." He sighed and shook his head. In *Decisive's* previous patrols under his command, they hadn't encountered anything like the sort of massacre that had evidently taken place aboard *Carmela Día.* On their first deployment they'd found an abandoned system lighter, a much smaller ship whose crew was simply missing. Then, on the deployment just before *Decisive* went in for refit, they'd responded to a distress call from a container ship whose engines had been disabled by pirates who simply removed the most valuable cargo units while leaving the crew more or less unmolested. Today's grim discovery was an entirely different sort of crime scene. *It's murder—pure, brutal murder,* he told himself. *And the animals who did this are still at large.*

"We'll need the orbiters," Fraser suggested. The ship's launch was currently engaged with the boarding operations, but the two orbital shuttles were available. "We'll cover more space that way, and it's really a job for small craft anyway."

"Do so," Sikander ordered.

Girard glanced over at Gunner's Mate Waters, the petty officer of the watch. "Pass the word for Orbiter One and Orbiter Two crews to report to their boats for recovery operations."

"Aye, sir," Waters answered. He keyed the ship's intercom, speaking in a subdued tone. "Attention, all hands. Boat crews, man your boats for recovery operations."

"*Decisive*, this is Lieutenant Shah. We've reached engineering control." The Kashmiri lieutenant's face appeared in one of the windows of the boarding team's display as Shah reversed his cam to show his face. He led the second of the boarding teams currently searching the derelict freighter. "Chief Ryan's looking over the power plant now, over."

"*Decisive* actual," Sikander answered, keying the comm panel. "Have you found any of the crew?"

"No, sir. There's no one here, and it looks like the systems were secured before they left."

"How bad is the damage to the drive system, Mr. Shah?"

"It does not appear to be serious, sir. We'd have to replace the damaged drive plate for full acceleration, and I don't know if there are any spares on board. I have to imagine that replacement drive plates wouldn't have been left behind. But I think she'd run well enough with reduced acceleration on the undamaged plates, assuming Chief Ryan can get the power plant online."

"Very good, Mr. Shah. Have Chief Ryan restore power if she's satisfied with the condition of the generators. Your work will go faster with atmosphere and gravity."

"Yes, sir. I will keep you advised of our progress. Shah, out." Shah switched his camera back to its external view, returning to his work.

"Are you thinking about bringing her in?" Amelia Fraser asked Sikander.

"I see no reason to leave her out here, and we can spare a small prize crew for a few days. Besides, we need to pick up parts at Bursa after the trouble with generator two." Sikander tapped his comm panel again, switching to the last of the boarding parties. "Ms. Worth, what's the status of the cargo? What were they carrying?"

"Some sort of refined ore, Captain," Zoe Worth replied. She led the team searching the cargo holds. "Four holds are still full of the stuff, but the fifth is mostly empty. If I had to guess, I'd say the attackers didn't have a ship anywhere near big enough to take off the whole load at once."

"Very good, Ms. Worth. Make sure you check the lifeboats and emergency stores, too. I doubt you'll find anything, but it's worth a look."

Amelia Fraser frowned in thought. "You know, Captain, it occurs to me that the pirates who looted this ship know perfectly well they left behind eighty percent of the cargo. They might be coming back for the rest . . . in which case we could be waiting here for them to return."

"I'd certainly like to catch up with the people who did this," Sikander said grimly, considering the suggestion. *Of course, it might be weeks or months before someone comes back for more of the ore. And we won't be able to report that we've found the ship until we see if the attackers return to the scene, which means that anyone expecting* Carmela Día *won't know that she was attacked . . . and we've got a schedule to keep.* He shook his head in reluctance. "Setting a trap is a good idea, but I'm not sure that we can spend our patrol waiting for them to come back. We're expected in Dahar eventually. Let's take a look at some sort of trap operation later, though—I believe you might have something there."

"Yes, sir." If Fraser disagreed with his decision, she didn't let it show. "Who do you want to appoint as prize captain? Amar?"

Sikander thought it over for a moment. The opportunity to

command one's own ship, even if it was just a bulk freighter for a voyage of a day or two, was something that any junior officer would kill for. "Zoe," he decided. "She's junior for it, but we'll escort her into port. I'm just worried enough about our generator that I think I'd like to keep our chief engineer on board *Decisive*."

"I'll detail a prize crew." The XO made some notes on her dataslate.

"*Decisive*, this is Herrera. We've reached the bridge." Jaime Herrera's face reappeared in another one of the display windows. "The computer cores have been removed and the sensor records erased. I don't think we're going to get much out of—oh, the lights just came back on."

"*Decisive*, Shah. Power restored," Amar Shah reported. "We're restarting life support and bringing gravity online at ten percent standard." That would spare *Decisive*'s boarding team from making a sudden and unexpected acquaintance with *Carmela Día's* deck plates; at 0.1 g, they'd have plenty of time to orient themselves to the ship and get clear of anything about to fall to the deck.

"Thank you, Mr. Shah," Sikander answered. He returned his attention to Herrera, on the derelict's bridge. "Mr. Herrera, what's the status of the helm and navigation systems? Are they operable?"

"They're booting up now, Captain." Herrera turned away and spoke to the crewhands accompanying him. "Petty Officer Tolbin says the helm looks okay, although it's displaying some damage to the drive systems. The sensors need a hard reset, but I think she's flyable."

"No sign of the bridge crew?" Fraser asked him over the comm channel.

"No, XO. I think everyone was either shot on the mess deck, or spaced afterwards."

Sikander exchanged a look with Fraser. He hadn't expected

anything else, but they had to be sure. "All right, Mr. Herrera," he said. "Coordinate with Mr. Shah and get the navigation systems back online. We might as well bring her in."

In the end, *Decisive* recovered sixteen of *Carmela Día*'s dead—thirteen inside the ship, and five drifting in space nearby. While none of the ship's logs or records remained aboard, Zoe Worth and Jaime Herrera came up with the idea of making a careful examination of the ship's berthing compartments and counting bunks that had been slept in. Their best guess was a complement of twenty-one on the freighter's last voyage; as Michael Girard had predicted, the ship had been a little shorthanded. Sikander found himself wondering what lucky spacer had resigned his position or gotten herself fired at the exact right time. That left four crew unaccounted for—taken off by the pirates or left to drift somewhere *Decisive*'s boats couldn't find them, no one could say.

Sikander ordered the ship's master-at-arms to preserve all the evidence they could find. Unfortunately, *Decisive* had only three petty officers with master-at-arms ratings, and a freighter made for a big crime scene. Amelia Fraser had to detail a number of the ship's chief petty officers and junior officers to lend a hand. While the master-at-arms's improvised teams carefully documented everything they could, Amar Shah and his engineers got the freighter's engines working again, and *Decisive*'s sensor techs restored basic navigational systems on the bridge. Nineteen hours after the Aquilan destroyer had arrived on the scene, *Decisive* and *Carmela Día* set course for Bursa's inner system and got under way.

Given the damaged freighter's limited acceleration, a journey that would normally take *Decisive* a day stretched out to three. Sikander resigned himself to the plodding pace, and kept the destroyer close by *Carmela Día*. Fraser's suggestion about setting a trap was fresh in his mind, and perhaps if they got lucky another pirate might mistake two sensor contacts in close company for one big one. Sikander also instructed Girard to refrain from notifying the local authorities about their discovery, at least not until they were a lot closer to Bursa. If anyone was monitoring the local system patrol's communications, he saw no need to announce *Decisive*'s presence.

On the second day of their passage, Sikander joined his reduced wardroom for dinner at the customary time: Amelia Fraser, four of his six department heads, and ten of his fourteen division officers. Reed Hollister noticed his arrival first, and came to his feet. "Attention on deck!" he called out as Sikander entered the room.

"Please, be seated," Sikander told his subordinates, and took his place at the head of the table. One of the small perks of being the captain was that meals weren't served until he arrived, and usually appeared on the table within minutes once he sat down. He glanced over at Grant Edwards, seated near the head of the table. "What's on the menu tonight, Grant?"

"Chicken ravioli, I believe," Edwards answered. Meal planning and preparation fell under the Supply Department's purview. Like most supply officers, Grant Edwards had a large department to run and many different demands on his time—he rarely presumed to tell his mess specialists how to do their job. Sikander suspected that Edwards only checked on the menu just before dinner so that he'd be able to answer the question if Sikander happened to ask about it, which was the way things worked on just about every ship in the fleet.

"Excellent," Sikander told him, maintaining the time-honored routine. He had to be careful about showing disappointment over a meal; he'd served on ships where the mere suspicion that the captain didn't care for dinner could send the mess specialists into paroxysms of panic. In this case, Sikander wasn't trying to spare anyone's feelings—he rarely ate pasta, but he liked it well enough when the galley served it. He waited patiently while the stewards brought out generous plates of ravioli, green salads, and the various sides and accompaniments, then made a point of sampling his dinner. Wardroom etiquette dictated that junior officers waited until the captain started to eat before diving into their own dinners.

He quietly watched the other officers as he ate, gauging their mood. He liked to think that *Decisive* was generally a happy ship—he tried hard to be fair and even-tempered, and his department heads naturally took their cues from his command style. Conversation around the table seemed unusually subdued this evening, though. *It's the* Carmela Día *situation*, he realized. *Everybody spent hours yesterday looking for bodies and documenting the evidence of brutal murders. I should've anticipated the effect of that work.* Most of his younger officers—indeed, most of his officers, period—didn't have much experience with the sort of scene they'd encountered aboard the drifting freighter. His own experiences in situations like *Hector*'s desperate battle at Gadira and the chaos and confusion of the *warumzi agu* revolution in the Tzoru Dominion were the exception in Aquilan service, not the rule.

Time to change the topic, he decided. He looked down the table and spotted Grace Carter picking at her food. "Ms. Carter, it just occurred to me that I never asked about your brother's wedding," he said. The young ensign had taken leave for the family event shortly before Sikander had headed home himself. "I take it you saw him securely married off?"

Carter almost dropped her fork in surprise. "Umm, yes, sir," she replied. "Everything went off without a hiccup, and I have to say, I really like Isabel—er, that's Kyle's wife. She's great. I have no idea what she sees in him."

A soft ripple of laughter went around the table. "All three of my brothers managed to marry better women than they deserved," Sikander told her. "You can imagine my surprise." That earned another round of chuckles, and from there the conversation turned to a collection of wedding stories. Some he'd heard before—after all, he'd shared dinner stories with most of the wardroom for a year now, and some tales inevitably got recycled—but several of his younger officers surprised him with new ones, including a disastrously bad bachelor party that had very nearly gotten Reed Hollister and his cousins arrested. Sikander was just about to launch into the story of his cousin Amarleen and a wedding cake when the compartment's intercom—located near the head of the table, where the captain usually sat—chirped for attention.

"This is the captain, go ahead," Sikander answered, holding up one hand to excuse himself from the dinner conversation. The rest of the company quieted down.

"Captain, Bridge. Mr. Herrera speaking, officer of the deck. Sir, we're receiving a distress call. A mining post called United Extraction Sixteen reports that they're under attack by an unidentified vessel."

Sikander tuned out the dinner table around him, focusing on Herrera's report. "Where are they, Mr. Herrera?"

"The system's middle asteroid belt, sir, bearing zero-two-seven up ten, distance twelve light-minutes."

Amelia Fraser worked out the math in her head. "Twelve light-minutes? That's six and a half hours, or more like twenty for a zero-range zero-speed rendezvous."

Sikander nodded. His XO had figured the intercept faster than he had, but he'd already realized that whatever was going on at the United Extraction post would likely be over by the time *Decisive* arrived on the scene. "We don't have to make that choice for several hours yet. Mr. Herrera, set a course for minimum-time interception, full military acceleration. Signal the mining post that we're on our way, but don't tell them exactly when we'll get there."

"Aye, sir," Herrera replied. "Bridge, out."

The stars in the wardroom's exterior-view vidscreens reeled suddenly as *Decisive* spun to point her nose on an intercept course, and the surge in acceleration gently tugged at Sikander until the ship's inertial compensators caught up. "Captain, should we send an acknowledgment?" Amar Shah asked. "Whoever is attacking the mining station will hear it too. They might flee before we get close enough to overtake them."

"I hate to say it, but I hope that they do. As the XO just pointed out, we're hours and hours from the scene—there's nothing we can do to help the station. On the other hand, the attackers might break off once they realize we're on the way. As much as I'd like to catch pirates in the act, I can't think of anything else we can do to protect the people under attack." Sikander's expression tightened. "I'd rather not get to that post and find more bodies floating in space."

"What do you want to do with *Carmela Día*?" Fraser asked.

"Have her continue on her course," he decided. He glanced at the wardroom's vidscreens, where the bulk freighter was now rapidly falling astern. He had fifteen people on board the other ship, but the freighter had no hope of keeping up with *Decisive* and he couldn't spare the time to recover them. *There's no point in regretting that decision now,* he told himself. *We've seen nothing during months of patrolling. How could we expect two incidents in three days?* If he'd known that he might suddenly have to leave the freighter on its own he might have put a more senior officer in charge, but Zoe Worth could handle the job of seeing the ship into port.

He hurried through the rest of his dinner, and headed forward to the bridge to study the tactical situation. If he decided to bring *Decisive* to a rendezvous with the mining post, he'd need to "turn ship" near the halfway point of the run and begin decelerating. Or he could have his crew keep on accelerating past the halfway point in order to reach the vicinity of the station as quickly as possible, but in that scenario *Decisive* would flash by her destination in the blink of an eye. They might be able to fire on a hostile ship lingering near the post . . . but no pirate skipper would be likely to oblige him by neglecting to flee the scene when he saw an Aquilan destroyer coming after him hell-for-leather.

"What do you want to do, Captain?" Jaime Herrera asked, watching Sikander study the tactical display. He understood perfectly well the decision Sikander faced.

"Any indication that the station's attacker is turning away?"

"Not yet, sir. But it's a twenty-four-minute observation lag at this distance."

Sikander nodded. The speed of light dictated that anyone near the station wouldn't hear *Decisive*'s reply to the distress signal until twelve minutes after *Decisive* transmitted—and *Decisive* wouldn't see what the distant target did in response to *Decisive*'s reply for another twelve minutes after that."We'll push on a little past the turnover point, and aim for a flyby at a thousand kps. That should save a few hours over the zero-zero intercept, and I don't mind an hour or two of maneuvering to return to the scene after we overshoot. Designate the unknown attacker Target Alpha."

"Aye, sir. We'll plot it out." Herrera moved off to begin working on the navigation computers.

"You know, an ugly and suspicious thought occurs to me," Amelia Fraser murmured to Sikander. She'd followed him to the bridge, joining him in evaluating the situation.

Sikander raised an eyebrow. "What's that, Amelia?"

"We're not supposed to be here. According to our original

patrol schedule, we should be departing Tejat Minor today, and arriving in Bursa four days from now. Someone aware of our schedule might have figured that they had plenty of time to carry out an attack or tidy up a mess around a missing freighter before we unbubbled in-system. But the problem with the generator—something no one else knew about or might have foreseen—forced us to accelerate our timetable."

Sikander stared at his XO, considering the implications. "You believe that Zerzura's pirates know our patrol schedule? Good God!"

"It seems awfully coincidental that the first time in months that we've shown up ahead of schedule we find interesting things going on."

"You have a devious turn of mind, XO."

Fraser shrugged. "I have two small children at home, and that teaches you to cultivate a certain sense for mischief taking place out of your sight."

Sikander might not share his exec's maternal instincts, but he had some grounding in intelligence work. Earlier in his career he'd spent a tour of duty as the staff intelligence officer with Helix Squadron, on the Tzoru frontier. Intel officers generally didn't believe in coincidences; if this patrol seemed to be turning out differently than previous patrols it seemed logical to assume that it was because something had changed, and Fraser's observation seemed all too likely as he thought more about it. *So who knew our patrol schedule?* he wondered. *We did, of course, and Pleiades Squadron Operations. Our people wouldn't let it slip, not on purpose . . . but if Amelia is right, this has been going on for months. One leaked schedule could be an accident, but a year's worth? That's espionage or collusion.*

"Captain?" said Herrera, interrupting Sikander's ruminations. "Target Alpha is withdrawing. Looks like they got our message."

"Course and speed?" Sikander asked.

"System true, they're on course two-nine-zero, acceleration sixty-five g. It looks like they're running for open space, sir."

"They have to know we've got the acceleration to run them down," Fraser observed. "Are they on a transit course, Jaime?"

The big gunnery officer turned his attention to the tactical display and studied the navigation display for a moment. "You nailed it, XO," he said after a moment. "They're lining up for a transit to Tunis. Assuming they're showing us all the acceleration they have and they bubble up at ten percent c, they'll clear out an hour before we can bring them into firing range."

"I guess we're not going to catch any pirates today," Fraser said.

"Not today, XO, but we know where they're going, and once they spin up their warp ring we'll know when they're going to arrive," said Sikander. Ships traveling in warp didn't accelerate; they coasted, making their transit with whatever course and speed they had when they activated their warp generators. The faster a ship was going when it created its warp bubble, the more extreme their warp gradient . . . which meant that once *Decisive* observed the velocity at which the unknown ship activated her ring, Sikander's crew would be able to plot out a higher-velocity transit and get to the destination system on their quarry's heels, or maybe even a little ahead of her. "In the meantime, we might as well have Lieutenant Worth pick up our generator parts as long as she's bringing in *Carmela Día*. And let's see if the United Extraction outpost captured any good imagery of Target Alpha before she turned tail. I'd like to have a better mug shot in my pocket if we chase them all the way to Tunis."

Decisive arrived in the Tunis system roughly twenty-five minutes after Target Alpha's calculated arrival time. Sikander's bridge crew couldn't be exactly sure, because they didn't know where in Tunis their quarry intended to cut their warp generators—an extra few minutes in transit duration could easily make the difference between unbubbling near the system's Kuiper Belt or carrying clear through to the Kuiper Belt on the other side. In the absence of any better information, Sikander opted for bringing *Decisive* to a more or less middle-of-the-system warp termination, figuring that he at least wouldn't be entirely across the system from whatever destination Target Alpha was aiming for.

"Clear arrival, Captain," Ensign Carter announced from her post by the bridge's sensor techs. "Nothing within ten million kilometers."

"Very good," Sikander said. "You know what we're looking for, Ms. Carter. Remember, they'll be decelerating from a Bursa transit vector." As he'd hoped, the United Extraction post in Bursa had gladly transmitted imagery of their attacker to *Decisive* as the Aquilan destroyer raced past the station in pursuit of the pirate—a light multipurpose cargo ship of a sixty-year-old type, battered by years of hard use. Scores of similar ships could be found in any system of the Zerzuran frontier, although few were stripped for speed and fitted out with the sort of armament Target Alpha carried in its current career.

"Aye, sir. The sensors are coming online now."

"Mr. Girard, send our arrival notice to the local traffic authority. And ask them about any other arrivals in the last couple of hours."

"I doubt that pirates are in the habit of obeying local traffic reporting regulations," Jaime Herrera observed. He and the other Gunnery Department officers manned the weapons consoles at the aft end of the compartment—every man and woman aboard *Decisive* was ready for action.

"You're probably right, but it occurs to me that pirates might find it useful to pretend to be law-abiding citizens when they un-bubble in a new system. It would seem to be simpler than hiding all the time." Sikander studied the nav display showing Tunis's planetary arrangement, then returned to his battle couch and composed himself to wait. In fourteen years of active duty and the four years of midshipman training before that, he'd never been on a ship attempting an interstellar pursuit. It just didn't come up very often, although some rarely used sections of the Common-wealth Navy's tactical manuals offered a few suggestions.

"Sir, we're receiving a transmission," Girard said, interrupting his reflections. "It's CSS *Harrier*."

"*Harrier*?" Sikander glanced over to his operations officer. "I didn't realize she'd be here. Let's see it, Mr. Girard."

Commander Giselle Dacey's visage appeared in a comm win-dow near Sikander's seat. "Welcome to Tunis, *Decisive*—this is an unexpected pleasure. What brings you to this corner of Zerzura, Commander North? Over."

"Always nice to see a friendly face," Sikander remarked to Gi-rard. Giselle Dacey was an old shipmate—they'd served together on the Helix Squadron staff during the *warumzi agu* rebellion in the Tzoru Dominion. She was one of his fellow COs in Pleiades Squadron, a colleague who shouldered the same responsibilities and faced the same challenges he did on a daily basis, and the sitting Senator Kilgore to boot. She'd assumed command of *Har-rier* at Neda just a couple of months after he'd joined *Decisive*, and they'd shared a few fishing trips and barbecues during their off-duty days. Romance wasn't really in the cards; dating some-one in the same command structure rarely worked out well, and even though they each had their own ship, they both worked for Wilson Broward and saw too much of each other in squadron meetings to be anything but friends. "Where exactly is *Harrier*, Mr. Girard?"

"High orbit over Ben Arouz, sir. That's Tunis IV, the inhabited planet of the system. We're sixteen light-minutes away."

There wasn't much point in trying to hold a conversation with a sixteen-minute lag, so Sikander decided to keep his reply to the point. "Commander Dacey, my compliments. The pleasure is mutual—I'm glad to see *Harrier* here. We're in pursuit of a pirate vessel that attacked a mining station in Bursa. She should be only half an hour or so ahead of us. I'm sending along our imagery in case you detect her, over. Mr. Girard, if you'd be so kind?"

"Already on it, Captain."

"Thank you," Sikander said. He got up and walked over to the sensor technicians at their posts; on *Decisive's* bridge, the sensor watch consisted of three operators positioned at the forward end of the arrowhead-shaped compartment, with the sensor officer's station just behind them. "Anything yet, Ms. Carter?"

"No, sir." The young ensign gestured at several points on her display. "We've got a few high-speed contacts currently decelerating from transit terminations here, here, and here, but the vectors aren't right—none of these ships came from Bursa. Either we passed Target Alpha en route and she hasn't arrived yet, or she managed to get behind a sensor shadow before we unbubbled."

Sikander studied the display, frowning. There was a sizable gas giant not too far off their projected course line on the other side of the system . . . with a bit of deft maneuvering the pirate vessel might have slipped behind it in the twenty-five minutes between the two ship's arrivals, using it to screen a crash deceleration and vector change. *It's not impossible,* he mused. *They observed us maneuvering to begin our pursuit, and they might very well have guessed that we'd be on their heels when they arrived here.* Then again, that would require precision military maneuvering, and it seemed unlikely that criminals flying a beat-up old cargo hauler could pull off that sort of timing—Sikander didn't know if *Decisive* could have managed it. *In fact, it's likely their navigation is much worse than ours. Chances are they missed their planned warp termination by a wide margin, maybe even light-hours . . . in which case they might be so far from us that we haven't even seen them yet.*

There was a third possibility, for that matter: The pirate vessel might have departed on the Bursa-Tunis transit line, only to cut her warp generator somewhere in the interstellar space between the two systems. In that case, *Decisive* would have overshot them by literally light-years by heading toward the obvious destination. Powering and depowering warp rings required very expensive charges of exotic matter, and no captain would want to run the risk of stranding himself with empty fuel bottles years away from port. *But if this fellow had full magnetic bottles and decided he could spare the ring charge, he just might have done it. So are we dealing with a shockingly incompetent navigator, a brilliant helmsman, or someone rich enough or desperate enough to waste a charged ring?*

Sikander chose the first option. "Expand our search parameters, Ms. Carter," he told his sensor officer. "Assume Target Alpha missed her course by a light-hour or three, and look for high-speed targets on the outskirts of the system."

"Yes, sir," Carter replied. She turned to her sensor techs and started working out how to best survey the outer portions of the Tunis system. Sikander left her to her work, returning to his command seat and settling in to wait for results.

Half an hour after he'd replied to Commander Dacey's greeting, he received her answer: *Harrier* hadn't detected any terminal cascades from Bursa arrivals for most of the day. "But it's a fifty-fifty chance that our orbit placed us on the wrong side of the planet when your pirate arrived," she added. "We'll add your imagery to our database and make sure to watch out for that ship."

"What now, Captain?" Michael Girard asked as Sikander digested *Harrier*'s news.

"Wherever Target Alpha is, she isn't close by. Secure from general quarters and set the normal underway watch. Hold this course, standard deceleration. We'll loiter in the outer system for a bit and see if she shows up."

"Aye, sir." Girard began issuing orders.

Sikander stood, stretched, and made his way back down to his quarters to tackle some busywork while they waited for the Bursa pirate ship to make its appearance. But the rest of the morning passed without a glimpse of Target Alpha . . . then the rest of the day . . . and the rest of the day after that. *Decisive*'s operations specialists pored over the sensor records of Tunis's traffic control and compared their imagery from Bursa against scores of ships going about their business in the system, to no avail.

On the third day of their fruitless search in Tunis, *Harrier* departed Ben Arouz and met *Decisive* in the middle reaches of the system, her port call concluded. Giselle Dacey shuttled over to *Decisive* to visit Sikander as the two destroyers proceeded in company, joining him and Amelia Fraser for a working lunch. "I hate to say it, Sikay, but I think you lost your pirate," she told him when they finished their meal. "They cut their warp transit short or they overshot on purpose, and they're not going to show themselves in Tunis as long as either of us is here."

"I'm beginning to think that you're right," Sikander admitted. "They must have guessed that we'd try to unbubble on their heels, so they gave themselves a couple of light-hours of distance to avoid us. We should have tried to get here before them."

"In which case you still would have been hours away when they arrived, and they would have had plenty of time to run again when they spotted you waiting for them. It's hard to catch a ship that's got enough of a lead to line up a transit course, Sikay. Don't blame yourself for failing to do the impossible."

"Given that, how much longer do we want to stay in Tunis?" Amelia Fraser asked. "I don't think we can say we're in a pursuit situation at this point, and this is *Harrier*'s beat, not ours."

"Only until tomorrow," said Dacey. "We're scheduled to make transit for New Kibris."

"You might want to leave today," Fraser said to her. "I have a feeling that the troublemakers in New Kibris know exactly when *Harrier* is due to arrive. I bet you'd have a better chance of catching someone doing something they shouldn't be doing if you showed up a day early. After all, we didn't find any trouble until we unbubbled in Bursa a week ahead of schedule."

Dacey thought over Fraser's advice. "That's a good idea, Amelia," she finally said. "In fact, I think I'll do just that. I'm getting tired of plodding through system after system where everyone's on their best behavior. And if that's the case, I'd better get back to *Harrier* and kick things into high gear. Time's wasting, as they say."

Sikander nodded, and reached over for the comm panel by his seat. "Hangar? This is the captain. Ready Commander Dacey's launch, please. She's departing soon."

"Where are you headed next?" Dacey said as she stood up and brushed a few crumbs from her uniform.

"I suppose we'll resume our patrol in Bursa," Sikander said. "I've got a prize crew of fifteen sailors to pick up, after all. And we still need to restock our generator parts, which was the whole reason we got off schedule in the first place."

Fraser frowned. "I don't like the idea of getting right back onto schedule, Captain. If we return to Bursa now, we'll arrive just in time for the end of our planned patrol. How much do you want to bet things are going to be suspiciously quiet when we get there?"

"I can't say that you're wrong, XO," Sikander said. "God knows the first thing I'm going to do when we get back to Neda is tell Captain Broward that we need to either incorporate some randomness in our patrol schedules or sail under sealed orders so that no one knows when we're coming. But we've stretched our mission parameters as far as they can go with this side trip to Tunis. I'm afraid it's back to Bursa for us."

"I'll have the quartermasters work out a transit course as soon as we finish here," Fraser said. As executive officer, she oversaw the ship's navigation. "You know, by the time we get there, it'll be time to move on to Dahar."

"No one ever said the Navy was *efficient,* Amelia," Sikander pointed out.

Giselle Dacey gave a snort of sour amusement, and Fraser grimaced. "I know, Captain. I'm not saying that we have any choice about it—I just don't like the idea of going right back to what we know isn't working. It rubs me the wrong way."

"Me too, Amelia." Sikander rose to walk Dacey back down to her launch in *Decisive*'s hangar bay. "Perhaps *Harrier* will have better luck in New Kibris."

"We can hope," Dacey said. She shook Sikander's hand. "Thanks for lunch, Captain North. Good hunting to you."

"And to you, Captain Dacey," Sikander replied with a distinctly predatory grin. "We'll catch our pirate sooner or later. I promise you that."

8

CSS *Decisive*, Dahar System

*D*ecisive lingered in Bursa just long enough to pick up the
Carmela Día prize crew and the generator parts, and then
set course for Dahar. This transit was a short one: thirty hours
at the standard ten-percent warp gradient. Sikander's navigation
team cut the ship's warp generators seventeen light-minutes from
Dahar II—the major inhabited planet of the system, as well as the
capital of the Zerzura Sector—and set course for the orbital station of Dahar High Port.

It turned out that *Decisive* wasn't the only foreign vessel visiting Dahar at the moment: the Velaran cruiser *Vashaoth Teh* held
station in a medium orbit above the Caliphate planet, as did a
Dremish survey vessel named *Polarstern*. Sikander sent both
commanding officers the customary compliments, and studied
the Velaran warship with some interest. He hadn't encountered
any Electorate vessels in his previous Zerzuran patrols. *Vashaoth Teh* was either a poorly armed heavy cruiser or an oversized
light cruiser—the product of some strange design compromises,
perhaps—but she was one of the newer ships in the Electorate
navy and certainly outgunned any of the destroyers in Pleiades
Squadron. *Polarstern*, on the other hand, was an unarmed research ship registered under Dremark's survey service: fast and

roomy, with several large hangars to support the operations of workboats and beacon tenders.

"Make sure we capture some good imagery on both of those ships," Sikander told Girard as *Decisive* drew near to the planet. "I don't think we've seen much of the new Velaran cruiser yet, and it wouldn't surprise me if the Dremish ship doubles as an intelligence-collection platform."

"Yes, sir," said Girard. "I have to admit I'm not exactly sure what the survey ship is surveying out here, anyway."

"What about the Zerzuran squadron? Any changes?" Amelia Fraser asked the ops officer. A kilometer-long arm of Dahar High Port reserved for the use of the Caliphate navy served as the base of the Zerzura Sector Fleet, a mismatched collection of half a dozen old corvettes, gunboats, and support vessels. Each of Zerzura's major systems maintained its own customs and patrol craft, but those were meant for law enforcement, not defense . . . not that the Zerzuran fleet could seriously hope to defend the sector against a hostile destroyer, let alone an enemy battle line.

"*Hasan Rami* is absent," Girard replied. "Out on patrol, I imagine. Other than that, no changes."

"Hopefully she's having better luck than we are," said Sikander. Zerzura's paltry squadron reminded him of the decrepit defenses of the Tzoru Dominion, but at least the pasha's warships occasionally got under way. Some of the Tzoru fleets hadn't moved in decades. He returned his attention to the mottled green-and-ocher planet ahead of *Decisive* and the wheel-like outline of Dahar High Port, now coming into view above the nightside. "Let's have Reed take the conn for the docking maneuver. He's due for a turn, isn't he?"

"I believe so," said Fraser. She nodded to the petty officer of the watch. "Pass the word: Mr. Hollister, your presence is requested on the bridge."

Sikander relaxed at his station, keeping half an eye on the bridge team's conduct of the docking maneuver. One of his duties as commanding officer was to make sure the ship's junior officers qualified in a variety of ship-handling operations, but like many engineering officers Hollister spent most of his watch time in main control and rarely got the opportunity to practice. He was pleased to see that the young engineer managed the delicate maneuver competently with only a point or two of advice. "Well done, Mr. Hollister," Sikander said when the cradle arms thumped into place to secure *Decisive's* hull. "You could have used just a bit more thrust to close up those last few meters, but there's nothing wrong with the way you did it."

"Thank you, Captain," Hollister said, obviously relieved that he'd handled the docking properly. "I'll remember that for next time, sir."

I still need to decide what to do about Shah's letter, Sikander reminded himself. In *Decisive's* flurry of transits and the excitement of the chase, he'd let the reprimand sit on his desk. He was inclined to soften Shah's reprimand to a letter of admonishment— something that would put Hollister on notice that his department head was unhappy and establish documentation in case something else came up but wouldn't follow the young officer to his next ship or station. It wasn't fair to either of them to leave that unresolved . . . but then again, a little time for reflection might provide Shah with a better chance to evaluate Hollister's ability and Hollister with a chance to show what he could do. In fact, Sikander rather hoped that Shah would reconsider the reprimand without any help from him. That, however, was a problem Sikander could put off for a little longer. Now that they'd arrived at Dahar, it was time to pay attention to some of his diplomatic duties.

"Secure from docking detail and set the in-port watch," he ordered, stretching as he got up from his acceleration couch. He was scheduled to meet Special Commissioner Darrow when *Decisive* made port, followed by a visit to the pasha's palace. "The ship is yours, XO. Standard liberty schedule for the crew."

"Aye, sir," Amelia Fraser replied. "I'll see to it. Who do you want to bring along today?"

Providing his officers with opportunities to participate in diplomatic missions was another one of Sikander's responsibilities. "Mr. Girard, you're with me," he said. Since operations officers handled intelligence functions on board small warships such as *Decisive*, Michael Girard was the closest he had to a dedicated intelligence officer; his recent study of Zerzura's piracy troubles might be useful. *One more should be enough*, he thought, and made his decision. "And let's ask Dr. Ruiz to join the landing party. Since this is her first visit to Dahar, we'll let her play diplomat today."

"Very good," Amelia replied. "I'll call over to the station and reserve you a shuttle."

An hour after *Decisive* secured herself in High Port's docking cradle, Sikander and his officers, accompanied by Darvesh Reza, caught a public shuttle down to the city of Mersin. Below their shuttle, the morning sun painted the clouds veiling the planet's lowlands a pale gold-orange hue. The view was impressive, but the details of *Decisive's* weeklong visit occupied most of his attention—social occasions, attending various civic gatherings as a guest of honor, hosting tours of the ship, and more meetings with the Aquilan consul. Formal port calls served as an important tool of diplomacy in remote sectors such as Zerzura, and as commanding officer of an Aquilan warship, Sikander was expected to represent the Commonwealth in a positive light—and take careful note of what he saw or heard during his visit.

So much for chasing pirates, he reflected. *Instead we're going to spend the rest of our scheduled patrol in the one spot in this whole sector that doesn't have a piracy problem, going to the same parties and speaking at the same events every Commonwealth crew attends when they pass through Dahar. Don't we have more important things to do?*

"It's orange!" Carla Ruiz said, openly gawking at the spectacular view. "How is this world even habitable?" As a rule of thumb, the more exotic a planet's coloration, the less likely it was to harbor the sort of atmosphere humans could breathe.

"An altitude-segregated atmosphere," Girard told her. "The sea-level atmosphere is several times denser than standard, and tainted by nitrogen dioxide and more exotic compounds. That orange you see is more or less permanent cloud cover above low-elevation areas. But once you get about three thousand meters above sea level, the air pressure's close to standard and the heavier compounds are all below you. The highlands are actually quite terran."

Ruiz nodded, and turned back to her window. "This is really something. It's like the bottom of the atmosphere is a three-kilometer-deep ocean."

"Oh, there's an actual ocean down there, too. It's even mostly water. But humans don't go down to sea level unless they have to, and when they do, they go in pressure suits or armored crawlers. Some of the native wildlife is, well, big and hungry."

"There's a sightseeing tour if you are interested," Sikander suggested, setting aside his frustration with the effective end of the patrol. "I haven't done it myself, but I understand it takes three or four hours and doesn't cost too much. They do make you sign a waiver, though."

"Really? I'm in." Ruiz elbowed Girard. "What about you, Michael? Want to come?"

The fair-skinned operations officer turned red. "Umm, that's not for me. I can see the clouds just fine from up here, thank you."

When they landed at Mersin's transit hub, they found that the Aquilan consulate had sent a flyer to meet them. A short hop across the city brought them to the consulate itself, a spacious office that occupied two floors in an expensive high-rise. Special Commissioner Eric Darrow waited for Sikander and his officers at the building's rooftop landing pad. Beside him stood a graceful white-haired woman dressed in a long, flowing Daharan kaftan.

"Commander North, a pleasure to see you again. Welcome to Dahar," said Darrow, extending his hand to greet Sikander as he climbed out of the flyer. A lean, angular man of forty-five with close-cropped hair and a short goatee, Darrow served as something of a regional ambassador for the Aquilan Foreign Ministry; he tended to split his time between Dahar, the Velaran world of Meliya, and Neda, where Sikander had run into him on a couple of occasions. "Allow me to introduce you to Nola Okoye. She's our consul-general in this system."

"Mr. Darrow." Sikander shook Darrow's hand, then turned to the consul. "Ms. Okoye, it's good to meet you. This is Lieutenant Girard, Dr. Ruiz, and Chief Reza, my personal assistant." A quick round of handshakes followed.

"Why don't you all come inside?" Okoye said. "We've got a little time before we're expected over at the palace, and as it turns out we have excellent coffee here."

Sikander and his officers followed the diplomats to a comfortable sitting area inside the consulate; a coffee service was already set out and waiting. "How has your patrol been so far?" Darrow asked as he personally poured for the consulate's guests, serving the coffee in tiny cups after the local style.

"Eventful. We stumbled across a recently pirated ship in Bursa, and while we were bringing her into port, we received a distress call for a separate attack on a mining station." Sikander briefly summarized *Decisive*'s adventures over the last couple of weeks, describing the pursuit of the pirate vessel to Tunis and his reluctant decision to abandon the chase after his quarry's escape. "This is my fifth cruise in this sector, but it's the first time I've even come close to catching a pirate in the act. We were lucky enough to be in the right place at the right time, but not quite lucky enough to catch them."

"A shame they got away," Darrow observed when he finished. "It would be useful to our position here to present the pasha with some measurable antipiracy successes. Several other powers are cozying up to Marid Pasha and looking for ways to impress him."

"Dremark and Velar?" Michael Girard asked. "We saw *Polarstern* and *Vashaoth Teh* in orbit."

"Among others—Montréal and Cygnus have interests here too, even if their ships aren't in-system at the moment."

"I suppose I'm missing something," Carla Ruiz said. "Zerzura is just one province of the Caliphate, isn't it? Why does everyone care about impressing one provincial governor?"

"The Caliphate isn't like the Commonwealth, Dr. Ruiz," Okoye answered. "Their imperial system developed centuries ago when interstellar travel time made it impossible to exercise much in the way of central authority, so they built a government that dispersed power. Each sector is more or less on its own. The Caliphate appoints a vali, or governor, who stands in for the Caliph and runs the sector more or less as he sees fit."

"Which means that if a foreign power wants something in a particular sector, we have to talk to the official who runs that sector," Darrow added. "Our ambassadors at Terra are mostly ceremonial. The Caliph's court expects all of us so-called lesser powers to abase ourselves before the splendor of Old Earth, of course, but in fact very little of what is decreed on Terra matters.

The only real decision made on Terra is choosing who they send to run things out here. In the Caliphate, the person is the policy."

Sikander nodded. It seemed that Dr. Ruiz wasn't afraid to ask an elementary question or two—a rare quality in an officer still fairly new in her duty station. For his own part, he'd come to understand something of Zerzura's relationship to Terra during his time on Pleiades Station, but he'd never heard it explained in quite that way: *The person is the policy.* "In that case, what kind of person is Marid al-Zahabi?" he asked the diplomats. "This is my first opportunity to meet him."

"A problem-solver," said Okoye. "He's a highly regarded military commander—something of a war hero, really. He fought with distinction in the Suhail War twenty years ago, and later commanded the landing force that put down the Yeni Süphan uprising. That earned him his noble title and put him on the Caliphate court's radar. Six years ago he was appointed to assume the duties of governor here in Zerzura after his predecessor's corruption became too much for even Terra to overlook. He's been aggressive in dismissing some of the worst and most incompetent local officials, and since he doesn't get a lot of help from Terra, he's done what he can to encourage foreign business investment here."

"He sounds like exactly the man for the job," Girard said.

Darrow shrugged. "Marid Pasha is certainly about three cuts above the typical well-connected idiot who secures an appointment of this sort, but believe me, the Caliph's handlers didn't send him out here because they were concerned about Zerzura. I think that they saw a capable, well-liked leader with a lot of support in the army and decided that a fellow like that might start to get ideas if they let him get comfortable too close to home."

Sikander raised an eyebrow. "Have we seen any evidence of those sorts of ambitions?"

"Not really, no, but you'll notice that Marid Pasha doesn't get much backing from the Caliphate," said Darrow. "No one on Terra seems to be in a hurry to send him extra troops or warships or the sort of budget he needs to run Zerzura properly. Whether they want him to fail or they're scared of him succeeding I couldn't say, but either way Terra is laying the groundwork for an even bigger problem in Zerzura: It's an open secret in Dahar's diplomatic community that Marid Pasha is thinking about declaring independence."

"I see. Why take orders from Terra if you could just run the show yourself, and deal with problems as you see fit?"

"In all fairness, not all of us in the Foreign Ministry agree with Mr. Darrow's assessment," Okoye said. "I see Marid Pasha as a man trying to make the most of what little he gets. I think that he's content to let the independence rumors incubate in the hopes they'll encourage Terra to take more interest in his sector. Then again, I'm an optimist."

"And on that note, it's about time to head over to the palace for our luncheon," said Darrow. "Marid Pasha is nothing if not punctual—we don't want to keep him waiting."

The pasha's palace was only a few kilometers from the consulate, a flight of less than five minutes. Caliphate soldiers in khaki dress uniforms and wide blue sashes stood guard at the entrance by the vast landing pad; the mag rifles slung over their shoulders gleamed with gold filigree. A dark-haired man in a civilian business suit greeted the Aquilan party at the door and introduced himself as Jahid Saif, one of the pasha's advisors. He escorted them through echoing hallways to a splendid dining room where a mix of high-ranking Zerzuran officers and well-dressed civilians waited, and announced their arrival.

"Mr. Eric Darrow, special commissioner of the Common-

wealth of Aquila. Commander Sikander Singh North, commanding officer of CSS *Decisive* and Nawabzada of Ishar. Ms. Nola
Okoye, Commonwealth consul to Dahar." Then Saif nodded
toward a silver-haired Zerzuran in a plain high-collared tunic.
"Please allow me to introduce His Excellency the Pasha Marid
al-Zahabi, Vali of Zerzura and honored servant of the Caliph."

"Ah, come in, come in!" Marid Pasha said in good Standard
Anglic. "Mr. Darrow, Ms. Okoye, a pleasure to see you both
again. And welcome to you, Commander North." Tall and square-
shouldered, the pasha certainly possessed the bearing of a military
man; Sikander could well believe that he'd been a commander of
some distinction before accepting his political appointment. He
stood half a head taller than the other Zerzurans in the room:
Saif, a middle-aged woman in a modest business suit, a balding
army officer who wore a general's stars, and a stocky admiral in a
Caliphate naval uniform.

"Thank you, Your Excellency," Sikander replied. Then, to his
surprise, Marid Pasha crossed the room to shake Sikander's hand
firmly.

"I have hoped to meet you for long time now, sir," the pasha
said. "Your actions during *Hector*'s fight at Gadira showed exem-
plary courage and leadership. This is truly an unexpected honor."

Sikander faltered in surprise. "You've heard of me?"

"Oh, yes. At the time of the Gadira incident I commanded
the Caliphate's Fifth Military District. The tensions between the
Empire of Dremark and the Aquilan Commonwealth naturally
caused us some alarm, so I directed my staff to follow the story
closely. I am quite familiar with the part you played by continuing
to fight your ship after Captain Markham's death. Extraordinary,
really!"

"Er, thank you, Your Excellency. I merely carried out my duties
to the best of my ability." Sikander glanced over at Eric Darrow,

who gave him a subtle nod of approval. If the senior diplomat had expected anything like Marid Pasha's remarks, he was doing a masterly job of hiding it. "I had no idea the story had been published in the Caliphate."

"Duels between the warships of major Coalition powers are few and far between," the pasha said. "Tell me, Commander, why exactly did the Dremish force break off the action? I've watched tactical reconstructions of the battle a dozen times, but it's never been clear to me why Captain Harper withdrew. Damaged as his ships were, he still outnumbered you."

Sikander paused a moment, measuring his response. He supposed that he should feel flattered by the pasha's admiration, but he remembered the battle as something he'd *survived*, not as some daring exploit to boast about later. In fact, he rarely spoke of it—too many of his shipmates had died that day. "I'm not sure whether I can shed any light on that, Marid Pasha," he finally said. "I only know what I saw on *Hector*'s bridge, and I'm not at liberty to disclose some of the details. But I can tell you that Mr. Girard here landed a hard salvo on *Panther* and disabled her torpedo battery just before she withdrew. He was *Hector*'s fire-control officer at Gadira, and his excellent marksmanship likely influenced Captain Harper's decision to withdraw."

The pasha turned to Girard, taking stock of him. "Indeed? I hadn't realized that we were entertaining two *Hector* veterans today."

"Mr. North played a more important part in things than I did, Your Excellency," Girard said. "I was only an ensign at the time—I engaged the targets I was directed to engage."

"With some skill and coolness under fire, I suspect. Well, I am honored to meet two such noteworthy officers. Perhaps I can prevail upon you to share your recollections of the encounter at some point. I am sure there are a hundred details you could add to what the rest of us think we know about—oh, excuse me, I am neglecting my introductions!" The pasha motioned toward the other Zerzurans in the room. "Jahid Saif you have already met; he's my chief political advisor. My appointment secretary, Nenet Fakhoury, and General Karacan, commander of the Mansur Guards. And of course my naval minister, Admiral Torgut al-Kassar."

Another round of handshakes and pleasantries ensued, and then the pasha led them to the room's generous table. "Please, sit, make yourselves comfortable—lunch will be served momentarily. How was your voyage from Neda, Commander North?"

I suppose I'm going to tell this story a few times this week, Sikander realized. "It was eventful, Your Excellency," he said, launching into a somewhat abbreviated account of *Decisive's* patrol. True to the pasha's prediction, lunch appeared while he spoke—a dish of roasted vegetables stuffed with rice, accompanied by traditional-style flatbread, tahini, and mashed beans. Jahid Saif followed him in Anglic, but the other Zerzurans relied on translation devices; Sikander didn't trust his own Jadeed-Arabi well enough to try it out in front of a high official like the pasha. "Regrettably, the pirate vessel we pursued managed to elude us in Tunis," he concluded. "We resumed our planned patrol route, returned to Bursa, and then proceeded here."

"I am sure you'll have better luck next time," Marid Pasha said. "If nothing else, it seems that you interrupted the attack on the United Extraction station. That's better than nothing."

"I believe *Decisive's* success, limited as it may have been, illustrates the value of vigorous antipiracy patrols, Your Excellency," Eric Darrow said. "Imagine how much more effective they would be if we kept units on station in the systems that are actually under threat. An Aquilan base of operations in Bursa or Tunis would make it much easier to monitor local conditions, and prevent pirates from slipping back into the traffic patterns of legitimate shipping after they carry out their attacks. It would also bring all of Zerzura's major worlds within a single short transit of an Aquilan post. A few light patrol vessels in the right spot could be exactly what you need to deal with Zerzura's piracy trouble."

Admiral al-Kassar snorted and spoke in his native Jadeed-Arabi. "We take our sovereignty seriously, Mr. Darrow. You forget that your ships are granted passage through our territory in the spirit of cooperation, not because we require your protection."

"I do not mean to suggest otherwise, Admiral," Darrow said. "But piracy is, by definition, a crime that threatens everyone engaged in spaceborne commerce or industry, and we are all obligated to do everything in our power to put an end to it."

Sikander shifted in his seat, but said nothing. Sovereignty over the empty space that made up the vast majority of a planetary system was a complicated question. Everyone recognized that planets and stations belonged to *someone*, but different powers held to different standards about those parts of a system that weren't actually inhabited or exploited by some form of industry. The Commonwealth of Aquila defined sovereignty rather narrowly—in fact, by Aquilan rules, *Decisive* had spent most of its voyage in open space. Other powers tended to claim the entirety of a system. Sikander didn't share Torgut al-Kassar's view that Aquila's ships required permission to just pass through the Caliphate's systems, but he doubted that he'd help Darrow's point by bringing that up.

"Of course pirates are everyone's enemy, Mr. Darrow," Marid Pasha observed. "In principle I have no objection to what you propose. But I do have some practical concerns."

General Karacan nodded seriously. "Whatever facilities we make available to Aquila will certainly require extensive renovation or new construction. The expenses could be significant, and Zerzura's resources are limited."

"Terra doesn't provide us with much help, as the general points out," said the pasha. "I am not sure we can afford to build the sort of base you're thinking of."

"Improved security in Zerzura would certainly entice Aquilan companies to consider new investments in your systems, Your Excellency. In fact, I know of several major manufacturers that are looking for opportunities to expand their operations into this area." Darrow smiled thinly. "Our government could perhaps assist Zerzura by providing some development loans to help create the sort of security infrastructure we think is needed here."

That sounds a lot like a bribe, Sikander decided. He kept that thought to himself, too—it wouldn't be the first time the Commonwealth secured what it wanted by writing a check to the right person. At first blush, it seemed ridiculous to pay the Zerzurans for the privilege of taking care of their piracy problem. Then again, if Darrow aimed to establish Aquilan influence over affairs in this corner of the Caliphate, the polite fiction of a "loan" that Marid Pasha could use to buy the loyalty of whomever he needed to buy might be the cheapest and most efficient way to attain his goal.

If Marid Pasha read anything more into Darrow's suggestion than a sincere offer to help, he gave no sign. "We would be happy to examine any proposal you'd like to share with us. Simply forward your suggestion to my office, and I will review it with my advisors. Now, Commander North: Tell me about your *Decisive*. She is one of your Dauntless-class ships, isn't she?"

Nola Okoye grinned. "Be careful, Your Excellency. If you ask a captain to talk about his ship, you might have a hard time ending the conversation."

A ripple of laughter ran around the table; Sikander joined in. "I will try to limit my remarks to a few short hours, I promise. Now, what would you like to know?"

The luncheon moved on to a discussion about life on a warship, and from there to comparisons of the various homeworlds of each of the guests—the working part of the meal was evidently over. Sikander didn't mind; Marid Pasha was a gracious host, and he sensed that Darrow and Okoye were satisfied to have at least raised the possibility of strengthening Zerzura's ties to Aquila. Sikander extended an offer to provide the pasha and his staff with a personal tour of *Decisive*. Marid Pasha seemed very pleased, but deferred on setting a specific time.

At the end of their hour, the pasha stood and shook their hands again. "This has been a fascinating discussion," he said. "I hope that you will be able to join me later this week for our hospital benefit. It's a worthy cause, and I know that our guests will be delighted if some of *Decisive*'s officers could attend."

"We would be honored, Your Excellency," Darrow replied. "Thank you for your time, and the fine meal."

"Think nothing of it," the pasha replied, walking them to the door. "Jahid, will you please show our guests out?"

Sikander and his companions followed Saif back through the palace to the landing platform. The Zerzuran official had the guards there call for the Aquilans' flyer, wished them a good afternoon, and returned inside while they waited for their flyer to be brought up.

When he was certain the pasha's attendants weren't in earshot, Sikander turned to Eric Darrow. "What in the world was all that about Gadira, Mr. Darrow?"

"I don't know, Commander. I've never seen Marid Pasha warm up to someone quite like that. I can only guess that your reputation has preceded you."

"It might have been a veiled suggestion," Nola Okoye pointed out. "A way for the pasha to signal that he knows what happened at Gadira and he would be pleased by a similar development here?"

"With all due respect, Ms. Okoye, I doubt that very much,"

said Sikander. "I saw what happened in Gadira, and I cannot imagine how anybody would want that."

"Are you certain? I admit that I'm not intimately familiar with how the Gadira crisis unfolded, but is it possible there is some part of the story that provides a parallel here?"

Sikander thought hard, trying to find some analogy and falling short. He shook his head, giving up in frustration, but Michael Girard cleared his throat. "We helped Ranya el-Nasir to retain her throne by deterring Dremish aggression," he offered. "She represented systemic reform, cultural moderation, even a certain degree of autonomy from foreign influence. Maybe the pasha is saying that he has similar aims."

"Keep going, Lieutenant," Darrow said to Girard. "I think you might be onto something."

A new flyer approached the palace and set down not far away; Sikander supposed that their own vehicle had been held up for a minute or two to make room for the arriving party. He composed himself to wait a little longer, watching the new arrival while Michael Girard struggled to explain the Gadira affair of eight years past to Darrow and Okoye. A long-legged woman with hair of burnished copper climbed out of the new flyer, rather daringly dressed for an afternoon appointment at the palace, followed by a fit, good-looking man with sandy hair and sharp features, his eyes shaded from the bright day by fashionable sunglasses.

Otto Bleindel.

"I don't believe it," Sikander snarled, momentarily stunned. "What is *he* doing here?"

The anger in his tone silenced the debate behind him; everybody else turned to see what had his attention. Darvesh moved smoothly to the front of the little group, suddenly at Sikander's side and ready to interpose himself against any threat. "What?" Darrow asked sharply. "What is it?"

"That's Hanne Vogt," Okoye said. "I don't know the gentleman with her."

"He's a Dremish intelligence agent named Otto Bleindel," Sikander said. "We've crossed paths before—on Gadira, no less. The last time I saw him, he tried to run me down with a truck."

The Dremish envoys started toward the palace from their flyer, and realized that they were the object of Sikander's attention. Annoyance flickered across Hanne Vogt's face, but Bleindel actually met Sikander's eyes and smiled. "Now, this is a surprise," he said in Standard Anglic. "I wonder if Marid Pasha is having a laugh at our expense."

Vogt gave Bleindel a stern look, then nodded to Darrow. "Commissioner Darrow. What a coincidence to see you here."

"Special Envoy Vogt," Darrow replied, nodding as well. "Imagine my surprise."

Sikander took a half step forward, fists clenched at his side. Otto Bleindel had more or less single-handedly stoked the Caidist rebellion on Gadira into a planetary civil war, causing thousands of deaths. The Dremish agent was still wanted on that planet; Ranya el-Nasir's security forces would happily extradite him from whatever system or world he happened to be captured on. "You have much to answer for, Mr. Bleindel," he said.

Bleindel did not flinch, but he did glance over at the Caliphate soldiers standing guard by the palace entrance. "I see you haven't forgotten me, Mr. North. I have to say that I'm a little flattered. Unfortunately, whatever you have in mind, this wouldn't seem to be the time or place. We are guests of Marid Pasha, just as you are."

Darvesh set a cautionary hand on Sikander's shoulder. "He is right, Nawabzada," he murmured softly. "This is neutral ground. We have no authority here."

"Eric, Nola, I would love to stay and chat, but I'm afraid I have an appointment," Vogt said to the Aquilan diplomats. "I am sure we'll see more of each other soon. Otto?"

"Coming," Bleindel replied. He offered Sikander a sardonic bow, and then followed Vogt into the palace. Sikander stood and stared after the Dremish envoys until they disappeared from view. Behind him, the flyer Vogt and Bleindel had arrived in lifted off and headed for the palace's parking area. The consulate's flyer appeared just behind it, taking its place on the palace landing pad.

"You are full of surprises today, Commander North," Darrow observed as they boarded their flyer. "What exactly is your history with this Bleindel?"

"He's a professional provocateur: terrorist, saboteur, assassin, a specialist in the sort of operations the Dremish government denies. If he's here in Zerzura, you can expect that the Empire of Dremark is up to no good."

"It's no secret that Dremark is paying a lot more attention to the Caliphate these days," Okoye observed. "Dremish companies are competing for some of the same markets and government contracts that our own companies have their eyes on, certainly. But we haven't seen anything to suggest that the Dremish are doing anything in Zerzura other than cultivating a relationship with an influential governor, which is more or less what we're doing."

"Then perhaps we're not looking in the right places," Sikander told her.

Okoye frowned, but allowed Sikander's remark to pass. Darrow cleared his throat after an awkward moment. "Well, I think that your friend Bleindel was right about one thing: Our little meeting on the landing pad was no accident. Marid Pasha wanted us— and the Dremish too, I suppose—to see that there's another player in the game. He hopes to incite a bidding war, and that means we'd better take another look at our aid package and incentives to make sure our case is compelling. There goes my afternoon."

"Drop me off at the transit center, if you don't mind," Sikander said. "I think I'll return to the ship. Mr. Girard, Dr. Ruiz, feel free to take the rest of the day off and see the town, if you like. There's nothing on our official schedule until tomorrow."

"Thank you, sir," Carla Ruiz said. "I think I'll do that. Come on, Michael, you can show me around."

"Okay, but we are *not* doing the sea-level tour," Girard said to her.

Sikander paid little attention to the flight back up to Dahar High Port. He spent the rest of the afternoon brooding over the significance of Bleindel's presence in Zerzura and what sort of underhanded scheme the Dremish agent might be working on. He even spent an hour retrieving various official reports about the Gadira incident to remind himself of exactly how Otto Bleindel had been involved in that crisis. Unfortunately, the best information came from the various investigations conducted after the event by the Gadiran intelligence services, and the Aquilan reports stored in *Decisive's* info assistant cited only a handful of those. *I probably know more about Otto Bleindel's role in the Gadira trouble than anybody within a hundred light-years,* he realized. *And I only met the man twice.*

Shortly before the dinner hour, he was interrupted by a call from the ship's quarterdeck. "Captain? This is Sublieutenant Haynes, officer of the deck. Sir, a Ms. Elena Pavon is here to see you."

Sikander glanced at the comm panel. "I don't believe that I know anyone by that name. What does Ms. Pavon want with me?"

"She says that she represents Pegasus-Pavon Shipping, sir. She'd like to talk to you about pirates."

Carmela Día's *shipping line,* Sikander recalled. He didn't really want to set aside what he was doing, but if the matron of a Zer-zuran shipping line had gone to the effort of coming up to Dahar High Port to see him, he couldn't very well put her off. *Show the flag,* he reminded himself. "Oh, one of *those* Pavons. Very well. Have the messenger show her up to my cabin, please."

"Aye, sir," Haynes replied. "They're on their way."

"Darvesh, please put on some tea and coffee," Sikander said to his valet. He took a moment to tidy up the various reports and folders sitting open on his desk while Darvesh busied himself with preparing a tray of refreshments.

A few minutes later, the messenger of the watch knocked on his door. "Ms. Pavon, Captain," he said, and stood aside to let his guest enter. Sikander came around the corner of his desk ready to greet the matron of the Pavon line, only to be startled by the discovery that Elena Pavon was strikingly beautiful: tall and athletic, with a graceful neck and a perfect oval face, not much older than thirty or so. She wore a black pencil skirt and a bold red blouse, and her wavy hair was as dark as midnight.

She marched into the cabin and fixed her gaze—challenging and confident, with eyes of a warm brown hue—on him. "Good afternoon. I am Elena Pavon, regional director of the Pegasus-Pavon line," she said. "You are the commanding officer?"

"I am," Sikander said, recovering his balance. He liked to think that it took more than a pretty face to impress him, but he really had expected that an important shipping line executive would be comfortably middle-aged and rather more businesslike in her attire. "Commander Sikander Singh North, Commonwealth Navy. What can I do for you, Ms. Pavon?"

"I wanted to thank you for recovering *Carmela Día*. She represents a substantial investment for my family, and we had all but written her off as a complete loss. Can you tell me anything about what happened to our ship?"

"Please, have a seat," Sikander said, nodding toward the cabin's sitting area. "Would you care for some coffee or tea?"

"No, thank you." She took a seat on the small couch, and simply waited for him to go on.

Direct, too, Sikander added to his observations about his guest. It struck him as refreshing after the circuitous conversation with Marid Pasha and his advisors. "We don't know for certain where *Carmela Día* was attacked," he began. "We found her abandoned in the outer reaches of the Bursa system, with no sign of her attackers nearby." He went on to describe the condition of the ship and the crew, skipping over the more gruesome details—whether Elena Pavon wanted to know more about that or not, *he* didn't care to dwell on that part of the story.

"Thank you, Commander North," she said when he finished, her face fixed in a steely scowl as she digested the details Sikander had chosen to include.

"I wish we could have done more, but the perpetrators were long gone by the time we discovered the wreck." Sikander poured himself a cup of coffee from the service Darvesh had set out for them; Elena changed her mind, and took one too. "I'm surprised that you heard about *Decisive*'s part in the business so quickly. We only arrived yesterday."

"Our office in Bursa dispatched a courier to notify me when your Sublieutenant Worth brought in our ship. I learned about *Carmela Día*'s recovery a few days ago."

Sikander nodded—that made sense. Zoe Worth had continued into port while *Decisive* was on its way to Tunis, so a courier departing from Bursa soon after her arrival would have had a significant head start on him. But it said something about Elena Pavon that her company had offices in multiple star systems and that she was important enough to have a courier dispatched to notify her of *Carmela Día*'s recovery. "Is there anything else I can help you with?"

"Finding the bastards who killed a Pegasus-Pavon crew and blowing them out of space would be a good start," the shipping executive said, sighing in frustration. "Someone has to do *something* about this outrageous situation, Commander. These attacks are ruining businesses that depend on interstellar commerce throughout the sector. It has to stop."

"I agree, Ms. Pavon, and I assure you that the Aquilan Commonwealth would be happy to help. But we need more patrols and more intelligence. Our squadron at Neda can only keep two or three ships on station in Zerzura at a time, and that's not enough to adequately cover the sector's systems. If we had some leads to follow we might be able to strike directly at the pirates or their bases, but so far they've left us little to work with."

"I might be able to help with that," Elena Pavon said. "I have agents watching markets in every system within fifty light-years to find out who's selling our cargo. When I learn who robbed us and killed our employees—and I will, I promise you—I intend to send you that information so that you can take the appropriate action on it."

"Not the Zerzuran authorities?"

"They're useless," Pavon said. "In fact, they're worse than useless—they're probably corrupt. It's the only explanation for the success the pirates have had in this sector."

Sikander considered Elena Pavon's claim. That might explain Amelia Fraser's observation about the pirates' apparent familiarity with Pleiades Squadron's patrol schedules. *Or it could represent the work of Otto Bleindel*, he realized. Arranging for the pasha's officials to overlook pirate attacks certainly seemed like the sort of operation the Dremish agent might be engaged in. Sikander couldn't imagine what the Dremish would have to gain from abetting piracy in Zerzura, but he wouldn't put it past them.

"That's a serious charge, Ms. Pavon," he said after a moment's thought. "I am afraid I can't rule it out, although I can think of a couple of other explanations for Zerzura's problem with pirates. I promise you this, though: If you provide me with actionable intelligence about the people behind *Carmela Día*'s attack or any other acts of piracy in this region, the Commonwealth Navy will deal with them—sternly."

"Excellent." Pavon stood, and smoothed her skirt. "I will let you know when I learn something. And I would appreciate it if you did the same for me, Captain. Good afternoon."

"Of course." A little taken aback by the sudden conclusion to the discussion, Sikander rose as well to see her out. Evidently Elena Pavon was not in the habit of wasting much time after she'd said what she had to say. "Darvesh can show you back down to the quarterdeck. Good afternoon, Ms. Pavon."

9

SMS *Polarstern*, Dahar System

V *ashaoth Teh* is beginning her warp transit," Leutnant Martin Holm reported to Otto Bleindel in *Polarstern*'s comfortable passenger lounge. The big, stoop-shouldered officer served in the Imperial Survey Service, the science and research organization of the Dremark Empire, but he also held a rank in the Imperial Security Bureau, as did every other officer in *Polarstern*'s permanent crew. In public Martin Holm played the part of a conscientious mariner who happily conveyed various scientific missions and monitoring equipment to wherever they needed to go, but in the privacy of the survey ship's VIP quarters there was no need for any pretense. "The package is secured aboard Launch Dora, Senior Agent. Captain Fischer says that we can depart anytime."

"Excellent," Bleindel replied. He rose from the comfortable chair where he'd been reading while he waited for the Velaran cruiser to leave, and slipped his dataslate into his coat pocket. "In that event, I would like to get under way at once."

"Yes, sir. I will notify the launch crew." Holm saluted and withdrew.

"Be careful, Otto," Hanne Vogt said, standing to see him off. "I know there's no need to state the obvious, but I will anyway: If conditions in Meliya don't match your requirements, abort the operation. After our little encounter with the Aquilans at the palace yesterday, I find that I'm concerned with the amount of Commonwealth interest in this region. Eric Darrow wouldn't be here if Aquila wasn't serious about finding Marid Pasha's price."

"Caution is my middle name. I didn't survive so long in this career by trying to do things when I wasn't sure how they would turn out." He offered her a precise half bow. Their working relationship was predicated on two things: respect for each other's competence in their chosen fields, and—at least in Otto's case—unbending resolve to keep things strictly unemotional. In another setting, Hanne Vogt was someone he would have liked to get to know quite a lot more intimately, but Otto Bleindel *never* mixed business with pleasure. He'd always felt that one needed to be absolutely clear-minded in his line of work.

"Commander North's reaction upon seeing you yesterday suggests otherwise," Vogt drily observed. "He seemed familiar with your work, which means that something didn't turn out the way you planned in your previous interaction with him."

"I will see you in a few days," Bleindel replied, choosing to let the diplomat's remark pass. He shouldered a small traveling bag, and headed down to the hangar bay to join the rest of his picked team—Martin Holm and two specialists from *Polarstern*'s crew—aboard a launch. The moment the hatch closed behind them, he filed Vogt's concerns away and gave them no more attention. In his judgment she had good reason to worry about Aquila's Zerzuran diplomacy, but that was her job, not his. He had a mission to carry out, and simple professionalism demanded that he give the task at hand his complete attention.

At Dahar High Port, Bleindel and his small crew transferred their equipment from *Polarstern*'s launch to a storage facility just long enough to change their clothing and assume the new identities he'd prepared for them before hiring an orbital skiff to ferry them over to the warp courier *Asfoor*. Couriers made their money by carrying news and time-sensitive business information from system to system, but many of the tiny ships also offered passage to individuals who needed to get somewhere fast and didn't care about traveling in comfort. In the case of *Asfoor*, the passenger accommodations consisted of two cramped cabins with two bunks each and a cargo compartment not much bigger than the kitchen in Bleindel's apartment back home.

The courier's captain, a thin middle-aged Cygnan who wore her hair in a ponytail threaded through an old cap, came to check on Bleindel and his comrades when *Asfoor* got under way. "Welcome aboard, Mr. Liddle," she said, extending a hand. "I'm Perla Sozzini, ship's captain. We're now accelerating along our transit course and expect to activate our warp ring in about four and a half hours. That should give us a fifty-six-hour transit to Meliya. You're welcome to spend time in the crew lounge or other common spaces, but the engine room is off-limits to passengers— there are some safety concerns, as I'm sure you can imagine—and we really can't accommodate more than one guest on the bridge at a time. You're welcome to visit if you like, but if our watchstander is busy and he or she asks you to leave, we'll need you to return below."

"I understand," Bleindel said. The name Liddle was part of his operational cover. For that matter, so was Icarus Technologies, the firm for which Mr. Liddle purportedly worked. "We'll make sure we stay out of your crew's way."

Sozzini smiled without much humor. "*Asfoor* is tiny, Mr. Liddle. We get in our own way even when we don't have any passengers aboard. Anyway, you're on your own for breakfast and lunch—you can help yourself to anything in the pantry or the cold storage case with the blue door. I'm afraid it's not much more than prepackaged frozen meals and a selection of spreads for toast and such. Oh, and you're welcome to join the crew for dinner, although it's whatever our cook fixes. We'll probably eat in two shifts because we only have six seats at the mess table."

"We understand that we're not paying for fine dining and four-star service, Captain."

"Good." Sozzini glanced around the tiny cabin, perhaps making sure that Bleindel and Holm hadn't somehow managed to trash it already after an hour's occupancy. "So what does Icarus Technologies do, anyway?"

"Advanced materials manufacturing," Martin Holm replied, making use of the cover story. If anybody bothered to check, they'd find a small company called Icarus Technologies listed in Dahar's regional business directories, and not much more than that. "We're based in Neda, but we've got a customer in the Electorate who requested urgent consultation about a problem. We're bringing special samples to Meliya to meet our local sales representatives."

"Okay, then. Just let me know if there's anything you need." Sozzini went back to her duties, her curiosity evidently satisfied.

For two and a half days, Bleindel had his team carefully survey the cramped passageways and compartments of the tiny ship and keep watch over their special equipment under the guise of stretching their legs or making themselves comfortable in the crew lounge. He instructed Weiss and Mayer, the other two members of the team, to avoid unnecessary conversations with the crew—not much of a difficulty, since neither specialist spoke much Jadeed-Arabi—and stick to Standard Anglic when they talked among themselves. For their own part, Asfoor's crew of seven seemed content to leave their passengers alone. They had their own duties to attend to, after all.

When they reached Meliya, Bleindel noted with some satisfaction that *Vashaoth Teh* occupied her customary berth at the planet's orbital dock. Meliya's spaceport was constructed around a small asteroid that had been towed into a high orbit; the military section of the spaceport consisted of a set of docking cradles fashioned from the upper surface of the rock, and an adjoining supply depot. *Asfoor* assumed a higher orbit a few hundred kilometers from the station, and Sozzini offered the courier's launch to ferry over her passengers.

"How long do you expect to remain in Meliya?" he asked the courier captain when his team was ready to depart.

"Twenty-four hours," Sozzini said. "We turn things around pretty quickly here. If you need to arrange passage back to Dahar, we come through Meliya about once a week."

"Depending on what our local representatives tell us, some of us might actually go back to Dahar with you tomorrow."

"Well, you know our rates. If no one books the guest bunks before you decide, we'd be happy to accommodate you, Mr. Liddle."

"I will let you know," Bleindel told her.

The flight from *Asfoor* to the station took only half an hour. He spent the trip in the launch's tiny cockpit, watching the station—and the moored Velaran cruiser—growing larger and larger in the armored glass windows. Bleindel had made this same trip just two weeks ago, studying the normal traffic patterns and quietly working out the logistics of his scheme. Fortunately, everything seemed to be exactly where he expected it to be—he'd been worried that some unannounced arrival or unexpected bit of maintenance work in the wrong part of the station might upset his plans. *Conditions are exactly as required*, he mentally noted for his report to Vogt. *So there!*

The launch nestled into a public-access docking cradle. Bleindel tipped the *Asfoor* crewman who'd piloted them to the station, then helped his small team with their personal luggage and the awkward cases containing their mission's special equipment. The cases did indeed hold authentic-looking material samples in case anyone demanded an inspection . . . but, as Bleindel's earlier reconnaissance had established, anything small enough to be carted around in a wheeled case didn't need to pass through any sort of station security screening on arrival. He led the others to a self-storage facility on one of the station's higher levels, and let himself into a small unit he'd rented during his last visit.

"Is this it?" Holm asked, looking around at the ugly little locker.

"This is it. We are exactly twenty-two meters beneath the centerpoint of the naval dock here." Bleindel nodded to Weiss and Mayer, the weapons technicians he'd brought along for the mission. "Assemble the device. Holm and I will keep watch."

"Yes, sir," Weiss replied. "Give us half an hour." She and Mayer began opening cases and removing the compartments holding the fake samples. Beneath those, heavily shielded secret compartments held the carefully arranged components of a Vampir warp torpedo's microfusion-bomb warhead.

"Take your time," said Bleindel. "We're not in any great hurry." He and Holm moved into the passageway outside the storage locker and made a show of fussing over the sales samples from one of the cases just in case anyone happened by . . . but no one did. It was the middle of the workday by Meliya Station time, and no one had any pressing need to retrieve anything from a locker during the time that *Polarstern*'s weapons techs were engaged in their work.

Forty minutes later, Weiss emerged from the locker and handed Bleindel a small remote such as one might carry for a private flyer's doors and ignition. "It's ready, sir," she said. "The button on top doesn't do anything, but this small catch here"—she demonstrated it for him—"opens the case, and the real button is this, right here. Press and hold it for three seconds, and you start a one-hour timer. You'll see a little green light here to show that the device has confirmed the signal. Press the hidden button five times quickly, and you detonate it immediately. Needless to say, you want to be at least four hundred meters away when you do that."

"Will the remote's signal penetrate the station interior?" Holm asked.

"It should, but I wouldn't count on it if you're more than a kilometer or two from the station. It's a surprisingly strong transmitter for its size, but there's a lot of rock around us."

"Understood," Bleindel said. He stepped into the storage locker to examine the installation; the techs had tidied up, returning the material samples to their travel cases and arranging the cases in the back of the locker. He took a moment to fix a button-sized vidcam on one wall of the locker so that he could keep an eye on the device, then pulled down the locker door and secured the lock. "Good work. Let's go get something to eat—we've got some time to kill."

They returned to the station's commercial corridors, this time carrying only their personal bags, and found a completely forgettable station restaurant offering a passable selection of pub fare. Bleindel ate well, enjoying the taste of a meal prepared with somewhat fresher ingredients than those available in *Asfoor's* tiny galley. Just in case anybody was inclined to listen in on their conversation, Holm started a vigorous discussion on the state of Neda's professional-soccer season with Mayer, who held up his end fairly well. Weiss picked at her meal until Bleindel discreetly tapped her foot under the table. "Relax a little," he told her quietly. "We don't want to be conspicuous."

"I know. I just . . . there are a lot of people here."

"All of whom are passing through, Luna. Many of them won't be anywhere nearby later." Well, the restaurant staff probably would be, but Bleindel kept that observation to himself; Torpedo

Technician Luna Weiss didn't need to hear it. When the time came to settle the tab and carry on with the operation, he made sure to give their server an average tip. It might have been pointless, but there was no reason to leave the young Meliyan fuming about a stingy customer for what remained of his shift.

After their meal, Bleindel used the station's info assistant to book return passage for four aboard *Asfoor,* and commed Sozzini to confirm. "It turns out our local office had someone waiting to pick up our samples," he told her. "I wouldn't have brought my sales team along if I'd known. We'll be heading back to Dahar with you after all."

"No problem, Mr. Liddle," Sozzini replied. "I can send our launch over to pick you up this evening, or very early in the morning. Which do you prefer?"

"This evening, please."

"Okay. Meet you at the public docking cradles at . . . 2200, station time. Enjoy the rest of your visit."

Now that the bomb was in place, Bleindel was anxious to be on his way. Unfortunately, he didn't think he could do much to push Sozzini for an earlier departure without raising suspicions, and arranging different transportation would create more loose ends to take care of later. He resigned himself to wasting a few more hours on the station, and instructed his team to split up and look like bored travelers trying to entertain themselves for a few hours while awaiting their departure. Luna Weiss he kept with him, though. He didn't really think she would give away anything to the sleepy Electorate security guards on the station, but he wasn't in the business of taking unnecessary risks. He took her to a cinema on the station's lower levels to watch a holofilm, then turned around and bought tickets for the next available show to keep her occupied until it was time to leave. In between, he sneaked peeks at the security locker's buttom-cam feed to make sure no one took an interest in the travel cases they'd left inside.

At 2200, Bleindel and the others met *Asfoor's* launch at the docking ring, and carried their bags back on board. While Holm distracted the pilot by complaining about the lack of a good pub on Meliya Station, Bleindel quietly opened the remote and held down the trigger button until the tiny green light came on. "Well, let's be on our way," he announced.

When they returned to the courier ship, he issued one more set of instructions to his team, and then went up to the tiny pilot-house. He found Perla Sozzini there, reviewing the ship's sailing plan. "Mr. Liddle," she said, acknowledging his presence. "You're welcome to take in the view for a bit if you like, but I'm afraid I'm a little busy. I have a long pre-transit checklist to complete and some documents to file with Meliya Traffic Control before we depart."

"Please, don't let me interrupt you," he said. The pilothouse did offer a good view, in fact; *Asfoor* was too small for her bridge to be buried in the center of the hull, and the ship actually had real windows—small and armored, but windows nonetheless— that looked out on the warm green curve of the planet below and the glittering pinpoints of ships and boats in flight. Bleindel located the dark mass of Meliya Station with its blinking nav beacons, and quietly manipulated the window controls to augment the image. He didn't have to wait long.

Precisely on time, the uppermost level of Meliya Station blew apart in eerie silence two hundred kilometers away. The blast swallowed *Vashaoth Teh's* midsection in an eruption of shattered rock and steel that hurled away docking cradles that massed hundreds of tons. Even through the protection of the smart glass that composed the bridge windows, the flash seared *Asfoor's* pilothouse and left spots dancing before Bleindel's eyes. When his vision cleared, he could make out the Velaran cruiser drifting amid clouds of molten debris, twisted and tangled in the wreckage of its docking cradle. *Amazing the ship is still in one piece,* he mused. *Twenty meters of rock and steel must have been enough to absorb quite a lot of the warhead's detonation.* Then again, warships were quite well armored.

"Holy shit!" Sozzini cried out, staring at the distant station in astonishment. "What the hell was *that?*"

"Someone detonated a microfusion warhead on Meliya Station," Bleindel told her. Then he drew a small mag pistol from his pocket and shot her in the head with a low-velocity round.

More pistol shots chirped through the tiny ship's passageways below. The Dremish agent eyed Captain Sozzini's slumped body, twitching in the pilot's acceleration couch, and decided that no more shots were needed. He didn't derive any particular enjoyment from killing her—or whatever unfortunate passersby and spaceport workers and Velaran navy personnel he'd just wiped out with the bomb in the storage locker—but he needed *Asfoor* to complete the operation, and he simply couldn't leave any witnesses who'd be able to tell anyone where his team had come from or where they'd gone. No, the courier ship would never be seen or heard from again . . . but that, of course, would reinforce the story he intended to leave behind for the Meliyan authorities.

Martin Holm appeared at the pilothouse door, pistol in hand. He took one glance at Sozzini, and holstered the weapon. "All targets accounted for, Senior Agent," the big lieutenant said. "The ship is secure."

"Good. Any difficulties?"

"Mayer is wounded—the engineer had a weapon and a moment's warning when we forced the hatch. Weiss is taking care of him."

"I'll see what I can do for Mayer in just a moment. First give me a hand with the captain."

The two men removed Perla Sozzini from the seat in which she'd died, setting her down on the deck at the back of the cramped bridge. There would be time to tidy up later, but right now Bleindel had things to do. He took his dataslate from his jacket pocket, and forwarded a message he'd composed earlier to the ship's communications system. In a few hours, it would be delivered to several news agencies down on the planet after bouncing through dozens of comm hubs . . . just the sort of thing a group of radicals might do in order to safeguard their true location when claiming responsibility for an attack.

Holm glanced at the text scrolling across the comm display. "Who the devil is the Meliyan Human Revolution?" he asked.

"Oh, I made them up," Bleindel said, and grinned. The Velaran Electorate security forces would turn Meliya upside down for weeks chasing after that particular fiction. In fact, he wouldn't be surprised if his imaginary terrorist group lingered on in police files and intelligence summaries for years after the authorities took stock of the manifesto he'd attached to the message—he'd always had a knack for revolutionary literature. "Let's get out of here, Leutnant. Set course for Dahar, if you please."

"Aye, Captain," Holm said. He activated the ship's maneuvering console and powered up the drive plates, confidently spinning *Asfoor*'s bow toward its new course. It was the reason Bleindel had brought one of *Polarstern*'s officers along on the mission—he needed someone who knew how to pilot a ship and plot a warp transit.

Two and a half days later, the Dremish agents abandoned *Asfoor* in the outskirts of the Dahar system, where a launch from *Polarstern* waited to pick them up. They pointed the empty courier ship toward interstellar space, and set her on her final course into the void.

10

Mersin, Dahar II

fter days of entertaining various dignitaries aboard *Decisive* and attending events ranging from school graduations to business-association banquets to local parades, Sikander was more than ready to be on his way. He didn't mind the parties and official affairs all that much—he'd become accustomed to those sorts of occasions growing up, after all, and he'd long ago learned that time passed much more comfortably when he made an effort to enjoy them—but he couldn't shake the feeling that he and his ship were simply playing parts in a small spectacle that no one of importance was paying attention to any longer. As long as he was making his carefully rehearsed remarks at some little gathering or chatting with the local business leaders at another, he was conspicuously engaged in doing exactly what he was supposed to do . . . and *Decisive* was making no progress in the effort to secure Zerzura's shipping routes or counter whatever scheme the Empire of Dremark had in mind for the region.

He bumped into the Dremish diplomat Hanne Vogt once or twice; they exchanged no words beyond the absolute minimum acknowledgment the occasion called for. Otto Bleindel simply dropped out of sight altogether, which made Sikander wonder what exactly he was up to. Elena Pavon, on the other hand, he encountered two more times within five days of her visit to *Decisive*: first at a cocktail party at the Montréalais consulate in Mersin, and then again at a ceremony dedicating a new academic building at Dahar Planetary University. On the first occasion he had only a moment to chat with her before he was steered away into a conversation with the Montréalais consul, but at the reception following the dedication ceremony they found themselves virtually alone in a gallery room adjoining the reception area . . . or as alone as either of them normally was, since Darvesh and Elena's personal assistant hovered nearby.

"Ms. Pavon, you look lovely today," Sikander told her. He meant it, too—she wore a Zerzuran-style djellaba in a vibrant blue and black pattern, noticeably more form-fitted than the customary fashion on Dahar. "I'm curious: What is your connection to the university?"

"My family has supported Dahar's university for generations. In fact, there's a library building across campus named after my grandfather." She shrugged. "We also give to schools in Nuevo León and Meliya and half a dozen other worlds as well, but since Dahar is the capital of the sector and the seat of Zerzura's government, well . . ."

"It's an opportunity to make a good impression in a place where you do a lot of business." Sikander nodded. "It's much the same for my family, although we tend to take an interest in institutions a little closer to home."

"Kashmir, Jaipur, or Ishar in particular?"

"You're familiar with Kashmir?"

"Not really," the heiress said. "I confess I did a little research after I visited your ship and read your official bio—it's included with the press kit your consulate issued for *Decisive*'s port call. First Kashmiri to command an Aquilan Commonwealth warship? That's impressive."

"I'm not entirely sure whether I find your interest flattering or unsettling."

"You should be flattered, of course. I stopped by *Decisive* to see if I could sting someone into finally taking some effective action about our piracy problems. I expected to find a pompous ass in command of an Aquilan ship, or perhaps a dull policeman who wouldn't believe what I told him about what's been going on behind his back. Instead, I found you."

"Sipping cocktails at a party days after you asked me to take some action." Sikander waved a hand at the reception, encompassing the entire planet in the gesture. "This must be frustrating for you. I know it doesn't look like it, but I take your concerns seriously. My operations team is scouring reports of attacks and ship data registries to turn up any lead we can, but frankly, we can't do much until we develop better intelligence. I am sorry that it's taking a while."

"Naturally I'm anxious to see results, but I haven't heard anything new from my investigators either," Elena said. "Like you, I have some diplomatic responsibilities—so to speak—to look after while I'm in Dahar. I only spend a few weeks here each year. But I hope that when I do give you something, you'll be ready."

"Nothing would make me happier than having a reason to skip five more days of receptions and making remarks. Unfortunately, pirates don't like to show themselves when the Navy's in the area, Ms. Pavon."

"I can imagine. And please, call me Elena."

"Elena, then. I'm Sikander, or just Sikay."

Elena Pavon smiled warmly. "Well, Sikay, if you're looking for something different to do while we're waiting, I have a suggestion: Come up to my family's coffee orchard at Mount Kesif tomorrow. We're just starting to hull this season's crop, and many of the local growers bring their own fruit to our mill. It's something of a local celebration."

Sikander mentally reviewed his schedule, and decided there was nothing he couldn't miss—Amelia Fraser would serve as a more than adequate replacement for the morning meeting at the consulate, and he had not yet taken any time off from his official duties. "I'd like that very much," he told her.

"Good! In that event, I'll see you tomorrow. I'll have Omar send you directions—it's about a hundred kilometers south of Mersin. Noon?"

"I'll be there," Sikander promised.

The next day, he had his crew break out the captain's gig—the smallest of *Decisive*'s various launches and orbiters—and changed into his dress whites. Aboard Aquilan warships, the gig was traditionally at the captain's disposal for whatever he or she saw fit to do with it; Sikander told himself that he was cultivating positive relations with the local business community, not that he really needed to justify an afternoon off. Pilot First Class Kersey flew Sikander and Darvesh directly from Dahar High Port down to the sunny highlands south of the planetary capital, and made a wide, generous turn around the Mount Kesif plantation so that Sikander could take in the view before they landed in a field a few hundred meters from the old stone farmhouse and mill in the middle of the property. Sikander was surprised to see dozens of ground cars and light trucks parked near the buildings, with a small crowd of Dahari thronging tables that had been set up beneath canopies or listening to a band that played some local variety of folk music.

"It seems to be quite the occasion," Darvesh remarked to Sikander as they debarked from the gig.

"Elena said it was something of a local tradition." Sikander took a deep breath, enjoying the warmth of the sunshine and the brilliant blue sky. High golden-brown mountainsides cupped the plantation, forming a three-sided bowl that faced to the south; green coffee trees marched up the slopes and away down the valley in even rows. The air smelled clean and earthy, with a strong whiff of roasted coffee instead of the exotic compounds found in Dahar's lower elevations. *I see why people settled here now*, he decided.

He and Darvesh started off toward the house at the center of the orchard, following a dusty lane. Elena Pavon descended from the house's grand porch to greet him when they reached the gate. "Sikay! Welcome to Mount Kesif. I'm glad you decided to come."

"It's beautiful here," he said. "You know, for all the coffee I've enjoyed over the years, I have never actually set foot in a coffee orchard. Are they all this pretty?"

"Oh, we're a small specialty grower, really," Elena replied. "Just over those hills there's an industrial grower with fifteen hundred hectares under cultivation. Mount Kesif is more of a family retreat than a big business, although I'm proud to say that we've won our share of medals and our plantation manager turns a tidy profit by selling into the gourmet market. When I'm on Dahar I work in downtown Mersin, but I spend my weekends up here."

"My family has something similar—a ranch on Srinagar at a place called Chittar Creek, although I don't get to visit it very often." Sikander fell in beside Elena as she strolled around the house, while Darvesh moved off to give them some privacy. "Thank you for sharing it with me."

"If all you ever see of a planet are the spaceports and big cities, you haven't really *seen* it. I have a feeling you don't find much opportunity to explore some of the worlds your ship calls at."

"You're not wrong about that. It's good to walk on grass and dirt every now and then."

"Well, we have plenty of that here. Very expensive dirt, I might add—prime coffee acreage is Dahar's most valuable real estate." Elena slipped her arm around his. "Come on, let me show you around a little."

Sikander allowed her to lead him in a tour of the plantation's working buildings—big storage sheds filled with crates of fresh-picked coffee cherries, the pulping room where an old machine stripped the fruit from the bean, the open-air drying sheds with long tables covered in parchment beans, and the mill itself, where the dried beans were hulled, graded, and sorted. They also met quite a few of the Pavons' Mount Kesif neighbors, who'd come to enjoy the daylong barbecue and harvest festivities. Some were wealthy dabblers like the Pavons, others were managers and buyers who worked in the area, and a few were small plantation owners who lived year-round on their property, maintaining family operations that in some cases went back for generations. The food was excellent, the music was good, and Elena proved to be a delightful guide; Sikander managed to forget all about pirates and Dremish spies for a couple of hours.

He was just about to suggest a return to the buffet for another helping when his comm unit beeped at him. "Excuse me, please," he said to Elena. "I'm afraid I have to take this."

"I understand." Elena turned back to the gathering, moving off to greet some neighbors who'd just arrived.

Sikander found a quiet corner of the plantation's wraparound porch and answered the call: "This is Commander North."

"Captain, it's Lieutenant Commander Herrera, command duty officer. Sir, we've just received word of a major incident in the Meliya system. The Velaran cruiser *Vashaoth Teh* was destroyed at its moorings by a bomb. Some Meliyan separatist group is apparently taking credit for the attack."

"Dear God. Any idea of the casualties?"

"No, sir, not yet." Herrera's tone had none of his habitual humor; his voice was as harsh and abrasive as gravel. "The ship's complement is listed as three hundred and fifty-five, though. And from what I'm seeing in this news footage, it looks like the bomb did a lot of damage to the orbital station where *Vashaoth Teh* was docked. I have to imagine there are civilians dead, too."

Sikander glanced up at the sky, as if he could somehow spot *Decisive* at its docking cradle in Dahar High Port. Suddenly the Mount Kesif coffee orchard seemed not quite real, a pleasant daydream from which he'd been shaken awake. "Secure the ship and the access points to the docking cradle immediately, Mr. Herrera. We're tied up to a station, too."

"Already done, sir."

"Good." Sikander didn't think it likely that a local separatist group could pull off multiple attacks in different star systems, but he had no intention of allowing his ship to be caught off guard in case he was wrong about that. He stood in silence for a moment, rapidly reviewing *Decisive's* orders for the current deployment to make sure he understood what action he'd be required to take. Pleiades Squadron operated under a fairly comprehensive set of standing orders; the requirement to respond to incidents such as what Jaime Herrera had just described to him was one of those. "Go ahead and recall the liberty party. We'll need to get under way as soon as possible."

"It's three and a half days to Meliya, Captain. By the time we get there, rescue and assistance operations will be a week old."

"I know, but the squadron's standing orders dictate that we investigate and offer whatever help we can. Show the flag, as they say. If nothing else, we've got trained damage-control teams and heavy cutting equipment—perhaps we can help pick up the pieces." Sikander shook his head, trying not to imagine what his team would find on a station shattered by a bomb big enough to take out a cruiser. "I'll return to the ship immediately. North, out."

He set off in search of Elena, and found her chatting with another well-dressed woman by a table covered in coffee beans. Elena took one look at his expression and excused herself from her conversation. "What's the matter?" she asked.

"I am afraid I have to go," he said. "We just received word of a separatist attack in Meliya—a Velaran cruiser was destroyed by a bomb. *Decisive* is the closest Commonwealth ship, and we're expected to render whatever assistance we can."

Elena paled. "We have offices and a major cargo facility on the ground there."

"The attack targeted the orbital station—your people are probably fine. I'm afraid I don't have any more details than that, but I'm sure the news is breaking throughout Dahar as we speak." He paused, and took her hand. "Thank you for inviting me to Mount Kesif. I am truly sorry that I can't stay and enjoy the rest of the afternoon."

Elena grimaced. "It's hardly your fault," she said, and then she leaned forward to give him a kiss on the cheek. "Be careful, Sikay. I hope to see you again soon."

"Me, too," he said, and hurried back to his shuttle.

Decisive announced her arrival in the Meliya system with a spectacular high-speed terminal cascade eighty hours after Jaime Herrera's call interrupted Sikander's Mount Kesif visit. The greater a ship's transit speed the more energetically its warp bubble collapsed when the warp generator cut off, and thanks to some particularly aggressive acceleration during the departure from Dahar, *Decisive* arrived in the Velar Electorate at nearly one-sixth the speed of light. Sikander did his best to project complete confidence in the ship's navigation during the tense moments before arrival, but he didn't miss the sighs of relief from the bridge crew when Ensign Carter and her sensor crew confirmed a clear arrival.

"We missed our mark by four light-seconds, Captain," Michael Girard reported. "We're eighteen light-minutes out from Meliya Prime."

"Very good navigation, Amelia," Sikander told his XO. In practice it was the ship's senior quartermaster who worked out the details of most warp transits, but Amelia Fraser personally checked his math and oversaw the process.

"Thank you, sir," said Fraser, acknowledging the compliment. "Sometimes you just get a little lucky."

"Perhaps, but pass along a well-done to your team anyway," Sikander told her. "Mr. Girard, depower and retract the warp ring, and transmit our arrival notification. Set course for Meliya Prime and secure from transit stations when you're ready."

He pulled up a tactical window at the console by his command seat, and quietly studied the Velaran planet while the bridge crew changed over into their normal underway watches around him. A small near-terran world orbiting a Class K star, Meliya Prime had been settled by the Terran Caliphate six centuries ago during the same wave of colonization that brought humans to Zerzura. Meliya had remained part of the Zerzura Sector for almost five centuries, until the neighboring Velarans seized the planet shortly after the humans and Paom'ii of that region unified under the Electorate. *But it's been more than a hundred years since the Velarans took the system,* Sikander thought. *Meliya assimilated into the Electorate generations ago, and the Paom'ii are happy to let the planet's humans manage their own affairs. So why did the Meliyan Human Revolution choose this moment to strike?*

"Captain, the orbital station's now coming into view," Fraser told him. She nodded at the bridge's central display; powerful hull cams trained on Meliya Prime magnified the imagery by a factor of several hundred. Sikander stood and moved a little closer to the display anyway, hands clasped behind his back as he took in the scene.

Where there should have been a domed city in space, a great debris field now tumbled above the planet. At first he thought the whole station had been literally blown to bits, but then the captured asteroid that served as the station's foundation came into view. To Sikander's surprise, the side of the spaceport that faced the planet seemed surprisingly intact, as did several docking terminals ringing the station's imaginary waist. But a seventy-meter crater marred the large naval terminal on the station's upper surface, surrounded by rings of wreckage, twisted alloy, and the shattered hulls of Electorate navy workboats and patrol craft trapped in what remained of their docking cradles.

"God," Amelia breathed, standing next to him. "How big was that bomb? And what did it do to the rest of the station?"

"The station's almost two kilometers across and that rock is mostly nickel-iron, XO," Jaime Herrera pointed out. "That's a lot of mass to absorb a bomb blast. It would take a pretty serious explosion to make a crater that big in hard rock, though . . . maybe a kiloton or two?"

"Where's *Vashaoth Teh*?" Sikander asked.

"One moment, Captain." Michael Girard consulted with the bridge's sensor specialists, and highlighted a battered and blackened length of hull in the middle of the wreckage. Sikander barely recognized the handsome burgundy-and-silver warship he'd seen in orbit above Dahar only ten days ago. *Vashaoth Teh* remained secured to the station by her bow, but her stern floated free in a mass of cables and twisted conduits. Heavy scabs of rock and steel scarred her flanks—the cooled remnant of molten debris from the blast—and near the ship's midpoint the hull had been wrenched through a ten-degree bend. Sikander could only guess that the ship's aft section had been hit so hard that it had to give way before the forward portion could begin to move, a grim testimony to the power and placement of the bomb.

Decisive's bridge fell silent as Sikander and his officers stared at the imagery. After a moment, Girard cleared his throat and continued. "That's not quite all of her. Several smaller pieces are part of the debris cloud around the station—weapon mounts and drive plates sheared free from the hull, I think."

"Thank you, Mr. Girard." Sikander studied the debris field for a moment, not entirely certain where *Decisive* could even begin to help. *It's worse than Bathinda,* he realized. The sight of the Velaran ship tangled in the wreckage of its moorings took him back thirteen years to the day the KLP's strike at the port turned deadly. It had been a sultry afternoon, hot and humid even by Jaipur's standards, and Sikander remembered the smell of smoke in the air—

—as he stands on the concrete pier, surrounded by his father's retinue. The burned-out hull of the container ship Blue Horizon *lies in the shallow water only twenty meters from its intended mooring place. Sikander wonders how the KLP strikers managed to get a bomb powerful enough to hole the ship on board before it had even docked. Perhaps the radicals hid the weapon in* Blue Horizon's *cargo at its previous port of call, or maybe they placed a mine on the seabed. But either way, the attack not only prevents the ship from unloading—it escalates the Bathinda situation into something much more dangerous than a troublesome labor dispute.*

"How many dead?" Nawab Dayan asks his escort commander, Colonel Nayyar.

"Five crewmen are unaccounted for, Nawab," Colonel Nayyar answers. A stocky woman of fifty with iron-gray hair, she wears a

khaki-colored dopatta around her face in addition to the turban worn by male soldiers of the Jaipur Dragoons. "All of them worked in the engineering spaces, so it is presumed that they drowned when the ship settled on the bottom. The fire on the upper deck most likely prevented their escape. They were all Kashmiris."

Sikander finds himself imagining the scene: water rushing in, flames and smoke above, a horrible choice of how to meet death. Five men had been sentenced to a terrible fate because they had the misfortune of serving on the container ship that the Seastar United transport line—owned by Aquilans, but operated by Kashmiri employees—sent into Bathinda in defiance of the port workers' strike. Does Devindar know the people who did this? he wonders. Does he support it?

If Nawab Dayan is thinking the same things, he gives no sign of it. Instead he paces toward the seaward end of the pier, gazing out over the waters of Diamond Bay. At least fifteen more sea transports ride at anchor in the heat and the haze, waiting for the weeks-long strike to end so that they can unload their cargoes. Sikander follows him, while Colonel Nayyar leaves the two Norths to a moment of privacy.

"What are you going to do, Father?" Sikander asks after a moment.

"I am not sure," Nawab Dayan replies without looking at him—one of the very few times Sikander has ever heard anything less than certainty from the ruler of Ishar. "I had hoped to restrain both the governor-general's office and the KLP long enough to simply outwait the strikers. But this—" He glances back at the wrecked ship by the pier. "—this means we are out of time. The Chandigarh Lancers are certain to be ordered into action against the strikers now. They will not be gentle . . . but the strikers brought it on themselves by sinking that ship."

"Seastar United provoked them by attempting to open the port without negotiating in good faith," Sikander points out. "I wouldn't be surprised if they sent that ship into port for exactly that purpose—

to force the strikers to do something that would then justify action by the King family troops. For that matter, the governor-general's office might have told Seastar to send Blue Horizon into port."

The nawab gives Sikander a sharp look. "You've been talking to your brother."

"I don't agree with everything Devindar says, Father, but that doesn't mean he is always wrong."

Nawab Dayan smiles a small, wry smile then. "No, not always," he agrees. "It makes one wonder, though, who sank that ship and why, doesn't it?"

"You don't really think—?"

"What I think is not as important as what people think I might think. Right now it might be useful if I expressed some doubts about responsibility for this attack. And for that suggestion, I suppose I owe Devindar my gratitude." Nawab Dayan sets a hand on Sikander's shoulder, and turns him back toward Colonel Nayyar and the waiting guards. "Let us hope that cooler heads prevail."

"Captain?" Amelia Fraser asked.

"Sorry, XO. I was just trying to figure out where we should start." Sikander pulled his gaze away from the imagery of the devastation, realizing that he'd been staring at the display while thinking about that long-ago day in Jaipur. He gave himself a small shake. "Let's find out who's in charge over there and ask them how we can help. It's going to take a few hours to decelerate and make orbit, so we might as well put that time to good use. Assemble the officers and chiefs in the wardroom in ninety minutes to go over our rescue and assistance plans."

At first, Sikander was not entirely sure what *Decisive* could do—as Jaime Herrera had predicted when the news reached Dahar, the

Aquilan destroyer arrived on the scene almost a week after the attack. The Meliyan authorities had already evacuated almost two thousand civilians from the damaged station, and those who had been injured were being treated in various hospitals around the planet. But as *Decisive* assumed an orbit close by the station, a few needs became apparent. Portions of the station remained inaccessible due to collapsed passageways, hull breaches, loss of power, and bent or jammed hatches and lifts. Those were all problems a warship's damage-control teams knew how to address, and since the Electorate naval depot had been virtually destroyed by the bomb, *Decisive*'s engineers represented a very welcome pool of trained personnel and equipment. Sikander put Amar Shah in charge of the ship's rescue and assistance team, since damage control was principally an Engineering Department function.

Several small craft that had been docked at Meliya Station remained adrift in various dangerous orbits; Zoe Worth and the Flight Department took on the job of using *Decisive*'s boats to corral them and help with clearing navigational hazards. Grant Edwards had his mess specialists set up field kitchens to support the salvage teams working on the evacuated station. And Sikander directed the Operations Department to investigate the bomb attack itself, collecting sensor records from ships that had been in the area and performing detailed battle-damage assessments to reconstruct exactly where the device had been situated and whether anything could be learned about its characteristics. Many of the station's records in the damaged areas were in no condition to be reviewed, since the explosion had naturally erased quite a good deal of the evidence. But Sikander trusted Michael Girard to figure out something—after all, in their first tour together aboard CSS *Hector*, Girard had displayed a knack for solving mysteries.

For his own part, Sikander spent most of his time dealing with the Velaran authorities, who proved difficult to work with. The person in charge of the situation was the senior surviving officer of *Vashaoth Teh*, a Paom'ii who called himself Meritor Pokk Skirriseh. Only one of the cruiser's duty sections had actually been on the ship when the bomb went off. While very few of those on board had survived the bomb, their shipmates on liberty elsewhere in the station or down on the planet's surface—including the meritor—had escaped injury. Sikander introduced himself with a vid call, conveyed the Aquilan Commonwealth's sincere condolences for the loss of life, and explained the ways in which his engineers and deckhands were ready to help.

"Your concern is noted," Meritor Pokk replied when he finished. The Paom'ii blinked rapidly; Sikander wasn't sure how to read his expression, but he thought he detected irritation in the alien's tone of voice. "We must of course approve all actions your damage-control teams undertake on the station. You may submit them in writing to the Meliyan System Defense Command for our review."

Sikander clamped his mouth shut. *We're trying to help!* he silently shouted at the alien on his comm display. "As you wish, Meritor," he grated. "We will be in touch."

"That's not very friendly," Amelia Fraser observed when Sikander cut the connection. "It makes you wonder how the human half of the Electorate puts up with it day in and day out."

"Perhaps they grow on you with a little time," Sikander said. "You'd better put the ship's office on the job of documenting and submitting everything we're trying to do. It's their station and I suppose we have to do it their way."

Decisive soon fell into a round-the-clock routine of emergency operations. Half a day after they arrived in Meliya, a Velaran navy salvage ship turned up. Naturally, Meritor Pokk issued an updated set of priorities when the new Velaran crew joined the effort. The day after that, the Montréalais assault ship *Dixmude* arrived in-system and likewise contributed damage-control teams to the job of restoring access to the station. Sikander directed his sailors to make room for the newcomers and do their best to respect the Velaran process, such as it was.

On the third day of their rescue operations, Amelia Fraser stopped by his cabin while he was reviewing the latest Velaran micromanagement of *Decisive*'s damage-control teams and wondering exactly how much more assistance the Commonwealth Navy was expected to provide. "Got a moment, Captain?" she asked, knocking at the side of his door.

"Come on in. What's on your mind, Amelia?"

"I've been keeping an eye on the rescue and assistance details, and I'm worried about the way our people are pushing themselves—specifically, Reed Hollister. He's been over on the station for sixty-four of the last seventy-two hours. He's returned to *Decisive* a couple of times to sleep an hour or two, and then he goes right back over." Amelia took her customary seat across the desk from Sikander. "Dr. Ruiz just told me he managed to slam his hand in a hatch this morning and damn near broke it. She thinks it's fatigue, pure and simple."

"Everybody in engineering's working port and starboard shifts at the moment, aren't they?" Twelve hours on and twelve hours off was not as easy as it sounded, but at least everyone should have been getting a few hours of sleep every day.

"They are," Amelia confirmed. "But it seems that Reed's stretching his shifts by six or seven hours a day."

"Have you talked to Mr. Hollister about this? Or Mr. Shah?"

"No, not yet. I just got the report from Dr. Ruiz."

Sikander leaned back in his chair, drumming his fingers on the desk as he thought over the situation. "Do you think Mr. Shah is punishing Mr. Hollister by assigning him extra work?" he asked.

Amelia shook her head. "No, I don't think that's it. I think Reed is punishing himself. He's trying to win his way back into Mr. Shah's good graces by working himself to the point of exhaustion."

"That seems plausible," Sikander said, and sighed. "All right, this has gone on long enough. It's time to address the situation."

"Should I call in Mr. Hollister or Mr. Shah?"

"Call them both in." Sikander tapped through the open documents on his dataslate until he found the one he wanted, while Amelia summoned the chief engineer and the power plant officer to his cabin. The final report on the failure of generator two was not as conclusive as he would have liked—there was just no way to say for certain whether the faulty weld for the magnetic flux sensor in the generator chamber should have been caught by Hollister. In Sikander's eyes, that sounded like a mistake, not malfeasance. He pulled up the draft of the letter he'd just about finished, and satisfied himself about the wording.

A few minutes later, both Amar Shah and Reed Hollister stood before his desk. Both men looked tired; Hollister had dark circles under his eyes and a bandage wrapped around his left hand, while Shah's customarily spotless uniform showed dark smears of soot and stains from hydraulic fluid. "You wished to see us, sir?" Shah asked.

"Have a seat, gentlemen." Sikander allowed the engineering officers to get settled. "I know you're both working very hard, so I'll keep this brief. First things first—Mr. Hollister, you're on medically restricted duty for that hand. You're to remain on board *Decisive* and rest for the next twenty-four hours, or more if Dr. Ruiz tells you to."

Hollister grimaced, but nodded. "Yes, sir."

"Very good. I apologize for putting this off for the last couple of weeks, but our patrol has taken some unexpected turns and I've allowed some things to get pushed aside that should have been dealt with in a more timely fashion. Regarding the failure of generator two: Mr. Hollister, I am issuing you a letter of admonition in regards to your certification of the weld test inspection report. I don't know if the shipyard worker performed the test incorrectly and you just missed it or if you didn't realize one of the sensors had been overlooked, but if you sign off on a repair action, we must be absolutely confident that the repair was indeed performed correctly."

Hollister's shoulders, already slumping with his fatigue, slumped further. "Yes, sir." Shah shifted in his seat, but said nothing.

"This is an admonition, not a reprimand," Sikander continued. "As long as this remains an isolated incident, the letter will be removed from your personnel jacket on the completion of your tour."

"It's a warning, Mr. Hollister," Amelia said. "But it's a warning that remains between us for now."

"As far as I am concerned, the incident has been addressed," Sikander said. "I will say no more about it, and I expect you to carry out your Engineering Department responsibilities capably and competently going forward. You may return to your duties, Mr. Hollister."

"After you rest that hand, that is," Amelia added.

"Well, of course," Sikander admitted. "Thank you, Mr. Hollister. You're dismissed."

"Thank you, sir," Hollister said, and stood. He saluted with his good hand, his expression in some unsettled space between relief and embarrassment, and left.

Sikander waited for Hollister to close the door behind him before turning his attention to Amar Shah. "I consider Mr. Hollister's part in the generator two failure closed, Mr. Shah. No retaliation, no unreasonable expectations. Are we in agreement about that?"

Shah frowned. "I have some misgivings, Captain, but it is your decision. I certainly will not attempt to undermine it."

"Good. Mr. Hollister deserves the opportunity to regain your confidence, and he needs to know that you're not holding that mistake over his head for the rest of his tour. Give him a clean slate, Amar. I think he'll impress you, if you let him."

"Yes, sir. Is that all?"

Sikander glanced at Amelia, who took her cue. "Almost," she said. "Mr. Hollister is clearly exhausted, and from what I've seen in the last day or two, so are the rest of your junior officers. Exhausted people make mistakes or get hurt."

"My whole department is working hard," Shah said. "I don't believe that I am asking anything of my junior officers that I'm not asking of anyone else—or myself, for that matter. I've been over on Meliya Station fifteen or sixteen hours a day since we arrived."

"It speaks well of your whole department that they're pushing themselves so hard to help strangers," Sikander said. *Especially strangers who are working so hard at being difficult about it*, he added to himself. "But it's time to start taking care of our people, and that means enforcing end-of-shift turnovers and reasonable amounts of rest."

"I haven't asked anyone to go without sleep, sir."

"No, but they're doing it because you're signaling that you see the need, whether you mean to send that message or not."

Shah started to protest, but checked himself. "All right, sir. I see what you mean. I will direct my officers and chiefs to make sure shift rotations are followed and that we're not sending exhausted sailors back to work. And I will remind them that they're included in those orders."

"Good. In that case: Carry on, Mr. Shah."

"Thank you, sir." The Kashmiri engineer stood and saluted, then left.

Sikander allowed himself a sigh of relief, and slumped back

in his chair. "Did that all seem to hit the right note?" he asked Amelia.

"I think so," she answered. "I'm pretty sure Amar is going to take a good long look at how he's using his people and make sure they get more rest. But I think Reed could use a shot in the arm. He probably feels like he let everybody down, and he's the kind of person who takes that sort of stuff to heart."

"We'll keep an eye on him," Sikander decided. "Discreetly, of course."

Later that evening, Sikander wandered up to the bridge to get out of his cabin for a bit and see how the watch team was doing. He found them engaged in the job of systematically cataloging every piece of debris in orbit and directing the ship's small craft toward anything that had the remotest chance of posing a danger to ships operating near the planet. It would probably take weeks to really clean up Meliya's orbital approaches, but as long as *Decisive* was on station there was no reason not to lend a hand. The subdued voices and quiet efficiency of the watch team spoke to the meticulous nature of the work, but Sikander found it strangely relaxing: It was just the right amount of white noise to let him listen to his own thoughts for a time.

"Captain, we've got a personal transmission for you," said Grace Carter, interrupting Sikander's ruminations. The young ensign had the watch at the moment. "Commercial message traffic, sir. It must have come in on the most recent courier ship."

"Personal transmission?" Sikander straightened up in his command station. Ordinary civilian correspondence between people in different star systems generally consisted of text messages or recorded vids carried in a courier's info storage, but sending notes to distant stars wasn't cheap, especially if the recipient wasn't exactly where they were supposed to be. He wrote his mother once a week when *Decisive* was in port, but most of the family's messages for him were held at Neda until he returned from wherever he'd gone. Very few people would have known to forward a message for him all the way to Meliya. "Send it to the ship's info assistant. I'll read it in my quarters."

He went back to his cabin to retrieve the message . . . and was more than a little surprised when Elena Pavon's face appeared on the vidscreen. "Hello, Sikander," she began. "I hope this message reaches you in good time—I'm recording this two days after *Decisive* departed from Meliya. To come straight to the point, my people have come up with a lead about the *Carmela Día* attack: Some of her cargo was sold in Tunis by a company called Venture Salvage. Our investigators in Tunis tried to locate a headquarters or point of contact for the salvage company, and found nothing. But they did discover that Venture Salvage owns a mining operation in the Zafer system, which is not all that far from Meliya. It seems that Venture bought the installation a few years ago when the original operation shut down, but there is no record of the Zafer operation being put back in service. Since Zafer is otherwise uninhabited, my people think it's possible that someone bought the facility to serve as a pirate base.

"I wish I could tell you that we're certain you will find pirate activity there. It's entirely likely that the mining operation is just an abandoned facility or that Venture Salvage itself is just a recycled front of some sort." Elena gave a small shrug. "But it's the first real lead our investigations have turned up, so maybe it's worth checking out. I'm attaching copies of our documentation to this message so that you can see what we have.

"I don't know whether you can look into this or not, but I'm holding on to this information until I hear from you—I don't want to share it with anybody who might warn the raiders that you're coming, if they are really in Zafer. Reply to me at the Pegasus-

Pavon offices in Dahar if you want me to give this information to someone else." Elena bared her teeth in a hungry smile. "But I think you want to get these bastards yourself, Sikay. Good hunting." The recorded message ended.

Sikander leaned back in his desk chair, gazing at the blank screen. "Now *that* is interesting," he said aloud. He took a few minutes to review the reports and images Elena had attached to her message, and decided that what she'd sent him was very, very interesting indeed. It was a long shot, perhaps, but there wasn't much more that they could do at Meliya that the Velarans couldn't do for themselves; *Decisive* could move on in good conscience.

It's time to hunt pirates again, he decided, and tapped his comm unit. "XO? Come on up to my office, and bring Master Chief Vaughn. I think we've got somewhere we need to be."

11

CSS *Decisive*, Zafer System

C lear arrival, Captain!" Ensign Carter called out from her station by the bridge's sensor techs. "We've got a small carbonaceous asteroid three million klicks ahead—it's already passed in front of us, it's not a collision danger. Lots of other small bodies within a light-minute or so, but nothing that impinges on our course."

"That's a cluttered screen," Jaime Herrera said, studying the array of icons and vector arrows populating the bridge's main display. "Rocks everywhere, it seems. Good thing we came in at a jog instead of a sprint."

"I thought that it might be a good idea, Guns," said Sikander. On departing Meliya, he'd naturally leaned toward the idea of another high-speed transit to reach Zafer as quickly as possible . . . but after a little consideration, he'd decided to do the exact opposite, and chose a low-speed transit. It added thirty hours to their transit time, but it also meant that when *Decisive* cut off her warp generator she was moving only half as fast as she would have been during a standard-speed transit. And that in turn meant that Sikander wouldn't have to spend hours and hours decelerating before he could think about executing tactical maneuvers in Zafer. Coming in hot would have carried *Decisive* hundreds of millions of kilometers across the destination system while she spent hours bleeding off her transit velocity.

Plus, the Zafer system was full of rocks. The odds of a collision would have been very small even in a high-velocity arrival, but very small was not the same as negligible, and the consequences of impacting an obstacle at ten or fifteen percent c were not to be taken lightly.

Sikander studied the bridge display, getting his bearings. Zafer was big, young, and bright compared to the sun of any system likely to harbor a world suitable for human colonization—a dazzling blue-white Class A star only about three hundred million years of age, surrounded by a dozen massive worlds and the smashed remains of two or three more that now made up a very rich set of asteroid belts. None of the worlds or their moons was remotely habitable, but systems such as Zafer could be valuable for space-based extraction industries. The challenge was getting the metal to market; a mine operation in an uninhabited system needed a particularly rich claim to work and a hungry industrial market nearby to make the trip worth the cost of the ring charge. Most mining companies settled for working less valuable in-system strikes that didn't add a warp transit to the operation's bottom line, so the fact that Venture Salvage's predecessors had tried to make a go of it in Zafer said something about the mineral wealth of the system . . . and the fact that they'd given up said something more about the economics of mining remote systems.

"Anything moving under power here, Ms. Carter?" Sikander asked the sensor officer.

"No, sir. But we've got a line of sight on the old mining installation, and it looks like several ships are moored there. Distance one point four light-minutes, bearing three-four-three up ten."

Close by, ahead of us, and not far off our transit-termination course, Sikander noted. *Decisive* had unbubbled in pretty much the exact spot he'd planned to arrive: less than an hour from the target, ready to seek an engagement. "Very well. Mr. Girard, set course for the installation, zero-zero intercept," he ordered—the standard naval terminology for reducing the distance to the target to zero, and arriving there at zero velocity in order to dock.

"Aye, Captain. Helm, come left to course three-two-five up eight," Girard ordered. Evidently he'd already calculated the interception. "Sixty percent standard deceleration."

"Ms. Carter, let's have a look at our mining post, please."

"Aye, Captain." Ensign Carter adjusted her sensor controls, creating a large new window in the bridge display to show the highly magnified view of the mining post they'd come to investigate. The facility consisted of a bunker-like structure blasted out of the hard rock in the scarred flank of a ten-kilometer asteroid, surrounded by a sprawling automated refinery. An industrial cargo pier consisting of an open framework of heavy girders jutted two kilometers into space; three small ships occupied a dock originally intended to accommodate massive bulk freighters ten times their size. Warm yellow light spilled out from the slit-like windows in the habitat bunker and the cargo dock's control tower.

"That facility doesn't look as abandoned as it's supposed to be," Herrera said.

"No, it doesn't," Sikander agreed. "But remember, it's possible that this is a legitimate mining operation. Mr. Girard, do any of those ships look familiar?"

"Checking now, sir," Girard replied. He studied his own console at the tactical officer's post. "Their transponders report them as *Qarash*, *The'eb*, and *Mazuz*. I'm comparing their registrations now."

"Would pirates use transponders?" Herrera wondered.

"If they wanted to blend in with ordinary shipping without attracting attention, they certainly would," Sikander pointed out. "At some point they'd want the ability to call on a civilized port and convert stolen goods into credits." He rubbed at his jaw, thinking about how to proceed as the minutes ticked by and *Decisive*'s momentum carried her toward Zafer's supposedly abandoned mining station. Venture Salvage might not realize they'd done business with pirate vessels . . . or they might *claim* that they didn't know that the goods they'd bought had come from a pirated vessel, in which case it was not very clear just what sort of action CSS *Decisive* was empowered to take to determine whether the station's occupants were actually guilty of something. Any commanding officer of the Commonwealth Navy could certainly intervene to stop an act of piracy in progress, pursue a ship he detected engaged in such an act, or even force a ship previously identified as a pirate to surrender for inspection. But outside of Aquilan territory, it was much less clear whether he had the authority to demand any sort of cooperation from people he only *suspected* of piracy.

Then again, it might not be clear to whoever's on that outpost that I can't, Sikander reminded himself. "Mr. Girard, give me a comm channel for an open broadcast, please," he said, and waited for the indicator light on his console before continuing. "Attention, all ships and stations in the Zafer system. This is Commander Sikander Singh North, commanding the Aquilan Commonwealth starship *Decisive*. We are making our approach to the Venture Salvage station located on the asteroid designated—" He paused to check his navigation display. "—Zafer B0177. Stand by to receive our boarding party. We have intelligence that indicates this station actively supports piracy in neighboring systems. Any ship presently docked at the Venture Salvage installation that attempts to get under way will be fired upon. Give up peacefully and I will guarantee you the opportunity to defend yourselves in the appropriate court of law. But if any captives currently held on your station come to harm before our boarding party arrives, we will hold all persons on your station individually and jointly responsible, and carry out summary justice. I advise you to choose carefully. *Decisive*, out."

Jaime Herrera's eyebrows climbed almost to his hairline. "Well, Captain, that's pretty clear," he said.

"It seemed best to be direct about it," Sikander replied. He made himself sit back in his command couch, crossing his legs and keying the ship's command circuit. "Did I miss anything, XO?"

Amelia Fraser was not on the bridge—she was back in *Decisive*'s auxiliary bridge, the traditional post for the ship's second-in-command during action. The idea was that she could continue to fight the ship from that position if enemy fire took out the bridge. Since Sikander had anticipated that they might find themselves in a shooting situation shortly after arrival, he'd ordered the ship to full battle stations shortly before arrival. "Clear and unambiguous," she confirmed over the command circuit. "I'd be shitting bricks over there if I was a bad guy, but you're going to owe someone an apology if it turns out this is just an unregistered mining operation."

Sikander snorted and started to reply, but Michael Girard suddenly called, "Captain! We've got movement. It's *Mazuz*, the outermost ship moored at the station."

"Perhaps I wasn't as clear as I thought I was," said Sikander. He glanced at the tactical display; *Decisive* was still millions of kilometers from the station, but gobbling up the distance by a thousand kilometers each second; they'd be in firing range in ten or fifteen minutes. *Mazuz* might build up enough speed to prolong the inevitable for a few minutes, but nothing in space was going to outrun *Decisive* with the kind of velocity advantage Sikander held, not from a standing start. "Mr. Girard, adjust our intercept course to head off *Mazuz*."

"Intercept *Mazuz*, aye. Weapons, designate *Mazuz* Target Alpha. Helm, come right to course . . . zero-one-one, down five. What about the Venture Salvage station, sir?"

"The station isn't going anywhere. We can come back to board her after we make sure *Mazuz* doesn't get away." Sikander looked back to his gunnery officer. "Mr. Herrera, we'll try to cripple her ring and drive plates when we come into range. We want to capture her if possible, not blow her out of space."

"Aye, Captain," Herrera replied. "We'll have the firing solution ready."

Minutes crawled by, while Sikander watched the geometry of the encounter taking shape on the tactical display. Most naval battles embodied the old military adage to hurry up and wait; ships easily spotted each other at distances measured in tens of millions of kilometers, unless something like a planet got in the way or someone managed to hide in the sun's glare. But kinetic cannons were unlikely to score hits at ranges of more than twenty or thirty thousand kilometers, so most of the battle consisted of waiting to get into range . . . at which point things started happening *fast*. Sikander himself had been in more space battles than most Aquilans—four, by his count—but even so, the waiting weighed heavily on him. The only other officer with battle experience on the bridge was Michael Girard, but then again, the fight at Gadira had been very atypical; *Hector* had started off that fight by exchanging fire at point-blank range with the Dremish *Panther* while both ships were in orbit above that planet.

This is the first real action for virtually everybody else on the ship, he reminded himself. They'd fought through plenty of tactical simulations—every hand aboard an Aquilan warship practiced their battle drills. Simulations, however, did not feel the same as the real thing. *It might be a good idea to settle some nerves before K-shots start flying.*

He keyed the ship's general announcement circuit and spoke. "All hands, this is the captain. I'm pleased to report that we unbubbled exactly where we wanted to be, and we've caught several ships moored at the Zafer mining station. We ordered them to surrender, but one of them is making a run for it. We're going to chase her down before attempting to board the station. It looks like nobody over there wants any part of *Decisive,* but we might have to fire on the ship trying to escape or make a few pointed remarks to the outlaws on the station with our K-cannons. Keep calm, be alert, and remember: This is exactly what you have trained for. I have complete confidence in each and every one of you, so let's go get them."

Officers and crewhands manning the bridge's various stations exchanged quick looks or nervous smiles; shoulders relaxed, expressions lightened, and some of the tension building up in the compartment seemed to dissipate. *Not exactly the St. Crispin's Day speech, but good enough,* Sikander decided.

"Captain, we've got an identification on *Mazuz,*" Michael Girard said. If he was nervous, the only sign he gave was that his natural awkwardness was nowhere to be seen—it seemed that the more he had to occupy his attention, the less he worried about how he carried himself. "She's the same ship we chased out of Bursa."

"Target Alpha is Target Alpha?" Sikander sat up in his battle couch, and zoomed in on his own display. The stripped-out light freighter had been hidden by the structure of the mining post's dock, but now that she was clear of the asteroid the battered hull and gleaming weapon mounts were unmistakable. "This is shaping up to be an interesting day. I'm looking forward to—"

"Sir! We're being illuminated by fire-control systems!" Ensign Carter shouted from the sensor position. "The mining station is targeting us!"

"*The'eb* is getting under way, Captain," Girard added. "*Qarash*, too. Designating Target Bravo and Target Charlie."

"Damn," Jaime Herrera growled. "They're *all* making a break for it."

"Very well," Sikander answered, keeping his voice steady. *So much for giving up peacefully*, he noted. The mining station didn't concern him too much yet; *Decisive* was still hundreds of thousands of kilometers out of the range of just about any weapon he could think of. Two more ships getting under way, however, complicated the tactical picture significantly. He still outgunned the pirates by a comfortable margin, but if the targets fled on diverging courses—

"They're scattering, Captain," Girard reported. "They're taking courses at right angles to make us choose which one we're going to chase. Which should we go after?"

"Captain, I think we should stay on *Mazuz*," Amelia Fraser suggested over the command circuit. "If we divert after one of the other targets, she gets away, and we *know* that she's a pirate."

"I'd like to, XO," Sikander replied. He studied the evolving engagement, scowling; this had been a lot simpler when he didn't have multiple targets tearing off in different directions. Whether through luck, panic, or cold-blooded calculation, the pirates had struck upon the best strategy to make sure at least one of their ships got away, and maybe two if Sikander wasn't careful. Due to her head start in getting under way from the station, *Mazuz* now represented something of a stern chase—it would take *Decisive* longer to bring the first ship under her guns than it would to engage one of the others just now leaving. *We can engage* The'eb or Qarash *much faster,* Sikander realized. *And if we disable our first target quickly, we might have time to chase down the other before it escapes . . . but probably not* Mazuz.

He decided he wanted two ships instead of one.

"Tactical, change course to intercept *The'eb,*" Sikander ordered Girard. "If we can disable her quickly, we'll have a chance to add *Qarash* to our bag. Sorry, XO."

"Intercept *The'eb,* aye, Captain!" The operations officer quickly calculated a new course on his console. "Helm, come right to course one-three-three up thirty, deceleration at one hundred percent military power. Hold on, this may get a little bumpy."

Decisive spun swiftly end-for-end, rotating to aim her powerful drive plates almost ninety degrees off her previous course, and went to full military power—the maximum safe acceleration customarily used in battle maneuvers. The ship's inertial compensators lagged just a little behind the sudden shift in acceleration; Sikander felt his weight shifting in his battle couch and quietly checked his seat harness. No one on the bridge needed to see the ship's captain decelerate himself out of his command seat by neglecting to buckle in before hard maneuvers. *Decisive's* projected course line in the tactical display changed into a high, looping curve that would pass above and in front of *The'eb* before settling in pursuit of *Qarash.*

Sikander nodded in satisfaction; Michael Girard was already looking past the engagement of the first ship to put *Decisive* in a good position to go after the second. By age-old custom, an Aquilan captain allowed the acting tactical officer to maneuver the ship in battle and focus on the details of engaging each target while exercising command by negation—if Girard started to do something Sikander didn't approve of, he'd step in and cancel the tactical officer's orders. But so far Michael Girard had things well in hand, so Sikander deliberately distanced himself from the details and paid attention to the situation as a whole. *Mazuz* boosted recklessly away from *Decisive*, pouring every gram of thrust in her drive plates into a desperate effort to flee. The distance continued to narrow . . . but the closing rate slowed as *Decisive* diverted toward the two ships just beginning to pull away from the mining station, now less than a hundred thousand kilometers away. *Decisive's* course would carry her quite a bit closer than that to the asteroid as she maneuvered for her firing pass on *The'eb.*

That station illuminated us with fire control, Sikander remembered. "Mr. Girard, keep an eye on the asteroid installation. They might be thinking of taking a shot at us when we pass by."

"Yes, sir," Girard replied. "Ms. Carter, see if you can figure out what sort of armament they're hiding over there. Maybe they've got a K-cannon or two concealed somewhere in that cargo structure."

"Yes, sir!" Ensign Carter consulted with her sensor techs, redirecting the destroyer's vid systems to study the asteroid installation more carefully.

"Tactical, we're in range to try a shot on Target Bravo," Jaime Herrera reported from the weapons post.

"Captain, permission to engage *The'eb*?" Girard asked.

"Permission granted."

"Main battery, Target Bravo, general-purpose rounds only, aim for her drive plates," Girard ordered. "Engage!"

"Commencing fire," Herrera reported. A moment later *Decisive's* Orcades Mark IX kinetic cannons whined loudly and thumped, sending a quiver through the hull behind the bridge. Given *Decisive's* hard braking maneuver, only the aft mounts bore on the target, but that still represented four powerful K-cannons, any one of which was easily enough to cripple a light freighter no matter how it had been rearmed or reinforced for its new career.

The first salvo sailed wide as the pirate vessel desperately jinked away from the K-shot. "Four misses," Herrera growled. "Next salvo, salvo aft!"

"Very well." Sikander wasn't surprised; he knew from years of experience that landing first-salvo hits on targets at long range was harder than it looked. When the range shortened and *Decisive* got into position to box its target with full broadsides, Herrera and his team would start scoring.

"Target Bravo is returning fire!" Ensign Carter announced—hardly necessary, since *Decisive's* bridge lit up with attack warnings from its automated systems. "Light kinetic cannons, velocity fifteen hundred kps."

"Helm, evasive action as needed," Michael Girard coolly ordered. "Maintain current course otherwise."

Sikander chose to let Girard's order stand. The real measure of a kinetic cannon's power was the speed at which it could hurl its projectiles, and while no one would want to be anywhere near the impact point of ten kilos of tungsten alloy moving at close to one percent of the speed of light, any reasonably agile ship with a few seconds' warning could accelerate or decelerate enough to make a slow-moving K-shot miss by hundreds of meters. At their current engagement distance, *The'eb's* shots had a flight time of ten or eleven seconds—far too long to pose a serious threat to his destroyer, which meant his tactical officer was perfectly correct to focus on the pursuit and dodge only when he had to. *The'eb* would have to get a great deal closer to *Decisive* to land hits. But just to remind Girard that *The'eb* might surprise them with a coordinated salvo, he asked, "What's her armament, Mr. Girard?"

Girard paused to study the enhanced imagery of the ship firing on them—a light freighter like *Mazuz*, but of a different class, with stubby airfoils for better handling in atmosphere. "Two K-cannons forward in casemates, and a third K-cannon mounted in a turret aft, sir," he reported. "She's engaging with the turret, but she'll have to turn toward us to bring the other weapons into play."

"I doubt she'd try it. Thank you, Mr. Girard. Carry on."

Decisive's K-cannons continued to thump away, launching their projectiles at nearly twice the velocity of the pirate's weapons. Sikander was accustomed to the main batteries of cruisers, firing shots every ten or fifteen seconds. Lighter weapons could sustain higher rates of fire, though, and *Decisive's* destroyer-weight cannons threw metal downrange every seven seconds. Even with her aft batteries alone, the destroyer could put a formidable volume of fire on a target . . . and, unlike a purpose-built warship, a converted freighter couldn't stand up to very many hits at all. *The'eb* managed to dodge the first three salvos that came her way, but a single shot in the fourth salvo smashed into her port side aft, punching clear through the hull to blast a ten-meter exit hole on the opposite side. Shattered drive plates spun away into space amid gobbets of white-hot metal and a cloud of venting atmosphere.

"Got her!" Herrera shouted from his console. "Direct hit on Target Bravo, midships aft. That had to have got an engineering space."

"Target Bravo's acceleration is falling off," Ensign Carter reported.

Sikander glanced at his own display, verifying the report. Sure enough, the pirate vessel's engines went dead, leaving her coasting along with the speed she'd already built up in her short run. "Mr. Herrera, see if you can get rid of that turret next," he told his gunnery officer. "No point in letting them have a chance of landing a lucky—"

"Weapon launch from the mining station!" Carter suddenly shouted. "Multiple weapon launches! Missiles inbound!"

"Damn!" Sikander swore. He'd expected some sort of attack

from the mining structure, but not at this range—even after their brief exchange of fire with *The'eb*, the station was still a good thirty thousand kilometers away. On his display, a ragged volley of fifteen small arrowheads appeared near the asteroid, crawling away from their launchers on brilliant plumes of exhaust. "Where were those hiding?"

"Launch canisters hidden in standard cargo containers, Captain," Grace Carter answered. "I'm sorry, sir. I didn't realize they were weapon emplacements."

Clever, Sikander observed. Missiles were mostly obsolete as weapons systems, but they did have a couple of advantages over more modern systems: They were cheap, and they didn't need much of a power supply compared to something like a laser or a K-cannon. If the missiles could catch *Decisive*, they could hurt her, obsolete or not. "I remember reading about old antiship missile systems designed to fit in standardized cargo containers, but I never thought we'd see one," he said to the sensor officer. "It's something of a poor man's shore battery. Well, now you know what to look for. Mr. Girard, what's the flight time on that missile salvo?"

"About three minutes, sir." Girard peered at his own display, studying the new threat. "Secondary battery, switch to antimissile defense. Engage as needed."

"Antimissile defense, aye," Herrera replied. At the console next to his, Sublieutenant Robert Ellis—the ship's assistant gunnery officer—went to work. He controlled *Decisive's* secondary battery of UV lasers. The lasers couldn't kill ship-sized targets fast, but they were more than capable of burning down a small target like a missile. In fact, point-defense lasers were the reason missiles were generally considered obsolete: self-powered weapons in real space just couldn't survive the defensive fire of their intended targets. Warp torpedoes had replaced antiship missiles generations ago in the Aquilan navy . . . but people who couldn't afford warpedoes had to make do with older weapons.

"It's official," Amelia Fraser said to Sikander over their private circuit. "They're throwing the kitchen sink at us."

"They would've been wiser to hold their fire a little longer," Sikander replied. "They might have given us a very unpleasant surprise if they'd waited until we were within a couple of thousand kilometers."

"I don't think they're used to targets that can shoot back, Captain."

"No, I guess not." Sikander checked his tactical summary, and saw that *Decisive's* battle management systems had identified the weapons as old Montréal-built AM-5 Faucon missiles with metallic-hydrogen rocket motors and five-hundred-kilo warheads of molecular explosive—dangerous enough in their day, perhaps, but according to the summary, the Faucon had gone out of production seventy years ago. *Decisive's* induction drive could sustain significantly higher acceleration than the old chemical rockets; the destroyer could avoid the entire salvo simply by outrunning it. *Ah, that's it,* he decided. *They hoped that the missile salvo might make us turn away, and give* The'eb *a chance to escape.*

It didn't work—one by one, *Decisive's* lasers reached out to melt the missiles, setting off their warheads in a rippling wave of distant explosions. The last weapon in the salvo was still two thousand kilometers short of its target when Sublieutenant Ellis burned it out of space.

"Well done, Mr. Ellis," Sikander said. "Mr. Girard, have the main battery neutralize any more missile canisters you can spot on that asteroid when we don't have something more important to shoot at. Sooner or later we're going to circle back around to the installation, and I don't want to worry about missiles in our face when we're getting ready to board them."

"Aye, sir. Main battery, split your fire. Engage the target emplacements on the station, general-purpose rounds."

"Split the battery, aye," Herrera acknowledged. *Decisive's* forward turrets opened up on the asteroid station, thumping away as the powerful electromagnets of each K-cannon hurled their deadly projectiles into space. It was a long shot for *Decisive's* Mark IX weapons, but unlike an enemy ship, a weapon emplacement on an asteroid couldn't evade fire—the salvo's flight time was a little longer, but the tungsten penetrators would hit just as hard. Four brilliant blooms erupted in the mining station's exposed structure, each representing the impact of a tungsten rod whose destructive power could be measured in kilotons. One round struck near the end of the cargo dock, vaporizing the last two hundred meters of its structure; two more flattened portions of the old refinery structure the size of city blocks; and the rest blasted molten craters from the barren rock of the asteroid where clusters of cargo units had been bolted to the surface.

Sikander winced at the blinding impacts. *That might have been a little more firepower than we needed,* he realized. "Let's reduce the power on any more shots we take at that station, Guns," he said to Herrera. "And don't target anything too close to that habitat—I have to imagine there's intelligence to collect somewhere inside."

"Er, yes, sir," Herrera replied. "Holding fire on the station until we see something else to engage down there."

"Hit on Target Bravo," Sublieutenant Ellis reported. He'd taken over the fire on *The'eb* after disposing of the missile volley, freeing Herrera to deal with the station. "Sir, we just knocked out her turret. Should we cease fire?"

Girard looked over to Sikander. "Captain?"

Sikander nodded. "Cease fire on Target Bravo, but continue to track her. If she accelerates or fires again, resume the engagement, but first let me see if I can convince these fellows to give up. Open a comm channel for me, please."

"Channel open, sir."

"Attention, all ships in Zafer. This is *Decisive*. Cease fire and cut your acceleration to zero, or we will fire upon you until you are disabled or destroyed. Zafer Station, shut down your fire-control radar or we will scrub your installation off that rock. *Decisive*, out." Sikander settled back and waited to see the results of his ultimatum.

"We're in range of Target Charlie, sir," Jaime Herrera reported. "Your instructions?"

Sikander looked over to his tactical officer. "Are they still running, Mr. Girard?"

"*Mazuz* and *Qarash* are still accelerating, sir. *The'eb* is dead in space. Umm, Zafer Station just shut down their fire-control systems."

Mazuz Sikander could do nothing about—the first pirate to escape the station had taken advantage of his decision to catch the other two vessels by making a beeline for the edge of the system. *Qarash*, on the other hand, was well within his grasp. "Make sure to record *Mazuz's* course and speed. That looks like a transit acceleration to me, and I'd like to know where she's going when she bubbles up. As for *Qarash*, I want a warning shot, and a warning shot only. Give me a salvo ten kilometers across her bow."

"Shot across the bow, aye," Herrera replied. He keyed up the targeting commands, and tapped the firing key again; a single K-cannon in the forward battery thrummed loudly, sending its projectile hurling ahead of the last fleeing pirate ship.

A minute passed, while Sikander waited to see if the third pirate ship would continue its futile flight or not. The geometry of it was simply impossible for *Qarash*—*Decisive* would overtake her in less than ten minutes, and she was already well within the range of Sikander's K-cannons. *Even the most desperate or inept captain on the other ship has to be able to see that too,* he told himself. He felt Jaime Herrera's eyes on him, and then Michael Girard's as well, as they waited for the inevitable order to resume fire.

Amelia Fraser spoke over their private link. "Captain, we're going to overshoot her if we wait too much longer."

"I know," Sikander replied. He started to give the order to fire— and then Ensign Carter interrupted him.

"Target Charlie's acceleration is zero!" she announced.

"Incoming audio transmission, Captain," Girard reported.

"Let's hear it," Sikander said. "Mr. Herrera, hold your fire."

The bridge's speakers crackled with a faint hiss of static, and then a man spoke in a rapid stream of Jadeed-Arabi. *"Decisive,* this is *Qarash.* We are peaceful traders—hold your fire! We surrender, we surrender! Do not, repeat, do not shoot!"

The tension on the bridge passed with a sudden wave of sighs and grins. Sikander savored relief for a moment, and then keyed his comm console to reply. *"Qarash,* this is Commander North. My tactical officer will soon send you maneuvering instructions to arrange a minimum-time rendezvous. You are to comply with his orders completely and without delay. Do you understand? Over."

"Yes, yes, we understand. But this is all a terrible mistake—"

"I doubt that, *Qarash.* Next: Direct *Mazuz* to cut her acceleration and heave to. If you want to surrender, you all have to surrender, over."

The voice from *Qarash* grew shrill in panic. "They won't do that for us! Please, we can't make them come back!"

Sikander cut the comms and switched over to his command circuit. "What do you think, XO?"

"You know the saying about honor among thieves, Captain,"

Amelia replied. "If I were on *Mazuz*'s bridge, I'd keep on going, and to hell with all my former friends in Zafer."

"I would too, but it was worth a try." Sikander switched back to the ship-to-ship comms. "Very well, *Qarash*. We accept your surrender. Stand by for additional instructions. *Decisive*, out."

12

Mersin, Dahar II

Marid Pasha met Elena Pavon in his working office, a spacious library with floor-to-ceiling windows that looked out over the orange-tinted clouds roiling over the lowlands beyond Mersin. She followed the pasha's appointment secretary Nenet into the room, and took more pleasure than she should have from the act of ignoring the Zerzuran woman's disapproving looks. Elena wore a perfectly modest pantsuit in a pearl-gray hue, and if it was tailored for a more flattering fit than the frumpy dark dress that Nenet Fakhoury considered acceptable business wear, that was Nenet's problem, not hers.

"Ms. Elena Pavon of Pegasus-Pavon Shipping, Marid Pasha," Nenet announced in a painfully neutral tone.

The pasha looked up from behind his vast desk—real Terran walnut, or so it appeared at first glance—and set down the dataslate he'd been reading, rising to greet her. "Ms. Pavon, what a pleasure to finally meet you," he said warmly. He had more silver than black in his hair, but his face showed strength rather than age, and she realized that he was quite tall when he straightened up to his full height. "I confess that I have been looking forward to this appointment all afternoon."

"As have I, Excellency," Elena replied, reaching out to shake his hand. "Thank you for seeing me."

"Oh, it's nothing. Do you know Admiral al-Kassar?" The pasha gestured toward a stocky naval officer with gold braid on his shoulders, sitting in one of the guest chairs in front of the huge desk; the admiral stood to greet her. "I asked him to join us since your note indicated your business today concerned the Zerzura Sector Fleet."

"I do know the admiral." Elena shook Torgut al-Kassar's hand too. "We met at the Founding Day celebration a few weeks ago."

"Very good, then. Can I have Nenet get you some coffee or tea?"

Elena resisted the temptation to send the older woman off to fetch her something to drink. "No, thank you, Pasha."

"Straight to business, I see. Well, I can appreciate that, I am sure your time is quite valuable. How can we help you today, Ms. Pavon?"

"I wanted to speak with you about the two Zerzura Sector Fleet gunboats that have been scheduled for decommissioning: *Kartal* and *Pelikan*, I believe."

"You're well informed," said Marid Pasha. "I didn't realize that our naval administration had made any public announcement about the ships to be scrapped."

"We haven't," Torgut al-Kassar said in a dour tone.

"My company does a lot of business with various shipyards in the sector; the news is common knowledge among local yards," Elena explained. "I have to admit that it surprised me, though. Given the difficulty of maintaining patrols in Zerzura's outlying systems, I'm afraid I don't quite understand why you'd want to get rid of any hulls at all."

"The Kartals are old and somewhat worn-out," Admiral al-Kassar said. "They were commissioned forty-five years ago, and it's becoming prohibitively expensive to maintain them. I am afraid they have outlived their usefulness."

"Do you plan to replace them?"

"Well, yes, we do," Marid Pasha said. "I don't want this to be generally known right now so please don't share what I'm about to tell you, but . . . we've reached an agreement to purchase a small number of surplus warships from the Empire of Dremark. They're not brand new, of course, but they *are* significantly newer—and more capable—than the old Kartals."

"Really?" Elena glanced at the admiral, who nodded in confirmation. She'd heard plenty of speculation in Dahar's news programs about the ongoing visit of a Dremish envoy and Dremark's apparent interest in expanding its commercial ties to Zerzura, but this was the first she'd heard about any sort of military aid. *Business as usual for a Caliphate governor on a budget, or a step toward Zerzuran independence?* she wondered. Either way, it seemed that Dremark was ready to put some money on the table in order to secure Marid Pasha's friendship. "I'm pleased to hear that. How long will it take you to bring your new units into service?"

"A few months, most likely. They should be arriving in a week or two, but it will take a little time to refit them for our needs and replace some of the older systems."

"That's the other reason we're decommissioning the Kartals," Torgut al-Kassar added. "We need the manpower tied up in the older hulls to crew our new ships, and as you can imagine, there is quite a lot of retraining involved for our sailors. They need some time to become familiar with the Dremish engineering and combat systems."

"Naturally," Elena said. "Pegasus-Pavon crews require similar training cycles when we bring a new hull into service. I look forward to seeing your new ships on patrol."

"Does that answer your questions about the Kartals, Ms. Pavon?" Marid Pasha asked.

"It certainly satisfies my curiosity, but that's not exactly why I asked you about *Kartal* and *Pelikan*. You see, since they're old and worn-out and you're going to scrap them anyway"—Elena carefully refrained from smiling, since Torgut al-Kassar had volunteered that very assessment of the gunboats just a moment ago—"I would like to buy them from you."

"Buy them?" Marid Pasha raised an eyebrow in surprise. "I'm not sure what use they would be to Pegasus-Pavon. They're certainly not big enough to serve as freight carriers."

"No, they're not. I don't need additional cargo capacity at the moment, but I *could* make good use of a couple of armed patrol craft, ships I could post near crucial shipping hubs to discourage pirate attacks. I have observed that pirates don't like to show themselves when warships are present—well, after the attack on *Vashaoth Teh*, the lack of naval protection in this whole region is now a crisis. *Kartal* and *Pelikan* might not be frontline combat units any longer, but I think they'd do a good job of discouraging attacks wherever they're stationed."

The pasha exchanged a look with the admiral, hesitating before he answered. "I'm not sure I care for the idea of privately owned navies roaming our territory looking for pirates," he finally said. "It sounds like a terrible tragedy just waiting to happen."

"Terrible tragedies are taking place every week somewhere in Zerzura," Elena pointed out. "I'm glad to learn that you've got plans to reinforce your squadron here in Dahar, but I can't wait months and months for help in places like Bursa or Tunis—or Meliya now, I guess. I need a *solution*, and it sounds like you've got two ships you can spare."

"They won't be available as swiftly as you might like," Torgut al-Kassar said, frowning. "The process of demilitarizing the hulls will take quite some time."

"I don't believe you understand what I want them for, Admiral. The gunboats are useful to me as is. All I need are hulls that are in one piece and carry enough armament to put my crews on an even footing with the pirate vessels we're encountering."

"And I don't believe *you* understand what the admiral is telling you," Marid Pasha said in a dry tone. "Caliphate law requires us to remove certain types of systems from a warship when we decommission her—cryptographic materials, certain weapons, military-grade sensors and communication systems, things that we're not allowed to just hand over to civilians."

"My staff has been looking into the relevant laws," Elena replied. *And ways to get around them, for that matter.* If Torgut al-Kassar didn't want to sell her a ship armed with kinetic cannons, she had other ways to obtain serviceable weaponry. General Karacan, commander of Dahar's ground forces, was perfectly willing to sell surplus artillery pieces for the right price, although it might not be a good idea to point that out at the moment. "We believe that we can work within those restrictions."

"You are persistent, Ms. Pavon," the pasha said. "I have to ask: Under what authority do you think your gunboat fleet can operate in Caliphate territory?"

"We'll commission them as privateers, Pasha. You have the power to issue a limited letter of marque that would empower private citizens to serve as pirate hunters. Or in this case, antipiracy patrols."

"I do?"

"The legal authority is there, even if it's rarely used. For that matter, the Velar Electorate and the Principality of Bolívar have similar laws governing letters of marque." That was Elena's little way of suggesting that she might have other options available if the pasha said no. She leaned in to make her pitch. "But as far as I know they don't have ships they're planning to decommission—ships that are right here in Zerzura, I might add. Marid Pasha, you have two ships you're about to sell for whatever the scrapyard pays—say, a quarter-million credits per hull. I'm ready to purchase them both today for two million credits."

"It would cost you fifty million each to buy your own gunboats!" Torgut al-Kassar protested.

"Well, yes, but these are old and worn-out, as you explained. And you're about to throw them away, so why not get something for them?"

"I commend you, Ms. Pavon. You have a real gift for thinking outside of the box." Marid Pasha squared his arms on his desk like a battlement. "But, in all seriousness, we need to consider your offer with some care. I *am* worried about the legalities of the thing."

"As you wish," Elena said. She stood up. "There is an expiration date on the offer, though. If I don't hear back in thirty days, I'll move ahead with securing my patrol craft from another source. It will cost me more and take more time since the ships aren't in-sector, so I'd prefer to take your hand-me-downs instead. But I can't wait forever."

"I understand. One way or another, we will get back to you. Good afternoon, Ms. Pavon." Marid Pasha smiled, and motioned for Nenet Fakhoury to return. The secretary showed Elena to the door.

Well, that was harder than I thought it would be, Elena reflected as she followed one of the ubiquitous palace attendants back to the landing pad. *I'm offering the pasha five times the scrap value of those old clunkers and real assistance with the single biggest problem facing the sector, so what's his objection? Am I too young and female to be trusted with something that shoots?* In theory, the Caliphate placed few restrictions on the sorts of jobs women could hold and treated them no differently from men under the law. No one on Dahar objected to Elena's leadership role in the regional offices of Pegasus-Pavon or the influence she wielded as a powerful and wealthy businesswoman. But in practice, a certain degree of chauvinism lingered even centuries after the Caliphate had officially abolished the legal restrictions on women that its worlds had inherited from the Quranists who settled them. Few women in the Terran Caliphate chose military careers, or advanced to senior rank even if they did.

Omar Morillo waited for her in her luxury flyer, busy with the dataslate on which he kept her schedule and managed her correspondence. "Well, how did it go?" he asked as she climbed in.

"They had some difficulty in wrapping their heads around the idea—I caught the pasha completely off guard, and he really didn't know what to think. Al-Kassar didn't like it at all, but then again he strikes me as the dictionary definition of military inflexibility, so I didn't expect anything else." Elena shrugged. "Overall, it came down to a tepid we'll-think-about-it."

"Home, or back to the office?"

"The office, please. I need to distract myself with some work," said Elena.

Omar murmured a few words to the pilot, and the flyer lifted off smoothly from the palace landing pad. Elena paid little attention to the beautiful late-afternoon sunshine glinting on Mersin's towers as they turned southeast and headed toward the city's business district. "I really don't understand their resistance to the idea," he mused. "They're disposing of the assets anyway. If we spend a lot of money to drag broken-down gunboats off to some other system where they accomplish nothing at all, what does it matter to the pasha?"

Elena shook her head. "It's a threat to the bureaucracy. The pasha might not care, but I guarantee you that Admiral al-Kassar and the Zerzura Sector Fleet would be pretty embarrassed if our privateering scheme actually works."

"There might be something to that," Omar admitted.

Pegasus-Pavon's Dahar office occupied several floors in a high-rise ten kilometers from the palace. Elena's pilot settled the flyer into her reserved space in the rooftop garage; she chewed on the problem posed by the defensiveness of government bureaucracies throughout the short lift ride to her floor and the walk through the busy common areas of the corporate office to her own suite, a magnificent corner unit. On one wall a vast vid display showed a map of the company's Meliyan-Zerzuran region with icons representing the estimated locations of each Pegasus-Pavon ship in port or in transit. On the opposite side of the office, generous windows faced north and west, back toward the pasha's palace, gleaming gold in the afternoon light. Elena threw herself down in her comfortable chair and spun around to glare in its direction while she replayed the conversation in her mind. *This might be impossible,* she realized. *People have been trying to fix government stupidity since the Egyptians started cutting stone for pyramids. Why do I think I can get better results?*

With a sigh of exasperation, she abandoned the fight for the day and turned her attention to the work that had piled up on her desk while she'd been looking into buying her own little fleet. She generally trusted the managers and specialists who handled the day-to-day affairs of the office, but as the local representative of the Pavon family she kept her eye on strategic concerns, executive staffing questions, reinforcing the values of the company . . . and thinking outside the box from time to time, as Marid Pasha had observed. The afternoon slipped away as she dealt with the messages and correspondence that had made it all the way to her desk; she hardly noticed until her comm device chirped, indicating a message to her private address.

Elena glanced at the display; she didn't recognize the sender, but the subject line read *More information on Venture Salvage*. Curiosity won out; she tapped the icon to read further. The message was brief:

> You don't know me, but your agents hired my firm to look into Venture Salvage last month. I have evidence that implicates one of your competitors in Venture Salvage's activities. Can we meet at 6:30 pm at the Mersin offices of Pegasus-Pavon? You need to see this as soon as possible.
>
> Yusuf Rahim
> Rahim Investigations, Izra, Dahar

"What in the world?" Elena murmured, eyes narrowing in suspicion. None of the agencies working for Pegasus-Pavon should have had her private address, but then again, if this information was as urgent as the sender claimed, maybe he'd decided to go straight to the top. And it was already five thirty . . . *Rahim must be in town, or on his way.*

She punched Omar's icon on her comm unit. "Did we hire a detective agency named Rahim Investigations?" she asked when he answered.

"Let me check," he replied. His office was just down the hall from hers—within shouting distance, if she were so inclined. A moment later he appeared at her door. "We did. Why do you ask?"

"I just received a direct message to my private address from Mr. Rahim. He says he wants to come by at six thirty and tell me something about what he's found. And he's making it sound important and a little cloak-and-dagger, to be honest."

"That's not how our contractors are supposed to work," Omar

said. "I'll tell him to follow the reporting procedures our people set up when they hired him."

"He says it's urgent."

"People have a habit of developing an amazing sense of urgency when they're dealing with excessively rich clients. This guy's probably going to try to convince you that you need to give him a few hundred thousand credits so that he can go get the really good dirt."

Elena tapped a finger on her chin, thinking. Pegasus-Pavon had competitors, certainly—Suvar United and Grupo Constelación came to mind—but the major shipping lines had worked out their positions decades ago. Rate wars hurt everybody, so they mostly stuck to their own hubs and tacitly shared the routes whose control wasn't obvious. *Suvar United is run by the al-Kassars*, she reminded herself. *Is that what's going on here? Is Torgut al-Kassar suppressing pirates only when they threaten his brother's company? That would explain quite a few things.*

"I'll see him," she decided.

"Okay, then," Omar said. "But how much do you want to bet that I'm right?"

Elena dismissed him with a wave of her hand, and sent Rahim a quick reply: *6:30 is fine. I'll be waiting for you.* Then she returned to her work, determined to clear as much off her desk as possible before the mysterious meeting.

She did her best to put the whole thing out of her mind for another forty-five minutes, and largely succeeded. But at 6:20 P.M. she received another message: *Apologies, running late. I will be there at 7:00.* "Who in the hell do you think you are, Yusuf?" she growled at her comm unit. She didn't have any particular obligations for the evening—a somewhat unusual situation, really—but she *was* getting hungry, and she looked forward to a quiet evening at home with good take-out food and some classic cinema. *Fine,* she replied. *Let me know when you arrive and I'll meet you in the lobby.* She turned on her office lights and resigned herself to another half hour of catch-up work.

At six thirty Omar wandered into her office. "Where's our mysterious visitor?"

"Running late," Elena replied. "He says he'll be here at seven."

"Tell him to come back in the morning."

"I'm already here, and it's only another half hour."

Omar settled down in one of the guest chairs of her office with his dataslate to keep at it while they waited. Elena appreciated the company—the office could be pretty lonely after the staff knocked off and headed home, especially after it got dark.

Seven o'clock came . . . and went. Elena gave up all pretense of working, and flipped on the local news station on one of the office vidscreens. Then, at 7:10, she received one more message. *Can't make it; will explain later. I will be in touch soon. Sorry, Yusuf Rahim.*

"Oh, you must be kidding!" Elena snarled. "He just canceled on me!"

"After wasting an hour of my evening," Omar observed. "Oh, I just can't *wait* to hear Mr. Rahim's story. Shall we go?"

"Let's get out of here," Elena agreed. She secured her office while Omar called her pilot to warm up the flyer, and the two of them walked out through the now-deserted corporate office. She fumed the whole way up the elevator ride, profoundly annoyed by Rahim Investigations and already planning the scalding tirade she'd unleash on the man if and when he ever found his way to the office.

The rooftop garage was as empty as one would expect an hour or more after most people in the building left for the day. Elena spotted her parked flyer and headed that way, Omar trailing half a step behind her. She was *hungry,* damn it, and—

A man dressed in black stepped out from behind one of the concrete support columns just as she passed, and shocked her with a handheld stunner.

Elena collapsed in midstride, losing all control of her muscles. She hit the garage floor hard enough to see stars and tried to scream, but all that came out was a sound like *gyuhhh!* To her surprise, she actually remained conscious—she could hear a desperate scuffle behind her, and she saw two more strangers in black run past her, weapons in their hands.

Have to get up, she told herself.

Not a chance in hell, her arms and legs answered, still convulsing from the shock. But she managed to twist herself onto her side.

Behind her, Omar Morillo danced away from the man who'd stunned her, lunging and twisting to avoid contact with his weapon's sparking electrodes while the two new assailants closed in. Elena couldn't imagine how he could stay on his feet for more than another second or two, but then he reached inside his coat and produced a snub-nosed mag pistol, a small and highly concealable self-defense model. She hadn't even realized that he carried a weapon.

He stopped dodging, set his feet, and calmly shot the first attacker between the eyes. The tiny pistol's chirp echoed shrilly through the garage, loud as a siren. Then he pivoted and dropped a second attacker with two point-blank shots in the center of the chest.

The third man got to him.

The black-clad attacker lunged forward even as Omar turned the gun on him, and rammed the stunner into the center of Omar's chest. The weapon made a sharp snapping sound, and Omar collapsed in a mass of twitching arms and legs.

"Son of a bitch!" the remaining attacker snarled. He kicked away Omar's pistol, then kicked him in the ribs hard before backing off to speak into a comm piece fixed to his shoulder. "The assistant was armed. He shot Mert and Haluk. I'm going to need a hand here."

Elena couldn't hear the reply the man received, but it didn't improve his outlook. He muttered another curse, glanced at Elena to check on her, then returned to kick Omar again. "You've made quite a lot of trouble for us, you little bastard. We only need that whore you work for. Too bad for you!"

The convulsions gripping Elena's muscles eased; she realized that she could just barely think about moving again. Slowly, she rolled onto her belly. *They attacked us with stunners*, she realized. *And they waited until the office was empty to make sure no one was going to be around. This is a kidnapping!* And that meant her attackers had transportation somewhere nearby, likely on its way this very moment.

She didn't have much time at all.

Grunting with effort, she dragged herself forward on her elbows. The third attacker should have heard her . . . but he was occupied with aiming cruel kicks at Omar while the Bolívaran lay helpless on the floor. Elena groped her way to the place where the first attacker had fallen, and she grasped his stunner with shaking fingers.

"Hey," she croaked.

The last kidnapper wheeled back to face her—and she shocked him on the top of his foot with the stunner. He let out a strangled cry and collapsed in front of her, so she hit him again, jabbing the electrodes against his left ear. The stunner let out a brilliant *snap!*

of electricity, and the man thrashed wildly in uncontrollable convulsions.

Above the garage's landing platform, a light-cargo commercial flyer came into view. As much as Elena would have liked to stay where she was and continue shocking the last living kidnapper, she doubted that she could spare the time. Staggering to her feet, she grabbed Omar's arm and dragged him back toward the elevator, mere meters behind them.

The door slid shut just as two more men in black utility uniforms leaped out of the sliding side door of the light-cargo flyer and lunged for her. Elena punched the button for the ground-floor lobby, and collapsed across Omar's body. Every muscle in her body ached, like she'd just gotten over a full-body charley horse. *Well, that's pretty much what hand stunners are designed to do.*

Omar let out a small wheeze. "I told you it was somebody who wanted your money," he said. "Kept you . . . at the office late . . . to make sure no one would be around. You sure . . . fell for that."

"Oh, shut up," she told him. "You were right, I was wrong. There, that's it."

"Not by a long shot . . . I'm going to enjoy holding this over your head. . . . Help me up."

Elena struggled to her feet, and helped Omar to his. The assistant took out his comm device and punched in an emergency code. "This is Morillo," he wheezed. "Get security down to the ground-floor lobby. Someone tried to kidnap Ms. Pavon, and they know we're in the elevator."

"Who would do this?" Elena wondered aloud. Someone after an heiress's ransom? Or did it have something to do with her efforts to push the pasha's government into taking action against Zerzura's pirates? She couldn't believe that anyone could have found out about her plan to outfit privateers; she'd held that close to the vest until the meeting with Marid Pasha. *No, that's not it,* she decided. *Whoever attacked me knew enough to use the name of one of the investigators we hired. And that means they might also know what our investigators told us.* "The pirates, of course. They came after me because we got close to them."

"What was that?" Omar asked. He really was a mess, with a split lip streaming blood down his chin and a hunched posture that hinted at some cracked or broken ribs.

"I think someone knows what we found out about Venture Salvage. And this was their way of making sure it didn't go any further."

Omar nodded, and spat out a mouthful of blood. "The Rahim message was bait."

"Are you okay?" Elena asked.

"Not really, no. I'm going to need a big raise."

"We'll see about that," Elena promised him. Then the elevator doors opened, and she sighed in relief at the sight of a lobby full of building security guards.

13

CSS *Decisive*, Bursa System

ecisive made the warp transit from Zafer to the Zerzuran system of Bursa in a little less than five days. Sikander observed the usual arrival routine on the bridge, with the added anxiety of a second ship to worry about: the captured pirate *Qarash*, now under the temporary command of Jaime Herrera and a small prize crew. *We're going to need to carry a bigger crew if I have to keep parceling out prize detachments,* he reflected as the arrival countdown ticked away. If *The'eb* had been in any condition to make a warp transit, Sikander would have been hard-pressed to come up with a crew for the second pirate without leaving *Decisive* undermanned . . . especially since the destroyer now carried eighty-seven prisoners locked in hastily cleared crew berthing spaces and guarded around the clock. He'd decided to tow the crippled *The'eb* back to Zafer Station and leave her moored there with her weapons and drive disabled until someone else could return to salvage the damaged ship and shutter the pirate base for good.

"Clear arrival, sir!" Ensign Carter reported as *Decisive* unbubbled.

"Very good." Sikander studied the now-familiar navigational display for Bursa; *Decisive* had arrived a few light-minutes out from Bursa IV and its inhabited moon. "Is *Qarash* with us?"

"Not yet, sir," Michael Girard said. "She could—oh, wait, there she is. Zero-nine-five relative, distance fifty light-seconds. It looks like she missed her transit-arrival mark by a little bit."

"I'm not surprised," Amelia Fraser observed. "Civilian-grade navigational systems aren't quite as accurate as what we've got to work with."

"Oh, I'm not going to let Jaime off that easily." Departing Zafer on parallel courses and identical acceleration, the two ships had planned to arrive in Bursa together. Naturally Sikander had spent much of the last five days imagining things that could go wrong on the prize ship while *Decisive* and *Qarash* were unable to communicate with each other in their own warp bubbles. He owed his gunnery officer a little good-natured ribbing about his navigation after days of worrying about *Qarash*. "Mr. Girard, depower and retract the warp ring, and send our arrival notice to Bursa Traffic Control."

"Aye, Captain," Girard replied. "Shall I set course for Bursa orbit?"

"Please do, and signal *Qarash* to follow us in—standard acceleration. The sooner we get these prisoners off our hands, the better I'll like it." The commonly accepted convention for dealing with captured pirates, ships and crew alike, was to take them to the nearest recognized planetary authority and hand them over to be charged and tried under local laws. The Meliya system in the Velar Electorate was actually somewhat closer to Zafer than Bursa was, but given the damage to Meliya Station—and Sikander's preference for a route that led more directly back toward Neda, now that *Decisive* was supposed to be concluding her patrol and heading home—he'd chosen to bring his prize into the Zerzuran port instead. "And please give me a channel for the Bursa Flotilla headquarters. It's Kaptani Hanan, correct?"

"Yes, sir. The comm system's yours."

"Thank you." Sikander had spoken briefly with the Caliphate navy officer who commanded the Zerzura Sector Fleet's local detachment when *Decisive* had returned to Bursa to pick up the *Carmela Día* prize crew. He silently composed his message for a moment, and then opened the comm window on his console. "Good afternoon, Kaptani Hanan. This is Commander North of CSS *Decisive*; my compliments. Please be advised that we are escorting a captured pirate to Bursa orbit. The vessel *Qarash* is currently under the command of an Aquilan prize crew. We also have eighty-seven prisoners apprehended during our raid on a pirate base in the Zafer system. In accordance with international antipiracy agreements, we are remanding both *Qarash* and our prisoners to your custody. We'll also turn over to you the evidence we gathered from the scene. My report is appended to this message." Sikander glanced over at the navigational display, confirming their course and position. "We should reach orbit later this evening. If you have any special instructions for the transfer of the prisoners or the prize, please advise us. *Decisive*, out."

Sikander decided to wait for a reply on the bridge, and busied himself for a few minutes with a review of the intelligence summary Michael Girard's team had compiled during the warp transit. A thorough search of the captured ships and station had turned up more stolen cargo than *Decisive* could easily haul back to civilization, so Sikander had directed his master-at-arms to select a good set of samples for evidence while his intelligence specialists connected the dots between the loot they'd discovered at Zafer and goods reported stolen from pirate attacks throughout the sector. They'd also separated their prisoners for brief interviews to see if any of their captives had anything to say, but the interviews hadn't provided much information—the captured pirates had denied any knowledge of wrongdoing, sat silent, or claimed to be legitimate miners who'd sue the Aquilan navy for millions of credits over "illegal detention" and the "use of excessive force" as soon as they got their day in court. Sikander would have worried about that a little more if his people had found any signs that the Venture Salvage "employees" at Zafer were actually operating the mining station. He'd personally interviewed a handful of the prisoners who seemed to be in positions of authority with no better results than his masters-at-arms, so he'd decided to let the authorities in Bursa sort it all out. Destroyer crews weren't police, and as much as he would have liked to see if his people could get *something* out of their Zafer prisoners, Sikander had no reason to believe they'd do a better job of it than Bursa's planetary authorities. Ultimately, his crew had caught two pirate ships and cleaned out a pirate base; conducting prosecutions was someone else's job.

After half an hour, the local naval commander's reply arrived. Kaptani Hanan was a taciturn, hard-looking fellow with a black beard and a habitual scowl, but today he looked more than a little surprised by Sikander's message. "Good afternoon, Commander North," he began. "We are not aware of any pirate vessel by the name of *Qarash*, but it's likely that we just haven't seen her in Bursa before. Please bring your prize to the naval station; we'll be happy to take her off your hands and transfer your prisoners. You are to be congratulated, sir—it's been a long time since someone caught one of our corsairs in the act. Bursa Flotilla, out."

"Our pleasure," Sikander said aloud, not bothering to transmit the remark. He stood and stretched. "Mr. Girard, I'll be in my cabin. Call me if anything interesting happens."

A few hours later, *Decisive* and *Qarash* moored in the docking cradles of a rather old and cramped naval station built around the hulk of an old battleship that had been decommissioned fifty years ago. Kaptani Hanan came to greet Sikander as the station's military police—hastily augmented by a number of ordinary sailors issued sidearms, or so it appeared—took charge of the prisoners *Decisive's* crew marched down to the accommodation tube. "Is this the same lot you chased away from the United Extraction mining post a couple of weeks ago?" Hanan asked as they watched the prisoners file by.

"Probably not," Sikander said. "*Mazuz* was the ship we interrupted at United Extraction. She got away from us at Zafer. Most of these men we found aboard *Qarash* and *The'eb*, and some we captured on Zafer Station."

"How did you find the pirate base, anyway?"

"We had a tip about a front corporation called Venture Salvage—they bought the mining rights to Zafer several years ago, and never actually put the place into production." Sikander glanced at the Zerzuran captain. "I don't suppose you have any Venture Salvage holdings here in Bursa? If the pirates used it as a front in one system, they might be using it in others."

"I am not familiar with any operation by that name, but I'll have my staff look into it," Hanan said. "Will you be able to stay to provide additional statements or testimony, Commander?"

"I'm afraid we're only in port for a day or so. We're already overdue back at our home base. As soon as we fill our magnetic bottles and replenish our stores"—feeding eighty-seven prisoners during the transit from Zafer had sorely depleted *Decisive's* food supply, and the dizzying number of transits during the last six weeks had used up quite a lot of the exotic lithium-c *Decisive* used to generate warp bubbles—"we have to be on our way again. The report I'm providing to your station includes sworn statements about what we found at Zafer. But if you need any of us to testify for a trial, send word to Neda, and we'll do our best to return for the proceedings."

"God willing, your statements should suffice to convict these men." Hanan offered Sikander his hand. "We will take it from here, Commander North."

Once the prisoners were off-loaded, Sikander had *Decisive* shift to Bursa's commercial spaceport for refueling and replenishing, and authorized a few hours of liberty for the crew. He didn't bother to go over to Bursa Station, remaining in his cabin to work on the Zafer after-action report—shots fired in anger, even against state-less criminals such as pirates, required a great deal of explanation to the Admiralty. Amelia Fraser had prepared a first draft of the report, but a commanding officer was ultimately responsible for every piece of official correspondence transmitted by his command, and as much as Sikander trusted his XO, he still wanted to review it for himself.

He was still at it early in the evening when Michael Girard knocked on his cabin door. The redheaded operations officer had a troubled expression on his face. "Captain? We just picked up some news from the latest courier arrival. Apparently there's been another pirate attack—Meliya, this time."

"Weren't we just there?" Sikander set down his dataslate and rubbed at his eyes. "Damn. I'd hoped that we'd dealt with all the active pirates when we neutralized the base. Did *Mazuz* circle back to attack Meliya after she fled Zafer?"

"No, sir, it looks like we're dealing with a different group here. Two pirate vessels working together ambushed a Grupo Constel-ación container ship the day after we departed for Zafer: *Duquesa*, one hundred and eighty-seven thousand metric tons. The pirates hijacked twelve cargo containers and shot the captain dead on the bridge."

"If it was the day after we left, that definitely rules out *Mazuz*, as you say. She wouldn't have beaten us to Zafer, even with our slow transit. This group must have waited for us to leave before moving against Meliya."

"But one day after our departure is too soon for someone in Meliya watching our movements to summon pirates waiting in a nearby system," Girard pointed out. "Either the pirates were hiding in Meliya when we were there—which seems unlikely, since we had several days to observe the system—or their arrival had nothing to do with our departure. The fact that they happened to show up after we left might be a coincidence."

Darvesh appeared in the doorway leading to the small galley that adjoined Sikander's cabin, a tray with two cups of coffee in his hands. Naturally, he'd long ago learned the preferred beverages of *Decisive*'s senior officers. "Or the pirates responded to some event or circumstance we simply are not aware of, Mr. Girard," he observed, offering a cup to the operations officer. "It only seems to be a coincidence because we do not know what led them to make their move."

"I believe that I'm with Darvesh on this," Sikander said. He stood and came around his desk to take the second cup from the tray, stretching his legs as he worried at the puzzle his operations officer had just brought to his attention. "I spent enough time as an intelligence officer in Helix Squadron to stop believing in coincidences. And we already suspect that someone is spying on us."

Girard stood still, thinking hard; the natural uneasiness that marked most of his personal interactions dropped away as he grappled with the problem, and a look of intense concentration sharpened his expression. Sikander knew him well enough to remain quiet and let him develop whatever thought had come to him. "If it's not a coincidence," the operations officer said slowly, "then the only other explanation I can see is that someone knew we were going to receive information that we would choose to act on, information that would cause us to leave Meliya."

"Someone? Who?"

"Ms. Pavon. She sent the message, didn't she? And Grupo Constelación is Pegasus-Pavon's largest competitor."

"You don't think that Elena Pavon intentionally lured us away from Meliya?" Sikander said, surprised. He stopped in his pacing, examining the ugly possibility that Michael Girard had just suggested to him. He didn't think the charming woman who'd invited him to the coffee orchard at Mount Kesif could be capable of that sort of duplicity, but how well did he know her, really? *It's clear that we're all missing something about what's going on in Zerzura,* he reflected. And Elena had sought him out directly, engaging him as an ally and cultivating his friendship . . . or something more. *But she came to see me* after *she learned what had happened to* Carmela Día. *She was angry about that. Furious, even.* No, the Elena Pavon who asked him to help bring the criminals who'd murdered her people to justice was not likely to consign another crew to a similar fate, not even if they were competitors.

He turned back to Girard. "I just don't see it, Michael. The information she gave us turned out to be good. If Elena Pavon actually meant to use the pirates to damage her competitors, I don't think she would have given us a useful tip—she would have sent us off to some completely empty system. Besides, the pirates are hitting Pegasus-Pavon harder than anybody." Sikander resumed his pacing. "But that does makes me wonder who else knew about Elena's message. Zerzura's pirates seem to be exceedingly well informed. If they knew she'd sent us a tip about Zafer—"

"—they might have guessed that we'd leave Meliya to chase it down," Girard finished for him. He shook his head. "Good God, Captain. What if pirates fed the information to Ms. Pavon in the first place? Maybe there are multiple gangs at work here, and one of them figured they could use us to wipe out some of *their* rivals?"

"Congratulations, Mr. Girard. You just made my head spin." Sikander leaned against the front of his desk, arms folded. "All right, I believe I've entertained all the suspicions I care to entertain for the day. But go ahead and take another look through the intelligence we collected from Zafer and see if you can find any evidence of rival pirate groups."

"Yes, sir. I'll check the transcripts of our prisoner interviews, too." Girard finished his coffee, and headed back to his work.

Sikander nursed his coffee a little longer while he thought about Elena Pavon. "Darvesh, what do you think?" he finally asked.

"About what, Nawabzada?"

"Did Elena Pavon send us to Zafer so that pirates could ambush her competitor's ship?"

"I believe you have already worked out the answer to that question for yourself, sir."

"That's not an answer."

"It is, Nawabzada. The question you are really asking is whether I *believe* Ms. Pavon is the sort of person who could conceive a scheme to use Zerzura's pirates to attack her rivals and arrange for the attack to take place after diverting you to another target. I have no reason to think that I know her any better than you do." Darvesh shrugged. "Could she have feigned her outrage over the attack on her ship? I suppose that a masterful liar and manipulator could do so convincingly, but in my experience such people are thankfully rare. No, you do not doubt Ms. Pavon's story, Nawabzada—you doubt your judgment where she is concerned."

"Am I that transparent?" Sikander asked.

"You are drawn to powerful and confident women, sir." Darvesh gathered up the coffee tray. "The thing that surprises me is that you are finally beginning to recognize that."

Forty-nine days after departing for a forty-day patrol, *Decisive* returned to the Pleiades Squadron home port at Tawahi Island in Neda. Sikander relished the sight of the warm yellow sands and the brilliant tropical waters in the bridge's sweeping display screens, and found that he almost couldn't wait for the destroyer to make its stately descent to the surface—after all the troubles and complications of their long cruise, he was more than ready for some shorter workdays and actual weekends that featured a little fishing or golf. If Neda was not exactly Kashmir or New Perth, it was home of a sort, and no one could complain about the weather.

"Helm, come left to course three-five-three, down fifteen," Ensign Carter ordered. The sensor officer had the conn for the landing maneuver, another junior officer practicing her ship handling. Sikander tried hard not to dwell on the idea of twenty-six thousand tons of steel moving at a thousand kilometers per hour in the hands of someone who'd graduated from the Academy less than a year ago, and studiously adopted an expression of mild interest in Grace Carter's approach. "Atmospheric maneuvering: all engines, ahead one-half."

Sikander shifted in his command couch, and decided that a little helpful advice wouldn't hurt the ensign's ego too much. "Take your time, Ms. Carter. I appreciate your enthusiasm, but we don't want to greet the base with a sonic boom. It's not too early to slow down a bit more."

"Er, yes, sir," Carter replied. "Helm, all engines, ahead one-third."

"Atmospheric maneuvering, all engines ahead one-third," Quartermaster Birk at the ship's helm replied.

"We've got gravity helping us now," Sikander continued. "The planet wants us on the ground sooner rather than later. Speed is what gets you into trouble with docking maneuvers, both in space and on the surface." *Or that's what Captain Garvey told me a hundred times or so when I was an ensign on* Adept, *he recalled. Not that I listened very well. Then again, I suppose captains have been telling ensigns to be a little more careful with their ships since navies sailed the waters of ancient Earth.*

"Yes, sir. I'll remember, sir."

"You're doing fine, Ms. Carter," Sikander said in the most reassuring tone he could manage. He even managed to remain silent when *Decisive* splashed down hard enough to raise a two-meter wave in the mooring basin . . . which, fortunately, was not lined with spectators waiting for the ship to dock. Ensign Carter winced, but she remembered the rest of the mooring commands well enough, and finished up the landing sequence without any more trouble.

"Not bad, Ms. Carter," Sikander told her when she finished. "A little less speed next time; twenty-six thousand tons have a certain amount of momentum, after all. Secure from landing detail and establish the in-port watch, if you please. XO, pass the word: General liberty for all hands not in the duty section."

"My pleasure, Captain," Fraser replied. "Shall I tell the squadron we're on our way?"

"Please do. Meet me on the quarterdeck in fifteen minutes— I'm sure Captain Broward is anxious to hear what we've been up to for the last seven weeks." Sikander returned to his cabin with a few more gray hairs than he'd had an hour ago, and changed from his shipboard jumpsuit into the working whites Darvesh had laid out for him. Then he headed down to *Decisive's* midships hangar, which doubled as its main access point when she was tied up alongside a pier. Naturally, Amelia Fraser was already waiting for him, and she'd ordered the quarterdeck watch to summon one of the base's courtesy flyers for the trip over to the squadron headquarters building.

"Commander North and Lieutenant Commander Fraser to see Captain Broward," Amelia told the squadron receptionist when they entered the building lobby.

"Welcome back, sir, ma'am," the admin specialist replied. "The captain watched you land. He told me to send you in 'just as soon as your feet were dry,' as he put it."

Sikander exchanged a look with his exec. "Make a note, XO: Let's make sure we don't wash off the pier the next time we set down," he told her. Then they headed back to Broward's office.

Wilson Broward stood at his window, gazing over at the slip where *Decisive* was moored. Sikander marched in and saluted. "Good morning, sir. I am pleased to report *Decisive's* return to base."

Broward turned and acknowledged Sikander's salute, but his brows drew together in an unhappy expression. "So I see. You're almost ten days overdue, Commander—I was about to send out a search party. The last position report I received from *Decisive* was postmarked Meliya, and you indicated that you were heading for some place called Zafer . . . which, I note, was not on any patrol route I approved. Where exactly have you been with my destroyer?"

"It's a long story, sir, but the short version is that we were diverted by the terrorist attack in Meliya, where we received some actionable intelligence about a pirate base. Your standing orders required *Decisive* to investigate—and I think you'll be surprised by what we found."

"We did file a position report from Bursa just a week ago, sir," Amelia added. "We must have beaten the report home."

"Hmmph. Well, it wouldn't be the first time communications in this sector lagged behind events." Broward moved over to his desk and keyed the intercom. "Petty Officer Martinez, clear my schedule for the rest of the morning. Apparently I'm in for a long story."

"Yes, Captain," the admin specialist who ran the office replied. "I'll reschedule your eleven o'clock."

"Thank you," Broward replied. He looked back to Sikander and Amelia, and nodded at the chairs in front of his desk. "Well, let's hear it. You have my undivided attention."

Sikander drew a deep breath, and launched into a verbal summary of the major events in *Decisive*'s cruise: the trouble with generator two and the diversion to Bursa, the discovery of *Carmela Día* and the pursuit of Target Alpha to Tunis, the visit to Dahar—and his encounter with Otto Bleindel in the pasha's palace, which required a fair bit of background all on its own—the rescue and assistance operation in Meliya, and finally the tip about the Zafer base and the successful raid. "We left one pirate vessel disabled at Zafer and handed another over to the Zerzuran authorities at Bursa, along with eighty-seven prisoners," he concluded. "I'm afraid that one ship got away from us, though."

"We recorded *Mazuz*'s course just in case it turns out she was running for another base," Amelia added. "One line of bearing isn't much of a clue, but it's a start."

"Well." Broward slowly digested the news for a moment. Sikander glanced at the clock on the wall and realized he'd been talking for more than an hour . . . but the squadron commander's expression had gone from vexed to troubled to thoughtful during the course of his verbal report. "Well. You've had an eventful cruise. I don't even know where to begin with my questions."

"I'm almost finished with the complete report. I'll send it along later today; it should cover any details I've overlooked." Sikander offered an apologetic shrug. "I am sorry that we got ahead of our regular situation reports, sir. I used my best judgment in responding to some very unusual events."

"As a commanding officer should." The squadron commander leaned back in his expansive chair, thinking. "All right, pending a review of your written report, I'll endorse your decision to divert from your scheduled patrol. While you should have brought *Decisive* back home after your trouble with the generator, it seems that your decision to remain on station led to you being in the right place at the right time to stop the mining outpost attack in Bursa and eventually identify the attacker. Maybe it was a lucky break, but we've been waiting months for one of those. You showed some initiative and made sure you didn't miss it."

"Speaking of lucky breaks, sir, I can't help but notice that we started catching up to pirates the minute events upset our schedule," Amelia said. "I think that Zerzura's pirates are aware of our intended movements and have been using that information to avoid Pleiades Squadron."

"My XO makes a good case for it, Captain," Sikander said. "Someone is telling the pirates where we're going and when we're going to be there. It explains why the squadron's had so little luck at pirate-hunting over the last few months, and why *Decisive's* luck suddenly changed."

"Surely you don't believe that the pirates have a spy in my headquarters?" Broward said sharply.

"I don't imagine that any Aquilan personnel are involved, although I suppose it's possible that someone's managed to plant a listening device in the office or set up a backdoor into the squadron's information systems," Amelia answered. "Local contractors look after the janitorial services, after all. No, sir, I think it's much more likely that the pirates have friends in Zerzura's planetary governments or security establishments. Paying a spaceport administrator or a corrupt security officer for information on our expected arrivals and departures would seem a lot easier than spying on us here."

"So you're saying that the Zerzuran authorities are helping their pirates to stay out of our way." The squadron commander's scowl returned. "Damn. That's even worse than a spy on our base because we can't put a stop to it! How can we do anything about cleaning up the sector if the cops and the robbers are on the same side?"

"It's probably a small number of informants and sympathizers, not systemic corruption," Sikander pointed out. "But until we identify the sources of the leaks, we shouldn't provide advance notice of our port visits to anybody in Zerzura."

"Or we could incorporate more uncertainty in our schedules," Amelia suggested. "Instead of requesting a port visit in Tunis on the fifteenth, tell the planetary governor's office we'll be there sometime between the twelfth and the eighteenth. Or just be rude and start showing up a day early here or a couple of days late there—all we really need is a little more unpredictability, sir."

"The Caliphate's likely to give our Foreign Ministry an earful about that," said Broward. "They're already touchy about Aquilan patrols in their systems."

"How long will it take for a complaint from Zerzura to reach Terra and for someone in the Caliphate bureaucracy to act on it, sir?" Sikander asked. "I think we could shake things up for at least three months before someone officially told us to mind our manners."

"Under most circumstances I'd agree with you, Sikander. Unfortunately, I've already received instructions to be very careful about Zerzuran sensibilities. The Foreign Ministry wants us to be on our best behavior while our man in Marid Pasha's capital tries to convince the pasha that Aquila can be a better friend than Dremark."

"Mr. Darrow." Sikander nodded. "I had the opportunity to speak with him several times during our stop at Dahar. And, as I noted earlier, we actually ran into the Dremish envoys while we were there."

"Then let me share some news about that you probably haven't heard yet." Broward's frown deepened. "Two days ago, our intelligence dispatches reported a major deal between Dremark and Zerzura. It seems that the Imperial Navy has agreed to sell Marid Pasha's government three old cruisers: *Zyklop, Drachen,* and

Meduse. They're already on their way to Dahar, along with a repair ship to assist in fitting them out."

"Three *cruisers?*" Sikander made no attempt to manage his
surprise. That would be the most powerful squadron within a
hundred light-years—the pasha's new fleet would outgun Pleiades
Squadron two or three times over. For that matter, three heavy
cruisers could defy the entire Bolívaran fleet or a substantial portion of the Velaran fleet, too. "What in the world does Marid Pasha need that much firepower for?"

"That's the question, isn't it?" Broward said. He glanced out the
office windows at the row of Aquilan destroyers moored alongside
Tawahi Island's concrete quays; their white hulls gleamed in the
tropical sunshine. "Those cruisers might be old, but then again,
most of the squadrons and fleets in this region of space are making do with ships of the same vintage. Certainly no pirate in Zerzura is going to be able to stand up to even one of the pasha's new
warships."

"Using heavy cruisers for antipiracy patrols is just one step removed from swatting flies with sledgehammers, isn't it?" Amelia
observed.

"I suppose the pasha wants to make a statement." Broward gave
a small shrug, and returned his attention to Sikander and Amelia.
"But until Marid Pasha gets his new ships in service, we'll keep
on doing our best, and we'll mind our manners while our diplomats try to top Dremark's offer. Smashing up a pirate base is a
good start, though. Welcome back, Commander, and enjoy some
well-deserved rest. It sounds like you and your crew earned it."

Decisive shifted into its in-port schedule: officers' call at 0730, a
workday that started at 0800, lunch at noon, knocking off around
1700, dinner at 1800 for anyone who chose to remain on board,

and an informal department-head gathering at 1900 after most of the crew and the more junior members of the wardroom had gone ashore for the evening. Officers with families living on base or in the town nearby usually skipped dinner to get home earlier, although Amelia Fraser and Jaime Herrera often stuck around long enough to check in at the department-head gathering—it was something of an unwritten rule in the Commonwealth Navy that a ship's senior officers and leading petty officers started their days before anybody else and were the last to head home in the evening. Sikander had certainly paid his own dues in long days during his department-head tours, although he tried to encourage his own senior staff not to overdo it when they'd just returned from a seven-week patrol. He made a point of canceling the evening gathering a couple of times a week and heading for his Tawahi Island bungalow at 1705 promptly just to make sure his people had no reason to stick around.

Ten days after their return, Michael Girard presented his findings about the *Vashaoth Teh* bombing to the department-head meeting. He brought along Ensign Jay Sekibo, the ship's communications officer and one of the division officers in his department. "I apologize for the long delay," Girard began. "Frankly, planning the Zafer raid and analyzing our intelligence take from the pirate ships we captured pushed the Meliya bombing to the bottom of my department's to-do list. Fortunately Mr. Sekibo kept the investigation on his radar, and I think he's turned up something important."

"An understandable conflict of priorities," Sikander admitted. "Very well, then. Mr. Sekibo, what did you find?"

Taller and more slender than the already tall and slender New Caledonians and High Albionans who made up much of *Decisive*'s wardroom, Ensign Sekibo was a young aristocrat from Great Fionia, the son of the Senator Surmsey. Most Aquilan populations

represented a centuries-old blend of the regional Terran pheno-
types, but Great Fionia's people retained a little more of eastern
Africa in their makeup than most other Aquilans. If Sekibo was
nervous about briefing Sikander and the ship's department heads,
he gave no sign of it. "I don't believe the bombing was a suicide
mission, Captain," he said, pointing a remote at the nearest vid
display to pull up his report. "This is a sensor log we downloaded
from the station's records when we arrived on the scene. You see
this signal, here? It's a simple short-range transmission of a nu-
meric code: 62463791. It carries no other information, and repeats
that code continuously for about five minutes before fading out.
Note the time stamp, sir: It's *exactly* one hour before the bomb
went off underneath the Velaran cruiser."

"That looks suspiciously like a remotely triggered timer," Amelia Fraser said.

"That's what my team thought, too, ma'am." Sekibo advanced
the presentation he'd prepared. "Here's a sensor log from *Duali-
fin*, a freighter that was in an orbit close by the station at the time
the signal was sent. You'll see that they recorded the signal for a
considerably longer time. We think that the transmitter left the
station shortly after it was activated, but the ship *outside* the station continued to pick up the signal for a few more minutes until
it passed out of range."

"The message the Meliyan Human Revolution released went
out of its way to praise the 'martyrs of the cause,'" Amar Shah
said. "What sort of suicide bomber uses a trigger with a one-hour
delay and then leaves the scene of the attack?"

"Someone who's not very interested in the suicide part of the
plan," Jaime Herrera said. "Damn. I have to say, it comforted me
just a little bit to think that the assholes who'd set off that bomb
had erased themselves from existence."

"How did you work this out, Mr. Sekibo?" Amelia asked the comm officer.

"I had Petty Officer Jackson and Petty Officer Morton check back through the sensor data we copied from the station, looking for anything out of the ordinary. It turns out that the station recorded hundreds of routine transmissions an hour, and the Meliyan authorities shared more than seventy hours of recordings leading up to the bombing. It took our people a while to find the anomalous signal."

"Good work, Mr. Sekibo," said Amelia. "Make sure you put in Jackson and Morton for some extra recognition, too. That must have been some tedious work."

"Thank you, ma'am. I will."

"If the claim of martyrdom is a lie, there might be other claims in that message that are less than truthful," Sikander said thoughtfully. "For example, anything the Meliyan Human Revolution said about how they came by a microfusion warhead."

"Or the claim that there's such a thing as the Meliyan Human Revolution in the first place," Michael Girard said. "While Mr. Sekibo was poring over comm logs, I went and took another look through news reports and our own intelligence files for anything about radical groups operating in Meliya. Sir, no one ever heard of these people before they managed to destroy a Velaran warship. It's a very impressive debut, so to speak—most radical groups need years to build up that sort of capability."

"A false-flag operation, then," Amar Shah said with a frown. "That begs the question of who is really responsible for the attack. And what did they hope to achieve by blaming it on Meliyan radicals?"

I have a guess, Sikander thought, but he kept it to himself. As convenient as it would be to blame Otto Bleindel, he didn't *know* that the Dremish agent was actually responsible . . . and it was generally a bad habit to assume you knew the answer to a question just because it fit nicely with your preconceptions. Maybe Bleindel had something to do with it and maybe he didn't, but until Sikander could form a guess as to *why* the Dremish would have wanted to wreck a Velaran cruiser, he needed to make sure he kept looking for answers. *Then again, just because it's what I expect to find doesn't mean that it's wrong.* Between the evidence of corruption in Zerzura's security apparatus, terrorism in Meliya, the dark suspicions Michael Girard had raised about what Elena Pavon stood to gain from the pirate attack on the Grupo Constelación freighter, and the specter of Dremish adventurism, he was more than ready for an answer or two.

He sighed and pushed his turmoil aside. "That's the next step, Mr. Shah. We think we know who didn't do it, so let's see if we can develop some leads about who might be responsible. If Mr. Sekibo is right about someone leaving the station after starting the timer, that's the place to start looking."

"Aye, Captain," Girard replied. "But small craft of all sorts were coming and going from the station almost constantly, including regular orbiter service to cities down on the surface."

"Do what you can, Mr. Girard. In the meantime, let's share our findings with the Meliyan authorities. Mr. Sekibo, please draft a message for Meritor Pokk Skirriseh that summarizes your discovery, and include the relevant portions of the sensor logs." Sikander paused, thinking over the implications of Jay Sekibo's discovery and what it might mean for the Aquilan squadron based at Neda. "I'd better have a word with Captain Broward, too. I have a guess or two about who might be responsible for a covert operation like the one you've just pieced together, and I'd sleep better if I knew we were keeping our guard up here on Tawahi."

The next day, another of Pleiades Squadron's destroyers returned home: Giselle Dacey's *Harrier,* finishing up her own extended patrol in Zerzuran space. Sikander sent a friendly message welcoming his fellow captain back to base, and invited Dacey and her exec to a barbecue at his home whenever it was convenient for them. He didn't expect a reply for a few hours, so he went back to the day's work: answering the Office of Construction and Repair's queries about the failure of generator two, and trying to get Neda Naval Shipyard to prioritize a very thorough inspection of each and every weld in *Decisive's* power plant. But to his surprise, she called him from the squadron headquarters shortly after *Harrier* landed.

"Sikander? I'm here with Captain Broward, going over *Harrier's* patrol," Dacey began. "He tells me that you found that ship you chased to Bursa in the Zafer system about twenty days ago."

"The *Mazuz,*" Sikander answered. "She got away while we were dealing with *The'eb* and *Qarash.* Did you spot her somewhere else?"

"I think so," Dacey said. "Eight days ago, in Tejat Minor. She arrived shortly after we did. We got a good look at her arrival vector, which didn't line up with any other Zerzuran systems."

"That's interesting. We got a good look at her departure vector when she made transit out of Zafer, and she wasn't headed for any known port when she left." Sikander grinned at his empty cabin. One line of bearing provided direction, but not distance. Two lines of bearing from separated locations meant that they might have a fix on where *Mazuz* had gone after fleeing Zafer. And if that spot wasn't any known port or outpost, it could very well be something that served as another pirate base.

Captain Broward joined in the conversation, raising his voice to be picked up on Giselle's comm unit. "Commander North, why don't you come on over to my office, and bring that navigational data with you. I'm very curious about where exactly this

Mazuz went in those twelve days between *Decisive*'s action in Zafer and *Harrier*'s encounter in Tejat Minor."

"I am, too, sir," Sikander said, getting up from behind his desk. "I'm on my way."

14

CSS *Decisive*, Unknown System

ecisive cut her warp generator and returned to the rest of the universe with her battle stations fully manned six days and ten hours after departing Neda. Sikander had experienced longer transits, and he'd experienced transits that he knew were likely to carry him into a fight soon after arrival, but he'd never spent the better part of a week hurtling toward a destination that he knew *nothing* about—and, for that matter, no one else aboard the destroyer had, either. Even at Zafer *Decisive*'s crew had known they'd find an old mining station . . . but today, the only thing they knew for certain about the nameless red dwarf where the transit lines established by the pirate ship's departure and arrival intersected was that no one had recorded a visit to the system since a Terran Caliphate survey ship had looked over the place more than two centuries ago. Finding no valuable resources or useful worlds, the surveyors had moved on to more interesting targets without even bothering to name it.

Well, we're here now, thought Sikander. *We'll find what we find.*

"Clear arrival, Captain," Ensign Carter reported. "*Harrier* bears zero-nine-five, distance nine million kilometers."

"Very well," Sikander answered. As at Zafer, he'd opted for a longer transit so that *Decisive* would arrive with a lower velocity and be able to maneuver aggressively that much sooner if need be, and he'd succeeded in persuading Giselle Dacey of the advantages the slower approach offered. "Mr. Girard, depower and retract the warp ring. Let's take a look around."

"Aye, sir."

Sikander let his operations officer see to the process of securing from the warp transit while he studied the system in which *Decisive* had just arrived. The sun was a Class M red dwarf—not surprising, since something like seventy-five percent of the stars in the galaxy were of the same type—and its planetary system consisted of three barren rocks in close orbits around their dim parent star, plus a frigid neptunian-type gas giant with a well-developed ring system and a number of moons, orbiting about 2.5 AU out. Nothing in the system seemed remotely appealing for human habitation, although of course dome-and-tunnel stations or space-based habitats could be built almost anywhere someone cared to set one up. *So why here?* he wondered, staring at the display. *Strategic positioning?* That could be enough—the red dwarf and its paltry collection of planets happened to be located less than a week's transit from four of Zerzura's five major systems. Dozens of other empty systems in the region were similarly convenient to inhabited worlds and busy trade routes, but pirates looking for a secret hideout had to pick one sooner or later, didn't they?

"*Harrier* actual calling, sir," Ensign Sekibo reported from the communications station.

"I'll take it," Sikander replied. He keyed the unit on his own console. "This is *Decisive* actual. Go ahead, over."

"*Decisive, Harrier.*" Giselle Dacey's voice was crisp and professional on the comm circuit. "I propose we split up and search independently. I'll come to course three-three-zero down twenty, you continue on as you're going. We'll cover more ground that way, over."

"*Harrier, Decisive.* I concur and will keep on in this direction for a bit." Dacey was a little senior to Sikander and therefore in overall command, but when two captains of equal rank operated together, the etiquette of the situation meant that orders tended to be couched as suggestions. She would refrain from giving Sikander direct orders, and in return Sikander intended to follow her lead. He didn't mind; as it turned out, he trusted Giselle Dacey's judgment. "We'll stay in touch. *Decisive,* out."

The two destroyers flipped to point their most powerful drive plates in the direction of their travel, *Harrier* about sixty degrees off *Decisive's* heading, and started braking from their transit-emergence velocities—even with a low-speed transit they'd unbubbled with inherent velocities approaching ten thousand kilometers per second, and if they did find anything in this system they'd need to bleed off a lot of that speed to avoid overshooting any points of interest. Sikander settled into his command station, watching his bridge team beginning the search; their course carried them in the general direction of the system's solitary gas giant, a few light-minutes ahead of their arrival point. An hour passed, and then two, as *Decisive's* quartermasters quietly updated the old charts for the system and the sensor techs studied their instruments for signs of human habitation—radio chatter, thermal signatures, the electromagnetic anomalies created by fusion power plants in operation, radar pings from the dense alloys of a ship's hull or a station's structure.

As the search dragged on without result, Sikander began to wonder whether the unknown system was nothing more than a convenient meeting point, a navigational dogleg where *Mazuz* had ended its flight from Zafer before maneuvering to line up a transit to its eventual destination in Tejat Minor. *If you believe an enemy is observing your transit, you might avoid fleeing straight back to your base,* he reminded himself. The Aquilan navy's operational doctrines called for two-leg or even three-leg fleet movements when it was important to conceal information about where a fleet had come from or where it was going. But it was also true that each time a ship charged its warp rings, it expended some difficult-to-replace exotic matter. The Navy maintained its own fueling stations and could afford to keep a ship's magnetic bottles topped off, but Sikander doubted that outlaws could openly purchase actuating material for their warp rings in the same systems where they hunted their prey. And if he was right about that, then Zerzura's pirates would want to keep their warp transits to a minimum, even if that meant a greater risk of discovery. *Mazuz* wouldn't have wanted to waste a transit just to deny *Decisive* a look at its transit course . . . probably. *But she might have done it once before when she evaded us between Bursa and Tunis*, he realized, and scowled at the empty sensor display.

He was just about to order his crew to secure from their action stations when the ship's tactical display suddenly updated with a new contact. "Thermal signature, range six million kilometers," Michael Girard said. "The gas giant's ring system, Captain. There's a station of some sort on the surface of a shepherd moon."

"A good hiding spot—plenty of sensor clutter with the rings, and the planet's throwing out a lot of electromagnetic activity. No wonder it took a while to spot them." Sikander smiled in satisfaction; his guess about *Mazuz*'s movements seemed better founded than it had just a few minutes ago. "Please pass our data along to *Harrier*, and take us in."

"Aye, sir. Helm, come left to new course two-nine-seven up five, maximum military acceleration."

Decisive's display rolled gently as the destroyer came to her new course, and Sikander felt the faint tug of her acceleration changing. He keyed his comm channel for the other destroyer. "*Harrier*, this is *Decisive*. It looks like there's an installation of some sort in the ring system of the gas giant. We're proceeding to investigate, over."

"Roger that," Dacey answered. "You're a few minutes closer than we are, but we'll be right behind you. Good luck, *Decisive. Harrier* out."

"We've got some better imagery for that station, Captain." Girard pointed at a screen showing the highly magnified view from one of *Decisive's* powerful hull cams. The station appeared to consist of a grounded freighter, surrounded by surface structures and domes— an outlaw fort built around the hulk of a large ship. "The grounded vessel is *Jalid Conveyor,* a bulk carrier that's been missing for several years now."

"One small mystery solved, I suppose," Sikander mused. The idea of using a grounded freight carrier as the basis for a surface fort made quite a bit of sense. Its power systems, sensors, and cargo modules must have been useful in setting up a habitat, and he had to imagine that it was difficult for pirates to sell a stolen ship of that size without risking discovery.

"Target separation, sir," Ensign Carter announced. "Two ships appear to be getting under way from *Jalid's* holds."

"They just now spotted us?" Jaime Herrera asked from his position at the weapons console.

Sikander shook his head. "I doubt it, Guns. They must have seen our terminal cascade when we arrived. They've been keeping dark and quiet in the hopes that we wouldn't spot them. But now that we've turned toward them—"

"They can see that the game's up," Herrera finished for him. He studied his display, and grinned fiercely. "They should've run when they had the chance, Captain. We'll be on them before they line up a transit, and this time we brought a friend."

"So we did. Mr. Girard, let me have a general channel, if you please."

Girard nodded to the comm techs on the bridge. "It's ready, Captain."

Sikander tapped the button. "Attention, all outlaw vessels and stations in this system. This is CSS *Decisive* of the Aquilan Commonwealth Navy. Surrender and prepare to be boarded. We will fire upon any vessel or station firing upon us or attempting to escape. This is your one and only warning. *Decisive*, out."

"They're still running, sir," Carter reported.

"We'll give them a minute to think it over. Mr. Girard, what can you tell me about those ships getting under way?"

"Designating them Target Alpha and Target Bravo, sir. Umm, Target Alpha appears to be a heavily modified salvage tug, definitely armed—I can see several K-cannon mounts—and fitted with improvised armor plating. She's big for a pirate. Target Bravo is a modified light freighter like we saw at Zafer . . ." Girard's voice trailed off for a long moment, and then he straightened up and swore. "I'll be damned! Captain, that's *Qarash*!"

"That's impossible," Amelia Fraser said over the command circuit. "We just handed her over to the Zerzurans! Are you sure about that, Tactical?"

"I'm certain, XO. I recognize the wear patterns on the bow plating. It's *Qarash*."

Sikander leaned forward, studying the imagery. He couldn't believe it either, but Michael Girard didn't make mistakes like that. Sure enough, the silhouette matched their earlier records, even down to the pattern of bare metal on the bow from particulate impacts during warp transits. "No, it's not impossible," he said slowly. "It's been three weeks since we left her in Bursa. That's more than enough time for someone to send a crew to retrieve *Qarash* and bring her here, if the local naval station was instructed to release the ship—or chose to do so on their own."

"So Kaptani Hanan simply handed the ship right back to the

pirates as soon as we went on our way?" Amelia's voice took on a tone of disgust. "Good God! I thought the Zerzurans might be quietly passing intelligence to their friends in the pirate fleet. But simply letting them go free? What in the hell is going on around here, Captain?"

"That's a question I'd like answered just as much as you would, XO. It certainly seems like compelling evidence for your theory about Zerzuran complicity." *And Elena Pavon's suspicions, too,* Sikander reminded himself. The Pegasus-Pavon director had sent her intelligence about Zafer to him instead of notifying the Zerzuran authorities because she feared the pirates might have their sources in the local security organizations.

If Amelia felt vindicated, she kept her I-told-you-sos to herself. Sikander glanced down at the inset on his display that showed the faces of the key officers in the command circuit; she'd quickly moved past her anger to cold calculation, her eyes dark beneath a knitted brow. "How high up does this go?" she asked. "Are we dealing with one rotten local commander, the whole Zerzuran fleet, or the pasha himself?"

"I intend to bring that up with whoever we find aboard *Qarash* . . . just as soon as we catch her again." Sikander returned his attention to the unfolding tactical picture, and called Giselle Dacey. "*Harrier, Decisive.* I think we're going to have to split up to intercept the two fleeing ships, over."

"*Decisive, Harrier.* I concur. You take Target Alpha; you're in a better position to cut her off. We'll deal with Target Bravo, over."

"*Harrier, Decisive.* We'll get Alpha, acknowledged. Be advised that Target Bravo is the pirate vessel *Qarash*—the same one we captured at Zafer, over."

Dacey paused a moment before replying. "Understood, *Decisive.* What the devil is she doing here? *Harrier,* out."

Sikander put *Qarash* out of his mind for the moment, leaving her to Giselle Dacey while he focused on the first pirate ship. "Mr. Girard, intercept Target Alpha. Cut her legs out from under her, but try not to destroy her outright."

"Yes, sir." Girard quickly examined the course projections. "Should we cut through the planet's ring, Captain? We'd knock twenty minutes off our time to intercept."

"What is the composition of the ring?"

"Dust and ice crystals, sir. It's less than ten meters thick."

Sikander thought it over for a moment. He wouldn't want to try it at something close to a warp transit velocity, but they'd had a couple of hours to decelerate now, and their speed relative to the particles that made up the ring wouldn't be much more than typical orbital velocities. As long as there weren't any sizable rocks in their path, they should be fine, and rings tended to be a lot more diffuse than most people thought. "Do it," he ordered Girard. "But make sure we pass through bow-first." *Decisive's* heaviest armor was on the bow, since ships traveling in warp bubbles encountered tiny specks of dust even in interstellar space.

"Helm, come right to course zero-zero-eight," Girard ordered, and then he keyed the general announcement circuit. "All hands, this is the bridge. We're about to pass through a bit of dust and ice. Prepare for minor bow impact in . . . ninety seconds."

"Sir, we're being illuminated by fire-control systems," Ensign Carter announced. "Target Alpha and the *Jalid* fort are both locked on to us."

"Weapons, illuminate the targets that are illuminating us," Girard said.

"Illuminating Target Alpha and the *Jalid* fort," Herrera replied. "Alpha's out of effective range, but we can take a shot at the fort."

"Very well." Girard looked over to Sikander. "Captain, what do you—"

"Laser attack, port side!" one of the sensor techs—Petty Officer

Diaz—shouted in warning. *Decisive* shuddered under the strike, as alarms sounded throughout the bridge and the damage-control display suddenly blinked red. A laser didn't deliver any kinetic energy to speak of and didn't hammer a hull the way a K-cannon shot did, but a sufficiently powerful weapon could vaporize a bit of hull, and that small explosion could give a ship a kick, or a series of small kicks in the case of a pulsed weapon.

"Helm, roll the ship," Girard ordered. "But make sure we're bow-on to the plane of the ring ahead."

"Aye, sir!" Chief Pilot Bell, the woman at the helm controls, answered. She expertly spun *Decisive* on her axis, rotating the area of hull under laser attack away from the point of contact to keep the weapon from burning through the spot where it had struck. A ragged, glowing scar of hot metal scribed its way around the hull as the ship turned away; the shuddering of hull alloy burning away into the void continued as the bridge displays rotated dizzyingly.

"What's hitting us?" Sikander demanded.

"A powerful ground-based system from the fort around *Jalid*, sir," Ensign Carter replied. "They burned out a lot of our hull cams on that side, but we've got imagery from just before it hit."

"It looks like some kind of converted mining drill," Amelia Fraser observed; she must have been studying the same imagery the sensor officer was looking at.

"We're more than a million kilometers from that moon!" Jaime Herrera protested.

"It's just a question of focus and power," Amelia pointed out. "They've got a whole moon to dump thermal energy into, so they're not worried about any kind of heat budget."

"Mr. Girard, please remind the pirates that forts can't dodge K-cannon fire," Sikander told Girard.

"Main battery, engage the *Jalid* fort," Michael Girard ordered. "General-purpose rounds—take out the laser battery!"

"Avoid hitting *Jalid* proper unless you see her attempt to get under way," Sikander added. "We want to preserve any intelligence that might be down there."

"Aye, sir—engaging the laser battery. Salvo port!" Herrera called out. An instant later, *Decisive's* eight K-cannons whined shrilly as their powerful electromagnets hurled a flight of g-p projectiles—designed to squash against soft targets for maximum damage, as opposed to hardened armor-piercing projectiles designed to pierce tougher targets—against the distant station. The recoil jarred the bridge. "Sir, at this distance, we've got a nine-minute flight time. Should I keep firing, or see whether the first salvo is effective?"

"Let's see what three salvos do," Sikander decided. Nine minutes of continuous fire would drop something like fifty more salvos on the target, and he had to imagine there wouldn't be much left of *Jalid* or the station built around the hulk if they kept throwing metal downrange during the first salvo's flight. "But give them one load of armor-piercing shot to make sure we get that damned laser."

"Ring impact in ten seconds!" Chief Bell called out in warning.

"Very well," Sikander replied. He activated the ship's general circuit. "All hands, brace for bow impact!"

Chief Bell turned *Decisive* at the last instant to point her bow directly ahead—and the destroyer plunged through the plane of the gas giant's ring in the blink of an eye, exploding out of the haze of dust and ice crystals in a spectacular display. The impact jarred the ship as scores of tiny grains peppered the ship's nose, but it was no worse than the shudder of the main battery firing. Sikander breathed a sigh of relief; the Admiralty was not very forgiving of captains who crippled their own ships through reckless maneuvers. "Well done, Chief," he said. "Mr. Girard, resume our pursuit of Target Alpha, please."

"Laser fire ceased, sir!" Ensign Carter reported.

"Our salvo's still on the way," Herrera said. "It wasn't us, sir."

Sikander had a guess, but he glanced at the aft-facing hull cams to make sure. "It's the ring. It's between us and the laser now—the dust and ice are attenuating the beam." Of course, it wouldn't be long before the laser's crew realized the same thing, which meant they might decide to change targets in the eight-odd minutes they had left before *Decisive's* salvo arrived. He signaled Giselle Dacey again: *"Harrier, Decisive.* Be advised there's a powerful laser battery in that surface fortification. We've got a few salvos on the way, but be ready to take evasive action, over."

"Decisive, Harrier, thank you for the warning. We saw them firing on you and sent them a salvo of our own. We're now engaging Target Bravo, over."

"Main battery, shift your fire to Target Alpha," Girard ordered. "We're getting close enough to try a long-range salvo or two."

"Shifting fire, aye," Herrera replied. *Decisive's* turrets slewed to their new bearings with the hum of training motors. "Salvo starboard!"

Herrera's first few salvos missed the fleeing pirate ship. The converted tug with its improvised armor was not a particularly agile target, but it was nimble enough to evade extreme long-range attacks. Its return fire was heavier than Sikander expected; at least one of its mismatched K-cannons was a cruiser-weight gun, significantly more powerful than anything *Decisive* carried. But the pirates lacked Aquilan fire control and experience in dealing with targets that could shoot back; *Decisive* jinked and twisted away from the incoming rounds, blasting away with her own kinetic cannons while dodging the pirate gunboat's attacks. On *Decisive's* fourth salvo, a single hit shattered one of the pirate's clumsy armor panels and damaged the ship's retracted warp ring. A moment later, the pirate altered course, bringing her full broadside into play.

"She's turning to fight," said Amelia over the command circuit.

"They've figured out they can't get away," Sikander replied. "Their mistake—a stand-up fight suits me well enough. Mr. Herrera, shoot out her weapons systems, if you please."

"We're on it, Captain," the gunnery officer replied. "You might want to take a look behind us. Our salvos should be arriving at the fort any second now."

"Thank you, Mr. Herrera." Sikander shifted his attention to the moon nearly two million kilometers behind them. The planet's rings no longer obscured his view—the pursuit of Target Alpha had carried *Decisive* above the thin bands of dust and ice. For a long moment, nothing happened. Then a ripple of powerful blasts racked the installation on the moon's surface; the dome containing the converted mining laser disappeared in a bubble of molten metal, and moon ice vaporized instantly to a thin plasma of white-hot hydrogen and oxygen. A few seconds later, too soon for *Decisive*'s second salvo, another line of explosions walked across the pirate fort, blasting the surface structures into incandescent wreckage. *Harrier*'s *fire*, Sikander realized. *And we've got two more salvos on the way to Fort Jalid.* The pirates' ground battery wouldn't trouble *Decisive* or *Harrier* again.

He returned his attention to the engagement in front of him just in time to see *Decisive*'s main battery score two more hits on the armored pirate. One grazed the pirate's forward turret, wrecking the stubby snout of the cannon mounted within; the second hit a little aft of the center of mass. "Target's acceleration dropping, sir," Carter called out. "Her power output just fell off, too. I think that last hit got one of her generators."

"Very well. Mr. Girard, hold your fire for a moment and give me a comm channel to that ship."

"Holding fire, aye, sir. You're on."

Sikander tapped his console. "This is the commanding officer of CSS *Decisive*, for the vessel twenty-five thousand kilometers ahead of me. Cease fire and heave to. We don't want to kill you, but if you force us to keep firing we're not going to be responsible for the consequences. Surrender, and you will receive a fair trial and the right to defend yourselves in court. If I have to give the order to resume fire, we're going to put eight armor-piercing rounds through your center of mass and keep doing so until you're disabled or destroyed. So which is it going to be? Over."

No one replied for a moment, but then the comm unit crackled, and a man replied in Jadeed-Arabi. "*Decisive*, this is *Balina*. Hold your fire. We surrender."

"*Balina*, this is *Decisive*. Your surrender is accepted. Reduce your acceleration to zero, and train your remaining weapons directly away from us. We are coming alongside to board you, over."

"We understand, *Decisive*. *Balina*, out."

Sikander let out a sigh of relief. "Mr. Girard, bring us alongside. Mr. Herrera, keep your battery trained on Target Alpha. If you see one of those cannons moving back into a firing position, resume fire immediately. I wouldn't put it past them to try something stupid when we approach."

"Aye, Captain. We'll keep her covered."

It took almost half an hour—matching courses and speeds could be tedious even if both ships cooperated to meet in the middle, and Sikander frankly didn't trust *Balina*'s ability to comply. While *Decisive* maneuvered to close the distance on the surrendered pirate vessel, *Harrier* successfully subdued *Qarash* with a few shots across the bow—apparently the pirates' understanding with the Zerzuran fleet in Bursa did not quite extend to getting the impounded ship back with its weapons ready for use, and they hadn't yet had the opportunity to rearm. "We're heading back to the moon installation to see what's left," Giselle Dacey told Sikander when she reported *Qarash*'s capture. "I doubt the laser crew survived, but our prisoners say that there were a couple of hundred people living in *Jalid* and the structures nearby, and not all of them had time to get to one of the ships."

Sikander checked his navigational plot. "We'll be there just as soon as I take my prisoners aboard and send a prize crew over to *Balina*—call it an hour or so. Congratulations, *Harrier*. I would say we've done a good day's work. *Decisive*, out."

He ordered the ship's security detachment—a force of twenty-five armed sailors under Zoe Worth's command—over to *Balina* in the ship's launch. *Decisive*'s K-cannons remained trained on the pirate vessel at a mere ten kilometers' distance to protect the boat in transit. Then, when the sublieutenant sent back her prisoners, Sikander went down to the hangar bay to see his captives for himself. Darvesh joined him, silently handing Sikander a sidearm as they waited for the airlock to cycle. "A routine precaution, sir," the tall Kashmiri explained. "They are criminals, after all."

"Thank you, Darvesh." Sikander had three masters-at-arms and a half-dozen armed crewhands around him already and didn't imagine that anyone aboard the launch was in any position to storm *Decisive*'s hangar, but it was Darvesh's job to prepare for the unlikely. If a little elementary caution reassured the valet, Sikander would allow him to have it. Amelia Fraser joined the group a few minutes later, and buckled on a sidearm of her own.

Decisive's sailors herded twenty or so pirates out of the shuttle and arranged them in a ragged line along one bulkhead of the hangar before carrying out several more on stretchers. Sikander studied the group, taking their measure. Most were ordinary-looking spacers, men in rumpled shipboard jumpsuits with the typical grease stains and worn patches sailors tended to accumulate in their working clothes, and at a glance they reflected the general phenotype common throughout the Zerzuran worlds: a blending of Terran ethnicities not too different from what Sikander saw in the Aquilans around him, if perhaps a little shorter and stockier on average. Only a handful were women, but that didn't surprise Sikander: Zerzura was Caliphate territory, after all, and cultural mores meant that relatively few women worked in space. Some glared at him angrily, but most stared at the deck or slumped in defeat.

They look so normal, Sikander realized. A thousand spaceports throughout the Coalition of Humanity were filled with millions of working spacers who looked just like these fellows. The prisoners he'd hauled in from Zafer had looked much the same. In fact . . . some of the prisoners *were* the same. He recognized one silver-haired fellow with a tattoo around his left eye, another one with thick arms and a heavy brow, a third man with a stork-like build who stood over two meters tall. "God is Truth! We caught some of these people in Zafer!"

"Apparently it wasn't just *Qarash* that was released in Bursa," Amelia said. "They must have let our prisoners go, too."

"We'll make sure they stay arrested this time," Sikander promised. Clearly they couldn't simply hand them back over to the naval authorities in Bursa . . . and he didn't see any reason to think that things would work out any differently in another Zerzuran system, either. Neda, on the other hand, might be a different story. He studied the ragged group of outlaws, and stepped forward. "You, there. Which of you is the captain?"

The pirates exchanged looks, but said nothing. Sikander sighed. "Look, I want one of you to speak for how you're treated and to answer for how you behave. I'll pick someone at random if I have to, but the job belongs to whoever was in charge."

One of the pirates—the older man with the silver hair—pointed over at the stretchers coming off the shuttle. "Al-Kobra. He's over there." The man he pointed out appeared to be unconscious, with a bandage around his head; Dr. Ruiz was already examining him.

"What happened to him?" Amelia asked the older pirate.

"There was a disagreement on the bridge," another man answered. "Al-Kobra wanted to fight it out. Some of us didn't think that was a very good idea."

"Well, you were probably right about that," Sikander said. *Al-Kobra, really?* His Jadeed-Arabi wasn't great, but "the Cobra" sounded much like it did in Standard Anglic. He looked over to Amelia. "We'd better confine him separately. There might be some hard feelings over that, and I'd rather not have prisoners killing each other now that they're in our hands."

Amelia nodded. "I'll see to it, Captain."

"Good." Sikander looked over the ragged group one more time, watching as *Decisive*'s masters-at-arms came forward to escort them to their temporary brig—ironically enough, the very same crew space where at least some of them had been confined before. "Let me know when we've got the *Balina* prisoners secured. We've got another pirate base to search, and I'm anxious to see what we find."

15

Do you have any idea what this is all about?" Hanne Vogt demanded of Otto Bleindel as the flyer whisked them toward the pasha's palace in Mersin. The early-morning sunshine painted the clouds that rolled up to the capital's island hilltops a fiery gold hue, but the diplomat ignored the view. Hanne Vogt was not a morning person, and the fact that she'd been awakened before sunrise by a call from the pasha's office did not put her in a particularly accommodating mood.

"Not really," Bleindel admitted, scowling. He didn't like to be caught off guard, especially in front of his nominal superior in the Empire's special delegation to Zerzura. Unfortunately, a curtly worded summons for Hanne Vogt certainly suggested that Marid Pasha was unhappy about something. He didn't *think* it had anything to do with the various clandestine activities his Security Bureau detachment had conducted in support of the Foreign Office's mission. After all, if the pasha's security forces had somehow figured out his part in the Meliya business or noticed his low-level collection efforts, they would have reacted in some way. "I've seen no sign that the Zerzurans are onto any of our operations, if that's what you're worried about. Whatever's going on today, it doesn't have anything to do with us."

"It's got *something* to do with us, since we're being called into the principal's office." Vogt crossed her legs and leveled a cold, thoughtful look at Bleindel. "Are you sure you haven't forgotten to inform me about an operation?"

Because he actually had a high regard for her competence and liked her better than most Foreign Office careerists he worked with, he told her the truth: "Hanne, there are many things that I don't inform you about. They're not relevant to the Foreign Office's mission to Zerzura, and the first step in preserving secrecy is not discussing things with people who don't strictly need to know. What I *will* tell you is that the reaction of the pasha's government is all wrong if you suspect that he's discovered some operation of ours that he objects to. If we were engaged in some hypothetical action carrying a risk of discovery—not that I am admitting that we are, mind you—and if the pasha had somehow learned of it, then the last thing he'd do is call us in to challenge us about it while allowing it to continue. Either he'd shut it down and scoop up all of our people he could catch, or he'd say nothing at all and initiate a counterintelligence operation. If you don't believe me when I tell you I don't think Marid Pasha is concerned about KBS activities, the pasha's summons should make it clear enough."

Vogt's eyes flashed dangerously—she was not accustomed to being explained to. "Fine, then. But you'd better remember that when it comes to things that might make my job here more difficult—say, a KBS operation that might leave the pasha furious at us if we somehow fuck it up—I define 'need to know' very broadly. And *I* am the head of the Imperial mission here."

"That's why I consulted with you about the Meliya operation. Which, I will point out, achieved exactly the results we hoped for." After sitting on Hanne Vogt's proposal of military aid for almost two months, Marid Pasha had suddenly warmed up to the idea when the Velar Electorate had announced the redeployment of a battle squadron to its Zerzuran border. He'd signed the deal within a week of *Vashaoth Teh*'s destruction.

"At five times the body count you estimated."

"I regret that, but it was important to make it look like the work of a terrorist group." There wasn't much more Bleindel could say; if he defended the number of casualties at Meliya Station as unexpected he would look incompetent, and if he played it off as unimportant he would look like a psychopath. He knew himself well enough to know that at some basic level he was able to dissociate himself from the consequences of his work . . . a trait that came in handy in his profession but provoked quite a bit of alarm in less pragmatic people if he let them catch a glimpse of it. Frankly, he would have preferred a smaller, more surgical operation too, but Aquila's unexpectedly determined efforts to win over Marid Pasha had forced him to put together the Meliyan operation in a hurry, and the basic premise of the thing—an audacious "terrorist" attack—had required a certain carelessness about collateral damage. In the end, he believed that a strong and secure Dremark was a force for stability in human space, and empires didn't grow strong or remain strong without people like him, people who could make difficult choices. Most of the time, Hanne Vogt recognized that his sort of work had a place in Imperial affairs; not all Foreign Office types did.

The flyer alighted on the palace landing pad. Hanne Vogt climbed out without another word to him; either she didn't believe his reassurances about the security of the KBS operations under his control, or she was still fuming about his explanation of things. This time, there was no carefully orchestrated "accidental" meeting at the palace door or a long wait in the antechamber with the beautiful aquarium. An attendant steered Vogt and Bleindel through the sunlight-filled corridors to Marid Pasha's working office without delay, and ushered them into his presence with a murmured introduction: "The representatives of the Empire of Dremark, Your Excellency."

Marid Pasha sat at his desk, reading through his morning mail on a holographic screen. "Very good," he replied. "Send them in."

"Good morning, Marid Pasha," Vogt said smoothly, gliding into the room. Her lingering irritation at Bleindel vanished from her face, replaced with a warm expression as if she suspected nothing to be out of place. "I didn't expect your invitation this morning, but it's a pleasure to see you, as always."

"Ms. Vogt, thank you for coming," replied the pasha, with a thin smile that failed to reach his eyes. He motioned to the chairs facing his desk. "Please, be seated. I wanted to speak to you about the delivery schedule for my new cruisers. It has become important to get them into service as soon as possible."

"Of course, Your Excellency," said Vogt, taking the offered seat. "We're happy to do what we can to accelerate the timetable, although I'm not sure what exactly is possible." She glanced over at Bleindel. "Otto, you've spoken with our people aboard *Neu Kiel*. What's your sense of the timing?"

"Well, they're just getting started," Bleindel said as he sat down beside Vogt. *Drachen*, *Meduse*, and *Zyklop* had arrived in Dahar just three days ago, accompanied by the repair ship *Neu Kiel*. He was no expert in naval construction, but he did have a keen eye for process management, and he had a rough understanding of the steps required to un-mothball the old cruisers, modernize their systems, and shift their operating systems from Dremish to Jadeed-Arabi. "Captain Beck did tell me that *Neu Kiel*'s conversion teams will be working from a fourteen-week refit plan with different jobs overlapping on different ships. *Meduse* is supposed to be ready in ten weeks, *Zyklop* two weeks later, and *Drachen* two weeks after that. I imagine that focusing efforts on one ship at a time could get the first into service a few weeks faster, but that might add to the time needed to finish the other two."

Marid Pasha shook his head. "Ten weeks is too long. I need at least two of those ships in service within a month. If we have to leave some of the refitting work for later, so be it."

"I don't know if that is feasible, but we can check with our technical experts," Hanne Vogt replied. She paused, making a show of carefully considering the pasha's request. "In our earlier discussions, you indicated that the timetable was acceptable. May I ask what's changed?"

"The Aquilan navy, Ms. Vogt. They've conducted two major raids within the last month, killing Zerzurans and seizing the goods and property of Zerzuran companies." The pasha's expression darkened. "In their zeal to suppress piracy in this region, they're bombarding mining outposts and seizing tramp freighters—Caliphate citizens whose safety is my responsibility. I can't have foreign warships roaming throughout my sector attacking my people under unsubstantiated reports of piracy. The sooner ships under my command can establish Zerzuran patrols throughout the area, the sooner I can tell the Aquilans to stay out of our territorial space."

"Two raids?" Vogt asked. "I heard about the unfortunate incident at Zafer, of course. What's the other one?"

"The Aquilan destroyers *Decisive* and *Harrier* raided a station at an unnamed system near Bursa last week," Bleindel told her. "They took two prizes with a couple of hundred accused pirates back to their base. The news just came in on last night's courier from Neda—it's in your morning intelligence summary." Which, of course, Hanne Vogt had not yet read, since Marid Pasha had decided to start everybody's day a couple of hours earlier than normal.

"*Decisive* was the ship involved in the Zafer situation," Vogt said thoughtfully. It might be early in the day, but she never forgot details. "That's Commander North's ship, isn't it?"

"It is." *Of course it's Sikander North again,* Bleindel added silently. *The man has a gift for complicating my work.* Captain Elise Markham of the Aquilan cruiser *Hector* generally received the credit—or the blame—for resisting the Empire's occupation of Gadira eight years ago, but Lieutenant Sikander Singh North had exposed Bleindel's role in arranging events and personally saved the sultan's niece so that she could rally Gadiran loyalists against the much more flexible sultan Bleindel had planned to put on the throne. He reminded himself not to let his annoyance at the Kashmiri captain affect his judgment, and continued. "I also have reports of *Decisive* recovering an abandoned freighter in Bursa and pursuing a suspected pirate to Tunis. Commander North's been a very busy fellow."

"Commander North's talent for finding pirates wherever he chooses to look is becoming a serious problem," said Marid Pasha. "I admire his zeal, but I've been informed that the 'Fort Jalid pirate base,' as the Aquilan press release describes it, is actually an unarmed research outpost operated by the Rihla Development Corporation. The so-called pirates he detained at Neda are ordinary workers and support crews."

Bleindel carefully noted the pasha's misrepresentation of events, but he maintained enough self-possession to keep silent. Nothing in the reports he'd seen late last night suggested that the Aquilans had made any sort of mistake at the Jalid base, as much as he would like to think that perhaps they had. For that matter, there wasn't any reasonable doubt about what the Aquilans had uncovered at the station in Zafer four weeks ago. Marid Pasha surely knew that as well as he did . . . but he'd just told the Empire of Dremark's representative that he doubted the justifications the Aquilan navy provided for its aggressive pirate-hunting. Either the pasha resented the usurpation of his authority, or he had some other reason to be embarrassed by the Aquilans' efforts.

Marid Pasha isn't angry about Aquilans chasing pirates, he realized. *He's angry because the Aquilans are* succeeding. *And he thinks that he'll be able to put a stop to that once he gets his new navy into operation.* That, of course, led to a very interesting question: Why would the governor of Zerzura want to protect the pirates? In Otto Bleindel's experience, the simplest answers were the best place to begin: *Because they're paying him, of course.*

He glanced at Hanne Vogt, wondering if she'd reached the same conclusion. Her expression gave little away, but she shifted in her seat and met his eyes for a brief instant before returning her attention to the pasha. "We can certainly understand your concern over that sort of reckless behavior," she said. "Obviously the Aquilans are receiving some very bad intelligence, or maybe they're trying to intimidate you with this sudden show of aggression."

Bleindel hid a smile—he should have known that she wouldn't miss something like that. He followed her lead. "I doubt that they'd admit to any mistakes with their intelligence. You'll notice that this time they took their illegally detained prisoners back to Neda instead of the nearest Zerzuran port. The Aquilans want to control the narrative, Your Excellency. Exaggerating reports of pirate activity may be an important part of their overall strategy for extending their influence in this region."

"I have enough troubles with the Velar Electorate and this Meliyan terrorist group they're blaming me for," the pasha complained. "The last thing I need is Aquilans drumming up accusations of piracy where it doesn't exist."

"We don't like it much either, but that seems like something you should bring up with Mr. Darrow," said Vogt.

"I will, Ms. Vogt, but let me be perfectly clear: The Caliphate government moves slowly, but sooner or later the bureaucrats back on Old Terra are going to demand explanations for the stories about terrorism and piracy reaching their ears. If Dremark is as interested in doing business in Zerzura as you've led me to believe, then you're going to need to help me deal with this problem, or you might need to make an accommodation with a different governor, one who is not so open-minded as I am." He leaned back in his chair, scowling. "Then again, perhaps I might need to make an accommodation with a different power, one that could be persuaded to adopt a more cooperative attitude toward antipiracy measures in exchange for the right sort of commercial privileges in my sector."

"There's no need for threats," Vogt said sharply. "You've already got three fine Dremish cruisers in your orbital dockyard, and there are more ships on the way. By the end of the year the Zerzura Sector Fleet will be more than capable of meeting your security requirements without any help from foreign navies . . . as well as discouraging those powers from more aggressive designs on Zerzuran worlds. Dremark takes care of its friends, Marid Pasha. Now, I'm not sure whether it is possible to bring even one of the cruisers into service within a month, let alone two, but I have the highest confidence in our technical experts and I know that they'll do their very best once I explain the urgency of the situation to them. Is that sufficient?"

"I suppose it will have to be." Marid Pasha stood, and motioned for his secretary; evidently the meeting was over. Vogt and Bleindel got to their feet as Nenet Fakhoury approached to show them to the door. "I will expect a preliminary answer about the delivery schedule later today, Ms. Vogt. Until then?"

"Of course, Your Excellency," Vogt said warmly, as if Marid Pasha had not just threatened to walk away from their deal and find a new partner, and allowed herself to be ushered out of the room. Bleindel gave the pasha a perfunctory bow and followed her out into the hall, where another attendant waited to escort them back to their flyer.

They said nothing until they were back in the security of the consulate's private flyer. The minute the door closed, Vogt threw herself back in her seat and crossed her arms. "The consulate," she ordered. The marine sergeant who served as their pilot acknowledged the order, and lifted off at once. "Now what in the *hell* was that all about?" she asked Bleindel.

Bleindel noted that they had returned to the same question that had been under debate on their way to the palace half an hour ago, and shrugged. "Is that a rhetorical question?"

"No, I really want to know the answer."

"This isn't about Marid Pasha making himself ruler of an independent Zerzura—or not directly about it, anyway. The pasha's in business with at least some of Zerzura's pirates, and the Aquilans keep hitting him in the wallet. He wants that to stop."

"Obviously." The special envoy shot Bleindel another sharp look. "Did we know about that before? Marid's association with piracy, I mean?"

"No, I'm afraid we didn't see that coming. I didn't figure it out until just now." Bleindel gazed at the palace dropping away below them, thinking aloud as he worked out the implications. "As long as no one was having any success in actually *catching* pirates, Marid Pasha could play the victim and claim that he just didn't have the resources he needed to deal with the problem. The situation suited him just fine: The pirates pay him off, then *we* pay him for the privilege of helping him fight piracy, an effort he intends to sabotage so the pirates can carry on while he asks us for *more* help. Losing the base at Zafer and a ship or two probably didn't concern him too much; the pasha had to expect that sooner or later some of his associates would find a way to get themselves into trouble he couldn't get them out of. But then last night he hears the news that the Aquilans knocked out another pirate base—"

"—and he goes through the roof," Vogt finished for him. "Damn it."

"We probably could have figured out the pasha's complicity if we'd known to look for a connection. But my team's directive"—a directive requested by the Foreign Office when they organized Vogt's mission in the first place, not that Bleindel saw any reason to remind her of that—"prioritized developing sources that could shed light on Marid Pasha's strategic alignment, not the regional nuisance of Zerzura's pirates. Naturally, that's where we focused our work."

"All right, I'm convinced." Vogt made a face. "Let's set that aside for a moment and consider the pasha's demands. Can we speed up the delivery of those ships?"

"Technically speaking, we've already delivered them. They're under Zerzuran registration now. But as to helping the pasha's navy to make them operational within a month, I couldn't say. I'll need to talk to Captain Beck, and I imagine he'll have to consult with his officers before he can give us an answer."

"Do it," Vogt said. "Marid Pasha's expecting an answer today."

"Is it really in the Empire's interest to proceed with the refits given what we've just learned about Marid Pasha?" Bleindel asked. "Or the additional transfers we've got planned, for that matter? We're handing a substantial fleet over to someone who clearly intends to do nothing about piracy."

"Moral qualms, Otto? I didn't think you were the type."

"Oh, I understand that sometimes you need to get muddy if you want to win the race. I'm just worried about the possible complications. If nothing else, our support for Marid Pasha's government is a potential scandal. The Empire won't look good if we're seen to be propping up a criminal strongman."

"The Foreign Office has worked with worse," the diplomat admitted. "As long as Marid al-Zahabi keeps his friends away from Dremish-flagged freighters, I can overlook local corruption. Zerzura is valuable territory, especially if the Caliphate finally falls apart. No, what worries me is that remark the pasha made about trying to make an accommodation with another power if we can't strengthen his navy quickly enough."

"I noticed that too, although it struck me as something of an empty threat. The Montréalais don't really want to be drawn into yet another regional commitment, our Meliya operation put an end to any possibility of engagement with the Velarans, and it's clear that Marid is furious at the Aquilans . . . who, as we've just seen, are highly committed to stamping out piracy wherever they find it, regardless of the consequences." The flyer swooped down to a handsome high-rise building only two blocks down the street from the Aquilan consulate; Bleindel could actually see the rival power's flag flying from the pole in front of the door as their pilot set them down on the Dremish consulate's landing pad.

"The Aquilans can be more flexible than you think if the stakes are high enough." Vogt remained seated, her eyes distant as she considered the problem. "Of course, it might take a while for that message to filter down to their navy. Military types tend to see things in black-and-white."

"They do, don't they?" Bleindel said . . . and that suggested a simple idea to make sure the pasha didn't suddenly reevaluate his relationships. He savored the notion for a moment, examining it carefully before he shared it with his Foreign Office colleague. "I think we can use that, Hanne. Since the Aquilans are so anxious to knock out pirate bases, let's help them find a few more. Marid Pasha is furious at their interference already. What will he do if they hit another one?"

"Assuming he doesn't roll over and try to cut a deal? Revoke their passage rights, ban them from Zerzuran ports, complain to Old Terra—"

"—and come to us for more help as soon as we can provide it," Bleindel added.

"And come to us for more help," Vogt acknowledged. She gave him a long look. "Why, do you know where to find a pirate base?"

"Not exactly," he replied. "But I'm good at making things up."

16

Tawahi Island, Neda III

The sweet smell of teriyaki fish kebobs sizzling on the grill wafted over the patio of Sikander's Tawahi Island bungalow. He eyed the skewers critically, turning a couple that looked like they were getting a bit too done on one side. He was not much of a cook—few Norths spent much time in kitchens, really—but early on in his naval career he'd decided to learn the basics of grilling for the purpose of hosting casual barbecues for shipmates and colleagues, and he'd actually come to enjoy it. Darvesh was much better at it, but the valet was happy to keep himself busy by seeing to all the sides and beverages for an evening cookout, and made sure to praise Sikander's efforts or offer the occasional tip without a hint of condescension. And, of course, it helped that the main ingredient—in this case, Nedan sunfin that he'd caught just a few hours ago—was as fresh as anyone could hope for. Sikander took a long pull from a bottle of the crisp helles-style lager he'd stocked for the day's occasion, and contemplated the sunshine, the palm trees, the ocean view, and the comfortable chatter of his guests with no small amount of satisfaction.

"Can I get you another one, Captain?" said Amar Shah, who happened to be standing near the cooler. He was a little over-dressed for the party, with long khaki pants and a designer shirt, but this was his first experience with one of Sikander's cookouts; Sikander himself wore shorts and an island-themed shirt with a bright floral design, while Amelia Fraser wore a sundress over her swimsuit and Michael Girard wore Bermuda shorts and a shirt even more garish than Sikander's, adding a brimmed hat; his red hair and pale complexion didn't mix well with Neda's tropical sun.

"Yes, please," Sikander replied. He'd earned it, after all, and so had the rest of *Decisive*'s officers in attendance. Normally ships returning from a two-month patrol would be able to stand down and adopt something close to a civilian work schedule, with full weekends for activities such as fishing trips and afternoon cookouts, but *Decisive* had been in port for only a long week before *Harrier* returned with the news that had sent Sikander and his crew right back out again on the Fort Jalid raid. Today's gathering marked the first time in more than three months that he'd had the opportunity to entertain, and he meant to enjoy it.

"I have to say, this corner of the island has a lot going for it," the Kashmiri engineer observed as he handed Sikander a fresh bottle of beer. "I see why you like the marina district."

"Are you thinking about buying a place on Tawahi?"

Shah nodded. His family was just as rich as Sikander's; he could afford anything on the island. "I intended to look into a condo somewhere along the West Beach strip soon after I arrived, but then we went to space only a few days after I reported for duty. I just didn't have much of a chance to see what was available before we left."

"West Beach is very nice, and you'd be close to the nightlife, such as it is around here. But I find that a boat slip in my backyard is hard to beat."

"I spend enough time on ships already, thank you," Shah said with an easy laugh.

"It's not the same thing," Sikander said, bemused by the engineer's relaxed attitude. The Shah he saw every day on *Decisive* was a results-driven, hands-on leader who pushed himself—and his subordinates—hard. This Shah was a man evidently quite comfortable in his own skin, and even though he'd sampled Sikander's beer cooler, it wasn't just a drink or two showing. Away from *Decisive* and out of uniform, Amar Shah was a Kashmiri aristocrat whose pedigree rivaled Sikander's own, and he knew it. Sikander wasn't sure how he felt about that; he liked to think that he didn't expect an unusual amount of deference from his officers in a social setting, but then again, most of them didn't really change their stripes in his presence just because they were ashore. *Well, that's why I host these gatherings, isn't it?* he told himself. *It's an opportunity to get to know my key people in a less formal environment. I shouldn't be put off when they let down their guard.* He poked at the grill, and gave Shah a small shrug. "Besides, it's not about the boat, it's about the fishing."

"Which is something else that I'm not very interested in—although naturally I wouldn't presume to criticize my superior officers' choice of pastimes," Shah said diplomatically.

"Good, because otherwise you wouldn't get to eat today." Sikander grinned to take the sting out of the words, and studied his handiwork a moment longer. On careful consideration, he judged the kebobs to be done but not overdone. He raised his voice and announced his findings to the dozen guests lounging around his patio: "Dinner is ready! Grab your plates."

"Dinner!" Amelia Fraser's children—Eric, five, and Ivy, three—shouted in chorus. Sikander had put on a couple of hot dogs for them, which usually suited them just fine.

"About time," Amelia observed. "I was beginning to wonder if you remembered how to work that thing, Captain."

"Food on top, fire on the bottom. It's not that hard." Sikander set the kids' hot dogs on a pair of plates, then loaded up a platter with the fish kebobs and carried them over to the serving table Darvesh had set up for him. He motioned for the Frasers to lead the way and see to their children, then followed them down the table to arrange a plate for himself—he'd found that no matter how much he insisted, many of the junior officers at one of his cookouts wouldn't think of helping themselves to the food until after they'd seen their CO make a pass through the line. He took a seat on the low stone wall that ringed the patio and pool, and watched as Decisive's officers—well, those who weren't on duty or busy with Saturday plans of their own—loaded up their own plates.

"Thank you, Captain. This is great," Jay Sekibo said, taking a seat on the wall near Sikander's spot. As one of Decisive's longer-serving division officers, he'd been to a few of Sikander's cookouts and was not overly nervous about bumping elbows with his commanding officer in a social setting . . . which was another one of the reasons Sikander hosted the gatherings to begin with. Not only did they build a certain amount of camaraderie in the wardroom, they helped him to introduce junior officers to the fleet's social life—a little bit of professional development that was easy to overlook. For that matter, it didn't hurt to show his department heads, who might not be all that far from commands of their own, something about domesticization of ensigns.

"My pleasure, Jay," Sikander replied. "We've had a busy couple of months, and everybody's been working a lot of long hours. I just wanted to do a little something to express my appreciation."

"Which just so happened to provide you with an excuse to spend the morning trolling for sunfin," Amelia's husband Jerrod pointed out from the table the XO and her family had claimed.

Sikander grinned—Jerrod Fraser had joined him on more than one of those fishing trips during his months at Neda. "Well, yes. That goes without saying." He went on to regale Jerrod with an account of the morning's fishing, after which the party conversation continued on to various other hobbies and interests. After dinner, Jerrod Fraser bundled up young Eric and Ivy and took them home for the evening bath and bedtime rituals, while Amelia lingered a little longer with the rest of *Decisive*'s officers.

Darvesh Reza appeared with Sikander's personal comm device. "A call for you, sir," he said. "I believe it's Ms. Pavon."

"Elena? I'll take it, thank you. Please excuse me, everybody." Sikander took his comm device from Darvesh and ducked around a corner of the house, seeking more privacy for the call. *What's she doing in Neda? I thought she was in Dahar.* The idea that Elena might actually be somewhere in the same star system brought a nervous flutter to his stomach—they'd shared only a couple of conversations and an hour or two enjoying the harvest celebration at Mount Kesif, but he'd sensed that they might be at the start of something very interesting. *I'm sure this is about Pegasus-Pavon concerns or perhaps another lead about piracy, not anything personal . . . or is it?*

He collected himself, and activated the unit's small vidscreen. "Hello?"

"Hi, Sikander, it's Elena." She smiled warmly at him from the tiny screen, her dark hair pulled back in a practical braid. "I just arrived on Neda, and I'm on my way down to Tawahi. Could I come by *Decisive*? I thought it would be nice to see you as long as I was in the system, and I have something I want to talk to you about."

"Umm, certainly, I'd like to see you too. But . . ."

"Oh, I'm an idiot. It's Saturday night there, isn't it? You must have plans."

"No, no, it's okay." In fact, now that he'd recovered from his surprise, Sikander decided that it was more than okay. He'd had to cut their previous date short because of the news from Meliya, and then he'd managed only a cursory message thanking her for the tip that led *Decisive* to Zafer. He was frankly astonished that Elena Pavon had any interest in resuming their acquaintance, if in fact that was what this was about. "It's not anything formal. I'm at home, hosting a small cookout for some of my officers. If you'd like to drop by, I can put a kebob on the grill for you."

"I'd love that. Are you sure I'm not intruding?"

"Not at all. My address is 204 Marina Loop Drive."

"Great. I'll be along shortly." Elena ended the call.

Did I just make a dinner date while I've got a houseful of guests? Sikander asked himself. Well, he had—if it really was a date, although he wasn't entirely sure it was. Apparently the situation with Elena Pavon was not as clear as he might have hoped. He sighed, second-guessing his spontaneous invitation, and returned to the back patio. "Ms. Pavon may be stopping by soon," he announced to his guests. "You may remember her from Dahar."

"Ah, too bad. I was just leaving," Amelia Fraser announced. "Time for me to get back home and tuck in the kids. But please say hello to her for me." She stood up and gave the other remaining guests a look that somehow got everyone else on their feet, too.

"Thank you, Captain, dinner was great," Michael Girard said. "I, umm, have a thing to get to."

"Me too, sir," Jay Sekibo added. "I'm meeting up with some friends later to hit the clubs. Good night, everybody."

Amelia Fraser ushered the rest of *Decisive*'s officers toward the door. Sikander saw them through the usual good-byes and thank-yous as they took to their flyers and ground cars, disappearing into the warm night. Amelia lingered only long enough to make sure her husband had collected all the children's' things.

Sikander eyed her suspiciously. "Would you care to explain why you chased off all my guests?"

"In the year that I've been serving with you, I think I've seen you make maybe three dates. There is no way in the world I'm going to get in the way of a fourth."

"I don't recall that an XO is supposed to concern herself with a CO's dating situation."

"Most of them don't need the help." Amelia grinned at him. "Good night, Sikander. Have fun—and don't even think about setting foot on the ship until Monday."

"Enough already! We'll resume this discussion at the time and place of my choosing, I promise."

Amelia replied with a raised eyebrow, and headed for her own flyer; Sikander returned to his patio to straighten up. Naturally, Darvesh had already cleared most of the plates and glasses and restarted the grill. "I understand Ms. Pavon may be joining us for dinner?" the valet said without a hint of amusement.

"It seems that way."

"Very good, sir. In that event might I recommend a fresh shirt, and perhaps a little cologne?"

"Not you, too." Sikander scowled at Darvesh, but he took his advice and retreated to his bedroom to change into khakis and a nice button-down shirt. The cologne struck him as a little too much, though. He finished changing just in time to answer the door when the bell chimed.

Elena stood on his doorstep, wearing a flowing knee-length summer dress with emerald green stripes and matching sandals; a luxury flyer whirred softly in the drive behind her. "I take it I missed the party?" she asked.

"I'm afraid my guests scattered suddenly—it was pretty casual, really. But I'm glad that you were able to stop by. Come on in."

"Thank you," she said. She followed him through the house and out onto the patio; the last embers of Tawahi's swift sunset glowed faintly along the horizon, and the colorful lights of the other homes ringing the basin glimmered across the water. "This is very nice. Do all Aquilan captains get waterfront homes?"

"I'm just renting it for the duration of my assignment in Neda. I think it's good to have a place to go home to each night when *Decisive's* in port—there's such a thing as spending too much time on your ship." Sikander nodded in Darvesh's direction. "Can I have Darvesh fix a bit of dinner for you? And get you something to drink?"

"Please. I'm hungry, although it's late in the morning by my ship's time."

"Brunch for you, and an after-dinner snack for me, then." Sikander poured her a glass of white wine that would go well with the kebobs and another for himself, and led her over to the patio table—cleaned up after the Fraser children and reset with two place settings by the efficient Darvesh, of course. "The last I heard, you were in Dahar. What brings you to Neda?"

"My security team convinced me that Dahar was growing dangerous for me. Well, the kidnapping attempt did that, but afterwards my security people told me that it might be a good idea to get off the planet for a while, and I agreed with them."

"Kidnapping? Good God! What happened?"

"Someone tried to grab me a few days after you raided Zafer: a gang affiliated with Zerzura's pirates, or so I believe. They arranged a bogus after-hours meeting at my office in Mersin, and tried to abduct me when I finally left the building. Fortunately my personal assistant is better armed than I thought he was. We got away from the team they sent to grab me, although the kidnappers fled the scene before the Mersin police got there. Anyway, after that I decided that I could catch up on some work back in Nuevo León—it's my family's headquarters. But when I heard that *Decisive* and another destroyer had raided a second pirate base, I decided to stop by and see what you'd found. You're sort of on the way back to Dahar."

"I'm glad that you are okay. And I'm glad that you decided to make the detour to tell me."

"If I'm being perfectly honest, I'm here to find some answers, Sikander. Seeing you is something of a side benefit." She took a sip of her wine, as cool as if she dealt with kidnapping attempts all the time. "First of all, I want to see if you happened to catch any of the people who tried to grab me in Dahar—a long shot, but worth a try. Second, and perhaps more important, I'm certain that the kidnappers knew that I passed you the tip about Venture Salvage. That was the bait they used for setting up the bogus appointment. I want to know who you told about Venture Salvage, and when you told them."

Sikander frowned. Evidently this was not the sort of date he'd hoped for, but he shifted his expectations and thought about the implications of her visit. "You think that someone on my end told the pirates where we got our tip from?"

"I see only three possibilities." Elena held up her hand and counted them off. "One: The investigators I hired to get that information left a trail for the pirates' allies to follow back to me. Two: Someone tapped my communications. Or, three: The Commonwealth Navy—possibly inadvertently—let the source of their intelligence slip. I'd like to know which it is before I go back to Dahar."

"I can see this is going to be a working dinner," Sikander said. "Let's start again, and see if we can build a timeline. Tell me everything."

"In just a minute," Elena replied, casting a longing look over at the grill. "Those kebobs smell *amazing*, and I'm going to insist on being fed before we go too much further."

They hurried through dinner; Sikander just picked at his own. Then they spent an hour or more poring over a calendar on Elena's dataslate, tracing out the timing of messages and events with the remains of their dinner shoved over to one side of the patio table. Together they were able to confirm that the kidnapping attempt had taken place the day before *Decisive* arrived in Bursa with *Qarash* and the prisoners from Zafer, which was the first time Sikander's crew had made any report of the action they'd taken; clearly the kidnapping was not in response to any Aquilan slip. On the other hand, the attempted abduction had occurred seven days *after* Elena received her investigators' report about Venture Salvage and sent off a message to Sikander, so it was definitely possible that someone monitoring her communications—or aware of her investigators' discovery—would have known to use Venture Salvage as bait.

And a comm tap of some kind would also clear Elena of responsibility for the attack on Grupo Constelación's Duquesa, Sikander realized. He'd mentally filled in those dates for himself as he went over Elena's story. *Somebody in Dahar who knew about the message Elena sent to me could easily have guessed that I'd leave Meliya exposed to go investigate Zafer, and passed word to their pirate friends to raid the system.* If that was the case, it was a bold play . . . but Zerzura's pirates were nothing if not audacious. Still, he was relieved to discover an explanation for the *Duquesa* attack that didn't require him to choose between coincidence and complicity on Elena's part. "There might be some possibility we're overlooking," he told Elena. "But it seems to me that you'd better assume that your communications aren't secure. Be careful what you say in any messages you transmit, and find another channel to warn people who regularly correspond with you that they should be careful, too."

Elena made a face. "Do you have any idea what a nuisance that's going to be? Half my workday consists of sending and receiving messages."

"Routine business matters probably aren't worth worrying about—it's pretty clear that Zerzura's pirates are already familiar with your ships' sailing schedules and cargo manifests. Just make sure to safeguard your personal schedule and travel arrangements for now."

"And invest in the best commercial encryption system I can find."

"It probably wouldn't hurt," Sikander said. "Although I can think of a few ways to use what you know against whoever's reading your messages. For example, you could send a fake message that indicates you'll be at a certain place at a certain time, then arrange for someone to be waiting in case the kidnappers make another attempt on you."

Elena nodded in appreciation. "That's clever."

"I served as a staff intelligence officer in the Tzoru Dominion a few years back. They covered some of the tricks of the trade during Intel School. If you think your enemy is listening in, you can say things you'd like him to hear."

"That's an answer for one of my two problems—or a way to find an answer, at least. Now, what about seeing if you happened to capture any of my kidnappers?"

"Do you know their names?"

"The two that Omar shot were called Mert and Haluk. I don't think they survived, but I did get a good look at three who did: the one I got with the stunner, and the two who chased me to the elevator when the transport flyer touched down in the garage. Show me your prisoners, and I'll see if I can pick them out."

Sikander rubbed at his chin. "I think I can arrange that, but I'll have to speak to the judge advocates, and they might need a statement from you. I'm afraid it might take a couple of days—it's Saturday night, as you noted earlier. Will you be staying in Neda for a while?"

"Captain North, I have a suspicion that you're looking for a way to keep me around." Elena gave him a playful smile over the rim of her glass before turning serious again. "Yes, I can wait around a few days, especially if it means finding out something about the people who tried to abduct me. My yacht's moored over in the civilian port."

"I'll let you know as soon as I set it up, then," he told her.

"Good. In that case, how about some more of this wine? It's been a long few weeks and my body clock is off by half a day."

They passed the rest of the evening—and the bottle—comparing stories of their homeworlds and their families. Sikander, of course, came from a large clan with dozens of cousins to go along with his four siblings; Elena was an only child, although the families of Pegasus-Pavon's board members had been allied for several generations and were the next best thing to blood relatives. As the third son in his family, Sikander had been sent off to the Commonwealth Naval Academy to find an honorable profession, since he wasn't expected to inherit Ishar's throne. Elena, on the other hand, had been groomed for her place in the family business from the time she'd finished elementary school, and couldn't imagine doing anything else.

When the time came to say good night, she paused in his doorway to kiss him warmly. "Thank you," she said. "Dinner was lovely. I'm sorry I had to bring up business."

"Think nothing of it," he told her, relishing the way she felt in his arms and the delicate scent of her perfume in his nose. "Are you sure you have to go?"

"Not really, but I think I'd better," she said, and kissed him again. "I'll see you soon, though. Good night, Sikander."

"Good night, Elena." He watched her climb into her flyer and lift off, then took a deep breath. After that good-night kiss he was fairly certain that the evening wasn't all about business. *Did she want me to try a little harder?* he wondered. *Or is it simply the game of savoring the anticipation?* That was enjoyable, too. There was a time when he might have viewed the evening as a disappointment, since it hadn't ended with Elena Pavon in his bed, but perhaps he was more patient than he used to be. Amelia Fraser was right about one thing: He'd spent the last year married to *Decisive* and had put any other ideas of romance on hold. Now that an alternative to the loneliness of command had appeared in the form of Elena Pavon, he found that he was anxious not to mess it up by rushing things. "If that's really where this is going," he murmured aloud. "Don't get ahead of yourself, Sikay."

As he'd guessed, it took him a couple of days to arrange for Elena to examine a lineup of the prisoners from Fort Jalid. He saw her twice in those two days—drinks at sunset at his favorite West Beach cabana bar, and a dinner for two aboard her warp yacht *La Nómada*, currently lying pierside at the large quay in Tawahi's picturesque harbor. Sikander had never imagined he could be awed by displays of wealth; after all, the North family had a fortune measured in multiple billions, and his own small part of the family trust made him fabulously rich for a naval officer. On the other hand, private starships such as Elena's cost hundreds of millions, and simply keeping the warp rings charged ran to millions of credits a year. With her hangar doors rolled open and stowable decking deployed above the waterline, *La Nómada* looked surprisingly like an oversized version of the waterborne luxury yachts he'd seen at Long Lake or thought about building at Mohali Qila.

The day after their dinner aboard *La Nómada*, Sikander received word that the base's master-at-arms office was ready for Elena's visit. He picked her up from her yacht in the middle of the afternoon, and took her to the brig. "You certainly know how to show a girl a good time," Elena observed as they landed in front of the fenced-off barracks building.

"This is your idea," Sikander reminded her. The Tawahi Island base had no brig facilities remotely large enough to handle the prisoners *Decisive* and *Harrier* had brought back; the base masters-at-arms had hurriedly repurposed an old barracks to serve as a cell block, erecting a fence around the building and stationing guards to keep order. Scores of men in prisoner jumpsuits sat in the improvised jail yard; a few played soccer on a half-sized pitch within the fence.

"What are you going to do with all these prisoners?"

"The judge advocate's office is still drawing up charges. Two hundred and three defendants sort of overwhelm the local office, though. And of course fifty different civilian lawyers are now involved, each with their own ideas about how things should work when Aquilan sailors capture Zerzuran pirates in open space after those pirates attacked ships registered in Bolívar and Velar. From what I hear, our prosecutors anticipate that the Zerzuran government's going to request extradition of the whole lot."

"So it might wind up being someone else's problem."

"After seeing exactly how long our Zafer prisoners remained locked up after we delivered them to Bursa, I'm not inclined to put a lot of faith in Zerzuran courts. I've already spoken with Captain Broward about making sure that we conduct the proceedings here, under Commonwealth law. But it seems that catching the pirates was the easy part of the job." Sikander led Elena to the mobile structure that served as the improvised brig's headquarters, and ushered her inside.

A stocky petty officer with a shaven head and a pistol belt greeted them at the door. "Good afternoon, Commander North," he said. "And you must be Ms. Pavon. I'm Senior Chief Master-at-Arms Vélez, base security. We've got a desk set up right here with a vidscreen for you to view mug shots of all our guests, ma'am. Take as long as you like, and let me know if you think you recognize anybody. Can I get you some coffee or tea?"

"Coffee, please," Elena said. She took the offered seat in front of the screen; Sikander pulled up another one beside her while Vélez retreated to fix a cup for her. One by one, she paged through the compiled images, scrutinizing face after face. The majority consisted of young or middle-aged men, with the dark hair and medium complexions one might expect from a random sampling of Zerzuran worlds. Sikander wondered whether Elena would really be able to pick out the individuals who had attacked her in Mersin even if any of them were here; sometimes surprise and fear etched an indelible image in the memory, and sometimes they left a confused blur.

"Huh," Elena said suddenly, pausing on an image. "I don't believe it."

Sikander glanced at the screen, and realized that he recognized the prisoner. "Al-Kobra," he said. "The captain of the pirate ship *Balina*, at least until his crew decided that they didn't particularly care to fight to the death on his behalf. Was he in Mersin?"

"Yes—at the pasha's Founding Day banquet. That's Gadi al-Kassar."

"Who is Gadi al-Kassar?"

"The al-Kassars own Suvar United Shipping." Elena stared at the screen, her mouth fixed in a thin and angry line. "His uncle Hidir is the president of the company. And his uncle Torgut just happens to run the Zerzuran fleet."

"Wait a moment. This man is a close relative of Admiral Torgut al-Kassar?" Sikander asked.

"And his brother Hidir, yes. No wonder Suvar United managed to avoid the damned pirate attacks and the Zerzuran fleet never seemed to catch anyone! It's the family business. Those dirty bastards!"

Sikander leaned back in his chair, wrestling with his astonishment. Gadi al-Kassar he hadn't ever heard of, but he'd met Admiral al-Kassar, and he certainly knew of Hidir al-Kassar and

Suvar United Shipping. Senior Chief Vélez glanced at the image on the screen, and made a note on his dataslate. "I had a feeling that al-Kobra wasn't the name his mother gave him," he commented in a dry tone. "Was he one of the men who tried to abduct you in Dahar, ma'am?"

"No, he wasn't part of that. But he's *important*—his family runs the biggest shipping line in Zerzura, and his uncle commands the Zerzuran fleet."

"That sounds like a problem that's above my pay grade," the master-at-arms said. "Okay, if he's a high-value detainee, we'll separate him from the others and let the intelligence types know. What else can you tell me about how you know him?"

"Not too much, really. I only met him once." Elena described encountering the al-Kassars at the banquet, and explained Suvar United's seeming good fortune in avoiding pirate losses over the last few years—Vélez didn't know much about Zerzuran carriers, after all. Then the senior chief had her complete her pass through the prisoner portraits, just in case she recognized anyone else. Elena scanned through the whole file twice, but Gadi al-Kassar was the only face she recognized.

"I'm sorry, Chief Vélez," she said when she finished. "I'd hoped I could pick out at least a couple more faces for you."

"You did just fine, ma'am," Vélez replied. "This al-Kassar character sounds pretty interesting. I wouldn't be surprised if the intelligence specialists or the judge advocates want to ask you a few more questions about him. Will you be staying in Neda for a while?"

"I can give you another day, maybe a day and a half, but then I need to be on my way. Finding an al-Kassar in the middle of all this changes everything. I have to consult with my family on Nuevo León—and I can think of some other things I need to see to in Dahar and Meliya, too."

"Dahar?" Sikander asked. "That strikes me as dangerous, Elena. If Admiral Torgut is involved in the conspiracy, you might be up against the Zerzuran government, not anonymous criminals. They don't need to kidnap you if they can just have you detained by the planetary police."

"Oh, you don't need to be worried for me," said Elena. She set a hand on his shoulder and gave him a small smile, but her eyes narrowed thoughtfully. "Mersin is the hub of our operations for five systems. I'll have plenty of protection there, now that I know what to watch out for. Besides, I *need* to talk to my people in Dahar. As you pointed out the other night, I can't be sure that my communications are safe, so I have to do it in person."

Sikander hesitated. Maybe Torgut al-Kassar didn't know about Gadi's involvement in piracy, maybe he did know but he chose not to interfere, and maybe the admiral was an active partner who had to keep his participation secret, but it was all speculation. It seemed to him that Elena had no real way of knowing just what the al-Kassars were prepared to do or how much support they had from other elements in the Zerzuran government . . . but he had a feeling that she'd resist any effort to dissuade her from going, and he suspected the harder he pushed her on the topic, the more determined she'd be about it. "Thanks, Senior Chief," he told Vélez. "If Gadi al-Kassar says anything that suggests Ms. Pavon may be in danger, make sure to let me know. I'll see to it that she's warned."

"Aye, sir," said the master-at-arms. "Take care, Ms. Pavon."

Sikander and Elena returned to his flyer. The late-afternoon breeze rustled through the near-palms that lined the boulevards of the naval base; he realized they'd spent a couple of hours reviewing the prisoner pictures and filling in the master-at-arms. "Where to?" he asked her.

"Beats me. I'm anxious to get going, but I did just promise your investigators that I'd stick around for another day." She shook her head. "I still can't believe it. I had my suspicions about Suvar United, but this is one occasion when I would rather have gotten it all wrong."

"It's possible that Gadi al-Kassar is the black sheep of the family. His uncles might not be directly involved in what he's been doing."

"Not a chance, Sikay. Pirates haven't touched Suvar United in years, and you told me yourself that the Zerzuran fleet isn't keeping pirates locked up. No, the al-Kassars are in this up to their ears—the challenge is proving that the others are just as guilty as Gadi."

"That might be hard to do. When they find out he's been arrested, the rest of the family will take steps to insulate themselves from anything he's involved in."

"Sure, but they can't convert hundreds of millions of credits of stolen goods and hijacked ships into cash without leaving a paper trail, which is the other reason I need to go to Dahar. It's where the evidence is."

"Assuming you find what you're looking for, what will you do with it?" Sikander asked. "If it's as bad as you think, the al-Kassars have little to fear from any Zerzuran court."

"Well, I'm still working on that part of the plan. Give me a few hours to digest all the implications, and I'll come up with something. Right now I want to go someplace where I can kick off my shoes, have a few good drinks, watch the ocean, and figure out what comes next."

Sikander could understand that sentiment . . . and he thought there might be another step in Elena's plan that she'd left unspoken. "At the risk of being forward, my house meets all those requirements," he offered. "I'd be happy to fix you dinner, too. After all, this might be my last opportunity to entertain you for a while."

She glanced over at him, and a smile crept back to her lips. "That sounds like just the place, then."

He lifted off and pointed the nose of the flyer toward his house, only fifteen kilometers away, before keying his personal comm. "Darvesh, I'm bringing Ms. Pavon over for dinner," he told his valet. "Set out something for the grill, and I'll fix it whenever we get hungry."

"Very good, sir. We have a couple of steaks that should do nicely; I will season them and leave them covered in the refrigerator," Darvesh answered. "I may take the liberty of stepping out to run a few errands. Call if you need me."

Darvesh was gone by the time they reached Sikander's bungalow; as promised, steaks and a side salad were waiting, along with a pitcher of sangria and two place settings on the patio table. "Oh, he's *good*," Elena observed, taking in the preparations as she slipped off her shoes. "You gave him a ten-minute warning, and he managed all this?"

"Darvesh Reza might just be the single most competent man I've ever known," Sikander admitted. "Something to eat, something to drink, or . . . ?"

"Or?" Elena raised an eyebrow, and turned to gaze out at the ocean view. The late-afternoon sun silhouetted her shapely figure through the lighter panels of her summer dress; Sikander stepped up close behind her, slipping his arms around her waist to nuzzle at the back of her neck while he caressed her. She sighed and leaned into him for a long moment before reaching around to find his mouth with hers. "Oh, *definitely* 'or,'" she murmured when their lips parted.

As it turned out, Sikander didn't get around to fixing dinner until much later in the evening.

17

Elena Pavon's *La Nómada* left Neda late in the following afternoon, climbing up and away from Tawahi Harbor with a silver sheen of water dripping from the gold and green hull. Sikander found an excuse to stretch his legs with a walk along the naval base's waterfront, watching the star yacht ascend on its crackling drive plates from across the bay until she disappeared from view. He wondered when he'd see her again—days, weeks, months, never? *Usually I'm the one flying off to the stars*, he realized, and shook his head at the strange irony of the situation. *How many times did I have someone watching* my *ship leave and wondering when I would return?*

He sighed, and turned his steps back toward *Decisive*. He didn't really know where his relationship with Elena was headed, but he knew himself well enough to recognize when he was a little infatuated, and he'd miss her. *The best distraction for a case of infatuation is good hard work*, he told himself; he certainly had no shortage of things that demanded his attention aboard his ship. He studied *Decisive* with a critical eye as he strolled back in her direction, noting the pitted armor at the bow, the fading red pinstriping that accented the Aquilan white-and-buff paint scheme, the scaffolding that clung to the hull above the long black scar cut into the ship's flank by Fort Jalid's laser. *She's mine*, he reminded himself. *And she's beautiful too.*

He noticed Amar Shah and Jaime Herrera engaged in a discussion near the scaffolding, and detoured from the brow to wander over to where they stood on the pier. "Gentlemen. What's caught your interest?"

Shah and Herrera turned and saluted. "Good afternoon, Captain," Shah said. He pointed at the looming K-cannon turret on the spine of the ship, fifteen meters above them. "The turret ring, there. Mr. Herrera is concerned that the damage it sustained might cause it to fail when we fire the number-three mount."

"A kinetic cannon kicks like a mule," Herrera said. "If a full-power shot cracks a weakened turret ring, we'd lose the ability to train the mount."

"I see. Have we done any resonance or integrity tests?"

"We did, sir," Shah said. "It's borderline between patching it and replacing it. But to replace the turret ring we'd have to remove the turret—"

"—and that's a job for the shipyard," Sikander finished. He frowned. Since *Decisive* just got out of the shipyard, she wouldn't be due for another visit for a year or more.

"I can't believe an outlaw's laser hit us that hard," Herrera observed. "That burn is fifteen centimeters deep in places. I think we would have been in real trouble if we hadn't gotten on the other side of the planet's ring. That was some quick thinking, Captain."

"No, Mr. Herrera, that was dumb luck. I didn't realize we were taking this sort of damage." Laser fire was much harder to dodge than incoming K-cannon rounds and theoretically outranged kinetic weapons by hundreds of thousands of kilometers, but a laser that could burn through an armored hull fast required a lot of power and generated a lot of heat. On board a ship, managing the heat of your own laser fire represented a serious challenge—but the Fort Jalid laser had a whole moon to dump its heat into. *That might be worth a memo to the Office of Construction,* Sikander realized. It was hard to see how that could be made to work with a shipboard mount, but as a ground battery on an airless body, it might be useful. "Patch it for now, but go ahead and write up the replacement request; we might as well start the paperwork. And let's do a little math and see if there's a power level at which it's still safe to fire number three, if we need it."

"Yes, sir," Herrera said. "We'll probably need to try a low-power shot or two to evaluate things, though."

"Next time we're in space, Guns," Sikander promised him. He clapped Herrera on the shoulder, and headed back aboard *Decisive* to throw himself into any work he could find.

For a few days, he succeeded in distracting himself with the ordinary routine of command: maintenance, training, planning for future deployments, the regular turnover of crew members moving on to new assignments and replacements showing up on board. He followed the prosecution of the Fort Jalid prisoners as closely as he could, although as one of the commanding officers present when the pirates had been captured, he was a key witness and couldn't overstep his role without causing headaches for the judge-advocate specialists building their case. He pored over reports of pirate contact from other ships in Pleiades Squadron, working with Michael Girard to see if they could spot anything the squadron intel team had overlooked. And, for the most part, he managed to put Elena Pavon out of his mind. Slowly, Sikander and *Decisive* returned to their in-port routine.

The week after Elena left, Michael Girard came to see Sikander with Jay Sekibo in tow. "Good morning, Captain," Girard said. "Got a moment?"

Sikander took note of Girard's quick stride and the frown of intense concentration on his face. Clearly, something had caught his attention. "Come on in, Mr. Girard," he replied. "What's going on?"

"Mr. Sekibo just informed me that we've received a response to the message we sent to the Velarans a few weeks ago. I think you're going to want to see this." He handed Sikander a dataslate, the message already cued for play.

Sikander took Girard's dataslate, and pulled up the correspondence—an old-fashioned text message, not the vid recording many humans would have used.

North, Commander of Destroyer *Decisive*:

We examined all sensor traces of the signal *Decisive* discovered and correlated it with small craft departures from Meliya Station as you suggested. There were two departures during the time window you identified. The first was an orbiter returning to the city of New Opava. All of the passengers aboard the orbiter have been interviewed and are no longer of interest to our investigation. The second departure was a launch from the courier *Asfoor*, which picked up four passengers before departing Meliya on a course for Dahar. We are informed that *Asfoor* has now disappeared, which means that none of the passengers aboard the launch can be accounted for. Attached you will find security cam recordings of the boarding area. You will review the recordings and inform us if you can identify any of the humans that boarded *Asfoor*'s launch one hour before the bomb explosion.

Pokk Skirriseh, Meritor

"Paom'ii don't waste words on common courtesy, do they?" Sikander said, rereading the message. "Has the *Asfoor* turned up anywhere since the meritor sent this?"

"No, sir," Ensign Sekibo said. "She was scheduled to arrive in Dahar weeks ago, but she's overdue. Dahar's system-control authorities now report her as 'presumed lost.'"

Pirates, again? Sikander wondered. He'd never heard of a courier falling prey to a pirate attack—drive couriers, even civilian versions, were *fast*. No pirate could have caught one that didn't want to be caught . . . but that was a mystery for another day. He turned his attention to the attached images to examine each one in turn: a thirtyish woman he'd never seen before, a man of about the same age with a military look to him, a bigger man who *definitely* looked like an operator, and—

"Bleindel." Sikander scowled at the dataslate in his hands. "Damn him! I *knew* he had to be involved in that Meliya business!"

Girard nodded. "I thought you'd find that interesting."

"Who is he, sir?" Sekibo asked.

"A Dremish KBS agent," Sikander replied. "A very dangerous one, I might add—Mr. Girard and I encountered his handiwork at Gadira eight years ago. We ran into him at the pasha's palace a few weeks ago."

"So the Dremish blew up *Vashaoth Teh*?" Sekibo whistled. "Damn."

Sikander stared the image on the small screen, thinking it through . . . and reluctantly shook his head. "No, Mr. Sekibo, this image doesn't prove that, as much as I hate to admit it," he said. "It's very, very suspicious, but it's circumstantial evidence. Yes, we see that Bleindel was at Meliya. That doesn't mean that he bombed the station. For all we know he was just passing through and narrowly missed getting caught in the blast."

"That's certainly what the Dremish will claim if we confront them with this security vid," Girard said, nodding. "But unless you record someone actually planting a bomb, how do you prove that they did it?"

"Demonstrate that they had the bomb beforehand?" Sekibo suggested. "Find a reliable witness who can testify that the bomber planted the device?"

"Neither of which we have here," said Sikander. He handed Girard's dataslate back to him. "Forward this to the squadron's intelligence desk—it might not be proof of Dremark's responsibility for the attack, but it's a certainly incriminating."

"Should I send a reply to the Velarans?" Girard asked.

"It's the policy of the Navy to cooperate with the investigations of friendly powers." Given the fact that Sikander had met Otto Bleindel publicly, there were no Commonwealth secrets involved, and while he could only guess at the diplomatic consequences of telling the Velarans that the Dremish agent might have been involved in the destruction of their cruiser, he had to imagine that it would make trouble for Bleindel—something he was inclined to do at the moment. "Thank you, Mr. Girard. And Mr. Sekibo, once more: Good work on the Meliya investigation. We wouldn't know about Bleindel's involvement if you hadn't found that signal."

Sekibo grinned. "Thank you, Captain!"

Sikander smiled at the younger officer's sheer enthusiasm, and watched him and Michael Girard hurry back to their work. *Was I that eager as an ensign?* he wondered. He returned his attention to the maintenance reports on his desk . . . but his attention was dozens of light-years distant. Regardless of what he'd just told his officers about proof versus suspicion, he *knew* that if Bleindel had been at Meliya, he must have been involved in the attack. The question was *why*—and Sikander simply didn't have anything more than guesses about that.

Late in the afternoon of the following day, Captain Broward summoned Sikander and Amelia Fraser to the squadron headquarters. "Ah, there you are," Broward said when *Decisive*'s officers entered his office. Sikander observed that Lieutenant Norton, the squadron's staff intelligence officer, was also present. "My apologies for stretching out the workday, but George here just brought some very interesting news to my attention. Go ahead, George."

"Yes, sir," Norton replied. He was a High Albionan, with the diffident bearing of a senatorial family that had represented the island of Falworth for something like two hundred years. Sikander found him somewhat standoffish, but as far as he knew Norton was good enough at his job. "We've received a report about suspicious activity in New Kibris: Specifically, outlaw ships are using an old Zerzuran naval depot at Bodrum as a fueling station and a transfer point for stolen cargo."

"Wait a moment," Sikander said. "This doesn't have anything to do with the message from the Velarans we sent over to you yesterday, or the Dremish agent who was identified in the security footage?"

"No, Commander," Norton replied. "We're looking into that, of course. This is something new."

Sikander hadn't expected that—he'd assumed that he'd been summoned to Broward's office to provide more context about Bleindel's activities. He leaned back in his chair. "I see. Go on."

"As I was saying, our source indicates that valuable cargo from several ships hit by pirate attacks over the last six months is stored at the Zerzuran depot. Naturally, we wish to verify this report."

"You're saying that this is a Zerzuran *naval* depot?" Amelia asked the intelligence officer. "As in a facility belonging to the Zerzura Sector Fleet and manned by Zerzuran military personnel?"

"Yes, ma'am. That is exactly what our report says," said Norton. "Bodrum is a minor supply depot and fueling station, not a fleet base per se. But as far as we can tell, it's an active post with a care-taker garrison of about sixty Zerzuran personnel."

"Are you so surprised?" Broward asked Amelia. "You handed *Qarash* and eighty-something prisoners over to the Zerzuran fleet at Bursa; the Zerzurans let them go as soon as you bubbled up and left the system. And I hear that Commander North's friend Ms. Pavon identified one of the prisoners over at the brig as the nephew of Admiral al-Kassar. Given that, the only questions in my mind are whether *any* of the Terran Caliphate forces in this region are honest, and whether Marid Pasha is personally involved in the scheme."

Sikander looked over to the staff intelligence officer. "What's our source?" he asked. He'd held the same position himself during his assignment to Helix Squadron, and his intelligence training had taught him that *how* you found out about something was almost as important as what you thought you'd found out. "Why are they only coming forward now, when everyone in the sector knows we've been looking for pirates for months?"

"I'm afraid that I am not at liberty to discuss sources," Norton said. "Suffice it to say that we consider it very reliable. As to why nothing was said before, my understanding is that our recent and highly publicized successes at Zafer and Fort Jalid—for which *Decisive* naturally deserves credit—have gone a long way toward puncturing the pirates' reputation for invincibility."

"You've shown everyone that the pirates are only human, Commander," Broward added with blunt approval. "We shouldn't be surprised if some highly visible successes encourage other people to come forward with what they know."

"No, I suppose not," Sikander said. He didn't care for Norton telling him to mind his own business, but he had to admit that it was a reasonable conclusion. The outlaws could easily be falling out with one another over the shock of losing outposts and ships, or perhaps not all of Zerzura's naval commanders could stand the idea of cooperating with the region's pirates—passing information to another power that would actually *do* something about piracy might be a whistleblower's way of striking back. "I take it that you'd like *Decisive* to investigate, sir?"

"You've demonstrated a real knack for paying attention to the right leads and doing what needs to be done," said Broward. "I wanted either you or Giselle Dacey for this job. I know I've been working *Decisive* hard lately, but *Harrier* just went into the yard for a couple of weeks, so it'll have to be you. I trust your judgment, Sikander."

"Thank you, sir." Sikander shifted in his seat, considering how the proposed mission would unfold. He wasn't familiar with the Bodrum depot, but he'd seen a number of similar stations. No minor post or patrol detachment in any of Zerzura's systems posed a serious threat to *Decisive*—that, of course, would change when the pasha's new cruisers entered service—but that didn't mean he had no reservations. "I want to make sure that I'm very clear on this, sir: You're ordering me to proceed to Bodrum and send a search party into the station to find pirated goods. Do we have the Zerzuran government's permission to conduct a search?"

"The last thing I want to do is warn someone that I'm about to search their facility for stolen goods," Broward said. "We already know that Marid Pasha's government leaks like a sieve, at least when it comes to our operations in their systems. Lieutenant Commander Fraser here convinced me of that weeks ago. So, no, I do not intend to ask them if we can have a look around."

"That worries me, sir. So far we've been operating in open space—international waters, so to speak. I have to imagine that Marid Pasha's government will see a search of one of their naval posts as a serious infringement of sovereignty."

"That depends on what you find there, Commander. I'm not

concerned about questions of sovereignty if the Zerzuran fleet is abetting piracy." Captain Broward pushed himself back from his desk, rising to pace over to one of the windows looking out over the row of destroyers moored in the basin outside. "Since you ask, I've already discussed the diplomatic implications with Admiral Thompson and Governor Blakeslee. Yes, in a perfect world, we'd run this all the way back to High Albion for approval. Unfortunately, that's a thirty-day round trip by direct courier, and I suspect that the first answer we'd receive is a long set of questions about what exactly we're proposing, meaning that it's really a *sixty*-day decision loop. Mr. Norton tells me that our intelligence suggests we need to move faster than that."

"Our source informs us that the pirates are preparing to shift their operations to better-hidden facilities by the end of the month," the intelligence officer said. "If we want to secure real, tangible *evidence* of the Zerzuran fleet's cooperation with pirates, we need to raid Bodrum before the stolen goods are moved somewhere else."

"I want to catch them at it, Sikander," Broward said, turning back to face his subordinates. "You're worried about the diplomatic consequences of boarding a Zerzuran station, but I'm worried about the consequences if we *don't*. Eric Darrow's dispatches from Dahar make it clear that Marid Pasha is cozying up with the Empire of Dremark in spite of our recent successes, and your report that a Dremish agent may have been involved in the *Vashaoth Teh* bombing certainly suggests that Dremark will stop at nothing to secure their strategic objectives in this region. Fine, then—if the Dremish are willing to fight dirty, we'll just have to do whatever it takes to stop them. Since we can't win the race for the pasha's friendship, maybe we can influence him with leverage of a different sort."

"Or start over with a different pasha," Norton added. "If we can prove that Marid Pasha actively supports piracy, or show that he's so incompetent that pirates can freely operate from his own fleet bases, the Caliph's court would have no choice but to replace him."

"Either way, we'll check our Imperial friends' designs on the Zerzura Sector while inflicting another serious setback to the pirates' operations," Broward said, nodding in agreement. "That's an opportunity we can't miss."

Sikander glanced over at his XO and met her eyes. Amelia gave the tiniest of shrugs, as if to say, *I'm not sure but I guess it makes sense,* or so he thought; after nearly a year of working with her every day he could read her pretty well. It wasn't too far off from his own reaction—having jumped headfirst into controversy more than once in his career, he thought he could recognize the signs of one here. On the other hand, the tiny Zerzura Sector Fleet's active participation in piracy would explain a *lot* of what had been going on the region since he'd taken command of *Decisive.* The idea of military professionals ignoring the sort of butchery he'd seen aboard *Carmela Día* or profiting from violent robbery sickened him. If that was what had been going on in Zerzura, it needed to be *stopped,* and he supposed that he didn't particularly care whose feelings got bruised in the process.

He looked back to Captain Broward. "I understand, sir. We can be ready to depart in a few hours."

Seven days and one high-speed warp transit after the conversation in Captain Broward's office, *Decisive* unbubbled in the Zerzuran system of New Kibris and began its deceleration maneuvers. Sikander studied the system with some interest after he'd satisfied himself that his ship had safely reached her destination—New Kibris was the only Zerzuran world he hadn't yet visited during his

tour at Neda. The planet represented a centuries-long terraforming project of a cold, dry, supermartian world. The old Caliphate
planetary engineers who'd started the process had succeeded in
unfreezing a narrow belt of ocean around the planet's equator
and building up a breathable atmosphere at low elevations, but
any point on the surface more than two thousand meters or so
above sea level lacked the oxygen or the warmth for human settlement—in a way, it was Dahar's opposite. Bodrum Naval Depot
was located on a tiny moonlet of the gas giant Tepegoz, twenty-
one light-minutes farther out from the system's semihabitable
world; it had been established more than a century ago to protect
and monitor mining operations exploiting the exotic ices found
in Tepegoz's moon and ring system.

"More rings," Amelia Fraser observed. "I didn't know pirates
were such romantics."

Sikander rested his chin on his hand. "I suspect they appreciate
the cluttered conditions more than the view. It must be hard to
keep track of exactly who's coming or going around here unless
you're right on top of the station. Mr. Girard, give me a zero-zero
intercept for Bodrum Depot, standard acceleration, please."

"Helm, come left to course two-four-four down five, standard
acceleration," Girard ordered. Naturally, he'd already worked it
out while Sikander was taking in the scenery. "ETA ten hours,
Captain."

"Roll over the watch in two hours so that everybody can get a
good rest before we set general quarters," Sikander told his tactical officer. "I'll be in my cabin."

He worked through a couple of hours of routine administration—reviewing enlisted promotion recommendations, today—
before taking his own advice and trying to get a few hours' rest.
Sleep proved more elusive than he would have hoped. He'd spent
most of the warp transit trying to visualize how events would

unfold at Bodrum, and after a week of thinking about Captain Broward's orders he still had no idea what to expect. At least he'd known that any ship he found in Zafer or Jalid would be a pirate; no honest spacers would have any reason to be in those uncharted systems. Today, though, he feared that Zerzura's pirates would be hiding behind denials and evasions instead of asteroids and ring systems, and he was keenly aware of the fact that he was poorly prepared for a confrontation of that sort.

Hours later, he was still staring at the ceiling when Darvesh quietly entered the room with his freshly pressed uniforms. The valet winced when he saw Sikander lying awake. "I am sorry, Nawabzada. I did not mean to disturb you."

"You didn't," Sikander told him. He sat up in bed and swung his feet to the deck. "I hardly slept."

"You are troubled, sir?"

"It's something that Captain Broward said before we left Neda." Sikander frowned at the deck plates, trying to pinpoint the source of his misgivings. "It seems to me that our pirate-hunting is turning . . . political. I was under the impression that we've spent the last year fighting Zerzuran piracy because piracy is bloody, cruel, and vicious, but Captain Broward reminded me that Aquila's interests are not quite as altruistic as I'd believed. Don't mistake me—if there are Zerzuran officers and officials getting rich from their support for piracy, I'll gladly drag them back to Neda in irons under any pretext. Still, I find myself wondering if we've been ordered to Bodrum because the Commonwealth Navy *stands* for something, or because Aquila is falling behind in this small corner of the great game and is ready to risk a bold play."

"The fact that Aquila finds advantage in dealing sternly with Zerzura's pirates does not mean that it is the wrong thing to do."

"All the same, I'd rather think of myself as a protector than a pawn," said Sikander. He rubbed the sleep from his face as if he could erase his unexpected doubts at the same time. "Damn it. I think Devindar's managed to get into my head."

Darvesh paused in his work. "I often disagree with your brother's rhetoric, sir. But I have never found fault with his cause or his reasoning."

"You think Devindar is *right*?"

"Nawab Dayan and Begum Vadiya have four admirable sons, sir. You should not be surprised by that."

"Admirable" was not a word Sikander expected to hear from Darvesh in connection with his brother's politics. He watched the tall Kashmiri return to arranging the pressed uniforms, remembering the argument in Devindar's kitchen at the end of his recent visit. "The last time I spoke with him, Devin told me that by serving here I endorsed Aquilan rule back home—that this uniform we wear stands for everything Aquila does, whether we personally participate in it or not."

"Aquilans are human, Nawabzada. All human institutions harbor potential for good and evil at the same time." The valet turned his attention to the cabin's small galley, and began to heat water for coffee. "I do *not* approve of the way the Aquilan governor-general discourages Kashmiri autonomy. I *do* approve of the effort Aquila is willing to put into suppressing piracy in this part of space. If that is not an entirely selfless enterprise, so be it, but we can see to it that our work secures a measure of justice for the dead of the *Carmela Día*. That is a worthwhile goal."

"It is, isn't it?" Sikander sighed and stood up, abandoning the attempt to rest. "Thanks, Darvesh. I'm up now. I might as well get dressed."

"Very good, sir." Darvesh handed him a fresh uniform and set out a pair of well-polished boots as though nothing in their conversation had been out of the ordinary. "Shall I fix you some breakfast?"

"Yes, please." *That's his way*, Sikander reflected. Darvesh found purpose in making the small routines of life important. *How many times has he told me that service has the value the servant chooses to give it?* Few people lived up to their words as honestly as Darvesh Reza did. "Eggs, toast, and coffee—it could be a long day."

Half an hour later, Sikander made his way back to the bridge well ahead of the scheduled arrival time. As *Decisive* drew near, Bodrum revealed itself as a misshapen, potato-shaped body two hundred kilometers long, orbiting just outside Tepegoz's rings. The naval station itself was built atop a two-kilometer rocky knob at one end, a spidery mass of habitats, docking cradles, cargo-handling modules, and fueling facilities; given the moon's feeble gravity, Bodrum had more in common with open-space orbital stations than typical surface installations.

Five hundred thousand kilometers and a little less than twenty minutes from their destination, Sikander had his crew set general quarters and don their battle armor. When all stations reported manned and ready, he took one last look around the bridge, taking in the tense and focused faces of his officers and crewhands. "I suppose we should announce ourselves," he said, and made a show of casually crossing his legs and relaxing in his battle couch for the benefit of the watchstanders around him. "Comms, give me a channel to the station, please. Bodrum Depot, this is Commander Sikander Singh North of the Commonwealth starship *Decisive*. You have probably noticed that we're heading in your direction; be advised that we intend to dock shortly. Please secure any small-craft operations you may have in progress and stand by for further instructions, over."

There was a long pause before anyone replied, and then the

face of a woman wearing the military cap-and-headscarf of a female officer in the Caliphate navy appeared in the display's comm window. She had a strong pattern of freckles across her cheekbones and dark, unfriendly eyes. "*Decisive*, this is Yarbay Rima Derki, commanding officer of Bodrum Naval Depot. I am not aware of any arrangements for an Aquilan warship to call at our facility. What exactly is the nature of your visit, over?"

"Yarbay Derki"—a rank equivalent to lieutenant commander in the Commonwealth Navy, Sikander reminded himself—"I am under orders to conduct a search of your station for stolen goods and evidence of pirate activity. Please direct your personnel to assemble in a common area and stand aside while my search teams do their work. Your cooperation would be very helpful, over."

Derki's nostrils flared in anger, and she drew in a deep breath. "Your *request* is highly unusual, Commander North. I cannot give you permission to dock until I determine whether my superiors want me to comply. Hold your position, over."

"You may consult with your superiors if you like, Yarbay, but I am proceeding with my search. I'm afraid it is not a 'request,' over."

"This is outrageous!" Derki snarled. "I don't know what sort of evidence of piracy you think you're going to find here, but this station is sovereign territory of the Vilayet of Zerzura and the Caliphate of Terra. Under what authority do you think you can land here and conduct a search?"

Sikander referred to a memorandum on his dataslate; he'd expected that very question and had made sure he didn't leave Neda without knowing what the answer would be. "The Neda governor-general's office and the Commonwealth Navy's Pleiades Sector Command have instructed me to conduct my search under the probable cause sections of the Interstellar Convention on the

Law of Open Space," he said to the Zerzuran officer. "Both the Commonwealth and the Caliphate are signatories, Yarbay Derki."

"Probable cause? What probable cause?"

"I will be happy to show you the letter authorizing my search in—" Sikander checked the ship's position. "—six more minutes. Tell your people to avoid doing anything foolish, and we will get through this as quickly and professionally as possible. *Decisive*, out." Then he cut off the channel, simply to make the point that he intended to carry through on things instead of talking about whether he could do them.

Another half minute passed, while *Decisive* continued to decelerate and the distance to the station steadily dropped. Then half the warning lights in the bridge suddenly illuminated at once. "Tactical, we're being illuminated by fire-control systems!" Ensign Carter shouted in alarm. "Bodrum Station is targeting us, sir!"

With what? Sikander wondered, forcing himself to remain seated calmly. His sensor operators had carefully studied the installation during their approach, determining that its defenses consisted of two old batteries of point-defense lasers—Bodrum was a support facility, not a hardened combat base. At a couple of hundred thousand kilometers, the small lasers could inflict some surface damage on *Decisive*, but nothing like what they'd endured from the repurposed mining laser at Fort Jalid.

"Weapons, illuminate the station," Girard ordered. "Target the weapon batteries. If they engage us, be ready."

"Illuminate the station, aye," Herrera replied from the weapons console. "It looks like only the one laser battery is trained on us, Tactical."

"Hold fire!" Sikander said, stepping in to make sure his combat team didn't meet the station's threat, small as it was, with lethal countermeasures. "Do not engage the target without my order."

"Aye, Captain," both Girard and Herrera replied.

He reopened the station communication channel. "Yarbay Derki, secure your fire-control system and point that laser somewhere else. I have ten times your firepower—if you attempt to engage my ship, your weapons systems will be neutralized before you even scratch our paint. Some of your people are likely to be killed over what amounts to token resistance, and we're going to be at your door in five minutes anyway. Trust me: You will regret it more than I will if you make me fire on you. *Decisive*, out."

The Zerzuran station commander did not reply—but thirty seconds later, the station's fire control switched off. Sikander sighed in relief. Searching another nation's military post was bad enough, but firing on it first to disable its defenses amounted to an act of war in his view. Despite Captain Broward's assurances and the support of the squadron commander's superiors at Neda, he sincerely hoped that he wouldn't have to fire a shot.

"Hard to argue with eight Mark IX K-cannons pointed in your general direction," Jaime Herrera observed.

"Yes, it is, but it proves nothing except that we have more guns," Sikander said; Herrera looked down at his console, chastened. *It doesn't hurt for my Aquilan officers to occasionally imagine themselves in front of the K-cannons instead of behind them. Jaime is a good man, but using firepower to win arguments is a bad habit.* Sikander shook his head in ironic amusement: Devindar was definitely in his head today. Darvesh's remark about the sons of the Norths came to his mind, and he found himself remembering the day Governor-General Braxton called at his father's palace in Sangrur. Nawab Dayan and his four sons had met the Aquilan viceroy, strolling together—

—on the sun-drenched terrace overlooking a peaceful vista of Sangrur. The jasmine is in bloom and the unrest breaking out in Bathinda seems like it belongs to another world. All the Norths

wear their finest military dress, although only Sikander's is Aquilan. Likewise the governor-general and his advisors wear immaculate uniforms and expensively tailored business suits; the "casual stroll in the garden" suggested by Jermaine Braxton resembles a military parade.

"This situation in Bathinda troubles me," the governor-general says to Sikander's father, with the blunt affability that is his trademark. "We can't have a city of ten million people immobilized by twenty thousand strikers. It's been the talk of all Kashmir for a week now, and there's no end in sight."

"It is difficult," Nawab Dayan admits. "But what would you have me do? People have a right to strike for better working conditions."

"They do not have the right to disrupt half a planet's commerce in the process. It's time to send in troops, Nawab Dayan. Today, before this gets any worse."

"In my judgment, the use of troops is a dangerous escalation," Sikander's father replies. "Better to wait out the strike, Your Excellency. Let Bathinda's store shelves remain bare a few more days, and I believe you will find public opinion turning against the strikers."

Braxton shakes his head. "If the KLP sees that they can shut down a major port any time they like, what will they choose to shut down next? Or, God help us, what happens if sympathetic strikes break out in other cities? The longer this goes on, the more likely it is to spread. We can't afford to be patient."

Nawab Dayan halts to take in the view as if he hadn't ever noticed it before, clasping his hands behind his broad back. "If the strike spreads to other states, then I will take whatever action the Khanate requires," he says without looking at his guest. "But until that time, Ishar is a sovereign state, and public order is my government's internal affair. I am not yet ready to send the port workers back to their jobs at bayonet-point."

The governor-general scowls. "Very well, Nawab Dayan. As you say, law and order in Ishar are your responsibility . . . until I declare an emergency, which I will do by the end of the week if you do not break up this strike. If I can't count on you to restore order, I will find someone who will."

"That is your prerogative," Dayan North says. Only someone who knows him well can recognize the anger in that deceptively mild tone. "But if you are concerned about the example the KLP is setting for people in other cities, you might also think of the example you would set for my peers if you intervene against my advice."

The Aquilan official's scowl deepens, but he suddenly turns away. "The end of the week," he says over his shoulder, retreating back to his waiting flyer. "Then something must be done!"

Devindar looks furious, but Sikander is not surprised; he knows where his brother's sympathies lie. Gamand, on the other hand, looks thoughtful. "I thought you favored breaking up the strike, Father," says Gamand.

"I did," Nawab Dayan replies, watching the Aquilan official and his entourage leave. Then, unexpectedly, he smiles. "But sometimes—not often, mind you—I am wrong."

"Captain?" Michael Girard interrupted his reverie, pointing at the Zerzuran base on the bridge's main visual display. "Which docking cradle, sir?"

Sikander scanned the depot's mooring spots. A few small craft clustered near one end of the station's row of cradles, so he picked one a short distance away. "The third one from the right, Mr. Girard. Set us down, and muster the search teams in the hangar bay. I want to get started before Yarbay Derki's superiors on New Kibris have a chance to tell her to do something stupid."

"Aye, Captain," Girard replied. He keyed the ship's announcing system. "All hands, prepare for mooring. Designated shore parties, report to the hangar bay and stand by to commence search and seizure operations."

"Very good, Mr. Girard," Sikander said, and settled back in his battle couch to await results.

Four hours later, he was still waiting: Sikander's search teams found none of the stolen goods reported in their intelligence brief in Bodrum Naval Depot, nor any sign that the goods had ever been there. Yarbay Derki's anger mounted hour by hour, as did the inquiries and protests of the Zerzuran fleet's New Kibris system commander. When his teams found nothing in the storage areas, Sikander dispatched Zoe Worth in *Decisive*'s launch to conduct a flyover search of Bodrum itself, just in case the missing cargo containers were stacked up in the shadow of a crater or buried under a few centimeters of regolith outside the base . . . to no avail.

"What do we do now, Captain?" Master Chief Felicia Vaughn asked Sikander. A broad-shouldered Orcadian, she served as *Decisive*'s command master chief and represented the destroyer's enlisted personnel in the command leadership team, which at the moment was huddled together in the hangar bay. Sikander, Amelia Fraser, and several of the ship's department heads had gathered at the ship's belly airlock to coordinate the search effort, only to watch frustrated sailors march out of the Zerzuran station, report their lack of results, then receive new assignments and march back in again. "Our people have been over every square meter of that depot twice now. If there's anything here, it's hidden pretty damned well. We're running out of places to look."

Sikander glanced over to Amelia. "Anything on the station security recordings?" There was a real question about whether *De-*

cisive could demand access to Bodrum's own recordings as part of their search, but since Yarbay Derki was already furious, he'd decided to have his people take a look. He wasn't a judge advocate, and he wasn't overly worried about preserving a future prosecution if the security records pointed his search teams in the right direction.

She shook her head. "Tolbin and Morton have gone back six months and haven't spotted any civilian vessels or a cargo transfer of anything other than normal provisions. If the pirates moved stolen cargo through here, they were careful to keep it off the vidcams."

"We could send in hull-cutting teams and burn through the bulkheads," Amar Shah suggested. "It might take a while to locate and open up all the structural voids in the station, but if there are secret cargo spaces, we'll find them, sir. It's just a matter of time."

"If," Sikander said, and ran a hand through his hair. "Somehow, I find it hard to believe that criminals operating in the friendly environment of a station run by their accomplices would go to the trouble of cutting and resealing bulkheads to stash their loot."

"Then we take the station crew into custody, separate them, and see if anyone feels cooperative when they think they might be in danger of going to prison," Shah suggested. "Someone can tell us where the cargo is concealed."

"You're overlooking the obvious answer, Mr. Shah: We haven't found anything because there isn't anything here to find."

"That would mean our intelligence is completely mistaken," Shah said.

"Yes, it would," Sikander said. "Or deliberately misled. But I think that's more likely than cargo containers welded behind bulkheads or security recordings so carefully faked our experts can't spot the loops or edits, don't you?"

Shah fell silent. Amelia Fraser folded her arms, and sighed. "Well, I think that brings us back to the master chief's question, sir," she said. "What now?"

"Call it off, XO. Tell our people to clean up their mess, collect their gear, and return to the ship. I'm afraid we're done here."

"The Zerzurans are going to raise holy hell over this," Amelia said glumly. "Well, I suppose it's not *our* fault. I'll have the quartermasters lay in a course for home."

"No, not yet," Sikander told her, giving voice to an idea that had been slowly taking shape in his mind as it had become clear that Bodrum was a dead end. "We'll return home by way of Dahar. I'm sure the Admiralty informed our diplomatic mission that we'd been ordered to search this station, but Mr. Darrow needs to know that we didn't find anything as soon as possible. And he might want me to personally apologize to Marid Pasha."

Amelia looked skeptical. "Do you think that would do any good?"

"I have no idea, but the pasha was familiar with my role in the Gadira affair and expressed a good deal of admiration for what I did there. I think that an apology from me might mean something to him."

"Or he might have you arrested on the spot, Captain," Master Chief Vaughn observed. "Nothing sours people like finding out that their heroes have let them down."

"We'll know soon enough," Sikander said. "XO, make preparations to get under way."

18

Mersin, Dahar II

I t was raining about as hard as Elena Pavon had ever seen it rain in Mersin . . . which, as it turned out, was not very hard at all. A damp, heavy mist clung to the city's mountaintops and high-rises, beading up on the windowpanes of her office. She didn't think it would do much to discourage the pro-independence marches and rallies taking place in the planetary capital today—crowds numbering in the tens of thousands were expected later in the afternoon despite the forecast. From her building, she could see dozens of banners featuring the heroically posed likeness of Marid al-Zahabi decorating store windows or looking down from billboards on every block. The newscasts and opinion shows playing on the vidscreens on the office's opposite wall all agreed that more and more Zerzurans supported the idea of independence from Terra, and a good number of them believed that Marid Pasha would be able to do more for Zerzura as a president instead of a governor.

They might not be wrong about that, Elena reflected. Certainly she'd long been frustrated by dealing with an outdated and inefficient bureaucracy designed by Caliphate officials back on Terra centuries ago; piracy wasn't the only challenge in Zerzura's business climate. If Marid al-Zahabi could do something about that, she'd gladly overlook whatever outsized political ambitions he might harbor. *In fact, we might need to boost our support for the pro-independence movements and put some more credits into campaign coffers. When the pasha gets around to making the separation official, it'd be smart to make sure he knows Pegasus-Pavon was behind him the whole time. We don't want the al-Kassars standing alone beside the throne.*

Omar Morillo appeared at her office door. "Ready to go?" he asked. His bruises had faded and his cracked ribs had largely healed from the scuffle in the parking garage more than six weeks ago, but he still moved a little gingerly as he held the door for Elena.

"I guess." Elena reluctantly abandoned her post by the window, and slipped her dataslate into the leather case she used in place of a handbag or purse. "Although I doubt the kidnappers would make another try, not after our security upgrades. And I've got a few calls I need to make—"

"—which you can do from Mount Kesif just as easily as you can from Mersin," Omar said firmly. "The first rule of personal security is don't be predictable. As long as we're in Dahar, regular office hours are out. We're rescheduling your afternoon appointments and leaving early today, and that's that."

Elena frowned, but did not argue the point any further. "Fine, then," she said. "Let's go." Omar had earned the right to micromanage her security arrangements, and it would have been stupid to go right back to business as usual in any event. She had to proceed under the assumption that her enemies could call upon the full resources of the al-Kassar family and Suvar United, and that meant they might be able to reach her anywhere in the system. As a result, a full-time professional security detail now guarded her office, her apartment, and the Mount Kesif plantation. She wouldn't be caught unprepared again.

Omar wisely refrained from commenting on her cooperativeness. He simply inclined his head, and led the way to the rooftop garage where her luxury flyer waited—a heavier and better-protected replacement for the flyer she'd been using just a few weeks ago. Two armed chase flyers hovered nearby, ready to escort her to her destination. "I can't imagine how much this is costing us," she muttered as they climbed into the backseat.

"It's significant," he admitted. "Then again, your father made it clear to me that I was to spare no expense when it comes to your personal safety, especially in Zerzura."

"Let's see if we can find a reasonable compromise sometime soon. I don't need a parade everywhere I go."

"Sure thing. Just as soon as the situation improves."

"Anything new from our legal team?" she asked as the skycade lifted off from the Pegasus-Pavon building and turned south through the mists wreathing the city. The minute *La Nómada* had arrived in Dahar, Elena had ordered Pegasus-Pavon's lawyers to begin proceedings against Gadi al-Kassar. She didn't need Gadi's money, of course, and she doubted that Gadi could be tied to the kidnapping attempt. The opportunity to ferret out Gadi al-Kassar's business arrangements and bank accounts with asset searches and discovery, on the other hand, might be very useful indeed.

"Since you ask, yes, we're making good progress," Omar said. "I received an initial report from our people less than an hour ago. It turns out that Gadi al-Kassar is a wealthy man—he's got dozens of accounts and investments to sort through. But the one that's caught our interest is something called the Rihla Development Corporation. No one seems to know what it is or what it does."

"Rihla Development?" Elena pulled out her dataslate and started searching; it took her only a few moments to make a cursory pass through Dahar's information systems. Her search bounced—

there wasn't any virtual storefront or public portal available. The name appeared only in public records listing businesses incorporated in the Dahar system. "Is it some sort of holding company or shell?"

"That's our guess," Omar said, looking over her shoulder. "Gadi gets a *lot* of money from Rihla Development, but this is all we have on them so far. We'll have to do some digging to find out where their registration forms are filed and what exactly they say they do."

"So let's dig, then," she told him. "I want to nail that son of a bitch to the wall, Omar."

"We've got thirty people on it, Elena. Before we're done, we're going to be able to account for every credit Gadi al-Kassar ever earned or spent. If he bought a candy bar in a vending machine twenty years ago, we'll document it. It's just a matter of time."

At Mount Kesif, Elena spent the rest of the afternoon looking after the plantation while she waited for Omar and the Pegasus-Pavon legal team to unearth more details. The coffee orchard always served as a welcome change of pace from Pegasus-Pavon strategic challenges spanning fifty light-years and involving eleven-figure profit-and-loss statements. A business that turned a profit of a few hundred thousand credits in a good year was a hobby, really, but Elena loved dealing in small and tangible things: discussing the irrigation strategy with her grower, consulting with the master roaster over the best way to bring out Mount Kesif's unique flavor profile, reviewing suggestions for a long-overdue new logo. Pegasus-Pavon was so big that she really spent most of her time and attention on the business of running a business; involving herself in the day-to-day operations of the shipping line was micromanaging. At Mount Kesif, she could literally get her hands dirty and tinker to her heart's content . . . and she'd discovered that her subconscious mind often continued to process the big problems while she distracted herself with solving a few little ones.

She did spend an hour late in the evening reviewing progress on the acquisition of the old gunboats *Kartal* and *Pelikan*. Before retreating from Dahar in the aftermath of the kidnapping attempt, she'd instructed the Mersin office to continue the effort to secure the two ships before they were scrapped. To her surprise, the Zerzura Sector Fleet hadn't shut down the transaction. Oh, they weren't in a *hurry* to transfer the gunboats, but they'd at least come back with a counteroffer and allowed her representatives to inspect the vessels in the orbital depot where they were currently being decommissioned. Given what she suspected about the al-Kassars, she couldn't imagine why Admiral Torgut had any interest in letting the deal go forward. *Maybe he intends to slow-walk the whole deal just to keep my time and money tied up in an effort he can stifle whenever he likes,* she decided. *Or maybe he's planning to pocket a big kickback in the process of helping me to "fight" piracy. He's probably laughing all the way to the bank!*

She directed her team to keep working on it just in case Torgut al-Kassar wasn't as smart as she thought he was, and went to bed.

The next day, Omar found her taking coffee and a late-morning brunch on the plantation house's wide porch. "Okay, boss, I think we've learned something about Rihla Development," he said with a grin. "And it's just about as bad as you could imagine."

"I can imagine a lot. What have you got?"

"Rihla Development is a privately held corporation registered in a tax-haven asteroid settlement in Dahar's outlying regions. They're a holding company with investments in real estate and legitimate businesses throughout Zerzura, established by Hidir al-Kassar five years ago with the purchase of a thirty-million-credit stake in a Tejat Minor bank."

Elena gazed off across the orchard, comparing dates in her head. "Didn't Suvar United lose a couple of ships to pirate attacks around five years ago?"

"Two old bulk carriers, yes. Suvar received a big insurance payout, and they haven't suffered another major loss from piracy since. Anyway, ever since its establishment, Rihla Development receives large infusions of cash from a variety of mysterious companies and corporations throughout Zerzura, turns that cash into legitimate investments, and pays its shareholders very handsomely. Guess who beside Gadi and Hidir is a shareholder?"

"A lot of people named al-Kassar, I imagine."

"Eight of them, in fact, including Admiral Torgut. A few other people I don't know, who might not actually exist. And Marid al-Zahabi, whose Rihla dividends last year were reported at sixty-three million credits."

"Oh, *shit*. The pasha, for sure?" Elena got up and paced away from the rocker where she'd been working. "Can we prove that Rihla's cash infusions come from illegal sources?"

"In a court of law? No, not yet. But I spent some time this morning chatting with a friend who works for a bank where we do a lot of business. Rihla Development keeps an account there, too. I asked him if Rihla ever received deposits from an outfit called Venture Salvage." Omar grinned again. "My friend told me that he could *never* disclose to me that Venture Salvage had made six large transfers to Rihla Development in the last two years."

"So what you're telling me is that we now *know* that proceeds from piracy flow from Venture Salvage—"

"—and a dozen other murky outfits—" Omar added.

"—into Rihla, where they're converted into legitimate investments and then paid out as gigantic dividends to the Caliphate governor of this sector, the admiral in command of the sector fleet, the president of Suvar United, and God knows how many more of their friends and cronies?"

"Short answer: Yes. Longer answer: A prosecutor would have a hell of a time proving that the money flowing into Rihla is dirty. Assuming that you could find a Zerzuran prosecutor who'd even give it a go."

"What do we even *do* with this?" Elena asked, momentarily overwhelmed by the sheer scale of the corruption. Any corporation doing business across multiple star systems had to deal with a certain amount of local corruption, but a sector government whose high officials moonlighted as pirate kings? It defied comprehension, really. *There's almost nothing we* can *do about it*, she realized. *Marid Pasha answers to no one in Zerzura.* There were no elections to think of, no opposition who could use it as a campaign issue, and not even much independence in the judiciary or the press to hold the pasha accountable. "We can't touch the pasha; he's the direct representative of the Caliph. The man can pardon anybody he wants, use his military authority to arrest whoever he needs to, or just expropriate everything under a Pegasus-Pavon flag in Zerzura and expel us from his little kingdom whenever he likes. In fact, I can't figure out why he hasn't done it already."

"He doesn't need to because you're not a threat to him. Not yet, anyway—you should be careful about how we pressure the al-Kassars. And while the law is in Marid Pasha's pocket, he still needs to keep public opinion in mind. He can't shut down the courts or start arresting people who accuse him of corruption without looking guilty as hell."

"I'd like to think so, but I'm not sure that Marid Pasha couldn't step on us whenever it suits him. If he spins it as standing up to an evil foreign corporation for the sake of all Zerzurans, the people in the streets might cheer him on. Have you seen the polling numbers lately?"

"I have." Omar made a face. "Damn. You're right—we need to find another mouse to bell the cat."

Elena didn't like to think of herself as a mouse, not even in a metaphor. "Let's reach out to the movers and shakers in the Caliphate court. If Marid Pasha doesn't answer to anyone in Zerzura, he might have to answer to someone on Old Terra." *Of course, who's to say that the next governor they send out to Zerzura would be any more honest?*

"Get the Caliph to fire Marid Pasha, got it." Omar made some notes on his dataslate. "You know, this might not be the sort of problem we can fix, Elena. Either we learn to live with it—minimizing our risks as best we can—or we write off the sector and look for safer places to do business."

"I'm not prepared to accept either of those answers." Elena paced across the porch, gazing over the even rows of coffee trees marching up the sunny hillside above the house. Omar remained silent, giving her space to think. *If this isn't a problem we can fix, then who can?* Even if she could convince the Caliphate court to intervene, that could take months, and the streets in Mersin were plastered over with banners calling on Marid Pasha to make a clean break from the Caliphate. She had to imagine that Marid would simply declare independence if Terra tried to remove him from power. No, what she needed was someone who could make it clear to Marid Pasha that it was in his own best interest to drop his support for the al-Kassars . . . even though they were paying him millions each month.

Well, no one's going to get paid for hijacking Pegasus-Pavon hulls if we pull our business out of Zerzura altogether, Elena realized. The question was, who could explain that to the Zerzurans and make them listen? And even as she examined that problem, she realized she might know the answer.

She stopped pacing and looked back to Omar. "Get me an appointment with the Dremish envoy," she told him. "I need to explain a few things to her."

Omar raised an eyebrow. "You really think she can control the pasha?"

"I think I can make her see why she ought to try."

"Okay. I'll make a couple of calls." Omar turned to go back into the house.

"Hold on. Set up a call with Alonzo Benady at Grupo Constelación first—I think I might want to talk to him before I approach the Dremish."

"Got it." Omar raised an eyebrow again at Elena's intention to speak with one of her chief competitors, but added it to his list of notes. "Anything else?"

"That'll do for now," Elena told him. She returned to her rocker and poured herself a fresh cup of coffee, already beginning to plan out what she'd say and how she'd say it.

The Grupo Constelación call took several hours to arrange— Alonzo Benady was busy with a board meeting and couldn't be interrupted. He turned out to be something of a hard sell, but eventually gave Elena a cautious agreement after she explained what she wanted. She expected it might take Omar days to book an appointment with the Dremish envoy after that, but surprisingly Vogt made herself available later in the afternoon. A little after four o'clock, Elena's skycade lifted off from Mount Kesif for the twenty-minute flight back to Mersin. They landed on the rooftop platform of the building housing the Dremish consulate, and Elena and Omar took the elevator down to the lobby.

"This is it," Omar observed, nodding toward an elegant

entranceway. Gold lettering on the plate-glass doors read "Consulate of the Empire of Dremark" in Jadeed-Arabi, with the Nebeldeutsch phrasing of the same name just underneath. "Last chance to change your mind."

"I think they'll be interested in what I have to say," she told her assistant, and headed inside. Two plainclothes Dremish security agents stood guard in the lobby, frowning at the rest of Elena's retinue—four private bodyguards who escorted her inside. Elena left the Dremish security and her own protection detail engaged in their professional stare-down, and headed for the receptionist at the lobby desk. "Good afternoon. Elena Pavon and Omar Morillo; we have an appointment with Ms. Vogt."

The receptionist, a Dahari, consulted the vidscreen in front of her and nodded. "Welcome, Ms. Pavon," she replied. "You're expected. Paul here will take you to the special envoy's office. Your detail can make themselves comfortable here."

"Thank you," Elena replied, and followed the young man indicated by the receptionist; Omar Morillo lingered just long enough to tell her bodyguards they could wait in the lobby, and hurried after her. The Dremish aide showed them through the working areas of the consulate to a comfortable corner office—nowhere near as vast as Elena's own in the Pegasus-Pavon suite a few kilometers away, but handsomely paneled and furnished nonetheless. Apparently the special envoy had claimed the permanent consul's desk for the duration of her mission in Zerzura.

Hanne Vogt met them at the door of her temporary office. "Good afternoon, Ms. Pavon," she said in Jadeed-Arabi. "Please, come in."

"Thank you, Envoy Vogt." Elena took note of Vogt's dark, expensive-looking designer pantsuit and her striking chartreuse blouse; the diplomat certainly had a sense of style. "This is my personal assistant, Omar Morillo."

"A pleasure to meet you, Mr. Morillo," Vogt said, shaking Omar's hand. "I must say, I am happy to see you both alive and well after that awful kidnapping attempt a few weeks ago. You must have been terrified."

"You heard about that?" Elena asked.

"You made the evening news. It's not every day that someone tries to kidnap an heiress." Vogt led them to a sitting area by the window; gray mist mantled the upper floors of the taller buildings outside.

"I had no idea," Elena said. She took one end of a small couch, and Omar sat beside her. Vogt took a seat across from them. "Thank you for seeing me, by the way. I'm sure you must be very busy."

"I have a feeling that you wouldn't call if your business wasn't something important. What can I do for you, Ms. Pavon?"

"Are you familiar with the al-Kassar family?"

"I've met Admiral Torgut, but I wouldn't say that I know him well," said Vogt. "I understand they're in the shipping business—competitors of yours, I imagine."

"They are," Elena said. "The admiral's brother is Hidir al-Kassar. He runs the Suvar United shipping line. Pegasus-Pavon is a bigger operation overall and we service a wider area, but here in Zerzura they're just as big as we are. In ordinary circumstances, that wouldn't present any special concern to me: Five major systems is a large market and there's room for everybody. But these aren't ordinary circumstances."

"How so?"

"Because the al-Kassars aren't just competitors, Ms. Vogt. They're the principal sponsors of piracy in this sector. In fact, Admiral Torgut's nephew Gadi actually captained the pirate vessel *Balina*, and I believe the rest of the al-Kassars are involved in other ways."

The Dremish diplomat gave a small frown. "That's quite an accusation. Can you prove it?"

"The Aquilan navy's holding Gadi al-Kassar on Neda right now; I saw him there myself. They captured him at the pirate outpost called Fort Jalid." Elena raised her hand, ticking off points on her fingers. "Gadi, his uncle Hidir, and Admiral Torgut are all shareholders in a holding company called the Rihla Development Corporation. We know that Rihla received large payments from another company, called Venture Salvage, which sold cargo stolen from our freighter *Carmela Día* and operated the pirate base at the Zafer system. Speaking of Zafer, the pirate ship *Qarash*—captured there and handed over to the Zerzura Sector Fleet base at Bursa—was immediately released, and turned up again at Jalid. I strongly suspect that the pirates were set free at Admiral Torgut's order, although we're still in the process of verifying the details."

"That's audacious," Vogt observed. "Assuming for the moment that I find your evidence as compelling as you believe it to be, why bring this to me?"

"Because Marid Pasha is involved, too. He's one of the principal shareholders of Rihla Development Corporation. He's made *millions* from the al-Kassars' piracy operations." Elena fixed a hard gaze on Vogt. "The al-Kassars I can handle, Ms. Vogt, but I need Dremark to deal with Marid Pasha. He's buying Dremish warships and signing fat Dremish contracts. The way I see things, you own him, and that means you're responsible for what he does."

"Zerzura is an autonomous vilayet within the Terran Caliphate. We don't 'own' anybody here."

"Oh, bullshit," said Elena. "Save that for the newscasts. I'm a businesswoman, and I'm here to talk business. If you can't do anything about the pasha, then I'm wasting my time, and yours."

Vogt's eyes narrowed almost imperceptibly, but she showed no other sign of anger, remaining silent for a long moment. "Go on," she said coolly.

"For a couple of years now I've been trying to work with the Zerzuran government to suppress piracy in this region. Ten days ago I found out that I've been trying to negotiate with the same people who are hijacking my cargoes and killing my employees— and yesterday I found out that it goes all the way to the top. I'm *pissed*, Ms. Vogt. So is Alonzo Benady over at Grupo Constelación. I'm ready to pull Pegasus-Pavon out of Zerzura completely, and I can get Constelación to follow my lead. Think about what happens to the economy of this sector if two-thirds of its shipping capacity suddenly goes away. Intersystem trade will grind to a halt—we'll put five worlds into the sort of depression that brings down governments. I don't know exactly what Dremark hopes to get from Zerzura, but I have to imagine that a sector in economic collapse isn't on your shopping list."

"Are you *threatening* me, Ms. Pavon?"

"That's one way of looking at it." Elena leaned forward and met the Dremish envoy's gaze evenly. "I would prefer to think of this as a friendly effort to make sure you're aware of the consequences of your new ally's unsavory habits. It's to my advantage to make sure the Empire of Dremark knows what it's buying in Zerzura, Ms. Vogt. I hope you can see it's to yours, too."

Vogt thought for a long moment before replying. "We have a great deal invested in Marid Pasha, Ms. Pavon. We can't lightly put that relationship at risk—or allow someone else to. *If* Marid Pasha's government is as complicit in piracy as you say it is, then yes, we would like our new friend to distance himself from those elements. Allow me to look into this a little more and think about the best way to proceed."

"I wouldn't think for too long," Elena said. It didn't escape her that Hanne Vogt hadn't actually committed to doing anything or even accepted her understanding of the situation. *Then again, she's a professional diplomat. If she lets on that she believes me, she'd have to take action . . . wouldn't she?* She decided to push just a little more. "The Aquilans know who they've got in their brig at Neda, so they're already aware of the al-Kassars' role in Zerzuran piracy. When Marid Pasha's involvement comes to light, I have to imagine that they'll bring it to Old Terra's attention . . . or take more direct action. Your investment in the pasha might be at risk."

"I wouldn't count on the Caliphate taking much of an interest in Zerzura any time soon. We're a long way from Terra." Vogt stood, and offered her hand. "Thank you for this frank and refreshing conversation, Ms. Pavon. I'll be in touch."

Elena scowled without reaching for Vogt's hand. "I need something more than that."

"I said I would look into your allegations and take the appropriate action. That's all I am prepared to say right now," Vogt countered. "Good afternoon, Ms. Pavon."

"I'll be waiting, Ms. Vogt," Elena replied. Clearly, there was nothing more to be gained by antagonizing the diplomat, so she forced a small, cold smile and stood. She just couldn't read Vogt well enough to tell whether she actually saw Marid Pasha's involvement as something that needed fixing. She glanced over at Omar, and her assistant gave a tiny shrug; he wasn't sure, either. "Good afternoon."

She and Omar collected her security detail in the consulate lobby, and then returned to her waiting flyer on the rooftop. "Well, that was interesting," Omar remarked as they climbed in. "I have a feeling she's not terribly surprised by what you told her— not happy, but not surprised. So what now?"

"Have *La Nómada* send the orbiter down for me—I think I'd better stay off-planet until we see what the Dremish decide to share with Marid Pasha and how he reacts to it." At Mount Kesif, Elena's security could spot anyone coming for her from a hundred kilometers away. In orbit, they'd see trouble coming from ten times as far . . . and they'd be ready to run, if it came down to it. Nothing in the pasha's fleet could catch *La Nómada* from a standing start.

Omar nodded in approval. "I was going to make that suggestion. I don't think Vogt would tell Marid to move against you—she's too smart for that—but if he doesn't like what she has to say, he might panic and overreact."

Sunset painted the hillsides a brilliant golden green by the time Elena's flyer and its escorts set down in the field beside the plantation house. High overhead, she could already make out the bright curving contrail of her yacht's orbiter against the darkening sky, and the distant roar of its descent echoed through the valley. She trotted up the wide steps of the porch and headed for her bedroom to gather up the materials for the various projects she'd been working on and make sure the household staff had packed up everything she wanted to take with her—Elena had no need to travel light, and never bothered to pretend that she saw any special virtue in being able to do so.

When she emerged from her room, she found her bags already on the way out to the orbiter, waiting in the dusty field that served as Mount Kesif's landing pad. She was just about to follow them when she noticed a bold new headline crawl on the living room's vidscreen, currently tuned to Dahar's leading business newscast channel: Aquilan Warship Threatens Zerzuran Naval Base at Bodrum * Sector Government Lodges Formal Protest * css decisive Arrives in Dahar After Conducting Illegal Search. "What in the world?" she murmured, pausing to take in the story.

The press-kit image of Sikander Singh North's face appeared

on the screen, followed by a montage of maps, a short clip of *Decisive* under way, and a moon or asteroid station she didn't recognize. Elena stood and watched, her leather working case forgotten at her shoulder as she tried to piece together what exactly had happened. She didn't think she was so infatuated with Sikander that she'd drop everything at the mere mention of his name—oh, she liked him well enough, and she looked forward to seeing him again. But she hadn't expected him to turn up in Dahar, or to see him on the news.

She lingered long enough that Omar came looking for her. "What's going on?" he asked.

Elena nodded at the vidscreen. "The Aquilans have apparently decided to start searching Zerzuran naval stations. The Zerzurans are pretty upset, as you might imagine."

"Oh, shit," Omar said, studying the screen. "What were they thinking?"

"I have no idea, but I bet Marid Pasha isn't going to take it well," Elena replied. *For that matter, the Dremish aren't going to like the idea of Aquila pushing around a potential client, either.* She could think of nothing that would push Marid al-Zahabi into Dremark's orbit more effectively than the sort of high-handed contempt for Zerzuran sovereignty the news channel was reporting. Hanne Vogt was probably on her way to Marid's palace already—and confronting him on corruption and support for piracy was not likely to be on her agenda.

"I think we just got pushed to the back burner." Omar could work out the implications just as well as she could. "You realize, of course, that this is exactly the sort of incident that Marid Pasha needs to move ahead with independence?"

"That's how it looks to me, too." Elena shrugged her satchel into a more comfortable position, and turned away from the news. "Let's get going—I think it's time to talk to the Aquilans again."

19

Dahar High Port, Dahar II Orbit

A few hours after *Decisive* returned to Dahar, Marid Pasha agreed to meet Sikander and Eric Darrow at the Dahar Naval Shipyard, an old facility that orbited twenty thousand kilometers above the Zerzuran capital world. No docking cradles had been available for *Decisive* at Dahar High Port—a sign of Zerzuran displeasure, Sikander guessed—so he'd directed his bridge team to assume a parking orbit nearby. He took the destroyer's gig over to the commercial spaceport to pick up Eric Darrow for their appointment with the pasha, accompanied by Amelia Fraser, Michael Girard, and Darvesh Reza.

The Aquilan diplomat didn't *look* angry when Sikander met him in High Port's public shuttle concourse, but his easy smile was nowhere to be seen this morning, and his manner was direct as he greeted *Decisive*'s party. "Commander North," he said. "I hope you'll forgive me if I say I'm not especially happy to see you under the circumstances. The Navy's really stepped in it this time."

"I can't say you're wrong, Mr. Darrow," Sikander said, shaking the diplomat's hand. He felt wretched about the situation; not a man or woman aboard *Decisive* didn't. Amelia Fraser winced at the diplomat's remark, while Michael Girard turned beet red and looked down at his shoes. Sikander, however, didn't have the luxury of remorse. Responsibility for *Decisive*'s actions ultimately rested with him. Whether the Admiralty found fault with his execution of the orders Captain Broward had given him—or simply decided it might be expedient to do so—was not in his hands. All he could do was move forward and accept the consequences without excuse or evasion, and perhaps provide one final example for the men and women under his command if it came down to that. "I hope I haven't made things more difficult by bringing *Decisive* to Dahar. My orders were to inform you of the results of our search as quickly as possible, and I felt that there was at least a chance that a personal apology to Marid Pasha might be helpful."

Darrow grimaced. "In all honesty, there's very little you could do to make the situation *worse*, so your presence probably doesn't hurt. Besides, the pasha's admiration for you gives us an opening we otherwise wouldn't have. He wasn't interested in seeing me until I indicated that you wanted to see him. Speaking of which, he's expecting us shortly—we'd better not keep him waiting."

"Our boat is right this way," Sikander said, nodding to the airlock where the gig was secured; the small group started in that direction. "Do you have any advice on what exactly I should say to Marid Pasha?"

"Make your apology and then stop talking. Don't speculate about what went wrong or what the Commonwealth should do to make up for it. To the extent that you can, try to avoid a specific admission that we were in the wrong: I'd rather hear you say 'I don't know but I promise we'll get to the bottom of this' than admit that you agree that we stepped over a line."

Sikander repressed a sigh. He'd never been very good at being evasive. "I have a feeling that the pasha isn't in the mood for any attempt to downplay the situation."

"Let me worry about that," Darrow told him. "I'll help you out if I have to. He's only giving us a few minutes, so I doubt that he's going to demand any kind of complete accounting of your actions."

Sikander hoped that the diplomat was right about that. They reached the airlock where *Decisive*'s gig was docked, and boarded the tiny craft; five passengers just about filled the cabin. "Dahar Naval Shipyard, Kersey," Amelia instructed Petty Officer Kersey.

"Aye, ma'am," the pilot replied, sealing the hatch. She smoothly accelerated away from the spaceport's docking ring, bringing the gig's drive plates to full power once she was clear.

"Did you see the summary of the Fort Jalid raid?" Sikander asked Darrow—the Commonwealth government's Neda offices provided regular intelligence reports to the diplomatic mission in Zerzura, as did the Admiralty. "It seems to me that Gadi al-Kassar's arrest and the mishandling of the impounded pirate *Qarash* show that we had good reason to mistrust the Zerzura Sector Fleet's leadership. We might owe the pasha an apology, but Admiral al-Kassar owes us some explanations."

"I did read the summary, but today's not the day to raise those questions," Darrow replied. "If Torgut al-Kassar is present when we meet with Marid Pasha, don't bring it up. It'll look like we're trying to deflect Marid by going on the offensive over an unconnected issue."

The issues seemed connected enough from where Sikander stood. However, he could understand Darrow's point; he decided to defer to the veteran diplomat. "Very well. I'll avoid the topic."

He fell silent, considering what he intended to say. Ahead of the gig, the Dahar Naval Shipyard steadily grew larger in the gig's cockpit windows. It was an old Terran Caliphate installation that had been towed into orbit two centuries ago to support Caliphate fleets operating against the Velaran Electorate during the wars of the time. After generations of infrequent work in maintaining

Zerzura's worn-out gunboats and corvettes, its open-space work cradles now housed the largest warships to visit since the long-ago wars for which it had been built: the ex-Dremish cruisers *Drachen*, *Meduse*, and *Zyklop*, plus the repair ship *Neu Kiel*. Sikander wasn't sure whether the pasha had chosen the site of their impromptu meeting to show off his new navy, to make the point that Aquila's representatives were no longer welcome in his palace, or because he cared to spare only a few minutes from his busy day and the shipyard visit best suited his schedule, but he supposed he should be grateful for any opportunity at all to speak with Marid Pasha given the outrage filling Dahar's news and opinion channels.

They docked at the shipyard's administration module, just a couple of cradles over from a gleaming white orbiter with gold trim that Sikander took to be the governor's official transport. Inside the airlock, the Aquilan party was met by a handsome, thirtyish Zerzuran in a good business suit: Jahid Saif, one of the pasha's aides. "Commissioner Darrow, Commander North," he said, nodding to them. "This way, please. I hope you'll forgive the setting, but you should understand that this is an informal exchange of views, and we are not prepared to entertain official discussion of any sort at the moment."

"We understand," Darrow replied. "Thank you, Mr. Saif."

Generations of infrequent use and short budgets had left their marks on the shipyard's admin spaces; the lights were out in some of the corridors they passed, and the air had the sharp, oily smell of recyclers in need of maintenance. Saif led them to a small, shabby passenger lounge near the docking rings, where two soldiers in the khaki dress uniforms of the pasha's personal guard waited. *Another sign of official displeasure?* Sikander wondered. *The pasha's handlers might want us to* know *that they don't care to make this a comfortable discussion.* He looked at the dusty plastic seats, considering whether he really wanted to sit down, but as it turned out he didn't have to decide: The interior door slid open just a moment later, and Marid Pasha entered the room. Torgut al-Kassar and the rest of the pasha's entourage followed just a pace behind Marid; the admiral glared at the Aquilan officers, but said nothing.

"Good morning, Your Excellency," Darrow said with a small bow, as if a disused passenger lounge were a formal audience chamber. "Thank you for agreeing to meet on such short notice."

Marid al-Zahabi folded his arms over his chest, glowering. "Mr. Darrow. I think my government's position has been made clear, so I'm not sure what you hope to add at this point. I have only a few minutes before I'm scheduled to inspect the work on my navy's newest acquisitions. Say what you came to say, if you please."

"Of course. We will get to the point, then." Darrow nodded to Sikander.

Sikander took a deep breath and faced the pasha. "Your Excellency, I would like to personally apologize for the misunderstanding at Bodrum Depot. Our intelligence was extremely confident that pirates were making use of the base for cargo transfers and resupply. Clearly, our intelligence was mistaken. I don't know how they came to make such a serious error, but we will figure out how this happened and make sure it doesn't happen again."

"I am disappointed in you, Commander," Marid said sternly. "What sort of intelligence would lead you to treat soldiers and sailors of Zerzura's military forces as criminal suspects? Or land armed troops in our sovereign territory? Those are not the actions of a friendly power."

"I know, and I am sincerely sorry that our sources led us to make such a serious error. Our intention was to help Zerzura suppress piracy in this sector, and we thought that's what we were doing." Sikander tried very hard not to look at Torgut al-Kassar as he said that, and did not quite succeed; the Zerzuran admiral actually smiled thinly at his words. "I will take this up with my superiors on my return to Neda, I promise you."

Marid Pasha exchanged a long look with his advisors; Sikander had the sense that he was waiting to see if they had anything to add. Jahid Saif returned the pasha's look without expression, and Torgut al-Kassar said nothing; the pasha returned his gaze to the Aquilan party. "I appreciate Commander North's personal apology," he said to Eric Darrow. "It speaks well of his character that he would be prepared to accept responsibility for his ship's actions. It seems clear to me, though, that his superiors directed him to act with blatant disregard for Zerzuran sovereignty; Commander North's apology is insufficient to the magnitude of the offense. As a result, I am immediately suspending all cooperation and passage agreements with Aquilan military forces. Commander, you have twenty-four hours to remove your ship from the Dahar system and set a course out of Zerzuran space."

Sikander remembered Darrow's advice to say as little as possible and clamped his mouth shut. The Aquilan diplomat, however, held up a hand in protest. "Your Excellency, with all due respect, a sector governor cannot suspend agreements between the Terran Caliphate and the Commonwealth of Aquila," he said. "However, in the interest of avoiding further local misunderstandings while this incident is fully investigated, *Decisive* will voluntarily withdraw to internationally recognized open space."

"I am not finished," Marid Pasha said. "Mr. Darrow, you and your special commission are hereby expelled from Zerzura. I have no interest in continuing a relationship with a partner that feels it can invade Zerzuran bases with impunity and meddle in our internal affairs. You have twenty-four hours to arrange passage from Dahar. I suggest you leave aboard *Decisive*, since she'll be heading in the right direction."

"You can't do this!" Darrow retorted. "You don't have the authority. I am accredited before the Caliphate Porte!"

"Then I suggest you go to Terra and make your protest there—you are no longer accredited in Zerzura. If you are still here the day after tomorrow, I will have my troops forcibly remove you." The pasha motioned to one of the bodyguards at his back, a hard-looking officer with a scarred face. "Major Terzi, our guests will be returning to their boat. Mr. Darrow, Commander North, you may rest assured that we will be conducting our own investigation into the facts of the New Kibris incident. If this debacle turns out to have been a sincere mistake, then I may reconsider my decision in due time. But until then: *Get out of my sector.* Good day, gentlemen."

Major Terzi silently motioned toward the passage through which the Aquilans had entered the lounge. Marid Pasha gave them one last withering look, then turned on his heel and stormed out without another word. The rest of his entourage followed him.

"Well, *shit*," Amelia muttered as the hatch hissed shut behind the Zerzuran party.

"Shit, indeed," Darrow said, and sighed. "Let's be on our way, Commander North. I have a lot to do in the next twenty-four hours, and then I suppose I'll need a ride."

After a brief detour through Dahar High Port to drop off Eric Darrow, Sikander and his officers returned to *Decisive*. He didn't trust himself to say a word about the pointed meeting with Marid Pasha, so he stormed back to his cabin and threw himself into the chair behind his desk. *So much for months of hard work*, he fumed. *Two pirate bases smashed, hundreds of outlaws captured, God knows how many lives saved from attacks we prevented simply by being present, and it's all for nothing because of one bad lead.* The truly infuriating part of the situation was that Torgut al-Kassar would doubtless keep those ex-Dremish cruisers parked at Dahar's dilapidated orbital station, where they'd do exactly nothing about piracy, allowing his friends to resume their depredations just as soon as Aquila's patrols ended.

Amelia Fraser let him cool off for the better part of an hour before she knocked at his door. "Mr. Darrow's office informed us that he'll be on board by 0900 tomorrow morning, Captain," she said. "How soon after that do you want to get under way?"

"The last possible moment to observe Marid Pasha's deadline," he said with a snort. "Let the Zerzurans stew a bit, damn them."

Amelia met his eyes. "It didn't matter what you said to the pasha, you know. Marid al-Zahabi had already made up his mind to expel our diplomatic mission and revoke our patrol agreement. It was out of your hands, Sikander."

"That doesn't mean I'm ready to accept the outcome. At least, *we* didn't need to be a part of that little scene. I don't know what I was thinking—we should have gone straight back to Neda instead of coming back to grovel in front of the Zerzurans."

"A sincere apology isn't groveling. We screwed up, we owned it, and we took our medicine. That's what honorable people do when they make a mistake."

Sikander grimaced, thinking of Torgut al-Kassar watching him go through the whole performance. Apologizing to a criminal for failing to catch him in the act didn't *feel* very honorable . . . but, as Amelia pointed out, the Commonwealth Navy *had* screwed up, and as the embodiment of the Commonwealth Navy in this particular corner of the galaxy at the moment, it had fallen to him to own it. *That's the job,* he reminded himself. *Leadership is about taking responsibility and setting examples. No one aboard this ship needs to see me sulking about that—not even Amelia.*

He took a deep breath, and composed himself. "All right, you've made your point. Let's get the department heads together to start our transit planning. But if we're supposed to be on our way by 1100, then I'm serious about not moving a millimeter until 1059."

"Not a millimeter until 1059, aye," Amelia confirmed. "We'll get them next time, Captain. Toads like the al-Kassars are going to get greedy and make mistakes—it's in their nature. You'll see." She saluted, and left to begin arranging *Decisive*'s next warp transit.

Sikander picked up his dataslate and headed for the bridge. Not much was going on as long as they were comfortably powered down in a parking orbit, but being around a few watchstanders and listening in to the routine system traffic seemed like a better idea than continuing to stew in his cabin, and he had some work to do—specifically, finishing his Bodrum Depot report for the Admiralty, now with an addendum describing the brief encounter with Marid Pasha. Chances were good that *Decisive* would beat the report home, given the circuitous routes messages took through the network of courier services linking the worlds of humanity, but after the last few months in Zerzura he'd lost a little confidence in his ability to predict where his ship would be in a few days' time.

He was just putting the last touches on the message when Zoe Worth—currently on watch as officer of the deck—called for his attention. "Captain? There's a civilian orbiter signaling us," the sublieutenant said. "It's registered to *La Nómada*, Principality of Bolívar. They wish to come alongside. Umm, Ms. Pavon is on board, and she says that it's important that she speak with you."

"Elena—er, Ms. Pavon—is here?" Sikander asked. He glanced over at the bridge display; sure enough, there was her yacht, now coasting into view in its own parking orbit a few hundred kilometers above *Decisive*. *I really shouldn't be that surprised*, he realized. Elena had told him that she planned to head in this direction as soon as she finished on Nuevo León, but in his hurry to consult with Eric Darrow and call on Marid Pasha he hadn't noticed *La Nómada* amid the rest of the system's traffic. "Very well. Tell the orbiter to come alongside, and bring Ms. Pavon up to my cabin. Ask the XO to join us, too."

He returned to his cabin and tidied up quickly—not that Darvesh ever allowed his quarters to become too cluttered—while the valet prepared coffee and tea. Then he took a moment to check his appearance in the mirror above the sink. He found that he was surprised by how much he was looking forward to seeing Elena, and a little regretful that he'd have to keep the unexpected reunion proper and professional. A captain enjoyed a few privileges most officers and crew didn't, but entertaining a romantic interest on the Navy's time was not one of them.

A knock at his cabin door announced Elena's arrival; the deck-hand escorting her opened the door and stepped aside. "Captain, your visitors," the young man announced.

"Sikander!" Elena said, and hurried over for a quick embrace. "I'm glad to find you here." A handsome, dark-haired man in a finely tailored business suit followed her in; Sikander recalled seeing him with Elena in one or two of their earlier encounters. *Omar, Elena's executive assistant,* he reminded himself.

"It's good to see you too," Sikander told her. Naturally, Amelia Fraser appeared at his door just in time to catch him with his arms around the lovely heiress. She raised an eyebrow, and managed to avoid smirking at him. He disentangled himself and nodded toward his XO. "Allow me to introduce my executive officer, Lieutenant Commander Amelia Fraser. Amelia, this is Ms. Elena Pavon."

"A pleasure to meet you," Amelia said, and shook Elena's hand. "I'm sorry I missed you a couple of weeks ago at Neda—I had to get home and see my children off to bed."

"The pleasure is mine," Elena said. "This is Omar Morillo, my executive assistant." Another round of handshakes ensued.

Sikander indicated the small conference table in the cabin's aft alcove, where Darvesh was setting out refreshments. "I have a feeling this isn't just a social call, and I'm afraid that we've been asked to leave the system soon," he said. "So . . ."

"So don't waste time?" Elena grinned, showing that she was not offended. She took a seat; Omar sat down beside her, while Sikander and Amelia took the opposite side of the table. "I understand. Let me begin by asking if you've ever heard of a Zerzuran company called Rihla Development Corporation."

"No, I don't believe so."

"It's a private holding company with only a dozen shareholders," Omar Morillo said. "Last year Rihla paid out almost half a billion in dividends from legitimate investments—investments funded by large transfers from shady outfits like Venture Salvage, the group that sold off *Carmela Día*'s stolen cargo and owned the so-called mining facility at Zafer."

"You're talking about a money-laundering operation that turns the proceeds from piracy into big checks for some very rich people," Amelia Fraser observed.

"Exactly," said Elena. "My legal team in Mersin unearthed the scheme when we started looking into Gadi al-Kassar's assets. He owns a six-percent stake in Rihla Development, but he's only a small fish. It turns out that the biggest shareholders are Hidir al-Kassar, Torgut al-Kassar, and Marid al-Zahabi."

"Whoa," Amelia said, sitting up straight. "*Admiral* al-Kassar and *Governor* Marid al-Zahabi? The two most powerful men in the Zerzuran government?"

Elena nodded. "And Hidir al-Kassar is the president of Suvar United, the largest Zerzuran shipping line. I see that you appreciate the magnitude of the problem."

"Good God," said Sikander. "We certainly had our suspicions about Admiral Torgut after you identified Gadi al-Kassar among our prisoners, but I didn't expect that a connection to Marid Pasha would turn up, too." He glanced over at Amelia. "Not three hours ago he looked me right in the eye and told me he was disappointed in me. Disappointed! That *bastard*."

"I told you they'd get greedy," Amelia said.

"You did. I didn't think it would be *today*, though." He thought about the implications. "No wonder Marid Pasha wanted to get rid of us. Everything we've been doing in the last three months has been a direct attack on his bank account!"

"Which certainly made it more attractive for him to cozy up to Dremark," Amelia observed. She snorted in bitter amusement. "Now I see why he wants those hand-me-down cruisers. He needs to keep us away from the people paying him off."

"One step at a time," Sikander said, returning his attention to Elena. "Before we go any further, you'd better explain what you know and how you know it."

"Show them what we've got, Omar," Elena said to her assistant.

Morillo nodded, and started a presentation on his dataslate— evidently he'd anticipated that a detailed explanation might be needed. For the next twenty minutes he walked Sikander and Amelia through the connections, showing them records of Rihla's tax filings, Venture Salvage's sale of stolen cargo, and Hidir al-Kassar's initial investment. "I don't know if we could make it stick in court," the assistant admitted when he finished. "We'd have to subpoena bank records to *prove* that Venture paid Rihla, which means a court would have to allow a suit to proceed or someone's being prosecuted over this whole affair. But we have informal confirmation that those payments took place."

Amelia glanced over at Sikander. "Maybe our intelligence on Bodrum Station wasn't as far off as we thought. This is our smok-ing gun."

"I suspect that depends on the court it's brought to," Sikander replied. "But it's certainly solid enough for an intelligence report. We don't have to prosecute the Zerzuran government—we just need to be able to document what they've been up to and take the appropriate action."

"That's the other thing I wanted to talk to you about," Elena said. "My options are limited. I've got everything I need to go after Marid Pasha and the al-Kassars, but that's dangerous for Pegasus-Pavon: The pasha could snap his fingers and confiscate our cargoes, revoke our commercial licenses, maybe even expropriate our ships and auction them off to his friends at Suvar. We lose if we go up against the Zerzuran government. I asked the Dremish to intervene, since they would seem to have some influence over the pasha, but they're in no hurry to rein in their Zerzuran allies. Hanne Vogt told me as much yesterday."

"You took this to the Dremish envoy?" Sikander asked sharply.

Elena shrugged. "Why shouldn't I? Dremark has more pull with Marid Pasha than Aquila does, and Dremark isn't *my* rival— I'm Bolívaran, after all. Unfortunately, it was a waste of my time. The Dremish are heavily invested in Marid Pasha, and Vogt has no interest in spoiling that relationship."

"No, I suppose she wouldn't." Sikander didn't like the idea of Elena looking for an accommodation with the Dremish, but he had to admit that he couldn't expect her not to do anything she could to protect her family's business. He hoped that his Dremish counterparts at least had the decency to feel ashamed when they overlooked the sort of criminal behavior Vogt was apparently prepared to overlook. "All right. What do you think we can do to help?"

"It seems to me that Marid Pasha is a problem for both of us," said Elena. "You can bring diplomatic pressure to bear on him. Press for Terra to recall him, threaten sanctions against Zerzura if he tries to declare independence, or at least see to it that he doesn't squash Pegasus-Pavon if we go public with what we know. If you can't get rid of him, you might at least get him to hold back his pirate friends and watch his step."

"That might be more difficult than it would have been a few hours ago," Amelia said in a sour tone. "The pasha just expelled our diplomatic mission and revoked our passage rights throughout the sector."

"Then you've got nothing to lose by confronting the pasha."

"It's not clear that pushing harder is in the Commonwealth's interest at the moment," Amelia replied. "It might be smarter to back off and find a different way to engage in this sector. Piracy isn't the only problem to keep in mind."

"I'm getting tired of hearing about the politics of the situation," Elena retorted. "It's not just about the bottom line, Ms. Fraser. People are dead—*my* people are dead. It's time someone *did* something."

She's right, Sikander decided, remembering the frozen bodies aboard *Carmela Día*. He hated the idea of letting the people behind such atrocities go unpunished; the more he thought on what he'd learned in the last few hours, the angrier he got, until he could actually feel a cold and razor-sharp resolve hardening in the center of his being. He stood abruptly and moved away from the table to stare at the vidscreen that served as the cabin's window. Dahar's nightside glimmered beneath *Decisive's* orbit, with a slim orange crescent of daylight creeping into view. *Politics be damned—we have to stand for what's right. By taking those payoffs, Marid Pasha made himself just as guilty of piracy as the murderers who shot down* Carmela Día's *crew in cold blood. We can't turn a blind eye to that just to stay a move ahead of the Dremish in this sector . . . who have their own crimes to answer for. And as Elena says, what more do we have to lose?*

He turned back to Elena and her assistant. "I agree with you," he told them. "I promise you that one way or another, we'll put a stop to what's been going on in Zerzura—and we'll see Marid Pasha answer for the blood on his hands. The al-Kassars, too."

Amelia looked up at him. "How, Captain? We're about to be personae non grata here."

Sikander wasn't exactly sure yet, but he didn't share that with his exec or his guests. "Not for another twenty-two hours yet," he said instead. "First things first: Elena, can we make a copy of Mr. Morillo's presentation and the supporting research? I need to show it to Mr. Darrow before we do anything else."

With a small smile, Elena set a datastick on the conference table. "I thought you might want one. Here's a copy of everything we've been able to document so far—I trust you'll make good use of it."

"I certainly hope to." Sikander scooped up the datastick and slid it into his pocket. "Next, I think you'd better leave Dahar as soon as possible. I don't know if Hanne Vogt will tell Marid Pasha about the case you're building against him, but if she does—or if he figures out your involvement based on actions we take— Zerzura could become very dangerous for you. Get out of Marid Pasha's territory until you know that it's safe to return."

Omar Morillo glanced over at his employer. "I've been trying to convince her of that for hours."

"Fine." Elena looked unhappy, but she nodded. "I have to go to our regional headquarters in Meliya anyway. Given what we've found out in the last few days, we need to take steps to minimize our exposure in Zerzura, and I can't take the chance of sending those instructions through Zerzuran message services—as you pointed out a few weeks ago, someone could be reading my mail."

"That's probably a good idea," Sikander agreed. If he were in her position, he'd certainly take steps to protect his business—and more importantly, his *people*—from Zerzuran retaliation. "I'll send word if anything changes, but in the meantime I'll feel better knowing that you're somewhere safe."

"So would I, I guess. And that means I'd better be on my way." Elena rose from the table, and came forward to give Sikander a fierce hug. He returned her embrace, ignoring Amelia Fraser's smirk. "*Get* these bastards, Sikander," she murmured to him. "They need to pay for what they've done."

"They will," he promised her. "Let me see you back to your boat."

"To borrow your exec's lovely turn of phrase again: Well, *shit,*" Eric Darrow said after Sikander finished explaining the whole Rihla Development revelation. They sat in Darrow's office in the Aquilan consulate, joined by Nola Okoye and Amelia Fraser. The special commissioner was in the middle of packing, and several storage boxes had been hastily cleared out of the way for the meeting; Okoye, on the other hand, planned to remain in Mersin. As a permanent consul, she wasn't part of Darrow's mission, and the Aquilan diplomats had decided that Marid Pasha's order of expulsion didn't cover the local consuls scattered throughout Zerzura's five major systems. Darrow blew out his breath and leaned back in his chair. "How confident are you about this information, Commander?"

"I know that we just embarrassed ourselves by acting on a bad tip, but Ms. Pavon presents a convincing case," Sikander answered. "I've got my intel specialists at work verifying the tax records in the planetary information systems to confirm the report. I don't think they are going to find that someone made this all up to embarrass us. Besides, all the pieces of the puzzle fit."

"Hanne Vogt saw all of this, too? And brushed it off?"

"Ms. Pavon came away with the impression that the Dremish

aren't in a hurry to jeopardize the relationship they've cultivated with Marid Pasha," said Amelia.

Darrow made a face. "Dremark's Foreign Office isn't afraid to double down on a risky bet—or cover up a mistake with a lot of angry bluster. I suppose it's a sort of loyalty to their clients, but it's one of the things I find especially trying in my Imperial colleagues."

"There's something else you need to know," Sikander said. "I'm not sure if the intelligence dispatches reached you yet, but we've confirmed that Otto Bleindel was at Meliya Station right before the bomb that destroyed *Vashaoth Teh* went off. It didn't come up before our visit with Marid yesterday, but in light of what Elena Pavon told me about Dremark's determination to stand by the pasha, it seems clear that Bleindel carried out the attack for his benefit."

"Human separatists *weren't* responsible?" Okoye's eyes narrowed, but she maintained her customary reserve otherwise. "The Meliya attack was the turning point in Vogt's negotiations with Marid Pasha. Our sources in the palace suggest that the pasha was happy to draw out our little bidding war until the Velarans started asking him pointed questions about the Meliyan Human Revolution."

"Which the KBS might have conjured up out of thin air specifically to force Marid's hand," Darrow observed. "Damn! I see that our Imperial colleagues have been busy. Commander, can you *prove* that Bleindel was responsible for the bomb?"

"All we can show is that he was there," Sikander said with a small shake of his head. "We let the Velaran investigators know who they've got on their security vid. They may turn up something more."

The two diplomats and the two naval officers fell silent for a moment, each considering the situation. Sikander found himself gazing out the office window; the pasha's palace gleamed in the distance, a fairy-tale castle that almost seemed to float in Dahar's gorgeous sky. It seemed impossible to believe that such extravagant splendor concealed such ordinary greed—or, for that matter, that Marid Pasha's sterling reputation as a hero and a reformer concealed such cold, calculating ambition—but the conclusion was inescapable at this point. The worst part of it all was that, as far as Sikander could see, Marid al-Zahabi might easily get away with it despite his promise to Elena Pavon. *The pasha answers to no one in Zerzura, and the Dremish have given him the fleet he needs to defy any enemy beyond his borders . . . unless that enemy is willing to bring a fleet that would trigger Dremish intervention in turn. So what is left?*

Amelia sighed and said aloud what Sikander was thinking: "Okay. We know Marid Pasha is corrupt and we know Dremark's been playing dirty. Now what?"

"We have what we need to expose Marid Pasha's corruption," Okoye said. "We present our findings to the Caliph's court. They'll remove Marid al-Zahabi from power, and the new governor—who, by the way, may be very interested to learn about Dremish bomb plots designed to sour Velaran relations with Zerzura—will certainly revisit any deals Marid al-Zahabi made with the Empire of Dremark."

"I wish it were that straightforward, Nola," Darrow said. "The problem is that Marid Pasha has all the popular support he needs to declare independence. By the time Terra orders his recall, he'll be the head of a sovereign nation under Dremark's protection. He'll thumb his nose at the Caliph and go right on with what he's been doing."

"I can't imagine that Terra would go along with that," Okoye said. "They'll treat it as a local rebellion, not a legal secession. They'll send a new governor with transports full of loyal troops to reestablish their authority."

"Except that Marid Pasha now has an ex-Dremish cruiser

SCORNFUL STARS • 357

squadron that can face down any force that Terra could reason-ably scrape together to subdue him," Sikander pointed out. "And once the pasha secedes and makes his alliance with Dremark of-ficial, I'm sure the Dremish will be more than happy to expand his new fleet." He'd assumed that the pasha wanted his expensive new fleet to challenge Aquila's patrols in his territory and keep Zerzura safe for piracy, but if Darrow was right, then the Terran Caliphate was one of those external powers Marid wanted the power to defy. *Checking our antipiracy efforts is only a side benefit for the pasha,* Sikander realized. He looked back to Darrow. "Are we going to recognize Zerzuran independence, Mr. Darrow?"

The special commissioner considered the question for a mo-ment. "We'll have to," he said.

"What? That's crazy!" Amelia protested. "We'll let Dremark pry a five-system sector away from the Caliphate and buy them-selves a pirate king in Zerzura?"

"Yes, it's crazy," Darrow said. "But, unfortunately, it's our job to deal with the facts as they are, not as we'd like them to be. I can't see a way to prevent the Empire of Dremark from winning this round of the great game. We'll just have to make up the lost ground somewhere else. If the Dremish believe they can sponsor Zerzuran independence to gain a strategically located client state, well, they can hardly complain if we encourage the Caliphate's Al-Ma'laf or Gurkani Sector to break away, too."

"Dear God," Nola Okoye breathed. "You're talking about the dissolution of the Terran Caliphate."

"That wouldn't be our choice, but if the Dremish are reckless enough to begin carving up the Caliphate, we *cannot* allow them to gain control of the whole thing," said Darrow. "We have to manage the disaster as best we can, and see to it that most of the Caliphate's worlds remain in friendly hands. What other choice would we have?"

Sikander shivered—that was the answer he'd feared when he asked about recognizing Zerzura. Aquilan diplomats and military planners had been quietly examining the possibility of a Caliphate collapse for decades as a sort of worst-case scenario. Most experts thought that it would precipitate a great-power war as younger, more vigorous nations fought over the Caliphate's carcass. He'd never really imagined that the long-feared day might actually arrive, though. *We four sitting in this office might be the only humans in existence who understand just how quickly disaster is approaching,* he thought. Somehow they needed to keep Marid Pasha from following through on his plan to secede or find a way to drive a wedge between him and his Dremish friends, and they needed to do it *now.*

"That's it, then," Amelia said. "We have to expose and remove Marid Pasha ourselves. We could be back here with all of Pleiades Squadron in three weeks. If we hurry, those Zerzuran cruisers won't be ready for service before we return."

Darrow shook his head. "If Marid Pasha declares independence and formalizes his alliance with the Dremish before your squadron gets here—which I imagine he will, within a matter of days—then it's just a quicker route to the same disaster. We can't remove a declared Dremish ally by force without starting a war; we'd need the Terran Caliphate to do it for us, and as Commander North pointed out a few moments ago, the pasha's new cruisers mean that's not going to happen."

"What if . . ." Sikander began slowly, thinking through an idea even as he started to speak. It was audacious, unexpected, even reckless, but he'd promised Elena Pavon that he wasn't going to let Marid Pasha's crimes stand, and he'd meant every word of that promise. *It could work,* he told himself, as the idea crystallized in his mind. *Elena's investigation proves that confronting piracy in Zerzura means confronting Marid Pasha—it's the only way we can bring those responsible for* Carmela Día *to justice. We'd have to move at once, and the diplomatic fallout might be too high a price to pay . . . but if disaster is inevitable anyway, then I'd just as soon fail while fighting to right at least one wrong.*

He took a deep breath, and finished his thought: "What if the pasha didn't have a fleet?"

20

CSS *Decisive*, Dahar II Orbit

Four and a half hours before Marid Pasha's deadline, CSS *Decisive* warmed up her drive plates and prepared to break orbit above Dahar. Sikander would have preferred to use more time rehearsing the mission at hand, but orbital mechanics could be unforgiving. Finding a window during which *Decisive*, Dahar Naval Shipyard, and Dahar High Port—one arm of which served as the base of the Zerzura Sector Fleet and Dahar's orbital defenses, such as they were—would all be in the optimal positions in their orbits forced him to dispense with several hours his people could have put to good use. If nothing else, a few hours' break between planning and implementation would have been desirable, but in the fifteen hours since his conversation with Eric Darrow in the consulate at Mersin, he and his senior leadership had found little opportunity for rest.

"Last chance to call it off," Amelia Fraser said to him as they headed for *Decisive*'s hangar bay. "I figure we're looking at sixty-forty odds that the Admiralty cashiers us both for this stunt, with at least a twenty-percent chance that we're court-martialed and spend time in prison before they throw us out of the service."

"It's my decision, Amelia," Sikander said. "I recorded a message for Commodore Broward taking responsibility for this whole scheme. They might bring me up on charges, but you should be fine."

"Oh, I'm pretty sure that they'll fire me for not stopping you, but I appreciate the thought. It'll be nice to spend more time with my children." They reached the hangar bay, and Amelia paused to offer her hand. "Good luck, Captain."

"And to you, XO," Sikander replied over their handshake. "You're the one who's going to have to clean up the mess if I'm wrong about this."

"Don't be wrong, then." Amelia gave him a quick grin, then preceded him into the hangar bay. "Attention on deck!"

Eighty-five Aquilan sailors divided into three detachments snapped to attention, standing in orderly ranks in the hangar. It was the only space inside the ship other than the mess deck that could accommodate that many people at once, and the group assembled here represented just over half of *Decisive*'s total crew. Each crewhand wore Navy battle dress, a mottled blue-gray urban-camouflage uniform reinforced by light armor panels, and carried a standard-issue mag rifle slung over his or her shoulder. In front of the sailors stood the officers assigned to command them: Lieutenant Michael Girard and Sublieutenant Olivia Haynes for the first group, Lieutenant Amar Shah and Sublieutenant Zoe Worth for the second group, and Sublieutenant Reed Hollister for the third.

"At ease," Sikander told them. The assembled sailors and officers relaxed their postures, turning their eyes to him. He took a moment to collect his thoughts, considering what he wanted to say—and, more importantly, what they needed to hear. "Good morning, everyone. I suppose you all know why you're here." A faint chorus of nervous chuckles rippled through the ranks; Sikander smiled, and continued. "I wish I could tell you that the battle dress and the small arms are just for show and that I really don't think you will need them, but I can't. There simply isn't much precedent for what we're about to do, and I have no idea how the other side is going to react. I hope to use the minimum amount of force needed to achieve our objective, and to that end I've issued instructions that all weapons are to remain set for non-lethal velocity unless we meet with armed resistance. Petty officers, make sure you check your squads' weapons and verify the power settings after we're done here.

"Assuming that everything works as we hope and we reach our objectives, I wish I could tell you that I'm confident that we'll be able to carry out Phase Two without a problem. I'm afraid that I can't make that promise, either. We just don't know enough about the condition of the target and the details of the systems we're taking control of. That's why we've made sure to include Jadeed-Arabi and Nebeldeutsch speakers in each detachment—we might need to stop and read the operating manuals in a hurry before we go any further." That earned another round of chuckles. "But I *am* confident about this: Whatever it takes to get this plan to Phase Three, you have the adaptability, the resourcefulness, and the sheer professionalism to make it work. You are the finest crew I have ever had the pleasure of serving with, and I am supremely confident in your ability to meet and overcome any obstacle that arises today.

"The spacers and ordinary citizens of this sector have suffered from brutal pirate attacks for years. They may not be our people, but they're people who need our help. Pirates—and those who support them—are the enemy of all civilized nations. Today we've got one good opportunity to strike a blow for those who can't." Sikander finished with a fierce grin. "So let's make the most of it!"

A raucous cheer broke out as the sailors assembled in the hangar bay shouted out their approval. Amelia waited a moment for the cheers to die down, and then called out in a high, sharp voice: "Boarding parties, attention! Boarding parties, to your boats!"

The sailors grabbed their gear and weapons, and headed for *Decisive's* small craft: both of the destroyer's sturdy VO-8 Cormorant orbiters, and the lighter launch. All three would be standing-room-only, but there was no help for it; Sikander just didn't know if circumstances would allow multiple runs, so he had to send everyone over at once. He turned to Amelia. "Well, time to be on your way, XO. Take care of my ship—not a scratch!"

"Not a scratch, I promise. Watch yourself over there, Captain." Amelia saluted, and then hurried out of the hangar—her place today would be on *Decisive's* bridge.

Sikander checked his own gear once more; he had a mag pistol holstered at his hip, but he'd decided not to carry a rifle to make sure he didn't forget that getting into firefights wasn't his job today. He watched the sailors crowding into the ship's boats, faces tense with worry or glowing with eagerness to meet the challenge of the unusual mission. Gunner's mates and masters-at-arms generally kept up with their small-arms practice and had at least a little tactical training, but most of the force was made up of volunteers taking on a job for which they were essentially untrained. *Rather like the Jaipur Dragoons at Bathinda,* he thought, trying to keep the worry he felt from his face. *I'm asking a lot of my people. They're willing and I know they'll do their best, but will it be enough?*

He remembered accompanying his father to his troops' deployment area a few hours after the *Blue Horizon* was bombed. Two battalions of dragoons mustered at a disused airfield on the outskirts of the city—

—standing in front of a row of grounded transport flyers in the long shadows of afternoon, arms clasped behind their backs in the position of parade rest. Nawab Dayan climbs up to stand on the back of a cargo tow car so that he can be seen more easily by the assembled

soldiers; Colonel Nayyar joins him on the narrow perch. Sikander and Gamand remain on the pavement with the rest of the nawab's command group. Sikander knows what his father has in mind, but he has no idea how the nawab will explain it to his soldiers.

"We are faced with a difficult situation," Nawab Dayan begins. His voice is strong enough to carry clearly to all the Kashmiri soldiers on the field. "This morning's attack on the Blue Horizon signals a new and dangerous phase in this dispute. Blood has been spilled; the governor-general has ordered the Chandigarh Lancers to secure the cargo facilities so that replacement workers can be brought in tomorrow to reopen Bathinda's port. The strikers are certain to resist any effort to disperse them short of deadly force." In fact, that's not all of it; Sikander also knows that the governor-general warned Nawab Dayan that he'd instructed the Srinagaran troops to begin mass arrests of strikers who refuse to return to work after the demonstrations are broken up.

Nawab Dayan continues: "I believe that this strike is the wrong way for Bathinda's port workers to bring about changes in their working conditions. It is confrontational and driven in large part by reckless rhetoric from a few radical voices. Worse yet, five people are now dead, and those murders demand justice. But the vast majority of the strikers are not responsible for the freighter's bombing, and those who aren't are within their rights to assemble and protest so long as vital services are not interrupted by their actions. We will take action to punish the guilty—and we will also take action to protect the innocent." He nods to Colonel Nayyar.

Nayyar steps forward and raises her voice: "Dragoons, attention! Stack . . . arms!"

Some of the soldiers glance from side to side, not entirely familiar with the rarely used command. But after a heartbeat of silent hesitation, the two battalions move forward to lean their mag rifles together in neat pentagons, hooking the bayonet rings to one another.

Within two minutes the entire force disarms itself and returns to its parade positions.

"Stand at ease!" Colonel Nayyar orders when they finish. "We are now going to board our transports and deploy to Pier Six, where we will bring a transport loaded with critically needed goods into port. Most of you will be assigned to perimeter security—your job will be to stand unarmed in between the demonstrators and the Chandigarh Lancers, and protect each from the other. Transportation and cargo-handling specialists will conduct the off-loading of the Fair Horizon. Additional fully armed units are standing by at deployment areas nearby; if they are needed, they will be called in. But until that happens, you will not respond to any provocation short of immediate physical attack."

"I am asking much of you," Nawab Dayan says. "It is a difficult thing for a soldier to not fight back. But tonight it falls to us to show both our Aquilan allies and our own independence movement that we wish to move forward in peace, not conflict. Your courage may provide the example—and the time—we need for cooler heads to prevail. Good luck."

That night, eleven Jaipur dragoons are injured by rocks and bottles thrown from the crowd . . . but the ship, just one of the fifteen waiting to make port, is unloaded. The strike leaders grudgingly return to the negotiating table the next day, while the governor-general refrains from ordering the Chandigarh troops into action. And, to Sikander's amazement, the crisis seems to slip by without becoming a disaster.

Until, of course, Devindar and his friends seize the statehouse—

"This is not your place, Nawabzada," Darvesh said quietly, bringing Sikander's mind back to *Decisive's* hangar bay. He spoke in High Panjabi, moving close and making a show of checking Sikander's harness to keep his words private. The Kashmiri bodyguard wore a small pakul instead of his customary turban, but was otherwise fitted out in the same battle dress the rest of *Decisive*'s sailors wore. "You should remain in command aboard *Decisive*. Leading this landing force is a job better delegated to your executive officer or one of your senior department heads— you are limiting your awareness of the overall situation, as well as exposing yourself to unnecessary risk."

"I am afraid that I disagree, Darvesh. I think I'm going to be needed over there."

"Do you lack confidence in your subordinates?"

"I believe that Fraser or Herrera could execute the plan perfectly well," Sikander admitted. "The problem is that I don't think this plan is going to work. There are too many things we don't know, and we haven't had a chance to properly prepare."

Darvesh frowned in disapproval. "That hardly reassures me, sir."

"My point is that something unexpected is going to go wrong, and when it does, I need to be on hand to recognize that moment and make a decision. Like it or not, you and I have had more experience with this sort of improvisation than any of my officers, and our experience may make a difference."

"There is nothing in that orbital yard that requires the son of Nawab Dayan to hazard his life."

"Perhaps not, but the commanding officer of CSS *Decisive* feels that he's obligated to do anything he can to give his people their best chance for success," Sikander told him. "If all goes well I don't expect a shot to be fired, Darvesh. Now let me do my job."

Darvesh's eyes flashed; he was as angry as Sikander had ever seen him. "Very well. But if all does *not* go well, Nawabzada, then I require you to let me do mine. Do not forget."

"I won't." Sikander headed for Orbiter One and the boarding team he'd decided to personally lead. Reed Hollister waited for him by the Cormorant's stern ramp; Sikander clapped the younger officer on the shoulder. "Are you ready, Reed?"

"Yes, sir, although I'm a little anxious about what we'll find. My college Nebeldeutsch is pretty rusty."

"It's better than mine, I promise you." Sikander couldn't manage much more than "good morning" or "thank you" in the language—he'd never found the time to study it, although he was able to get by in Jadeed-Arabi after years of off-and-on practice. He would have preferred to leave Hollister in charge of Decisive's power plant, since Amar Shah was leading one of the other teams, but the fact that the sublieutenant was an engineering officer who spoke Nebeldeutsch made him indispensable to the mission; Sikander had reluctantly left the destroyer's engineering watch in the hands of Ensign Warren, the auxiliaries officer, and senior enlisted personnel like Chief Power Tech Ryan and Petty Officer Cruz. "It'll come back to you if you need it. Come on, let's take our seats."

"Yes, sir," Hollister replied, and followed Sikander and Darvesh into the orbiter. Sikander paused to hit the button for the stern ramp, then continued on past the sailors filling the sling seats in the cargo bay to the orbiter's cramped cockpit. Hollister and Darvesh found places at the front of the cargo bay, while Sikander took the jump seat behind the pilot and copilot.

"Good morning, sir," Petty Officer Kersey said. "We're pre-flighted and buttoned up, and so are the other boats. We can launch whenever you like."

"Good." Sikander checked the Cormorant's tiny tactical display, studying the planet's space traffic one last time before launching. At the top of the display, High Port drifted by thirty-two thousand kilometers above Mersin in its geosynchronous orbit, a bright white-and-gray ring with cluttered piers. It didn't appear to be moving all that fast, but that was a mere illusion—High Port was pulling away from *Decisive* by more than a hundred kilometers every minute. The rusty-looking open-space scaffolding of Dahar Naval Shipyard in its medium orbit was moving nearly twice as fast as the Zerzuran spaceport. *Decisive*, only five thousand kilometers above the planet's surface, raced along fastest of all, but even so the destroyer wouldn't return to the area below the shipyard for another six hours without some rather obvious orbital adjustments . . . and Sikander didn't want to tip his hand too soon. The more warning he gave the Zerzurans, the more likely it was they'd decide to resist.

He keyed his comms and linked into *Decisive*'s command circuit. "Bridge, Captain," he announced. "We're ready in the hangar bay. Break orbit and get us under way, if you please."

"Break orbit, aye," Amelia acknowledged. She occupied Sikander's command position on the bridge. "Mr. Darrow wishes you luck, sir."

"Thank him for me," Sikander replied. Darrow and his immediate staff had come aboard just an hour before departure; the special commissioner was observing the day's operations from the bridge.

Decisive shuddered gently as her helmsman applied thrust, beginning the short climb up out of Dahar's gravity well. Sikander watched the tiny tactical display in the orbiter's control console while listening in to the routine chatter of the command circuit. With the smooth nonchalance of a ship making a completely routine departure, *Decisive* began to pull up and away from the planet below . . . and, apparently by coincidence, settled on a course that passed close in front of the Dahar Naval Shipyard in its orbit nearly fifteen thousand kilometers above them.

"Nothing but routine traffic on the tactical board, Captain," Amelia reported to him over the command link. "Sixty seconds to our waypoint."

"I'm watching from the orbiter's cockpit," Sikander replied. "So far, so good. Carry on."

Decisive continued climbing on its departure course. Sikander watched the distance to their deployment point tick down to zero, and silently whispered a prayer to steady his nerves. *God, I ask for success not for myself, but for these men and women who follow me into danger,* he concluded. *Don't let me lead them into disaster.*

The distance reached zero; Sikander spoke into his mic. "Bridge, Captain. Execute!"

Decisive spun suddenly on her axis, pointing her nose at the orbital shipyard, and roared to full military acceleration. A moment later, the hangar bay door slid open, and one by one the ship's boats launched. The Cormorant's comm unit picked up Amelia Fraser's broadcast from the bridge: "Attention, Dahar Naval Shipyard. This is the Commonwealth destroyer CSS *Decisive*. We are sending over a boarding party to impound the Zerzuran vessels currently docked in your facility under the authority granted by the Interstellar Convention on the Law of Open Space to confiscate vessels intended for use in or support of piracy. Any attempt to interfere with our boarding operations will be met with force. Attention, Imperial Navy vessel *Neu Kiel*. Please instruct any of your personnel currently at work in the shipyard or vessels undergoing refit to stand aside or return to your ship. We have no intention of boarding *Neu Kiel* or detaining your personnel. *Decisive*, out."

"The XO sounds like she means business," Kersey observed to her copilot. She gunned the orbiter's induction drives to cross the open space between *Decisive* and the Zerzuran shipyard as swiftly as possible. "Let's hope they believe her over there."

Sikander nodded in agreement behind her. He'd worked with Eric Darrow to script Amelia's challenge, hoping that by citing the letter of the law they'd maintain at least some justification for their action. Of course, they were stretching the definitions provided in the Law of Open Space treaty to the very limits of what might be considered a defensible action; the claim that *Drachen, Meduse,* and *Zyklop* were supporting piracy was thin, at best. He couldn't even imagine what sort of protests, disputes, and charges would be leveled at the Commonwealth Navy for this operation . . . but while the diplomats wrangled with the official protests, the three cruisers would be safely interned out of Marid Pasha's hands.

The three Aquilan craft split up as they raced across the open space between *Decisive*—now furiously decelerating to remain nearby—and the shipyard. The launch, under Michael Girard's command, headed for *Drachen*. Orbiter Two, with Amar Shah's detachment aboard, headed for *Zyklop*, and Orbiter One continued straight ahead for *Meduse*. Each craft jinked and bounced in frantic evasions as they approached their targets; Sikander felt himself thrown against his restraints, and hoped that anyone not strapped in behind him had managed to secure a firm handhold. He doubted that the Zerzuran shipyard had any defenses that could be swiftly manned, but the Dremish repair ship had point-defense lasers that could riddle any of *Decisive*'s boats if they were caught in transit.

An alarm buzzer sounded on the Cormorant's console. "Oh, shit," Kersey swore. "We're being illuminated by fire-control systems, sir!"

"Keep going," Sikander told the pilot. "Get us to the airlock!" *And let's hope they talk before they shoot,* he added to himself.

Decisive's own fire-control systems came to life, and her K-cannon turrets swiveled to point their deadly weapons at the *Neu Kiel*. "*Neu Kiel*, this is *Decisive*," Amelia snapped. "If you even *think* about firing on one of my boats, you'll receive a full salvo from my main battery at point-blank range. Are you sure you want to do that, over?"

"*Decisive*, this is Kapitan zur Stern Beck of His Imperial Majesty's starship *Neu Kiel*. Suspend your operation at once! You have no legal right to board this facility or any of the ships currently docked here. This is tantamount to an act of war!"

"Your protest is noted, sir, but this is between the Aquilan Commonwealth and the Zerzura Sector government," Amelia replied. "No Dremish property or personnel will be harmed today—so long as you don't fire on our landing force. So stand down and let's all get through this without any more trouble than we need, over."

"Good job, XO," Sikander murmured. He looked up from the tactical display to the orbiter's armored viewports, gauging the boat's position. The scaffolding and structures of the shipyard raced past in the glittering vacuum outside the cockpit windows, and then the long, lethal teardrop-shaped hull of *Drachen*, the first cruiser in line. She was tethered to the Zerzuran space dock by half a dozen personnel tubes and power conduits, but appeared intact otherwise. She might have been an old hand-me-down, but the formerly Dremish cruiser bristled with powerful K-cannons and cut an impressive silhouette even in the shipyard's scaffolding. Any one of the three possessed enough firepower to handle four or five *Decisives*; two of them together would be more than a match for all of Pleiades Squadron.

The Cormorant kept going—Sikander had left the closest ship for the slower and more fragile launch, steering for *Meduse* while Amar Shah in the second Cormorant made for *Zyklop*. Petty Officer Kersey toggled the orbiter's intercom. "We're coming up on the target," she announced. "It'll be a hard stop, so brace yourselves, everyone."

Sikander set one hand against the back of the pilot's acceleration couch, and tensed in anticipation. Kersey flipped the Cormorant end over end and rammed the induction drive to full emergency power, braking as hard as she could in the last few hundred meters of their flight before adroitly spinning the orbiter to line up its port-side airlock with *Meduse's* midships accommodation tube. Sikander flinched, holding his breath as the cruiser's side seemed to rush at the orbiter . . . and at the last instant, Kersey applied the attitude thrusters to slow down just enough. The contact was jarring, but not as bad as he feared: the sailors behind him swayed and stumbled, but no one was thrown off their feet. An instant later the automatic docking rings—standardized for virtually every ship and boat throughout human space—clamped shut, securing the orbiter to the cruiser's side. "Airlock's green!" Kersey shouted. "Go!"

Sikander unbuckled himself and stood. "Great flying, Kersey," he told the pilot. "I have no idea how we're not splattered over the side of that ship."

"Ms. Worth told me to get to the target *fast*, and then she said that she'd be awful mad if I turned the ship's captain into a bug on a windshield," the petty officer replied. "Go get 'em, sir."

Sikander made his way to the orbiter's airlock just as the last sailors in his detachment pushed their way onto *Meduse*. *They didn't have time to secure the airlock hatch on us,* he noted. *Good!* He'd been worried that whatever work crews happened to be on board the cruisers might have time to lock out the Aquilan orbiters and stall them at the airlock. His teams had brought heavy cutting gear and breaching charges to force their way through if they needed to, but that of course would have taken time he wasn't sure they could afford to spare. Just inside the airlock, his boarding detachment worked to sort itself out into its mission teams: main control, power plant, bridge, perimeter, and security. Twenty-eight sailors was a ridiculously small number of people to seize control of something the size of a cruiser, but they had the advantages of firepower and surprise; he hoped that would be enough.

"Mission teams, get moving!" Sikander called. "Mr. Hollister, call me when you secure the engineering spaces. Bridge team, follow me!"

He turned to the right and headed forward, following what appeared to be a major fore-aft passageway with Darvesh and six enlisted hands escorting him. *Decisive's* intelligence specialists had been unable to locate any sort of trustworthy deck plans or schematics for the Chimäre-class cruisers on short notice, so *Decisive's* sailors had to make do with a certain amount of guesswork about the ship's interior arrangement. The deck was covered in rust-red linoleum and the bulkheads were painted in eggshell white instead of the dark blue and taupe he would have expected inside an Aquilan warship, but otherwise *Meduse's* interior spaces didn't look all that different from *Decisive's*. Power cables and air lines lay in tangles on the deck, and portable work lights glared in one darkened compartment where some refit job seemed to be in progress, but the ship seemed to be in better condition than Sikander had hoped. *They made the transit to Dahar under their own power,* he remembered. *They couldn't have been in very bad shape if they did that.*

Just ahead of him, Comm Tech Jackson and Quartermaster Birk turned a corner—and suddenly raised their mag rifles as a chorus of shouts in Jadeed-Arabi erupted in the new passageway. "What the hell is this? Who are you? You can't be here!"

"Drop the wrench!" Jackson shouted back in the same language. "I mean it!"

Sikander started to push his way forward, but Darvesh threw out an arm like an iron bar to stop him. "One moment, sir," he said.

Jackson and Birk advanced slowly, mag rifles trained on their unseen opponents—and then Sikander heard the muffled thud of something heavy and metallic hitting the linoleum. Darvesh lowered his arm, allowing him to continue around the corner; there, he found a crew of five Zerzuran shipyard workers standing by a disassembled ventilation duct. The Zerzurans glared at the Aquilan sailors in confusion and fear, obviously surprised by their appearance. "What's going on here?" the foreman demanded.

"We're seizing the ship," Sikander told him. "Don't worry, no one needs to get hurt—we'll escort you to the station-side airlock and let you go. Leave your tools and gear here."

"You're out of your mind," the foreman snarled. "This is a Zerzuran warship! You can't possibly get away with it."

"Let us worry about that," said Sikander. He shifted back to Anglic. "Birk, Jackson, escort these gentlemen to the station, along with anyone else you come across. Secure the station access until you're relieved, then meet us on the bridge."

"Aye, sir," the two petty officers replied. They gestured at the work crew to lead the way, and headed down the athwartships passage. Sikander and the rest of his party continued forward.

They found the bridge eighty meters forward of the midships airlock and one deck up, a well-armored compartment in the center of the ship. The hatch stood open, with power conduits and cable runs as thick as Sikander's arm lying across the sill. Someone on the other side was engaged in an angry conversation in Nebeldeutsch, accompanied by the unmistakable crunching of armored glass breaking and heavy blows of metal on metal. This time Darvesh stopped him with a look before Sikander started to rush ahead. "Allow me, sir," the Kashmiri said quietly.

Sikander nodded his assent. Darvesh motioned to the next two sailors in their group—Electronics Tech Tolbin and Gunner's Mate Waters—to take up position by the hatch. Darvesh risked a quick peek, then stormed into the room with the two sailors just behind him.

Mag-rifle fire erupted in the compartment, followed by shouts of fear and panic.

Sikander drew his pistol and started in to back up the first group, but just as he reached the hatch a young-looking Dremish technician bolted out of the bridge in a blind panic and ran into him full-on. He went down on his back with the worker on top of him.

"Sir! Sir!" the *Decisive* sailors remaining in the passage shouted, hurrying up to aid him.

"Damn!" Sikander swore and twisted underneath the fellow, shielding his face and shoving his pistol under his hip to make sure the man couldn't grab it. The technician flailed and scrabbled, trying to get back to his feet—but before he managed to stand, the two sailors knocked him senseless with their rifle butts and pulled him off Sikander.

"Er, sorry about that, Captain," Sensor Tech Diaz said. "I didn't hit you, did I?"

"I don't think so," Sikander replied, getting back to his feet. He took a moment to catch his breath and examine himself for injury; the back of his head throbbed from hitting the deck when he'd been bowled over, and he'd bitten his tongue, but that seemed to be the worst of it. "For a moment there I was afraid you were going to shoot the fellow while he was wrestling with me. Thanks for holding your fire."

He placed his cap back on his head, and stepped over the cluttered hatch into the bridge. Darvesh, Tolbin, and Waters held a group of four Dremish technicians at gunpoint in a bridge that looked like it had just been hit by a K-cannon round. Three more Dremish sailors lay on the deck, unconscious or close to it after point-blank mag-rifle shots. Broken consoles, unconnected ducting, and shattered keyboards littered the space. "Good God," Sikander murmured.

"They were busy breaking up the place, Captain," Petty Officer Tolbin said. "A couple of 'em tried to rush Chief Reza, but that turned out to be a bad idea."

"They should regain consciousness soon," Darvesh said calmly. "They may wish they had not, though. I assume you apprehended the one that fled?"

"Let's just say he isn't going anywhere," Sikander answered. He looked over at the Dremish who remained on their feet. "Do any of you understand Anglic?" he asked.

"I do," one young woman wearing the chevrons of a third-class petty officer answered grudgingly.

"You and your people can return to *Neu Kiel*," Sikander said. "We'll escort you to the station and turn you loose. Do not attempt to come back on board—my sailors will be standing guard at the station access, and they'll stop you. Tell the others. Do you understand?"

"*Ja*, I understand. But what is going on here? What is this?"

"We're confiscating these warships from the Zerzura Sector Fleet. Your commanding officer can tell you more. Tolbin, Waters, show our guests to the door, and come on back as soon as you can. It looks like we have some work to do here."

The armed sailors shepherded the Dremish technicians out of the bridge. Sikander took one look at the assorted destruction and partial repairs cluttering the space, and decided that he wouldn't worry about the condition of the controls quite yet—that was why he had a boarding team of technical experts along. Instead, he keyed his comm device to check on what was going on elsewhere. "Mr. Hollister, this is the captain. We've secured the bridge. How are you doing in the engineering spaces?"

"We've secured main control and we've got teams sweeping the engine and power rooms, sir," Hollister replied. "One of the fusion generators is completely disassembled—we won't be able to do much with that. The others are shut down, but they look intact. I'd guess thirty minutes to bring them online."

"The sooner the better, Mr. Hollister. And remember we're likely to lose station power at any moment, so don't dawdle." Sikander switched to the operation command channel. "Mr. Girard, Mr. Shah, status reports, please."

Shah replied first. "We have secured *Zyklop*, Captain. Hardly anyone was on board, and it appears that little work has been done here. I believe the Dremish must have been concentrating their repair efforts on the other ships."

"Have you secured the station access?"

"Yes, sir. We are buttoned up. I am examining the condition of the engineering plant now."

"Very good," Sikander told him. "Mr. Girard, how are you doing?"

There was a long pause before *Decisive's* operations officer replied. "We have *Drachen's* main control room, but there's some organized resistance on the bridge and we're having a hard time getting in, sir. I think we've got all the work crews over here that Mr. Shah didn't find on *Zyklop*. We control the station-side airlocks but I'm just not sure how many other people are left on board."

"What's the material condition of the ship?"

"Good, sir. They're in the middle of a number of jobs but I think it's mostly accommodations and habitability at this point—it looks like the engineering plant is operable."

Sikander nodded, even though it was only an audio link. He'd thought it likely that the refit work on the three ships might be at different stages of completion. "If you need to, seal the bridge and cut its power, then shift your effort to securing the auxiliary bridge," he told Girard. "If we can't remove the work crews without resorting to extreme measures, lock them in and we'll deal with them later. Mr. Shah, since you're secure on *Zyklop*, I want you to detach four of your nontechnical personnel and have your orbiter ferry them over to *Drachen*. It sounds like Mr. Girard can use a little more manpower over there."

"Aye, sir," Shah answered. "We shall send them over at once."

"Thank you, Captain," Girard said. "Do you need help on *Meduse*, sir?"

"We've got the bridge and the engineering spaces, but we're still sweeping the ship. I'll let you know when we button up," Sikander replied. "Carry on, gentlemen."

"Captain?" Petty Officer Waters called. Sikander turned his attention to the gunner's mate, who stood by the ship's weapons consoles. "Sir, I hate to say it, but these are wrecked. The Dremish ripped out the control circuitry and smashed the boards before we got in. It'll take me hours to fix this, assuming the spare parts are on board and I can find 'em."

"I didn't really expect that we'd need the K-cannons today, Gunner's Mate," Sikander told him. "Leave that mess as you found it, and lend a hand with the nav systems and helm."

"Aye, sir," said Waters. He hurried off to join other petty officers working on *Meduse*'s bridge systems. The Aquilan sailors unceremoniously hauled down the incomplete ductwork and threw it into the passageway aft of the bridge with a loud crash before turning their attention to the ship's maneuvering controls.

Sikander moved over to the tactical display and dragged the dust cover off the console. After a few moments of guesswork, he found the power icon and turned it on. To his relief, he found that the display had been switched over to Jadeed-Arabi, so he could fumble his way through the start-up dialogue and initiate the various system updates it required—while he didn't think he'd need *Meduse*'s guns today, he did want to be able to see what was going on around him. Then, while he waited for the systems to warm up, he commed Amelia. "XO, Captain. We've got our boarding teams on all three cruisers and we're in the process of securing them. What's the situation outside, over?"

"Confusing, sir," Amelia answered. "Captain Beck of the *Neu Kiel* doesn't seem to understand that we've got K-cannons and he doesn't—he's demanding that we stop what we're doing and withdraw immediately. Admiral al-Kassar is on a different channel in what I can only describe as a frothing rage. On a more serious note, the Zerzuran gunboats *Penguen* and *Marti* appear to be warming up their power plants and making preparations to get under way from the naval facilities on High Port. The old monitor *Rahman* is showing signs of life, too. We don't think she can leave the dock, but she won't be entirely out of range for some time yet."

"Understood," Sikander replied. He and Amelia had spent some time talking over the possibility of Zerzuran resistance and how *Decisive* should respond to different threats. The gunboats didn't worry him too much—their K-cannons were significantly lighter than *Decisive*'s, and they carried only two each. But if they waited to open fire until they were at point-blank range, they could inflict some serious damage before *Decisive* destroyed them. The monitor carried two much heavier K-cannons, but she could be neutralized by the simple expedient of maneuvering to keep the shipyard between *Decisive* and those guns until her orbit carried her away. "Warn the Zerzuran gunboats to stay at least a thousand kilometers away, and send a shot across the bow if you have to. If they press on anyway, engage and disable them. I don't want to fire the first shot if we can help it, but that doesn't mean we'll allow them to stroll up and punch us in the nose before we take action."

"Warning first, engage if necessary, understood," Amelia said. "I'll try—oh, *shit!*" A chorus of alarms broke out in *Decisive's* bridge; Sikander could hear them over Amelia's mic.

"What?" he demanded. "What is it? *Decisive*, respond!"

For a long moment, there was no reply. Sikander clapped a hand over his earbud, trying to make out what was happening through the distant chaos of shouts and alarms. Then, just before he bolted out of the bridge to get back to the orbiter and see what had happened to his ship, Amelia came back online. "Sorry, Captain. *Rahman* took a long-range shot at us, and we had to evade. We're maneuvering now to get out of her line of fire. The gunboats are getting under way, too. I need to explain a few things to them, if you don't mind."

Darvesh was right, Sikander realized. *I'm deaf, dumb, and blind on this damned hulk. I should be on* Decisive's *bridge!* There was still time to amend that—he could return to the orbiter and have them rendezvous with *Decisive*. He could be back on board in ten minutes . . . by which time those gunboats would be close enough to hit the destroyer if he ordered Amelia to refrain from evasive maneuvers long enough to recover the orbiter. *No, I made my decision about this scenario when I chose to lead the boarding force in person. Amelia can handle the Zerzurans—she has to. Like it or not, I am stuck here for now.*

"Very well, XO—fight the ship as you need to. I'll keep you posted on our progress. *Meduse*, out." Sikander took a deep breath, forcing himself to slow down and project calm and confidence for the sailors around him before selecting the boarding team's comm channel. "*Meduse* prize crew, this is the captain. We are now moving to Phase Two of the operation.

"Make all preparations to get under way."

21

Dahar Naval Shipyard

The Aquilan navy's raid caught Otto Bleindel in yard super-visor Yarbay Gamal Mohamed's office with *Neu Kiel's* re-pair officer, Kapitan-Leutnant Marisa Kohl. The KBS officer had taken a launch from High Port over to the orbital shipyard first thing in the morning to assess the progress of the refit work on *Drachen*, *Meduse*, and *Zyklop*, a trip he'd made at least once a week for the last month and a half. It had become tiresome by the third visit, but Hanne Vogt insisted that he personally monitor the project, since Marid Pasha had made it very clear that he wanted his squadron as soon as he could get it. She didn't have the tech-nical background to know what questions she needed to ask the people who were actually doing the work, and so she relied on him to keep her up to date.

Just a few more weeks, Bleindel told himself as he watched Kohl and Mohamed argue about whether the power conduits supplying *Zyklop's* secondary battery of UV lasers required re-placement. Both engineers agreed that it was a job that should be done, but Kohl maintained that it was outside the scope of work outlined by the transfer agreement and therefore a job the Zer-zurans ought to take care of themselves at some later date, while Mohamed insisted that the pasha had a right to expect delivery of a fully functional secondary battery that wouldn't require additional expensive repairs within a matter of months. *I'll take a nice vacation—skiing, perhaps, preferably on some world where I won't hear a word of Jadeed-Arabi for my entire visit.* As far as he was concerned, his work in Zerzura had concluded once he arranged the Meliya affair and provided Marid Pasha just the right amount of prodding to cast his lot with the Empire of Dremark; the Security Bureau had better things for him to do then waste his time and talents serving as Hanne Vogt's project manager. *Then again, staying around long enough to help Sikander North embarrass himself in New Kibris and watching the Commonwealth get expelled from Marid Pasha's domain was worth a few weeks of drudgery, wasn't it?*

"Mr. Bleindel, what do you think?" Marisa Kohl suddenly asked, bringing him back to the matter at hand. She was a brilliant engineer but young for her position, and patience was not her strong suit. Yarbay Mohamed's refusal to moderate his demands brought an angry glower to her face.

Bleindel refrained from the temptation to tell both officers that he couldn't care less, and made a show of considering his answer while recalling the course of the conversation over the last few minutes. "Marid Pasha wants these ships ready for service as soon as possible," he said. "The laser batteries are functional, so let's not take them apart now. We can cover some of the cost of the future power-conduit replacement when Mr. Mohamed's technicians find the time to do the work." That would no doubt lead to a future argument about when and how much, but by then he'd be on his way to a new assignment that made better use of his abilities.

"That is acceptable, but I would need to have a letter to that effect," the Zerzuran officer said thoughtfully. "It depends on how much of the cost Dremark is willing to cover, of course—"

"Security alert, security alert!" the office intercom suddenly announced. "Armed craft are approaching the station! Muster the station defense force!"

"What in the world?" Mohamed growled. "There's no security drill on the schedule!"

Who puts security drills on a schedule? Bleindel asked himself. *People who have no reason to think they'll be attacked and who haven't bothered to plan for the unexpected, of course.* Complacency was not a uniquely Zerzuran sin—he imagined that plenty of Dremish support facilities and repair depots in quiet backwaters throughout the Empire were similarly unprepared for trouble. That, however, was his professional specialty, and at the first sign of Mohamed's confusion, he realized something was very much out of the ordinary.

"It's no drill," he snapped, and shot to his feet. The shipyard's command module, such as it was, was at the other end of the administration block and one deck above Mohamed's office; Bleindel covered the distance in less than a minute, sprinting past offices and passageways where Zerzuran clerks stood transfixed by the alarms or tried to recall what they were supposed to do in a security alert.

The command center occupied a small tower with armored windows looking out over the shipyard; the bright orange and mottled green dayside of the planet Dahar gleamed in the viewports across from the main hatch. Half a dozen Zerzuran techs and officers occupied the room, most trying to talk over each other on various comm channels or requesting instructions from superior officers. Bleindel ignored them all and went straight to the traffic-control display. The station's navigational sensors showed a lean warship in the buff-white-and-red colors of the Aquilan navy standing off a few dozen kilometers from the shipyard, while several small shuttles raced toward the station. Over the center's speakers, he heard a woman's voice speaking in Anglic: "—to interfere with our boarding operations will be met with force. Attention, Imperial Navy vessel *Neu Kiel*. Please instruct any of your personnel currently at work in the shipyard or vessels undergoing refit to stand aside or return to your ship. We have no intention of boarding *Neu Kiel* or detaining—"

"Who are they?" Gamal Mohamed asked, hurrying up to the display in Bleindel's wake.

Marisa Kohl followed only a step behind the Zerzuran. "The Aquilans," she answered, pointing at the display. "That's their destroyer *Decisive*."

"Activate your point-defense systems!" Bleindel ordered Mohamed.

"They were removed years ago—no one expected an attack in the capital's orbit!" the yard supervisor protested. "The only weapons we have aboard the shipyard are small arms for the security force. Our defense against naval attack is the Zerzura Sector Fleet, and they're docked at the fleet base." He pointed at Dahar High Port in the tactical display, ten thousand kilometers higher than the shipyard and rapidly falling behind as the shipyard's faster orbit carried it away from the system's defenses.

"Underpowered and undergunned patrol vessels," Kohl told Bleindel in Nebeldeutsch. "They could shoot down those boats if they were here, but they're no match for an Aquilan destroyer."

Bleindel nodded. There was no point in bemoaning the foolish cost-saving measures of years past that had led the Zerzurans to strip defensive systems they didn't think they needed, or in waiting for the pasha's gunboats to save the day. What was needed now was a clearheaded and frank appraisal of the situation so that he could determine what sort of action was necessary—or possible. He watched the symbols for the Aquilan boats split up, each heading for one of the three cruisers in the shipyard's work cradles, and listened carefully to the Aquilan officer's broadcast on the general comm channel.

The cruisers, he realized. *They're going to sabotage the pasha's new cruisers. Can we stop them? And do we want to?*

The answer to the second question was obvious: Those ships were the centerpiece of the bargain to reshape Zerzura as a Dremish client state. Their neutralization would leave Marid al-Zahabi without the navy he'd negotiated for. Even though the Empire had delivered on its end of the bargain by bringing the ships to Zerzuran space and turning them over, Bleindel didn't believe for a moment that Marid Pasha would reciprocate without those ships . . . and that meant everything he and Hanne Vogt had worked toward over the last six months was at risk. He wasn't about to let that effort go to waste; first of all, he was ready to move on from Zerzura and he had no interest in returning to square one with the pasha, but more important, he took a great deal of pride in his work, and he was not about to let it be undone without a fight. *That leaves only the question of whether we can stop the Aquilans*, he decided. And he had a couple of ideas about that.

He moved back from the chaos of the station's command center and tapped his comm unit. "*Neu Kiel*, this is Agent Bleindel," he said. "Give me a channel to Kapitan zur Stern Beck, diplomatic priority."

It took only a moment for Beck to respond. "Agent Bleindel! It's an outrage, an act of war! The Aquilans are boarding our cruisers!"

"I know, Captain," Bleindel replied. Technically, of course, the cruisers now belonged to the Zerzurans, but he didn't blame Beck for feeling a certain amount of ownership over the three ships after all the work his people had put into them. In fact, he shared Beck's outrage, although he didn't see the point in shouting about it. "I'm going to put a stop to this nonsense, but I need your help. Listen closely: First of all, I want you to signal Fregattenkapitan Fischer of *Polarstern* and advise her of what's going on her. Tell her to get here as quickly as she can and take up position near the shipyard."

"*Polarstern* is on the other side of the planet at the moment. I am not sure how long it will take her to power up her drives and get under way."

"Find out from Fischer, and let me know. Next, I need you to organize a landing force from your crew, issue them small arms, and send them to meet me on the station."

"The Aquilan commander has warned us against attempting to interfere with their operation, Agent Bleindel. She can turn my ship into a smoking wreck with one salvo."

That is a risk I am willing to take. Bleindel had bitter experience with Aquilans deciding to open fire instead of backing down, but that wasn't something Beck needed to hear at the moment. "*Decisive*'s captain is Commander North, and I promise you that he does not want to fire on *Neu Kiel* unless you pose a threat to his ship," he told the repair ship's captain. "Nor will he fire on your sailors if doing so endangers his own landing force at the same time. Our best bet to stop this illegal action is to get our own armed sailors onto those ships as swiftly as possible and *resist.* The Aquilans have the crew of a single destroyer to draw upon, and they had to leave enough people on board *Decisive* to handle her in a fight. That means they can't have more than a hundred sailors for their boarding parties, and most of those will be no better trained for close-quarters fighting than your own personnel. When the Aquilans see that they're not going to be able to seize the ships without a fight, they'll have to back down."

"Or they might threaten to bombard my ship if I don't withdraw my sailors," Beck said bitterly.

"Captain Beck, this is not a request. I am invoking Special Command Authority Case Blue-Three. Do you understand?" Bleindel didn't particularly want to resort to rank to solve the impasse—if nothing else, it identified him as something other than a Foreign Office technical advisor—but he did not have time to persuade *Neu Kiel*'s captain or search for the safest course of action. They needed to act swiftly, or not at all.

Neu Kiel's captain remained silent for a moment, perhaps too surprised—or frightened—to answer. Then he said, "I understand. I will call out the ship's self-defense force. That will give you thirty sailors with small-arms training."

"Captain, I want a hundred of your sailors under arms in ten minutes. Select them at random if you have to, but *issue them guns and get them moving.*" Bleindel considered the shipyard's arrangement of open-space scaffolding and enclosed work modules, and the relative positions of *Neu Kiel* and the three cruisers undergoing refit. Ironically enough, the many hours he'd spent plodding around the shipyard over the last couple of months seemed likely to serve him well; he actually knew his way around the place. "Muster your force at Machine Shop Two—your sailors can reach it through interior passageways and keep out of sight from our Aquilan friends. I'll meet your people there. In the meantime, I want you to get back in touch with *Decisive* and lodge every protest you can think of. List off every law and diplomatic protocol you think they're violating and let them think you're documenting everything they do. I want Commander North or his deputies completely distracted by your complaints."

This time, Beck did not hesitate. "Yes, sir. I understand. I am issuing the orders now." He paused briefly, and then asked, "What about the Zerzurans? They have hundreds of workers on the station, too. Can they help?"

"Most are civilians, and the Zerzuran military personnel aren't ready for anything like this—we don't have time to wait for them to figure it out. It's up to us, Captain." Bleindel cut the connection. He stepped back into the command center just long enough to signal Kohl to follow him, and then set off for the machine shop at a jog. The facility was reasonably close by the work cradles housing all three of the cruisers, and it was deep enough in the shipyard's structure that *Decisive* couldn't easily monitor any personnel movements there while standing off dozens of kilometers away.

It wound up taking twenty-five precious minutes for *Neu Kiel*'s sailors to equip themselves, hurry to the machine shed, and sort themselves out into improvised platoons and squads. Kapitan zur Stern Beck, however, had not stinted on his personnel—he sent the repair ship's trained landing force of thirty, and then a full hundred more sailors to boot. Half were armed only with mag pistols or stunners instead of the heavy firepower Bleindel would have hoped for, but it turned out that was unavoidable; the sailors had virtually emptied *Neu Kiel*'s small-arms lockers. The delay also provided him with the opportunity to quickly scout out the approaches to *Drachen*, *Meduse*, and *Zyklop*, and confirm that the accommodation tubes leading to the ships' airlocks were sealed.

He returned from his inspection of the access points to find *Neu Kiel*'s officers standing to one side of the machine shop, waiting for him: Kapitan-Leutnant Kohl, executive officer Korvettenkapitan Arnold, main propulsion officer Oberleutnant Sommer, and a handful of junior officers. "The station access points are closed, so we'll need to cut our way in," he told the naval officers. "Mr. Arnold, I suggest you take charge of the *Drachen* group. Ms. Kohl, you take a group to *Zyklop*. I'll take Mr. Sommer and the third group to deal with *Meduse*."

"What's our mission, Mr. Bleindel?" Arnold asked. He was a stout man who barely managed to stay within the navy's fitness requirements, but he carried his Gerst autorifle as if he knew how to use it. "What are we trying to do?"

"Get to the vital spaces of the ship and prevent the Aquilans from carrying out whatever sabotage they have in mind," the KBS agent said. "We'll begin with the bridge and the engineering spaces, and once we have those in hand, we'll systematically sweep each vessel and secure prisoners. Divide your detachments into three teams each: one for the bridge, one for engineering, and one team to capture the Aquilans' shuttles and prevent their escape. Get on board however you can, and shoot to kill if you meet with any resistance. Now, what will it take to force the hatches?"

"If they're locked, an hour or more with a high-powered laser cutting torch," Arnold replied. "These are heavy cruisers, Mr. Bleindel. The airlocks are armored."

"Damn!" Bleindel swore. "Could we blow them open instead?"

"I'm afraid it would take fifty kilos of molecular explosive."

"Find some, then. Time isn't on our side."

"I have an idea," Marisa Kohl volunteered. "The torpedo loading hatches. They're big enough to crawl through, and we've got external work shelters in place around each ship's bow—we can access the hulls without suiting up or being spotted."

Arnold nodded. "And the torpedo rooms on *Zyklop* and *Meduse* are currently unpowered," he added. "We can get in without tripping any alarms on their bridges. *Drachen*'s torpedo room has power, so opening the torpedo loading hatch will trigger an alarm. But her bridge is enough of a mess that the Aquilans might not notice the signal on the status board."

"That's a much better plan," said Bleindel. He had to imagine the Aquilans would be guarding the airlocks, but it was possible they might have overlooked an access point that wasn't intended for use by humans. "Oberleutnant Sommer, you're with me. Let's move."

The Dremish sailors assembled in the shipyard's machine shop broke up into the three groups and hurried toward their assignments. Bleindel allowed Leutnant Sommer to lead the way for the *Meduse* group, since he was not completely certain where to find the cruiser's torpedo loading hatch other than somewhere near the bow. In one ear he listened to Kapitan zur Stern Beck railing ineffectually at the Aquilan warship over the local comm channel; the Aquilans didn't seem to be listening, although he had to admit that if he were in their position he wouldn't be, either.

"Here we are, sir," Oberleutnant Sommer told Bleindel. The passage they'd followed from the machine shop ended at an airlock and a flexible accommodation tube, which in turn led to a temporary work shed clinging to the cruiser's alloy hull. Just a few millimeters of tough, translucent plastic stretched over a light frame separated the working space from the hard vacuum outside; Bleindel tried not to think about what would happen if one of the untrained sailors behind him accidentally fired off a few rounds while the group was crowded into the shed structure. The torpedo loading hatch itself proved to be two meters long and about seventy centimeters wide. Two sailors hurried to open a small panel next to the larger hatch, and activate the concealed controls. With a hiss of seals deflating, one end of the hatch depressed, forming a steep chute leading to a round hatch; he realized that the torpedoes would simply slide in like bullets in a sporting rifle's ammunition feed.

"Inside, and quietly," he ordered the sailors. One by one, they scrambled down the chute, through the round hatch at the bottom, and onto a semicylindrical receiving tray in the machinery-cluttered torpedo room. From there, it was simple enough to scramble down the two and a half meters to the deck. *So far, so good,* Bleindel decided. *We're on board without shots fired, and the Aquilans have no idea we're here. We might actually pull this off!*

When all forty-odd sailors in his group had assembled in the torpedo room, Bleindel addressed his improvised force. "Sommer, you take engineering. You there, Obermaat—my apologies, I don't know your name—head for the starboard-side airlock and get control of the shuttle, or at least block access to it so that the Aquilans can't retreat that way. I'll take the bridge. Once we leave this room, move fast: Speed and surprise are our best weapons now. Good luck to you."

He moved to the compartment's interior door, and cracked it open to peek out at the darkened passageway beyond. No one was in sight, but a string of portable work lamps provided at least a little illumination. Without hesitation he set out for the bridge, one party of armed sailors at his back; the other teams swiftly turned down different passages, heading for their own targets. Ideally he'd wait for them all to get into position before signaling an attack, but Bleindel doubted that all three groups would reach their targets undetected, so they'd just have to do the best they could.

He almost reached the bridge before the plan fell apart.

A sudden burst of mag-weapon fire erupted from somewhere aft of his group: the piercing buzzsaw whine of Gerst autorifles opening up, the heavier chirping coughs of Aquilan battle rifles, the rattle of high-velocity darts striking steel bulkheads and ricocheting down passageways, a dozen voices shouting at once in Nebeldeutsch and Anglic. *One of the other groups must have blundered into the enemy,* he realized. The Aquilan shots sounded off to him: too low in pitch. *Nonlethal rounds,* he realized, but before he could pass that reassuring news to his followers, the shots grew higher and shriller—someone on the other side recognized that they were in a gunfight now.

"Come on!" he shouted to his own team, and sprinted down the last passageway leading to *Meduse*'s bridge hatch.

An Aquilan sailor in battle dress stepped out of the bridge and caught sight of the charging Dremish. Bleindel fired at a dead run, and downed the Aquilan with a lucky hit—but a second Aquilan using the hatchway for cover opened up with a blistering spray of automatic fire, shooting half-blind down the passage. He couldn't help but hit somebody, and a *Neu Kiel* mate running shoulder-to-shoulder with Bleindel grunted and collapsed around a bad hit in the midsection. Bleindel threw himself behind a structural stanchion that offered at least some protection, while the sailors behind him hit the deck or leaped for cover of their own.

In the space of a few seconds a furious firefight broke out, as more Aquilans fired from the doorway to the bridge and Bleindel's own force returned fire. Mag rifles created no muzzle flash or gun smoke, of course, but showers of sparks from mag darts striking steel bulkheads rained down in bright curtains and weapon reports filled the passageway—high, shrill shots at full lethal power in response to the Dremish assault. Bleindel realized at once that his force was pinned down: Rushing a doorway defended by alert enemies with automatic weapons was a tactical challenge that simply had no good answers. *Think, Otto, think*, he told himself, ignoring the shouts and screams and roaring guns. *Either find another way in, wait them out, or screen your approach somehow.*

He looked back at Leutnant Sommer, crouched behind a water cooler in an alcove. "Is there another way into the bridge?" he called, raising his voice to be heard over the din.

"There are escape scuttles in the deck and overhead, but I'm not sure which compartments they're in," Sommer called back.

Too slow, Bleindel decided. Escape scuttle hatches were small, barely large enough for one person at a time. It might take several minutes for the sailors to find the neighboring compartments where the hatches opened, minutes during which their advantage of surprise would dissipate entirely. No, he needed an answer *now*, and that meant screening their assault. "Smoke!" he ordered the sailors. "Smoke grenades at the doorway, now!"

At least half the sailors crowded in the passage with him ignored his order, concentrating only on hosing down the bridge entrance with their autorifles. Others were already hurt and unable to comply, or couldn't figure out how to use the devices they'd been issued. But a few—just three or four, more than enough—found the smoke markers on their utility harnesses, pulled the pins, and hurled them down the passage. Dense white smoke billowed out, filling the narrow space.

"Go! Go! Go!" Bleindel shouted.

With a ragged chorus of shouts, the *Neu Kiel* sailors on the deck scrambled to their feet and ran into the smoke. Scathing mag-rifle fire blasted from the now-hidden doorway; blind or not, some of the defenders found targets, filling the hall with screams of panic and pain. Bleindel crouched low and advanced more slowly after the first wave of the assault, keeping one hand on the bulkhead to his left to feel his way forward. Mag darts cracked past him, close enough that he could *feel* them pass by. He stumbled over a motionless Dremish sailor bleeding on the deck, and stepped past another thrashing in agony with her hands clamped around a shattered knee. Then he found the edge of the hatch, turned left, and started making his way along the bridge's aft bulkhead as he searched for a target.

The smoke thinned around him, and he got his first good look at the scene inside the bridge. Dremish sailors groped blindly through the mist, firing wildly as they stumbled into the room. The Aquilans had pulled back from the entrance: Several crouched behind bridge consoles or acceleration couches, firing at the smoke-filled doorway. Across the room, Sikander Singh North stood behind the main tactical display, firing a mag pistol at the sailors attempting to storm the room.

No one had noticed Bleindel slipping to the side as he entered the bridge. He raised his autorifle and fixed the sights on the center of North's chest. One small part of him hesitated, wondering if the commanding officer of *Decisive* might be more useful as a hostage than a corpse . . . but Gadira was a blot on Bleindel's career that had followed him for years, and Sikander North was the single individual on whom he could blame that failure. He pulled the trigger—

—just as North's Kashmiri bodyguard hurled himself into the line of fire. "Nawabzada, look out!" Darvesh Reza shouted. The burst intended for *Decisive*'s captain stitched a lethal line across the tall Kashmiri's chest. He stumbled back into North and fell, taking them both to the deck.

"Damn!" Bleindel swore savagely and aimed another burst at the two men tangled on the deck, but he'd lost his shot—they were both behind the tactical display now, although his burst might have caught them on the ricochet. He started to move into a better position to clear his line of fire, only to find a storm of mag darts descending on his position from the other Aquilans on *Meduse*'s bridge. Rounds shrieked and sparked all around him, tearing up the row of acceleration couches he'd been using as cover.

Not optimal, he realized. *I'm the only Dremish target still standing in the room.* The sailors who'd made it through the smoke and the bridge hatch were all on the deck, or had been driven back into the passage outside.

"Right side of the bridge hatch!" Sikander North shouted. "He's back by the communications console!"

The KBS agent ducked back behind the best cover he could

find, looking for his next move . . . and then he found it. One of the escape scuttles Sommer had mentioned was on the deck just two meters from where he sheltered. He briefly considered holding his position and calling Sommer to make another attempt at the bridge hatch now that they'd gotten a foothold inside the compartment, but in a matter of moments one of the other Aquilans would find a clear shot on him, and that would be the end of that. He was not afraid to take a gamble if there was a hope of success, but staying where he was meant certain death, and would not make any difference in the effort to retake *Meduse.*

If we can't take the bridge, we might succeed elsewhere, he decided. He dropped a smoke grenade just in front of his own position, waited a moment for the smoke to thicken, and then crawled toward the hatch in the deck. He yanked it open and dove in headfirst as darts scoured the spot where he'd just been standing.

22

I am sorry, Darvesh. Sikander knelt on the blood-pooled deck beside Darvesh Reza, holding one lifeless hand in both of his. The bodyguard had died almost instantly, shot through the heart in the moment he interposed himself in the line of fire. He lay on his back with his eyes closed, a curious small smile fixed on his face. The rifle burst that had killed him had left his face unmarked; Sikander was strangely grateful for that. *This is my fault,* he silently told his fallen servant, mentor, confidant . . . friend. *You told me to leave this to someone else. I chose not to listen, so you had to come with me. And because I insisted on doing what I thought was my job, you had to do yours—just as you said you would.*

"Captain? Are you hurt, sir?" Comm Tech First Class Jackson sank down on one knee beside Sikander, looking at him with concern. "Sir, should I call for a corpsman?"

Sikander took a deep breath, and looked down at himself. He bled freely from a gash on his lower leg—a graze or ricochet from a mag dart, he guessed, although he hadn't even noticed the injury when he'd received it—but otherwise he seemed unhurt. "I'm fine," he made himself answer. "Chief Reza took the burst that was meant for me."

Jackson grimaced. "I'm sorry, sir. I know he's served with you for a long time. But I'm afraid there isn't much we can do for him now."

"No, there isn't." Sikander set Darvesh's hands across his chest, and stood. *Darvesh is dead*, he realized dully. *He warned me, and I didn't listen. Dear God, what now?* For a long moment the only thing he could do was to stare at Darvesh's face, replaying their argument in the hangar bay. There had to be a way to change this outcome, to go back and make the right decision instead of the wrong one, and then maybe events wouldn't lead to this inescapable conclusion. Nothing else seemed to matter at the moment other than figuring out how he could have avoided this . . . but then Sikander realized that he couldn't hear any weapons fire close by. The surviving sailors on the smoky bridge watched him in silence, waiting for their orders.

It's too much, he told himself. *I can't figure this out now.* Darvesh needed a better answer than he could manage at the moment, so Sikander made himself set aside his confusion, resolving to come back and work out the meaning of what had just happened as soon as he could. He turned away from his fallen friend and looked at Petty Officer Jackson. "What's our status? How many casualties?"

"Besides the chief, we lost Diaz and Waters," Jackson said. "Birk is wounded in the arm, but he's still on his feet. The Dremish backed down the passageway and around the corner." The comm technician shook his head. "They must've lost ten people trying to rush the bridge."

Sikander looked back at the compartment's entrance; five Dremish sailors lay dead or unconscious in the doorway or just inside the bridge, and he knew more were in the passageway outside. They wore ordinary working uniforms, not battle dress. *Ship's company pressed into service as a landing force*, he realized. Many of his own sailors were not much better prepared for a boarding action, but at least they'd had time to suit up with light armor and practice with their weapons before he'd launched his operation. Then he noticed that no Dremish bodies lay near the communications stations at the aft end of the bridge.

"Bleindel!" he snarled. He'd spotted the Dremish agent just in time to see him raise his autorifle. In one terrible instant he'd recognized his old adversary and realized that Bleindel had him in his sights, until Darvesh had stepped in between them. He hurried over to where the Bleindel had been hiding . . . and spotted the open scuttle in the deck. A small splatter of blood smeared the edge of the scuttle hatch. *Damn him! He got away again!*

He glared at the hatch, resisting the urge to rush off in pursuit—for all he knew Otto Bleindel could be waiting in the compartment below with his rifle aimed at the ladder to gun down the first person to follow him. Besides, Sikander had other things to worry about first. He backed away a step or two, and tapped his comm unit. "Mr. Hollister, the Dremish managed to get an armed force on board," he told the sublieutenant. "They are almost certainly heading your way."

Hollister took a long time to respond. "They're already here, Captain," he finally answered. His words came in a halting monotone. "We just repelled a group that tried to storm main control, and I think there may be some more out in the engine rooms. We're trying to ascertain whether the engineering plant is secure."

"Keep at least some of your people at work on warming up the power plant. I want to get under way as soon as possible—the longer we stay in this docking cradle, the more likely it is we'll have to fight off additional efforts to retake the ship."

"We'll do our best, sir. But we lost some people and I've got to post guards in case the Dremish make another try for the control room."

"Acknowledged. Carry on, Mr. Hollister." Sikander switched back to the command channel. "Mr. Girard, Mr. Shah, *Meduse* has been boarded by a number of armed sailors—Dremish from *Neu Kiel*, I think. If they're trying to retake this ship, there may be Dremish forces moving on your positions as well. Be on your guard."

"This is Lieutenant Girard. Captain, a party of Dremish sailors just boarded *Drachen* through the torpedo loading hatch. We've got serious fighting in the passageways near the torpedo room."

"Lieutenant Shah on *Zyklop*, sir. We also are under attack. Ms. Worth was forced to abandon the bridge, but we managed to keep the boarders out of engineering."

"Boarding parties, this is *Decisive*," Amelia Fraser said. "Do you need reinforcements?"

Sikander answered at once. "Belay that, XO. You don't have any more people to send over. The ship is already dangerously undermanned, and we handed out just about every weapon in the small-arms locker. *Do not*, repeat, *do not* attempt to send any more of the crew over to the shipyard. If we lose control of one of these ships, we'll evacuate our force to the other cruisers and disable the target we abandon with main battery fire, over."

Amelia hesitated just a moment before responding. "Aye, Captain. We'll continue to monitor the situation. Just so you know, we fired warning shots at *Penguen* and *Marti*—they're holding position a thousand kilometers away. *Rahman*'s orbit has carried her out of firing position. She won't be back around again until early tomorrow morning, but there's always a chance the Zerzurans get her under way too. I would advise being on our way before they do. *Decisive*, out."

We're trying to do too much with not enough, Sikander told himself. Amelia Fraser and Michael Girard had said as much during the mission planning, arguing that it would be safer and more certain to destroy the cruisers in place. *Decisive*'s K-cannons might not have had the punch to get through the cruiser's heaviest armor, but they certainly could have wrecked the warp rings and drive plates to immobilize the pasha's new squadron for months and months of repairs, and a warp torpedo with a zero-range detonation would have ensured that the pasha's cruisers never left their docking cradles again. On the other hand, killing hundreds of workers with a bombardment of the shipyard wasn't something that Sikander was prepared to live with, and Eric Darrow had strongly favored the idea of removing and interning the ships instead of destroying them. The special commissioner thought that temporarily confiscating ships was much less likely to be seen as an act of war than firing on them, and Sikander believed—or hoped, more accurately—that he was right.

He turned his attention to conditions on the bridge: Two of his enlisted hands stood guard by the bridge hatch, while the surviving technicians worked to activate the ship's control consoles. Electronics Tech Tolbin brought the main bridge display online even as he watched; the deck-to-overhead vid displays that ringed the compartment flickered to life, although some of the panels were shorted out by mag-dart damage and only the most elementary target data populated the screen. *Decisive* stood only twenty kilometers off, slowly orbiting the shipyard as she warily kept an eye on the Zerzuran gunboats in the distance.

It's good to be able to see what's going on outside, Sikander decided, *but it's not what I need to know right at this moment.* "Good work, Petty Officer Tolbin. Before you move on to more sensor systems, see if you can find the ship's internal security monitors and get them working. We need to see where the Dremish inside the ship are."

"Aye, sir," Tolbin replied. "Umm, it might take a minute. I'm not exactly sure what I'm looking for. Waters was our expert on security systems."

"Do your best," Sikander told him. He moved over to check on Birk, who was working on the helmsman's console. "Quartermaster, how are you coming along here?"

"Good, Captain," the petty officer replied. Much of his left arm was encased in a battle dressing, but he seemed to be alert and in good spirits. "We're still booting up the nav systems, but basic helm functions are ready. We can move whenever the engineering team brings the engines online."

"I understand. Thank you, Birk." He changed his comm channel again. "Mr. Hollister, your status?"

"Sir, the engineering spaces are secure, and we're bringing the generators up to full power. You should have engines in five minutes."

"That was fast. You did a complete sweep of the engineering spaces?"

"Not exactly, sir. We got the damage-control sensor system working, and we're using it to check which compartments are occupied."

"Clever thinking, Mr. Hollister," Sikander said. Damage-control systems included a sensor for each and every compartment of the ship to detect hazards such as vacuum, fire, radiation, or loss of power . . . as well as whether or not a particular compartment was occupied. He knew where all his people were *supposed* to be—and Reed Hollister had now figured out a way to determine which of *Meduse's* hundreds of compartments harbored people he couldn't account for. "Brilliant, in fact. Call your counterparts on *Drachen* and *Zyklop* and tell them what you've done, and then get over to the damage-control display. You're going to locate our Dremish holdouts and direct our search teams to the compartments where they're hiding."

"Aye, sir. I'm on it."

What am I missing? Sikander asked himself. He turned to look for Darvesh to ask the Kashmiri veteran's advice, as he'd done a hundred times over the last twenty years . . . and realized again that Darvesh Reza would not be able to help him now. He stared for a long moment at his friend and protector, lying still on the cold steel deck with his hands folded over his chest. *Darvesh would remind me that we have less than thirty people on this ship and can't reinforce our numbers, but more enemies might arrive at any time. Sooner or later they'll find another way in—the longer we remain in this docking cradle, the greater the danger.* Well, he might be able to do something about that.

He keyed the general boarding team channel again. "Attention, all boarding detachments. This is the captain. Jettison your accommodation tubes, release your mooring clamps, and use your attitude thrusters to get clear of the shipyard. Break things if you have to—if we remain tethered to the station, the Dremish and the Zerzurans will retake these ships."

Amar Shah replied on a private channel. "Captain, that will leave us adrift until we can start up the engines. And it will trap any remaining Dremish sailors on board with us."

"They had their chance to leave," Sikander told him—he'd instructed his boarding detachments to keep their prizes in the docking cradles as long as possible for that very reason, but now it was clearly too dangerous to linger. "We can put them off in lifeboats later if we need to. Detach from the station, Mr. Shah."

"Aye, sir," Shah answered. "We are jettisoning our tubes now."

Sikander turned his attention back to *Meduse*'s bridge. Distant clatters and thumps echoed throughout the ship as one by one the ship's accommodation tubes, the extensible passageways that linked her airlocks to the airlocks of the shipyard's docking cradles, decoupled. He hoped that no one was in them at the time; he was pretty sure that no Aquilans were on the wrong side of the airlocks, but if the Dremish or Zerzurans had teams preparing to assault through any of the tubes they wouldn't have had much warning before the seals were broken. A moment later, the cruiser rocked softly as Quartermaster Birk hit the attitude thrusters, releasing puffs of compressed gas to impart a gentle drift away from the station—the thrusters used nonpowered systems to ensure that a ship didn't lose all maneuvering capability in the event of a power failure. *Drachen* likewise detached; *Zyklop* followed suit a moment later.

"We're clear, Captain," Birk reported. "Still waiting on engine power, though."

"Very well. Petty Officer Jackson, Deckhand White, Deckhand Flores, you're with me. Everybody else, stay here and keep the compartment buttoned up—the Dremish may make another attempt to storm the bridge."

Petty Officer Tolbin frowned. He was the senior man left on the bridge. "Where are you going, Captain?"

Sikander picked up Darvesh's battle rifle and checked the clip. "I'm going to hunt down that murderous bastard Bleindel before he finds a way to kill us all," he said.

They started by clearing the compartment immediately below the bridge, even though Hollister reported that the internal sensors showed no body heat or movement. It turned out to be an equipment room housing the ship's inertial navigation system—something that could easily have been sabotaged to impede the Aquilans' ability to track the ship's course. Other than another splatter of blood at the bottom of the ladder leading to the bridge, they found no sign of Bleindel or any indication that he'd made any attempt to damage the delicate systems. Sikander guessed that Bleindel simply hadn't realized that the gyroscopes and tracking computers might be important; after all, the man was an intelligence operative, not a naval professional.

"He's bleeding, anyway," Petty Officer Jackson observed. "Someone must have winged him during the shootout on the bridge."

Where would he go? Sikander had to imagine that Bleindel would try to circle back to rejoin any Dremish assault groups he could find, which probably meant returning to the passageway just outside the bridge. But now they were a deck below that passage, and he might not know the quickest way back to that point. The blood on the deck plates led to the equipment room's door . . . and there Sikander found the discarded wrapper of a battle dressing. "Damn the luck. A blood trail would have made tracking him down a lot easier," he said. "Mr. Hollister, where are the Dremish?"

"There are a few outside the bridge, sir, but the biggest group now appears to be down on the mess deck—it's a central location where several main passages converge. I can see more near the port-side airlock where we docked the orbiter, too. Petty Officer Kersey reported that she had to seal the hatch a few minutes ago, but I haven't heard anything from her since."

"Which way, sir?" Jackson asked him.

Sikander doubted that Bleindel would return to the same spot where an assault had just failed—either he'd go for reinforcements, or he'd give up and attempt to escape. *If not the bridge, then is it the orbiter or the mess deck?* he wondered. Of those two possibilities, collecting reinforcements for another attack somewhere else presented the more dangerous threat. "The mess deck," Sikander decided. "Mr. Hollister, guide us, if you please."

"Turn left when you exit the hatch and head aft about ten meters. Go right at the T, and you'll find one of the main ladderways in another fifteen meters or so. You'll descend one deck and head aft."

"Thank you, Reed. Let us know if you spot any sign of someone moving around ahead of us." Sikander readied his rifle, and cautiously exited the equipment room; the passageway outside was cluttered with air lines and power cables, and the bulkheads had been stripped down to bare metal in preparation for repainting. He picked his way aft with Jackson and the two younger deckhands following him.

Amelia Fraser's voice crackled in his ear on their private channel. "Captain, Petty Officer Tolbin tells me that Chief Reza is dead and you're not on the bridge," she said. "What are you doing?"

"Dealing with a very dangerous loose end," he whispered back to her. He reached the T intersection, and peeked out to look right and left; no one was around, but he saw the steep metal stairs of the ladderway Hollister had mentioned.

"That's not your job, Sikander. Leave it to your subordinates. You've got a flotilla of four ships to command and I need your help to keep control of this operation. The commanding officer has no business looking for a gunfight."

She was right, of course. Fixing his attention on one small tactical problem instead of the whole operation was reckless and self-indulgent by any standard . . . but at the moment, Sikander didn't care. *Otto Bleindel running around loose on this ship is the biggest threat we face at the moment,* he told himself. If dealing with that situation just happened to give him an excuse to settle the score with the KBS agent, well, that wasn't his fault. "It's not up to you, XO," he replied. "Bleindel is here, and there's a real possibility that he'll retake the ship. Fend off the Zerzurans and keep an eye on our orbiters—the Dremish might be after our boats. I'll be back in touch soon."

He cut the channel, and continued to the ladderway in silence. Carefully he lay down flat on the deck so that he could peek at the passageway below. No one seemed to be waiting for them, so he retrieved his rifle and moved down the stairs. This passageway gleamed with a fresh coat of paint and shiny new linoleum on the deck; Sikander contacted Hollister again. "Mr. Hollister, is there a good way to get at the mess deck without being seen?"

"There's a hatch on your left, about twenty meters ahead of you," the engineering officer replied. He'd picked up on Sikander's hushed voice, and kept his reply to a whisper. "It leads to the galley. There are a couple of doors between the galley and the mess deck, and a pass-through too. No one seems to be in there."

Sikander motioned to his small team to move aft, weapons at the ready. No one appeared in the passage ahead of them. They came to the galley hatch, quietly opened it, and crept inside. The galley and the mess deck were dark, illuminated only by dim emergency lighting. He picked his way past the industrial stoves and ovens and around a large prep table to a position near the pass-through window, and paused to listen.

Several people in the room beyond the window seemed to be holding a hushed conversation in Nebeldeutsch. Sikander wanted to take a peek, but he simply couldn't chance it; he had no idea where the Dremish sailors were and whether any of them might be covering the galley entrance. Instead he turned back to Jackson, Flores, and White, all crouching behind him, and leaned in close to keep his voice to the barest whisper. "Ready flash grenades," he told them. "Mr. Hollister, on my signal, cut the power to the mess deck for about five seconds, then turn it back on."

"Just a moment, Captain. We're looking for the master power controls . . . got them. Ready when you are, sir."

Sikander armed his flash grenade, showing the sailors with him how to hold the lever clamped close to the casing in case they hadn't seen it before, and held it at the ready while they armed theirs. "Throw them in the room and make sure to look away," he whispered. "On the count of three. Mr. Hollister, be ready. One . . . two . . . *three!*"

The lights went out as Sikander popped upright. He hurled the small flash device in his hand through the galley's pass-through window out into the darkened room beyond, then dropped back down under the counter again. Beside him, *Decisive*'s sailors followed his example as the Dremish shouted in alarm or dove for cover. An instant later, a salvo of brilliant white flashes and deafening explosions echoed through the compartment. Sikander felt his way toward the nearest doorway, ears still ringing from the blasts, and reached it just as the lights came back on. Dremish sailors staggered to their feet or stumbled into each other, blinded by the flash grenades—and then the Aquilans opened fire. Three Dremish dropped in the first volley, then two more fell while trying to blink their eyes clear or firing wildly at targets they couldn't see. Sikander aimed and fired in cold efficiency. It might not have been fair, but the best way to keep more of his people from being hurt or killed was to neutralize the threat as quickly as possible; he'd wrestle with his misgivings later.

He dropped another sailor who peppered the wrong doorway with a long burst from her autorifle, and heard a cry of pain from one of his own men. He swept the muzzle of his mag rifle to the left, searching out the corner of the room . . . only to see the remaining Dremish sailors drop their weapons and raise their hands. "*Nicht schiessen! Ich gebe auf, ich gebe auf!*" they shouted. His translation device couldn't make out the details with several people shouting at the same time, but clearly they'd had enough.

"Sir, they're saying they want to surrender," Jackson called to Sikander, confirming his guess. Like many comm techs, he had a bit of language training.

"Hold your fire!" Sikander ordered. He kept his rifle to his shoulder, scanning the room again to make sure no one was about to un-surrender. Eight Dremish were down, several of them clearly dead. Five more remained on their feet, but their hands were in the air; the firefight seemed to be over.

Otto Bleindel was nowhere in the room.

"Damn," Sikander muttered—he'd guessed wrong. *Did he circle back to the bridge, or head for the orbiter?* "Flores, White, collect their guns. Petty Officer Jackson, keep the Dremish covered."

"White's hurt, sir," Flores replied. "It's pretty bad."

"Do what you can for him. Jackson, you collect the guns. I'll cover you."

The comm tech hurried out to gather the Dremish weapons, while Sikander motioned for the sailors who could move to gather in the middle of the room and do what they could for the wounded. *How many people have been shot on this ship in the last fifteen minutes?* he wondered. *Fifteen? Twenty? We've got one corpsman in the boarding party, and she's with the orbiter. Treating our own injured is going to be hard enough, but some of the* Neu Kiel *sailors need serious attention—the sooner, the better.*

Jackson returned with the weapons. "What now, Captain? What do we do with 'em?"

"We let them go," Sikander said. "We'll escort them to the nearest lifeboat and allow them to return to the station. We don't have the manpower to guard them, and we certainly don't have enough medical personnel to treat the wounded. Can you explain that to them for me?"

"Yes, sir," Jackson replied. He turned and addressed their captives; looks of relief flickered across a few faces.

That might be the right way to put a stop to this, Sikander realized. *Most of these sailors aren't trained for this and aren't willing to die for someone else's ships. If we can make that clear to them, they might choose to withdraw.* He thought it over for a moment, and called the bridge. "Petty Officer Tolbin, are you still secure up there?"

"Yes, sir," Tolbin replied. "We've got the hatch sealed, and the escape scuttles too."

"Is the ship's general announcement system working? And can you put me on?"

"Just a second. . . . Yes, sir, I think so. Let me know when you're ready."

"One moment," Sikander told him. He activated his translation device, and started to speak; the translator issued a stream of Nebeldeutsch in neutral tones. "Attention, Dremish sailors aboard this ship. This is Commander North of the Aquilan navy. *Meduse* is under our control. We have repelled your attempts to seize the bridge and engineering spaces, and we've captured the force assembled on the mess deck. You have no reasonable chance to retake this ship, and we are about to get under way. We don't want to take you prisoner and we have no ability to treat your injured, so I urge you to proceed to the lifeboats and leave the ship. Otherwise, we'll be forced to take you with us and hold you as prisoners until we reach our destination. Enough people have been hurt today—there's no point in anyone else getting killed. You have five minutes to comply. North, out."

"You can't just seize an Imperial warship!" one of the Dremish petty officers protested. "What gives you the right?"

"It's not an Imperial warship anymore. It's been transferred to the Zerzura Sector Fleet, and we have determined that the Zerzuran government is complicit in piracy. We're not going to let three heavy cruisers fall into the hands of a pirate regime." Sikander turned his back on the fellow and moved away for more privacy, then activated the command channel again. "Mr. Shah, Mr. Girard, I'm offering the Dremish forces currently aboard

Meduse the opportunity to use the lifeboats and debark before we get under way. You might try a general announcement to extend the same offer to the boarding parties you're dealing with. We don't want to take them with us and I doubt that they want to go, over."

"Aye, Captain—I'll speak to the group holed up in our torpedo room and see if I can convince them to leave," Michael Girard replied.

"This is Shah. I will make the announcement. We have recaptured the bridge and I believe we can hold all the vital spaces." The Kashmiri engineer paused, and then added, "Sir, I regret to inform you that Sublieutenant Worth has been killed in action. I think that *Zyklop* can still get under way, however."

Zoe Worth dead? Dear God, this is turning into a disaster. Sikander closed his eyes and took a moment to master his shock before speaking again—he had to project confidence and keep the mission moving ahead, or more deaths might follow. "Acknowledged, Mr. Shah. Give the Dremish sailors a chance to leave first."

Since Jackson seemed to have control of the room, Sikander moved to the galley entrance to check on his wounded deckhand. White sat on the deck leaning against an oven, his fatigue shirt pulled open to reveal a blood-soaked wound dressing over his shoulder; Flores knelt beside him, fumbling with the medical pack from her battle-dress utility belt.

"How are you doing, White?" Sikander asked, kneeling beside him.

"I've been better, sir," the young deckhand said through gritted teeth. "I'm sorry. Guess I should have ducked faster."

"Don't worry. We'll take care of you." Sikander set an encouraging hand on the wounded sailor's good shoulder, but he didn't like how pale the young man looked or the amount of blood soaking the bandage. "Do you think you could walk a short distance?

Corpsman Chang's in the orbiter, and I'd like to have her se
what she can do for that shoulder. Flores, help him out, please."

"I'll try," White said. Sikander and Flores helped him to his
feet, and Flores propped him up by positioning herself under his
good arm.

"Good man. Flores, take him to the airlock where we came in.
Mr. Hollister, I'm sending White and Flores back to the orbiter.
Keep an eye on their progress and make sure to warn them if
they're about to run into any Dremish holdouts."

"Aye, Captain," Hollister replied. "They should be okay, sir. I've
reestablished contact with Orbiter One, and it looks like White
and Flores have a clear path to the airlock. And from what I can
see here, most of the Dremish on board seem to be moving toward
the lifeboat stations—I think they're taking you up on your offer."

"Very well." *But where's Bleindel?* Sikander added silently. Of
course, Hollister couldn't tell from the damage-control system
which small blob of body heat and motion belonged to any specific person on board, even if he did have an idea of who Sikander
was looking for. Perhaps the Dremish agent had given up too, and
was making his way to a lifeboat like the others. He hated the idea
of Otto Bleindel slipping away again, but—

"Captain, I've got movement near the bridge," Hollister suddenly said. "Someone's in the equipment room one deck below,
and it's not one of ours."

Sikander heard Bleindel through the closed hatch—low scraping
sounds, an awkward metallic clunk, the dull clatter of something
dropped on the linoleum-covered deck inside. He paused in the
passageway outside, frowning. Clearly the Dremish agent was up
to something, and that could mean he was too busy to watch the

hatch. On the other hand, Sikander had seen Bleindel in combat before—a shoot-out in a warehouse on Gadira eight years ago. Despite being surprised by a contingent of Royal Guards, Bleindel had reacted swiftly and coolly, escaping in seconds. He wouldn't be easy to catch off-guard.

"What's he doing in there?" Petty Officer Jackson whispered.

"Nothing that we want him to finish, I'm sure," Sikander replied, likewise keeping his voice to a whisper. It was just the two of them; he'd reluctantly released the Dremish on the mess deck to find their own way to the nearest lifeboat, hoping that with wounded to look after and their weapons confiscated they wouldn't make any more mischief for his prize crew. As much as he wanted to confront Otto Bleindel and personally put a mag dart through his head, he recognized that two men going up against an expert combatant in a small room with one door was a terrible risk. Of course, there was the escape scuttle from the bridge . . . but if there was anything more dangerous than going in through a door watched by a capable enemy, it was descending a ladder into that enemy's room. Petty Officer Tolbin had the top of the scuttle secured; it seemed much better to Sikander to ensure that Bleindel remained locked out of the bridge than to try for some distraction that required opening that hatch.

We could wait, he told himself. The inertial nav systems were important, but there were ways to work around their loss if Bleindel sabotaged them. *Then again, how do I know he didn't bring a ten-kilo charge of molecular explosive on board? Or that he isn't in contact with someone on* Neu Kiel *who can tell him exactly how to disable a critical bridge function from that space and make sure this ship is unable to get under way?* What Otto Bleindel lacked in technical expertise, he more than made up for in resourcefulness and a talent for mayhem. Sikander couldn't afford to wait him out.

He looked over at Jackson. "Bleindel is very dangerous. Our

only advantage is that he doesn't know when we're coming through this door. We'll use two flash grenades, two seconds apart, and then we'll go in low—he may retain enough awareness to fire through the doorway after the bang. If you get a shot, take it without hesitation."

"Our grenades might do a pretty good job of sabotaging the nav systems in that room, sir," Jackson pointed out. "We could wind up saving the Dremish the trouble of wrecking the gyroscopes."

"That's an acceptable outcome," Sikander told him. "I'll crack the hatch and throw in my grenade. You count to two, then throw in yours. Make sure you look away from the door after you throw your device. After the second explosion, I'll go in and turn right. You go in and turn left."

Jackson nodded. They readied their flash grenades, drawing the safety pins and holding the levers tightly as they crouched beside the hatch. Then Sikander reached up for the handle and popped the hatch open just wide enough to toss his grenade into the room; the comm tech held his for two heartbeats, then threw his grenade in after Sikander's. A mag-rifle shot pinged against the hatch edge just above Sikander's head, and—*BANG!*—the first grenade went off. Sikander readied his battle rifle, and the instant the second grenade detonated, he threw open the hatch and dove in at knee height, scrambling to the right to duck behind a gyroscope casing as he looked for Bleindel—

—who crouched in a corner behind a two-meter-tall wheeled metal cylinder, a mag pistol pointing at the red-painted canister behind which he was hiding.

Metallic hydrogen fuel cylinder, Sikander realized. He trained his weapon on Bleindel but did not pull the trigger. "Jackson, hold your fire!" he shouted. "Don't hit the cylinder!"

Bleindel blinked his eyes clear and shook his head. "Commander

North," he said loudly, trying to speak over the ringing in his ears. "Yes, please don't hit the cylinder unless you wish to ruin everybody's day. It turns out that there are all kinds of explosives on board a ship undergoing a refit—I found this just down the passageway. I should point out that you nearly blew us all to pieces with those flash grenades."

"Damn you, Bleindel," Sikander snarled. "Lower your weapon and step out from behind that hydrogen, or I swear before God that I'll put a dart in that cylinder myself. It's exactly what you deserve."

"I'm not sure if a hundred kilos of metallic hydrogen exploding in this compartment would substantially damage the bridge, but I have to imagine it would wreck all the equipment in here," Bleindel said with a shrug. "I doubt that you'd survive, either. So I suppose you'll just have to go ahead and shoot."

"How exactly do you expect this to play out?" Sikander demanded. "You threaten to blow yourself up unless we surrender the ship to you? You don't strike me as the type."

Bleindel gave him an ironic smile. "In all honesty, I'm still working that out—I'd hoped to set the bomb and be on my way before you interrupted me. Give me a minute or two, and I'll see whether I can come up with a scenario where nobody else dies and I get what I want."

"Captain?" Petty Officer Jackson asked. He crouched behind an equipment cabinet a few meters from Sikander, covering Bleindel with his weapon. "What do we do, sir?"

Sikander hesitated a moment. The cylinder provided Bleindel with good cover, but it couldn't protect him completely. He was fairly confident that he could hit the Dremish agent without striking the cylinder, but whether he'd prevent Bleindel from being able to pull the trigger or not . . . *If Darvesh were here, he would remind me that Bleindel does not want to die,* he realized. *He believes that he's clever enough to figure a way out of this standoff. That gives me the advantage.*

The Dremish agent seemed to arrive at a decision. "Lower your weapon, Commander North. This is how it's going to—"

Sikander fired.

The mag dart caught Otto Bleindel in the jaw, shattering bone and teeth. He sagged back into the bulkhead behind him and somehow found the presence of mind to shift his pistol from the cylinder to Sikander—and then Petty Officer Jackson fired, punching two more darts into the Dremish agent and knocking him down to the deck. The heavy hydrogen cylinder spun in a half circle on its narrow base and fell to the deck with a resounding clang. Sikander flinched, but the cylinder withstood the impact.

The instant he realized that the hydrogen wasn't about to explode, he surged up from his crouch. Darting across the compartment, he kept his sights on Otto Bleindel, ready to fire again, but the Dremish agent had dropped his pistol. Bleindel tried to speak through his ruined mouth, spitting blood over his shirt. Then his eyes fluttered closed, and he lost consciousness.

"Holy *shit*, sir," Jackson breathed, moving up beside Sikander and kicking away Bleindel's weapon. "What happened to 'Hold your fire'?"

"I saw a shot and I took it. And so did you, for which I am grateful—good work, Jackson. Restrain Mr. Bleindel, if you please, and guard him until we can send someone to help you get him to the brig."

"Okay, sir, but I don't think he's going anywhere." The comm tech fished around in his utility belt for a set of tough plastic restraints.

Sikander waited just long enough to make sure that the Dremish agent was secured, and then tapped his comm device. "Bridge, this is the captain. Signal *Drachen* and *Zyklop* to prepare to get under way. And open that escape scuttle, I'm coming up." Then he hurried up the ladder to the bridge.

23

Meduse, Dahar Naval Shipyard

Under *Decisive's* watchful gaze, *Drachen*, *Meduse*, and *Zyklop* energized their drive plates and began to accelerate away from Dahar's orbital shipyard. A little more than an hour ago, Sikander had boarded *Meduse* with twenty-seven officers and enlisted personnel. Seven of his sailors had been killed in the Dremish attempt to retake the cruiser and four more were so seriously wounded that they couldn't help man the ship, leaving only sixteen people fit for duty in his prize crew. Michael Girard on *Drachen* reported that he'd only lost two sailors killed in action; he'd been fortunate enough to bottle up the Dremish boarding team in the torpedo room before they were able to mount an attack. Amar Shah on *Zyklop*, on the other hand, was down to only thirteen effectives, in part because he'd sent some of his people to help Girard during the initial seizure of the cruisers.

It will have to be enough, Sikander told himself. A heavy cruiser typically carried a crew numbering of three to four hundred . . . but during routine sailing, the bridge could get by with just a few watchstanders, as could the main control station in the engineering spaces. Warships needed their large complements to man weapon mounts and damage-control parties during combat, but he had no intention of getting involved in a fight with his flotilla of prizes. *Decisive* sufficed to protect his undermanned cruisers from the Zerzuran gunboats now tailing the mismatched Aquilan squadron until they could charge up their warp rings and began their transits.

He directed Master Chief Vaughn to take three crewhands—all he could spare at the moment—to remove their dead and wounded to the ship's wardroom and then conduct a methodical sweep of *Meduse* for any Dremish or Zerzurans remaining on board. Sikander had to imagine that at least a few *Neu Kiel* sailors hadn't been able to make up their minds about whether or not they should heed his advice, or were too badly wounded to get themselves to a lifeboat station and needed help.

"Boy, the Dremish didn't build these buckets for speed, did they?" Quartermaster Birk observed from his place at the helm. "I've got the throttle at the stops, Captain, and it looks like seventy-one g is all we're going to get. And even at that *Drachen* isn't quite keeping up with us."

"She's thirty-five years old and she was built to be tough, not fast. Still, you make a good point about *Drachen*." Sikander studied the tactical display, observing the slight deviation in each ship's vector, and got back on the command channel. "*Drachen, Meduse.* Mr. Girard, what's your best sustained acceleration, over?"

"*Meduse, Drachen.* Sorry, sir, but it looks like sixty-nine point six is the best we can do," *Decisive*'s operations officer replied. "We've got two drive plates out of commission and we're not going to be able to power them up without a few days of work, over."

"Understood," Sikander replied. "All ships, *Meduse.* Make your acceleration sixty-nine g. We'll extend our transit acceleration time a little bit to initiate warp at nine percent *c*, over."

"Make acceleration sixty-nine g, aye," Amelia Fraser, Michael

Girard, and Amar Shah responded in turn. Then Amelia added, "Captain, Mr. Darrow would like to speak with you. I'm giving him a private channel."

"Very good." Sikander selected the new channel while he watched the formation adjust its speed in *Meduse*'s display. "This is Commander North. How can I help you, Mr. Darrow?"

Darrow's angular face appeared in a comm window of the bridge display. "Ah, there you are. Commander, I suggest you initiate warp as quickly as possible. Marid Pasha is making some very ugly threats—I worry for the safety of Aquilan travelers and businesspeople in Zerzuran territory. If we leave before he escalates his language any further, he might not get around to making a threat he feels that he needs to act on. Can we begin our transit now?"

"We're not moving fast enough yet. At this speed, we'd turn a four-day transit into twenty-five days, and we simply don't have the stores for that—the only provisions on board these cruisers are what we brought with us." As it turned out, the Zerzurans hadn't seen the need to stock the storerooms of ships that were still undergoing refit. Fortunately, Grant Edwards had pointed out that possibility to Sikander during their hurried mission planning, and the boarding teams had brought a few cases of field rations for the trip. Otherwise, *Decisive*'s prize crews would have been facing a long and hungry warp transit. "We'll need another five hours of acceleration at a minimum before we can bubble up. I don't suppose it would help if you pointed out that we'll hold him personally responsible for the treatment of our citizens?"

Darrow shook his head. "A counterthreat would only escalate things more. I'll pass word to our consulates to issue a travel warning to Aquilan citizens, and I'll ask some of my colleagues from friendly powers to look out for Aquilans who need help. I'm sure they'll think we've lost our minds, but they might give me the benefit of the doubt once I provide a little more explanation. Please advise me if our departure time changes."

"Of course," Sikander replied. "We will do our best, Mr. Darrow."

"Captain, the Dremish survey ship is overtaking us," Petty Officer Tolbin reported. He manned the bridge's sensor console in place of Petty Officer Diaz. "Bearing two-zero-five down ten, range sixty thousand kilometers."

"*Polarstern?*" Sikander limped over to Tolbin's display to look for himself; the mag-dart graze on his leg was beginning to throb. *Polarstern* evidently had a better turn of speed than he would have expected from a survey vessel. Her acceleration wasn't too much less than what *Decisive* was capable of, and she was easily twice the destroyer's tonnage. *What does she think she's going to do when she gets here?* he wondered. *She might be fast enough to get in front of us and foul our transit course, delaying our departure by making us avoid collisions. But what would be the point?*

He called his XO again. "Amelia, what do you make of *Polarstern's* maneuvers?"

"I've been keeping an eye on her since she broke orbit and started pursuing," Amelia replied. "I'd say that she means to overtake us and maybe maneuver aggressively to make us change course. I don't want to fire on her, but if her movements put the ship in danger—"

"—we might have to take steps to defend ourselves," Sikander finished. *Polarstern's* surprising acceleration troubled him. The Dremish vessel appeared to be unarmed, but he'd heard speculation in various corners that the Imperial Survey Service's science ships doubled as surveillance platforms and might have hidden capabilities—covert minelaying, for example. *Could* Polarstern *get out in front of us and deploy a pattern of mines in our path? Would the Dremish be willing to damage or destroy the ships they're transferring to Zerzura to keep us from removing them?* It seemed to Sikander that if Dremark wanted to give Marid Pasha an operational navy they wouldn't want to damage the pasha's new ships. But, then again, he hadn't expected the Dremish to reboard their cruisers through torpedo loading hatches. He knew what rules of engagement he intended to observe today, but he'd had time beforehand to think through the risks and consequences of the operation. Marid Pasha and the Dremish commanders and diplomats in Dahar, on the other hand, had clearly been caught off guard by the seizure of the ships. *They probably haven't yet decided what the stakes are and how much they're willing to risk. That means they could easily stumble into a decision they'd regret—and us, as well.*

"Continue to watch *Polarstern*, but don't warn her off or take any aggressive action yet," he told Amelia. "We're in open space and she's free to go where she wants, right up to the moment that she does something to endanger our ships. Be ready for trouble— Naval Intelligence has been saying for years that those Dremish survey ships might have military capabilities. Now, what about *Penguen* and *Marti*? What are they up to?"

"They're closing and illuminating us with fire-control systems, Captain. They've fired a few warning shots, but they haven't been cheeky enough to fire directly at us yet." Amelia paused, studying her own tactical display aboard *Decisive*. "It looks like they're coordinating their movements with *Polarstern*. I think the arrival of the Dremish ship has stiffened their resolve."

Sikander nodded. "Very well. If *Penguen* or *Marti* close within two thousand kilometers, warn them once, then fire to disable if they don't immediately change course."

"Final warning followed by engagement at two thousand kilometers, understood." Amelia paused, then added, "That's pretty generous, Captain."

"I want to give them as much time as I can to make the smart choice." Sikander returned to the tactical display and zoomed out, looking for any other impediments in their path—it would be all too easy to get caught up in looking over their shoulders without noticing other threats getting into position ahead of them. Fortunately, nothing seemed to be in their way. No Zerzuran warships were in front of them, and their course didn't come anywhere near any of the stations, planets, or moons in the outer system where a clever commander might attempt to prepare an ambush. *At least we're not about to run into trouble,* he decided. *The question is whether trouble's going to chase us down.*

For the next fifty minutes, he watched the distance between his prize flotilla and the pursuing ships narrow, wondering about the next move in the deadly game taking shape. His cruisers steadied their bows on the distant point of light that was Meliya's sun and steadily built up their speed, increasing their velocity by a little more than two kilometers per second every three seconds. *Decisive* fell back slightly, interposing herself between the cruisers and the Dremish and Zerzurans following them. Sikander didn't care for the idea of his XO maneuvering to keep the destroyer in the most exposed position, but he refrained from ordering Amelia to make *Decisive's* safety her priority—he didn't want to second-guess her, and she knew perfectly well that none of the cruisers were capable of returning fire if the Zerzurans chose to attack.

When *Polarstern* and her Zerzuran allies drew within ten thousand kilometers of Sikander's flotilla, Comm Tech Jackson looked up from his position at the communications station. "Captain, *Polarstern* is signaling our formation. I, er, don't know how to forward it over to the tactical station with this set-up, but I've got her over here."

"Thank you, Jackson." Sikander crossed the bridge to stand behind Jackson's battle couch. He found himself looking at the

image of a woman in a Dremish naval uniform. She had a prominent gray streak in the dark hair above her sharp-featured face,
and her mouth was fixed in an angry scowl. "CSS *Decisive*, this
is Fregattenkapitan Valentina Fischer of His Imperial Majesty's
Survey Service vessel *Polarstern*," she began. "You have no legal
justification for removing those Zerzuran ships from this system.
You are flagrantly violating Zerzuran sovereignty and flouting the
norms of international relations, and I will not permit this to continue a minute longer. I order you to surrender *Drachen, Meduse*,
and *Zyklop* immediately."

"Shall I respond to that, Captain?" Amelia Fraser asked via
their private channel.

"No, I've got it," Sikander told her. He nodded to Petty Officer
Jackson. "Give me a channel, please."

"You're on, sir," the comm tech replied.

"Captain Fischer, this is Commander Sikander Singh North
of the Aquilan Commonwealth. I am in command of this force.
As my executive officer explained to Captain Beck of *Neu Kiel*,
these ships are prizes confiscated under the antipiracy provisions
of the Interstellar Convention on the Law of Open Space. If you
don't agree with that determination you're welcome to file your
protests with the admiralty court, but until a court orders us to
return these ships to the Zerzuran government they'll be interned
in a neutral system."

"What acts of piracy have those ships participated in?" Fischer
demanded. "You're *stealing* those ships, Commander, and in my
view you're committing an act of war. You have one opportunity
to cease hostilities and reconsider your actions before I put an end
to this outrageous provocation. Cut your acceleration to zero and
stand by to receive boarding parties—we are taking those cruisers
back."

"*Drachen, Meduse*, and *Zyklop* are not yours to take back,

Captain Fischer. And we are not 'stealing' them—our prize crews are sailing to the nearest neutral system to surrender these ships for adjudication. That system happens to be Meliya in the Velaran Electorate, which you may have already guessed from our transit acceleration course. There is no 'act of war' here."

"No act of war? You have dozens of dead Dremish sailors aboard those ships, and no doubt others whom I assume are now being held prisoner!"

Sikander met Fischer's gaze without flinching. "We took control of these ships using nonlethal settings on our weapons, Captain. *Neu Kiel*'s sailors weren't so careful when they attempted to seize them back. Your sailors initiated the use of deadly force, not ours."

Fregattenkapitan Fischer's glower should have melted the comm console. "This is your last warning, Commander North: Return those cruisers, or face the consequences."

"I am engaged in a lawful action against vessels under the flag of a government associated with piracy, Captain. Your objections are noted, but I am continuing on my course. North, out."

Meduse's bridge fell silent for a moment; Birk, Tolbin, and Jackson exchanged wide-eyed looks, but none of the enlisted personnel ventured to speak. On the command circuit, Amelia Fraser let out an audible sigh. "I don't think she's going to like that answer, Captain," she said.

"To be clear, Captain Fischer isn't entirely wrong," Amar Shah pointed out. "We're basing this action on a highly creative reading of the ICLOS piracy definition. An admiralty court could very easily rule against us."

"Not for a long time, Mr. Shah," Sikander said. The lawyers and the diplomats would spend months and months arguing over the fate of the impounded cruisers—time during which evidence of Marid Pasha's corruption would reach Terra, and the Caliphate might finally be prodded into doing something about the situation in Zerzura. "In fact, I'll settle for—"

"Captain! *Polarstern* is illuminating *Decisive* with fire-control radar!" Petty Officer Tolbin called to Sikander. At the same time, he heard shouts of consternation and alarms wailing on *Decisive's* bridge behind Amelia Fraser and more alarms from the other two prize ships.

Sikander swore and moved over to the tactical console. The Dremish survey ship put on another ten g of acceleration and surged ahead, while *Marti* and *Penguen* followed her in and opened fire with their light K-cannons. "Damn it!" he snarled at the tactical display. "What sort of weapons systems does she have?"

"I'm looking, sir. That's a Teller-D fire-control radar, so it's probably a medium-weight kinetic cannon." As an electronics tech, Petty Officer Tolbin specialized in fire-control and sensor systems; he fumbled with *Meduse's* unfamiliar console, and managed to train a high-power vidcam on the Dremish ship. "Got it, sir. She's got a false side concealing casemate-mounted K-cannons, just forward of her hangar bays."

An auxiliary cruiser, Sikander realized. *She's designed to pass as a research vessel and slip into enemy space without raising suspicions, then turn commerce raider if Dremark decides to start a war. She'll have at least a couple of point-defense lasers to go along with that hidden broadside, a torpedo tube or two, and maybe even that minelaying capability the Naval Intelligence Office suspects.* He grimaced as he considered what *Polarstern's* size and speed meant for this confrontation; it was entirely possible that she outgunned *Decisive. And with the two Zerzuran gunboats, Decisive is outnumbered as well.*

"EM blooms! She's firing, sir!" Tolbin reported.

"*Decisive*, evasive maneuvers! You're under attack!" Sikander shouted. His warning was pointless—*Decisive's* tactical systems would be shrieking with attack-detection alarms, and Amelia Fraser could certainly understand their meaning—but he couldn't help himself. He gripped the display, helplessly watching the Dremish attack develop. *I should be on* Decisive's *bridge!* he railed at himself. On *Meduse* he was only a spectator—he'd sidelined himself for the most serious fight *Decisive* was likely to face in his tour of duty.

Amelia Fraser didn't respond to Sikander, but she hadn't been caught sleeping. The instant *Polarstern* fired, the Aquilan destroyer jinked and dodged wildly. The range was close, but *Polarstern's* first salvo managed nothing more than a single graze across her back, a glancing blow that hurled a brilliant spray of molten droplets into the void but only seared a channel two centimeters deep in *Decisive's* armor.

"Velocity of those K-cannons?" Sikander asked Tolbin.

"One moment, sir," said the petty officer, studying the sensor display. "Thirty-two hundred kps. Damn, those are light-cruiser guns! Only three mounts on the broadside, though."

"So it would seem," Sikander agreed, his heart sinking. A K-cannon's effective range depended on the velocity at which the weapon could hurl its tungsten-alloy penetrator—large cannons generated higher muzzle velocities, which meant they covered more distance in the same flight time than smaller weapons. Small and nimble targets could dodge K-shots as long as the flight time measured at least a few seconds, but *Polarstern* was well within her guns' range; sooner or later, she'd score, and no destroyer ever built wanted to be on the receiving end of a cruiser's cannons. Sikander fought the temptation to get on the command channel to try to tell Amelia Fraser what to do. She understood how to fight the ship as well as he did, and he'd left her in charge of *Decisive.* It was up to her to conduct the battle for his ship's life.

Marti and *Penguen* split up, each swinging wide as they charged in closer, seeking to get within range of their smaller K-cannons. *Decisive* ignored the Zerzuran gunboats, turning to bring her full main battery to bear on the much more significant threat posed by the armed survey ship, and replied with a full salvo of her own. Eight Orcades Mark IX K-cannons fired as one, brilliant shot trajectories taking shape in the tactical display to show the line of fire. A single hit landed on one of *Polarstern*'s sliding panels, wrecking the false side and gouging the armored casemate behind it without punching through.

"*Meduse, Zyklop*," Amar Shah called. "Captain, what should we do? We've got to help *Decisive!*"

"Maintain course and speed, *Zyklop*," Sikander said, speaking to himself as well as his chief engineer as he worked out his responsibilities in the engagement. "Our job in this fight is to align these cruisers for warp transit and build velocity as quickly as we can. The longer we remain in Dahar, the longer *Decisive* has to remain here to protect us."

"But it's going to take us hours to reach any kind of transit velocity," Shah protested. "Surely there must be something we can do, Captain."

"Stay in formation, Mr. Shah. *Decisive* is in good hands," Sikander repeated, but he looked around *Meduse*'s bridge—he certainly shared Amar Shah's desire to help out. *We've got three heavy cruisers here. Any one of these ships could wreck* Polarstern *with a single salvo . . . but we don't have the manpower we need to operate the gun mounts, and* Meduse's *weapons console is completely disassembled at the moment.* Well, there might be a way around that problem, at least. Every Aquilan gun mount had some provision for firing under local control in case the bridge was knocked out by battle damage; he had to imagine that Dremish weapons systems incorporated the same level of redundancy.

He selected *Meduse*'s internal command circuit and called

Master Chief Vaughn. While she currently served as *Decisive's* command master chief, she'd come up through the ranks as a gunner's mate. "Master Chief, where are you right now?"

"Searching the crew berthing spaces for any more stowaways, Captain. What's going on?"

"The Dremish survey ship is firing on *Decisive*—it turns out she's armed like a light cruiser. We need to find a way to help out the XO. Can you take your team back to one of the after main-battery mounts and see about getting it into action?"

"Damn it, I knew that Dremish ship was up to no good," Felicia Vaughn replied. "Aye, sir, we'll give it a try. That means suspending our sweep for holdouts or survivors—I'll need all the hands I can get to operate a main mount. And I don't know if we have any ammunition on board."

"I understand. Maybe there are some practice rounds in the magazines. Have a look, and see what you find." It wasn't much, but at least Sikander felt like he was doing *something*.

He returned his attention to the battle developing behind *Meduse*. *Decisive* veered back and forth across the rear of the formation, evading vigorously while firing at high speed. She carried more guns than the Dremish auxiliary, and her lighter weapons could maintain a higher rate of fire—for every three-round broadside Captain Fischer fired, Amelia Fraser sent two eight-round broadsides back in return. *Polarstern* tacked more slowly, content to maintain the range instead of pressing too close. Sikander could see that it was a wise choice on Fregattenkapitan Fischer's part, considering the fact that she carried the heavier guns and closing the range would only improve the effectiveness of the Aquilan destroyer's weapons. *Marti* and *Penguen* charged forward boldly to make the most of their smaller K-cannons, until *Decisive* opened up on *Penguen* with her secondary battery of lasers and drove back the Zerzuran with a dozen glowing burns in her flanks.

"Good God," Amar Shah murmured over the command channel. "How much longer can *Decisive* keep it up?"

"Longer than you might think," Michael Girard told him. "It's hard to land a clean hit on a dodging target. During the fight at Gadira *Hector* dueled *Panther* for more than an hour."

"One lucky hit can change that in a hurry," Sikander warned. "If you have any trained mount crews aboard, have them try to get a gun into action—as Mr. Shah suggested, maybe we can find a way to help out without diverting from our transit course."

"Aye, sir," the two department heads said.

Decisive scored on *Polarstern*'s nose, landing a shot in the heavy bow armor that protected a ship from radiation and microscopic impacts during warp travel. The larger ship shrugged it off and replied with a fresh broadside of her own. Two of her K-cannons missed again, but the third hammered the Aquilan destroyer just aft of her midsection, blasting through the armor belt and causing an eruption of incandescent gas and shattered steel from her wounded side.

Sikander's heart hammered in his chest as he watched his ship stagger under the blow. "*Decisive, Decisive!*" he shouted over the command channel. "Damage report! *Decisive*, respond!"

No one answered for a long moment . . . and then Amelia Fraser's face reappeared in the comm window. Her expression was fixed in a tight frown of worry, but she seemed unhurt. "We lost generator two," she reported. "Power's out to mount three, but Chief Ryan's working on it. Dr. Ruiz confirms that we have several killed in action and some serious wounds—I don't know the exact number. We're still here, Captain, but we can't take too much more of that."

Do I order her to break off? Sikander thought furiously, search-ing for a way to carry out the operation while preserving his com-mand. If he ordered *Decisive* to turn away, the Dremish would be faced with the choice of pursuing the destroyer or continuing after the cruisers, their real target. Without *Decisive's* threat in her way, *Polarstern* could pull ahead of Sikander's cruisers and foul their transit course, forcing them to turn away . . . or perhaps Val-entina Fischer would decide that inflicting some damage on the cruisers to prevent their removal from Dahar was worth it, and shoot out their drive plates or warp rings. *That's what I would do,* he realized. *And when she reduces our maneuverability to zero, she can send over a boarding party at her leisure. If we lose* Decisive, *we lose this encounter—and likely the whole sector, too.*

"Very well," Sikander answered. "Carry on, XO. If you see an opportunity for a torpedo attack, take it."

"Understood, Captain. But those stupid Zerzuran gunboats are actually serving as a reasonably competent screen for *Polarstern,* whether they mean to or not. Should I shift fire and chase them off?"

"Stay on *Polarstern.* You don't dare let her take shots at you without having to dodge your return fire." Sikander tried to think of something else he might try if he were in her place, and came up with nothing other than *shoot faster and don't get hit.* He was pretty sure that Amelia Fraser could figure that out for herself.

"Captain, Master Chief Vaughn," his shipboard channel crack-led. "Sir, we've got the number-five mount manned and powered. There isn't much ammunition, but we can try at least a few shots. What's our target?"

Sikander straightened up and looked aft, as if he could some-how see the master chief through the bridge and all the compart-ments between him and her. He'd almost forgotten that he might be able to participate in the battle after all. "Hit *Polarstern* with whatever you've got, and keep shooting until you run out of ammo or I tell you to stop," he told her. "Fire at will, Master Chief!"

"Engage *Polarstern*, aye." A moment later, *Meduse*'s after turret swiveled into position and opened up with a dull, distant boom that set the deck under Sikander's feet quivering. Instead of the stiletto-like trajectory line of a normal shot, the tactical screen displayed a strobing blur that flickered through half a dozen flight projections before hammering into the Dremish auxiliary's flank. The blow struck her on her forward starboard-side casemate and left a ragged five-meter crater where one of *Polarstern*'s heavy guns had been mounted.

"We hit her, sir!" Petty Officer Tolbin shouted. "We knocked out one of her K-cannons!"

"That's more like it," Sikander said with a fierce grin. "Good shooting, Master Chief! What in the devil was that?"

"A big-ass combination wrench, sir. Only thing we could find around here that was about the same size and shape as a main-battery round. We're ripping up a power-distribution panel now to get at the bus bars, they might do. It's going to be hell on the actuating magnets, but it isn't my gun."

"Master Chief Vaughn, do you mean to tell me that we just hit *Polarstern* with a ten-kilo *wrench* moving at thirty-six hundred kps?"

Vaughn chuckled over the shipboard channel. "I bet it left a funny-looking hole in that Dremish bastard. Oh, wait, we just found a little crowbar. It's only a kilo or so but it's good hard alloy—we'll try that next."

Sikander gave a harsh bark of laughter. "Hah! Master Chief, you're a wonder-worker. Remember to document everything you jettison, that's impounded Zerzuran government property." Vaughn merely snorted in reply.

"Sir, *Drachen's* firing on *Polarstern!*" Petty Officer Tolbin reported. "And *Zyklop* is illuminating her with fire-control systems!"

"Good!" Sikander turned back to the tactical display. *Drachen's* shot went wide, missing the Dremish survey ship by a few hundred meters, but he didn't mind. Wrecking *Polarstern* wasn't the mission at hand—holding her off was all they needed to do. He had to imagine that the prospect of dealing with the intermittent fire of the heavy cruisers in addition to *Decisive's* constant barrage presented Fregattenkapitan Fischer with a much more complicated tactical picture than she'd faced just a few minutes ago.

"Captain, Lieutenant Shah," Amar Shah called. "We've got a fire-control system working aboard *Zyklop* but it's just for show, sir. We don't actually have anyone to man a turret. I'm illuminating *Polarstern* in the hope that they'll believe we might open fire at any moment."

"This is *Drachen*. We're bringing a second mount up to power, but we've only got a dozen K-shot in the magazine and we're firing in local control," Michael Girard said. "We won't be able to sustain our fire for long."

"Good work, *Drachen* and *Zyklop*," Sikander told his officers. "*Polarstern* might not appreciate your limitations. Keep at it—if we can force her to break off, we win."

"Mount five ready to fire again, Captain," Master Chief Vaughn announced.

"Fire!" Sikander ordered.

Meduse shook once more with the powerful recoil of the heavy K-cannon in her after turret. This time the sensors tracked a dozen outgoing shots at once, a mismatched collection of projectiles that blasted through *Polarstern's* patch of space like a sleet storm. "What in the world?" Sikander said, startled by the instant salvo . . . and then he realized that his gun crew must have loaded the K-cannon with an assortment of improvised projectiles in the absence of any standard penetrators. Bolts and hand tools and even ferrous metal shavings could all serve as ammunition in a pinch. They might not do much damage against a heavily armored target, but they'd already seen that *Polarstern* was a little thin-skinned, and just about anything moving at thirty-six hundred kilometers a second could inflict substantial surface damage. Most of the junk flew past the Dremish ship, but a thumb-sized hex nut impacted right in the middle of a drive plate and cracked it in half, while a tumbling screwdriver holed one of the ship's hangar bay doors and wrecked a launch in its docking cradle.

A moment later, *Decisive's* next salvo arrived. This time two Mark IX penetrators scored solid hits in the forward hull, hammering through the light armor to incinerate the captain's cabin and scythe through one of the repair lockers before blowing a three-meter hole on the opposite side of the hull. *Polarstern* shuddered under the rain of blows, streamers of molten metal spilling from her wounds amid jets of escaping atmosphere—and then she suddenly turned away, flipping end over end to point her main drive plates in the direction of her travel and decelerate with all her power. In a matter of seconds, the Dremish auxiliary began to fall behind the fleeing squadron.

"Captain, they're breaking off!" Girard exclaimed. "They've had enough!"

"So I see, Mr. Girard," Sikander said, and breathed a sigh of relief. He looked to see whether the Zerzuran gunboats intended to continue the action on their own—without the Dremish ship to draw *Decisive's* fire, they wouldn't last long. Their commanders quickly came to that conclusion for themselves; less than a minute after *Polarstern* broke off the action, *Penguen* and *Marti* likewise spun to point their bows away and begin braking.

Four and a half hours later, Sikander gave the order for his battered squadron to activate their warp generators and leave Zerzura behind them.

24

Baybars City, Meliya Prime

O mar Morillo's vid call woke Elena Pavon shortly after three in the morning. She did her best to ignore the insistent chirping of the bedside comm unit, but finally she rolled over in her luxurious bed and slapped the screen to answer. "Omar, you're fired," she mumbled through her disheveled hair.

"Well, I figured you'd fire me if I didn't wake you up for this," her assistant said with a shrug. Somehow he was awake, dressed, and alert despite the hour. "Since you were certain to fire me either way, I decided I'd at least savor the opportunity to drag you out of bed in the middle of the night. Turn on the news, Elena— you're going to want to see this."

Elena sat up, reaching for the vidscreen remote. No doubt Omar was getting an eyeful of her nightie, but it wasn't like he would be impressed. She activated the two-meter screen on the opposite wall of her palatial bedroom, and propped a pillow behind her back as she settled in to watch Meliya's planetary news channel flicker to life. The first thing she recognized was Meliya Station and the familiar green curve of the planet below. Three large warships painted in the black, green, and gold of the Zerzura Sector Fleet drifted on mooring tethers above the scaffolding that covered the damaged naval post on the station's upper surface, while the smaller teardrop shape of a warship painted in Aquilan white, buff, and red hovered nearby. Blackened scars pitted her flanks; Elena was no expert, but she could tell at a glance that the ship had been in a battle recently.

"Holy crap—is that the *Decisive?*" she asked Omar.

"And Marid Pasha's new cruisers, formerly *Drachen, Meduse,* and *Zyklop* of the Dremish navy. They unbubbled in-system about three hours ago and just made orbit."

"I don't get it. What are they all doing here?"

"If you'd actually *watch* the newscast instead of asking me to explain it to you, you'd find out," said Omar. Elena shot him a hard look; he sighed and went on. "Fine. As the crawl is reporting at this very instant, the Aquilans are surrendering the three cruisers as prizes to the lord arbiter's office to be interned under antipiracy laws. Apparently they seized the vessels from the naval shipyard in Dahar and brought them here to observe the legalities."

"You mean to tell me that Sikander North stole Marid Pasha's cruisers and handed them over to the Velaran government?" Elena stared at the screen in amazement. She'd figured that the Aquilan captain would do something with the evidence she'd handed him—after all, she knew that he shared her disgust at the Zerzuran government's corruption. *But seizing the pasha's new fleet? That certainly escalated in a hurry!* "Can the Aquilans do that?"

"Short answer: None of the talking heads on the newscast know, but the ships are here. Longer version: The Aquilan diplomat who was negotiating with Marid Pasha—Darrow, the special commissioner—claims that they can. He's here, too. In fact, he just issued a statement that establishes the legal underpinnings of the seizure and goes on to explain that Aquila's got proof that the highest levels of the Zerzuran government are complicit in piracy. I have to imagine that's based on the evidence we turned over to your friend Captain North, which means that Pegasus-Pavon's role in this whole affair may very well become public knowledge. I have no idea what that means for us, so I woke you up."

Elena slipped out of bed and reached for a robe, gazing out the window at the bright lights of Baybars City in the distance as she thought over the implications. Her snap reaction was that Marid Pasha was going to be *pissed*, and that he'd take it out on anybody involved in the situation. *That's what we get for trying to do our civic duty*, she fumed. *It's all going to blow up in our faces anyway. Marid Pasha's going to seize our shipping.* Then again, she'd already anticipated that possibility, so it wasn't like cooperating with Aquila had really cost her anything. Passing her information about Rihla Development over to Sikander North had just ensured that Marid Pasha paid a price for his unsavory business relationships . . . *a very public and humiliating price*, she reminded herself.

"Do we need to implement our Roanoke plan?" Omar asked, guessing at the direction of her thoughts. That was the worst-case scenario for the emergency withdrawal of Pegasus-Pavon assets and personnel from Zerzuran territory. The latest version was sitting on her desk in the Pegasus-Pavon regional headquarters building in downtown Baybars, waiting for her to give the order.

"Not yet," she said slowly, glancing back at the newscast. An inset window now appeared in the display, showing the Aquilan envoy—Darrow, she reminded herself—taking questions after his statement. "If the arrival of those cruisers is news *here*, I have to imagine that their sudden departure from Dahar is certainly news *there*, which means that everybody in Zerzura knows that the Aquilans are calling the pasha's government a pirate regime. And everybody in Zerzura also knows that Marid Pasha couldn't stop them from taking away his new fleet."

"You're thinking that the local decision makers will be distracted by the Aquila-Zerzura crisis."

"And the question of whether Marid Pasha can survive politically. No one in the Caliphate wants to back the wrong horse, and the leading power in human space just announced that they regard Marid al-Zahabi as a local criminal with delusions of grandeur. How much do you want to bet that Marid Pasha is already screaming to anyone who'll listen that he was doing his best to fight piracy until the Aquilans backstabbed him?"

"Sorry, but I don't think I'll take that bet."

Elena smiled to herself in the shadows by the balcony door. "Clever fellow. Notify the executive leadership team that we're going to meet as early as possible tomorrow morning . . . say, seven A.M. I want to know whether PR and Legal think we should acknowledge our cooperation with Aquila's investigation, or stay quiet about it. I'd also like Security and Operations to take a look at what happens if the Zerzura Sector Fleet gives up on enforcement altogether, not that they were doing much to begin with."

Omar glanced down at his dataslate and made some notes. "Okay, I'll pass the word to everybody and pick up the doughnuts and coffee. See you in a few hours, boss."

Elena considered going back to sleep, but she found that she was too awake to make that a possibility. The more she thought about it, the more exposed Marid Pasha seemed to be. *They say that sunlight is the best disinfectant,* she reminded herself. Well, the Aquilans had dropped a fusion bomb of sunlight on Zerzuran politics, and followed it up with an action so spectacular and unexpected that it would be impossible for Marid Pasha to shrug off the accusations as some sort of misunderstanding. More to the point, Marid Pasha and Torgut al-Kassar—and any other Zerzuran officials involved with Rihla Development or similar schemes—couldn't protect their pirate allies any longer. And *that* meant the murdered crewhands of *Carmela Día* and half a dozen other ships and posts might finally receive the justice they deserved. She brewed herself a pot of excellent Mount Kesif coffee and watched the sunrise while savoring that thought.

By the time the morning meeting arrived, Elena had already decided that Pegasus-Pavon didn't need to make any special effort to keep its role in the antipiracy investigation quiet. If Marid Pasha attempted to retaliate against the company for helping to establish the facts of *Carmela Día's* plundering, he'd only confirm that he had something to hide. Likewise, it seemed unlikely that pirates under the pasha's control—direct or indirect—could hardly target Pegasus-Pavon shipping without creating similar problems for Marid, so there was no need to implement the Roanoke plan quite yet. Elena's regional executives agreed that they could await developments, although the heads of security and operations recommended that they continue to vary their arrival and departure schedules until they were certain that the situation in Zerzura had improved.

Shortly before noon, Elena's receptionist called to inform her that she had an unscheduled visitor: Meritor Pokk Skirriseh. *What does he want?* she wondered, but kept it to herself. Instead she cleared her calendar for an hour—it never was a good idea to keep a Paom'ii waiting. "Send him in, and have Mr. Morillo join us," she told the receptionist. "Hold my calls until our guest is done with his business."

The Paom'ii officer shambled into her office and nodded to her. He wore a burgundy kilt and harness with silver fastenings, the alien version of the Velaran naval dress uniform; his people rarely dressed casually. Elena came from around her desk to greet him instead of offering him a seat—Paom'ii didn't much care for human chairs, either. "Meritor Pokk, this is an unexpected pleasure," she said. "How can I help you today?"

"Ninety days ago at the Founding Day celebration on Dahar, you asked Captain Szas to look into the disappearance of your ship *Carmela Día*," the Paom'ii said without preamble. "Captain Szas explained that we could not proceed to Bursa. You then asked us to urge the Zerzura Sector Fleet to redouble their efforts to find your missing ship. I regret that at the time I assumed the Zerzuran fleet was taking all appropriate steps and that your concerns were unwarranted. Today's news has now made it clear that you had good reason to be concerned about Zerzuran malfeasance."

I don't believe it, Elena thought. *Is a Paom'ii trying to actually* apologize *for something?* She took care to keep her expression neutral, and gave the alien a small nod. "In all honesty, Meritor, I didn't suspect that such highly placed officials would turn out to be involved. I thought I was up against routine bureaucratic indifference—that's why I asked for your help."

"The Aquilan envoy claims that a Zerzuran firm called Venture Salvage sold cargo stolen from *Carmela Día*. This claim serves as the critical link that directly ties those highly placed officials to an act of piracy. The Electorate government is greatly disturbed by this possibility, Ms. Pavon. I am required to ask if your company can positively identify the goods in question before the Electorate takes action on this matter."

"We can," she told Meritor Pokk. "There's no doubt about it—we've already identified the specific cargoes by planet and date of sale. I can provide you with our investigators' reports, if you like."

"That will be helpful. Have them sent to me today," Pokk replied, and turned to go. "Good day, Ms. Pavon."

Elena hadn't expected a thank-you, but she'd hoped that the surprise visit might at least shed a little light on whether the Velaran Electorate agreed with the Aquilan navy's actions or intended to do anything with the evidence that had been presented. "Just out of curiosity, Meritor: What's going to happen to the Zerzuran ships?"

The Paom'ii paused, glancing back over his shoulder. "It is a complicated situation, and the lord arbiter's office will require some time to make a determination. The ships may be returned to Zerzura. They may be returned to Dremark. They may be claimed by Aquila as prizes. Or they may be scrapped in an effort to find an outcome that satisfies no one, which might be the wisest course of action. I, however, intend to argue before the lord arbiter that the Electorate navy is entitled to compensation for *Vashaoth Teh's* destruction and that we should retain possession of at least one ship. After all, the Meliyan Human Revolution's claim of responsibility for the attack appears to implicate Marid Pasha's government, and they may have received some amount of technical assistance from Dremark's Security Bureau. Someone owes us a cruiser, Ms. Pavon."

"I see. Thank you, Meritor."

Pokk gave a small shrug, and continued on his way without another word. Elena sat down again, gazing after him. She was no diplomat, but one couldn't run a shipping line doing business in four stellar polities and dozens of worlds without developing some sense for the ebb and flow of international relations. *I can't even imagine how this is all going to sort itself out in the end. I wonder if Sikander saw this coming when he decided to take the pasha's ships.* She shook her head, amused that her Aquilan captain had managed to so completely surprise her. *Whatever else happens, Marid Pasha isn't going to declare independence without a navy . . . and the Dremish are going to think twice about giving him another one.*

She resolved to ask Sikander about it the next time she saw him. But *Decisive* departed the next day, and Elena didn't get a chance to see Sikander before he left.

Gunshots—the shrill chirping reports of mag-weapon fire, to be more precise—awakened Marid al-Zahabi an hour before dawn.

His eyes flew open and he rolled out of bed, instantly alert; he'd always had the knack for waking up fast. A concealed holster secured under the side of the bed he customarily slept on held a fine Cygnan mag pistol and a comm device. He drew the weapon, chambered a round, and moved over to crouch behind a large sofa that stood in the bedroom's sitting area, distantly noting the brilliant gold gleams of sunrise illuminating the marvelous cloudscape his windows overlooked.

"Major Terzi, report!" he snapped into his personal comm. "What's happening?"

Ibrahim Terzi, the commander of Marid's palace guard, took a long moment to answer. "Troops are moving on the palace, Excellency," he replied. "I do not believe we can ensure your safety. We must prepare to evacuate."

"Troops?" Marid demanded. "What troops?"

"Your own, sir. They appear to be soldiers of the Third Mansur Guards. General Karacan has issued a declaration stating that he's temporarily assuming the governorship and instituting martial law."

Several questions warred for Marid's attention at once—*What is the meaning of this?*, *On whose authority?*, *Which units remain loyal to me?*, and *Where are we evacuating to?*—but he silenced all of them with a single savage growl. He could work out those answers soon enough, if he managed to avoid arrest. In the meantime, every second he spent demanding Major Terzi's attention reduced his chances of remaining out of General Karacan's hands, and therefore his ability to fight for his governorship at least a little bit longer. This was an occasion for action, not useless shows of indignation. The first step was simple: Get dressed and get out of the palace before the disloyal troops secured the building.

"I will be ready in just a moment," he told Terzi. "Come get me." Then he hurried over to his closet and dressed himself. *It would be Karacan*, he fumed as he pulled on his clothes. The general was up to his eyeballs in his own unofficial activities, raking in a vast fortune from various creative military purchasing agreements and a willingness to look the other way when paid to do so. No doubt he'd come to the conclusion that moving against Marid was the surest way to appease the Caliphate jurists and news networks emboldened by the events of the last few weeks to examine questions of public corruption, and perhaps evade scrutiny for his own wrongdoing. *He might even hope that he'll be able to assume my governorship by being the loudest member of the mob coming after me, the miserable dog!*

He tapped his comm device again as he dressed, and called Torgut al-Kassar. "Admiral, I am shifting my command center to the fleet base. Make sure that the security stations and defensive systems are manned by troops personally loyal to you—many of our personnel may be confused about whose orders to follow."

The admiral scowled. "I'm working on that, but Karacan's damned broadcasts aren't making it any easier. My own flag lieutenant just tried to arrest me. Can't you shut down his access to the planetary comm network or issue a statement of your own?"

"I would prefer to do that from the vantage of High Port," Marid Pasha said. "In the meantime, I would like you to make sure that no one shoots down my orbiter on approach."

He cut the connection and headed for the door, fastening the last button of his military tunic as he emerged. Terzi and his escort—eight veteran soldiers, each of them a man who had served with Marid in campaigns going back almost thirty years—waited in the antechamber. The firing outside had died down; he hoped that meant his palace troops had repelled the Mansur Guards for the moment.

"The landing pad, Major," Marid said. "We must reach my orbiter."

"Of course, Your Excellency," the major said. He fell in beside Marid.

Marid took three steps, heading down the hall toward the palace's landing pad . . . and then froze in midstride as he felt the barrel of Terzi's mag pistol in his ribs. At the same time, six of the guards in his detachment suddenly pivoted to point their weapons on the remaining two. "You, too?" he said, glaring at his chief bodyguard.

"General Karacan gave me very specific instructions before sending his troops to secure the palace, Your Excellency," said Terzi. He carefully disarmed Marid, taking the pistol from his holster and tucking it into his own waistband. "I sincerely apologize, but the situation demands your arrest and replacement. I had no choice but to comply."

"What now?" Marid asked. "You're a fool if you think that Karacan is going to survive this. Whatever he promised you, Major, you're never going to see it."

"That may be true, but we have to start somewhere, sir. When evidence implicating General Karacan surfaces, I'll arrest him too." Terzi shrugged. "It's long past time for someone to clean up Zerzura. You used to be an honest man and an honorable commander; I'd like to think that part of you recognizes that this is necessary."

To his surprise, Marid found that the major's words stung him. He bit back on angry retorts and empty threats before he lost his composure, and simply nodded at the two guards who had remained loyal to him. "Lower your weapons, old friends," he told them. "I don't want your blood on my conscience. Let's go, Major."

Shoulders squared and head held high, Marid Pasha marched off to meet his fate.

Otto Bleindel woke up in a clean white room with windows that looked out over a brilliant blue sea. A pleasant lassitude seemed to infuse every centimeter of his body, although he was aware of a dull and distant ache on the left side of his jaw and additional soreness on the right side of his chest and in his right hip. *I'm sedated*, he realized. *Now why would someone do that?* It was a curious little mystery, but it didn't seem very important to solve it right away, so he gazed at a green palm frond waving gently in a breeze and thought about nothing at all for a long time.

After a while, a metallic clatter on the other side of the room caught his attention. With an effort, he rolled his head to look the other way, and saw that the doorway leading into the room was secured by steel bars. A round-faced woman in a white doctor's coat waited patiently while two soldiers in the green jackets of the Aquilan Commonwealth Marine Corps unlocked the door and escorted her inside. She came over to his bedside, and nodded in satisfaction when she saw that he was awake.

"Good afternoon, Mr. Bleindel," she said. "I'm Commander Soto, and I'm the doctor entrusted with your care. I have to say that you're looking much better today. I don't think you'll be staying with me much longer."

"Where am I?" he asked, and regretted it almost at once. Talking hurt his jaw—there was nothing distant or dull about the stab of pain that came from speaking aloud.

"Careful, there," Soto told him. "Your mandible—er, jawbone— was badly damaged by a mag dart, and while we manufactured a good fill for the missing bone, you still have some serious dental work ahead of you once the new bone finishes healing up. To answer your question, you're in the medical ward of the brig in the Tawahi Island Naval Base on Neda. You've been unconscious for most of the last two weeks, so I imagine that's a little disorienting."

"I'm a prisoner," he said, careful to move his mouth as little as possible when he spoke—a statement, not a question.

"I'm afraid so, although that hasn't made any difference in the medical care you're receiving. We are doing our best to help you recover from your injuries. What happens after that is not in my hands, but you still have your life, Mr. Bleindel. That was touch and go for a while."

"Injuries?" he asked. The trick to managing the sore jaw was to avoid using any more words than he absolutely had to.

"The jaw you already know about. You're fortunate that you were hit from the side; the dart passed through your mouth without hitting any vital structures, although I know it's very uncomfortable. You also were shot in the right hip—that one cracked your pelvis and required the surgical repair of your hip socket—and through your right lung, which very nearly killed you. Oh, and you also had a clean through-and-through in your left calf muscle, but that wasn't so bad. Fortunately the Navy corpsman who treated you aboard *Meduse* managed to keep you stable until *Decisive's* Dr. Ruiz was able to take over your treatment at Meliya. You owe your life to their efforts."

Meduse, Bleindel realized. *I was aboard* Meduse. *The Aquilans seized the cruisers in the shipyard, and we armed* Neu Kiel's *sailors to take them back.* Then the rest of it came back to him—the fight in the passageway outside the bridge, the escape scuttle, the search for something that could be turned into a bomb, the confrontation with Sikander North . . . "He shot me!" he snarled in anger, and instantly regretted it.

"Well, yes," Dr. Soto said. "That's what I was just explaining.

Can I get you anything, Mr. Bleindel? You're not ready for solid food, but we can bring you a protein shake or some pudding."

Bleindel waved her away. "Not hungry."

"I'll check back on you in a little bit," the doctor replied, evidently deciding to choose her battles. She retreated from the room, leaving Bleindel to his thoughts.

Two days after he first woke up—and half a dozen protein shakes later—Bleindel felt strong enough to sit up in bed, which provided him with a better view of the bars on the windows and bright sand beach outside. As much as he would have liked to surprise his Aquilan hosts by escaping from their medical ward, he had to admit that wasn't going to happen with his right leg immobilized from knee to pelvis and barely enough strength to reach for the attendant call button when he needed help relieving himself. That afternoon, Dr. Soto returned with a familiar face: a towering, brawny man in the uniform of Gadira's Royal Guard.

"You have a visitor, Mr. Bleindel," Dr. Soto announced. "This is Colonel Tarek Zakur of the Gadiran Royal Guard."

"I know him," Bleindel mumbled. His jaw did not hurt quite so much, but he was acutely conscious of the missing teeth.

"I'm pleased that you remember me," Tarek Zakur said. He grinned in a distinctly predatory manner. "Commander North was kind enough to send word to Sultana Ranya that you were in Aquilan custody; I came as quickly as I could. You may be interested to learn that you're being extradited to the Sultanate of Gadira to face charges related to certain acts of terrorism and insurrection during your last visit to our world."

"I want to speak to a representative of my government." That was the longest sentence Bleindel had spoken since waking up, but he deemed it worth the effort.

Soto nodded. "We sent word to your consul that you were in our custody, awaiting extradition. I believe she plans to visit later this afternoon, although I'm not sure what she can do for you—I'm a doctor, not a lawyer." She looked over to Tarek Zakur. "And, just so we're all clear, I'm not quite prepared to release Mr. Bleindel for transport. He won't be going anywhere for at least forty-eight hours."

The big Gadiran shrugged. "As you wish, Doctor. I'll wait."

25

To absent friends," said Sikander, raising his glass: dark, aged rum that represented the finest Navy spirit in his cabinet. He rarely drank hard liquors, but today was an exception.

"To absent friends," Decisive's officers answered, honoring the ancient toast. Fourteen of the seventeen officers under Sikander's command stood assembled on the patio of his Tawahi Island bungalow, resplendent in their dress whites. Jaime Herrera had drawn the short straw, remaining aboard the destroyer as the duty officer; he'd observe the tradition later. For Grant Edwards and Zoe Worth, however, the absence was more permanent. They would remain under the manicured green lawn of the Tawahi Naval Cemetery, where Sikander and his company had just said their final good-byes.

Sikander sipped the strong, sweet liquor, closing his eyes and savoring the taste as he thought of the fine people Decisive had lost at Dahar. Zoe Worth had been killed in the fight for control of Zyklop's bridge before the cruisers got under way; Grant Edwards had died aboard Decisive when a K-cannon round from Polarstern had wiped out the damage-control station that was his post during general quarters. Twenty-nine of Decisive's enlisted company had likewise fallen, killed in the gunfights aboard the cruisers or lost during the ensuing naval duel between the destroyer and the Dremish auxiliary cruiser.

Was it worth their lives? Sikander wondered. *Bringing down Marid Pasha and checking one small move in the great game?* Captain Broward seemed to think so; after overcoming his astonishment at the reports coming out of Dahar—and digesting a direct note from Eric Darrow on the circumstances surrounding the shipyard raid—he'd decided that the success of the mission warranted enthusiastic public praise, and showered Sikander with congratulations on what he described as "a textbook example of command audacity and initiative." Sikander knew that the squadron commander meant well, but he'd felt sick at heart about accepting Broward's praise for an operation that had left thirty-one of his ship's company dead. In the long run, he found it hard to believe that the questions of who controlled the Zerzura Sector or how they managed their affairs counted as vital interests of the Aquilan Commonwealth.

He looked up and saw the familiar faces of the men and women under his command, some staring at their feet, others gazing out over the ocean, one or two with heads bowed and tears on their cheeks. *If I have these doubts, they certainly do as well,* he reminded himself. *They're looking for meaning in this too.* And he realized that it was up to him to try to make the case that their friends and colleagues had not died for nothing.

He cleared his throat, thinking about what he wanted to say; the assembled officers looked up at him, waiting. "In my faith, we do not mourn for the dead," he began. "We believe that death is a necessary part of the cycle of existence, the moment when the soul is finally freed of the body to be reborn or to find union with God. Neither Grant nor Zoe shared that belief—nor did any of the others we lost, except for Darvesh Reza—but I'd like to think that they would not want us to grieve for them. Instead, we mourn for ourselves. Our friends have gone on ahead of us; we will miss them. My beliefs permit me to be saddened by that, even as I celebrate their lives and commend them to God's care.

"I wish that the cost of our victory was not so high. I wonder why they had to die at this time and whether it was necessary for us to fight at Dahar. Those are questions that have no easy answer. I think that all I can say is that we put on this uniform in the service of something greater than ourselves—not just the flag of the Commonwealth, although there is no shame in loving the nation in which you were born, but also in the service of certain ideals: to protect those who need protection, to stand against injustice, to carry ourselves with honor. Grant and Zoe lived those ideals, and lived them well. That's what I choose to remember today, and I find comfort in it. I hope you do, too." Sikander paused, and then nodded at the food and drink arranged on the serving tables; he'd borrowed the services of a couple of *Decisive*'s mess stewards to assist in the absence of Darvesh's expertise. "So honor their service, share some stories about better times, and raise a glass or two or three to our absent friends. They wouldn't want us to be sad for long."

"Well said, Captain," Amelia Fraser said. Then she glanced down at her empty glass and made a show of looking around. "Now where's the bar, again?" A ripple of chuckles passed through the somber gathering.

Sikander smiled—naturally, Amelia had seen that someone needed to punctuate the moment, and perhaps take one small first step in the healing process. "To your left, XO," he said. The assembled officers went for refills or made their way toward the buffet; a murmur of conversation began.

Even though he didn't feel very hungry, Sikander helped himself to a modest plate to signal to his junior officers that the buffet was not just for show. He also refilled his glass, but he switched to a cold lager: hard liquor in the middle of the afternoon was something best taken in small doses, in his opinion. He found a barstool at the house's kitchen-patio counter, and devoted himself to his food for a moment.

Amelia came up and took the seat next to his. "Good work, Sikander," she said quietly. "I think they needed this."

"I think *I* needed this," Sikander replied. "Are you ready to take command again?"

"Two weeks of yard time. I think I'll manage." *Decisive* had another date with the shipyard to repair the battle damage she'd suffered. In the meantime, Sikander had something he needed to see to, so he would once again leave his exec in charge during his absence. Amelia grew somber. "I'm sorry I got her all banged up, especially after you trusted me with the keys."

"Amelia, you did as well as anybody could have at Dahar. You handled *Decisive* brilliantly; I can't think of a thing I would've done differently if I'd been on the bridge and you'd been over on *Meduse*. My report to Captain Broward is very clear about that— and so is my endorsement on your fitness report." Sikander met her eyes. "You're more than ready for your own command."

"Thank you, Captain." Amelia took a deep breath, looking around the patio at *Decisive*'s surviving officers. "It'll be hard to leave, though."

"We've got you for a couple of months yet," Sikander told her. "Besides, the Navy is a smaller club than you think. You'll serve with some of us again—you'll see. Now, if you'll excuse me, I think I'll make the rounds and see how my guests are doing. For that matter, I think I could use a few good memories or funny stories, myself."

The next evening, Sikander returned to his bungalow late after a long day of meetings in the squadron office and a careful review of *Decisive*'s work orders for the upcoming return to Neda's shipyard. He was just settling into his favorite chair for one more pass through the ship's official report on "the Dahar incident" (as the raid on the shipyard was now being referred to in the newscasts and squadron correspondence) when he was interrupted by a knock at his door. He looked up in surprise; anyone from the ship would have called if they needed him for something, and everyone in the squadron office generally went home by dinnertime. He set down his dataslate and padded over to the door, checking the security cam more out of curiosity than anything else.

Elena Pavon stood on his doorstep, looking up at the cam with an impish smile on her face.

Sikander hurried to unlock the door. "Elena! This is a surprise."

"Well, I didn't tell you that I was coming." She moved into his arms and kissed him lightly, before pulling away again. "I hope you don't mind. Is this a good time?"

"The only thing you're interrupting is some paperwork, and it turns out that the Navy isn't in any danger of running out. Come on in—can I get you something to drink?"

"Please. A little white wine or sangria if you have it."

"I do." She followed him to the kitchen, and watched him rummage around in the refrigerator until he produced a half bottle of sémillon left over from the previous day's gathering. He poured her a glass, and then one for himself. "What brings you to Neda?"

"I'm my way back to Nuevo León to bring my father up to date on events in Zerzura. It turns out that Suvar United is in all kinds of trouble after Hidir al-Kassar skipped the sector, and there might be an opportunity for Pegasus-Pavon if we aren't too risk-averse. Anyway, I decided to stop by since you're sort of on the way." She sipped at her wine, and pointed the glass at him. "I'm a little angry with you, Sikander. You popped into Meliya and then bolted off so quickly that I didn't get a chance to see you. You couldn't take a moment to answer a message?"

Sikander winced. "I apologize for that. I was under strict instructions from Mr. Darrow to be on my way as quickly as I could after handing the Dremish ships over to the Electorate authorities. He was worried that *Decisive's* presence in the area was provocative—you should have heard the things the Dremish consul at Meliya was saying!—so he sent us back here. I didn't even look at my correspondence until we were bubbled up and on our way home."

She made a face. "Out of sight, out of mind, I suppose. What's next for you?"

"*Decisive* needs some repair work, so it's back to the shipyard. We won't be going anywhere for a while. In the meantime, the Admiralty is going to review every step I took to determine whether I was out of my mind when I decided to seize three warships that didn't belong to us and trade fire with the Empire of Dremark. Generally speaking, we're not supposed to risk starting a war without checking first."

"Your admirals think you went too far at Dahar?"

"*I* think that perhaps I went too far at Dahar. If I'd known that *Polarstern* was so heavily armed, I never would have risked the confrontation. I was fortunate that we got away with it—and my superiors are very much aware of that." Sikander took a sip, trying not to dwell on what that might mean for the continuation of his career. Eric Darrow endorsed his actions, which certainly helped . . . and a very narrow reading of his orders to take aggressive action against piracy just barely extended to keeping three major warships out of Marid Pasha's hands, once the pasha's involvement in Zerzuran piracy had been established. Captain Broward might have publicly endorsed Sikander's actions, but whether he would let Sikander out of his sight for the duration of his tour in Pleiades Squadron was far from clear. "There's another board of inquiry in my future, I'm afraid."

"Another?"

"Gadira, eight years ago. I have something of a reputation."

Elena laughed at that. "At least Neda seems like a pleasant place to wait while everything gets sorted out."

"It will be, when I get back," Sikander replied. "I have something I need to do back home first. I'm scheduled to depart for Kashmir tomorrow."

Elena frowned. "Oh. I have the most miserable sense of timing."

"It's not too bad—I should be back in about two weeks, and then *Decisive* needs another six weeks in the shipyard to repair the damage we suffered. After that? My tour of duty in Neda lasts another eight months." Sikander gave her a small shrug. "I'll be around."

"I might not be—I've got work to do in Dahar and Meliya after I finish in Nuevo León. Did I mention that the Zerzuran market is wide open for expansion these days?"

"I'm pretty sure the Admiralty's not going to let me anywhere near Dahar for the rest of my tour here," Sikander said with a bitter smile. *Why is it that I keep getting involved with women just before I have to leave?* he asked himself. Ranya el-Nasir, Lara Dunstan, Elena Pavon . . . the pattern might be familiar, but that didn't mean it hurt any less. "I guess that it's a good thing you decided to stop by today."

"So what now?" she asked.

There was an obvious answer to that question, but he realized—somewhat to his own surprise—that it wasn't what he wanted at the moment. "I lost a good friend at Dahar, one of the best men it's been my privilege to know," he said slowly. "Would you mind if we took the bottle down to the beach and just talked for a while? I could use the company."

"I'm sorry, Sikay." Elena's expression softened. "That sounds good. I think I could use something like that, too."

They spent the rest of the night on the cool sand, watching the dark ocean and talking beneath the stars.

Six days after saying good-bye to Elena, Sikander stood on the beautiful green banks of the Palar River on Jaipur at sunset and waited for Darvesh Reza's cremation to begin. It was a fine evening, warm but not humid, and the aromatic oils of the pyre filled the air with a rich and heady scent. In addition to the twenty or so members of the extended Reza clan who were present, a dozen of Darvesh's old comrades from the Jaipur Dragoons had joined the ceremony, standing a final watch over one of their own. Nawab Dayan, Begum Vadiya, Gamand and his family, and Sikander sat together on one of the low benches that faced the bier.

"You did well to bring him home, Sikander," his father said quietly as the granthi read the old verses from the Guru Granth Sahib. "His ashes belong on Jaipur."

"Thank you, Father." In Kashmir's New Sikh traditions, it was customary to cremate the deceased within three days of death if possible, but Sikander had decided that the delay involved with bringing Darvesh back to their homeworld was justified. He'd wanted to give Darvesh's family the opportunity to perform the funeral rites, and his own family a final chance to honor a man who'd stood beside them almost every day of the last thirty-five years. "It felt like the right thing to do."

As the sun slipped below the horizon, Darvesh's younger brother lit the pyre, since Darvesh had no children to observe the tradition. As the flames took hold, the assembled family and friends stood together to recite the ancient words of the Kirtan Sohila, the evening prayer; Sikander joined in, finding comfort in the unison of their voices: "Day after day, God looks after all beings. None can assess the price of the gifts, so how can the Giver be assessed? The day and hour of the wedding is fixed; gather and pour the oil upon the threshold. Bless the servant, so that union with the Master may be obtained. Into each and every home, into each and every heart, this summons is sent out; the call comes each and every day. Remember in meditation the One who sends the call, O Nanak. That day is drawing near."

The gathering fell silent as the flames grew brighter and louder, a brilliant blaze against the orange sunset. Sikander stood and watched for a time. When he saw the Rezas making their final gestures of farewell, preparing to return to their home for the days of readings from the Guru Granth Sahib that would follow the cremation, he stirred. "God is Truth," he murmured, and followed his family as they turned to make their way back home.

He found a young sergeant in the dress uniform of the Jaipur Dragoons waiting for him near the family flyer: one of Darvesh's nephews. Like his uncle, he was tall for a Kashmiri, standing half a head above the other dragoons in the household guard who accompanied the Norths anywhere they traveled in Kashmir, but he was broad through the shoulders and powerfully built, where Darvesh had been lean and bony. The big sergeant bowed to Sikander as he approached. "Nawabzada Sikander," he said. "I am Harman Reza, nephew to Darvesh. I hope that you will allow me to ask a favor of you in the memory of my uncle's service."

"In memory of your uncle's service you can ask me anything you like, Sergeant Reza," Sikander answered. "He saved my life on many occasions. I can't ever repay that debt, but I would like to try. What can I do for you?"

Harman Reza bowed again. "Please allow me to take my uncle's place by your side, Nawabzada. It would be my great honor to serve as your bodyguard and helper in your travels."

Taken aback by the younger man's offer, Sikander was not entirely sure how to answer. "Are you certain? I have no plans to retire from the Aquilan navy any time soon. We'll be away from home most of the time—I only spend a couple of weeks a year in Kashmir."

"I am unmarried. The travel does not deter me, sir."

Sikander considered the offer carefully. The Rezas had already made a great sacrifice on his behalf—not just in Darvesh's death, but also in his twenty years of service on distant worlds. Harman Reza might have the desire to see more of human space, but he would be missed by his family . . . and there was always the chance that, like Darvesh, he might not come home. Of course, the younger man would dismiss any concern for his personal safety—Sikander could see that much about him at a single glance—but how could he ask more of the Reza clan? "Does your family approve?"

"That is between me and my family, Nawabzada. But yes, they understand that I will be away for long periods of time and that my sworn duty is to protect you at all costs."

It's not a question of whether I can ask more of the Rezas, Sikander realized. *No, the question is how can I say no?* "In that case, Sergeant Reza, the honor is mine," he said. "I'll inform Colonel Nayyar that you are joining the household guard at my request. Make whatever arrangements you need to make tomorrow, and report to the palace the day after. I'm expected back aboard *Decisive* by the end of next week."

"Very good, sir," Harman Reza replied, a distinct note of satisfaction in his otherwise expressionless reply. He saluted, then strode away to rejoin his family.

Sikander watched him go, and sighed. Breaking in a new minder would doubtless bring all sorts of challenges. *I hope he can cook better than I can,* he told himself, and climbed into the luxury flyer; his father, his mother, and his brother had all waited patiently while he spoke to Harman outside.

"Is everything okay, Sikander?" his mother asked.

"I think it will be," he told her. "Let's go home."

ACKNOWLEDGMENTS

When you spend the better part of six months building a manuscript, it can sometimes be hard to see the forest for the trees. A good editor can help you find your way out of the woods; Jen Gunnels provided me with just the right amount of pointing in the right direction to sharpen up a key character or two and make this a much better story.

I've never had the pleasure of meeting him, but I would like to say that Larry Rostant knocked me out with amazing covers for my first three Sikander books. It's a rare pleasure to find that an artist has so perfectly captured the look of your character and your world. Likewise, my diligent copy editor, Terry McGarry, made this a better-looking book by catching dozens of small slips, including some sneaky continuity questions. Thanks, Terry.

Writing can be a lonely pursuit. It's easy to get caught up in what you're working on and forget to go do fun things with other people. Let me take this opportunity to say thanks to some good friends who help me keep at least one foot in the world outside my house. First, I'd like to thank Daniel, David, JD, and Mark for reminding me how much I enjoy racquetball after ten years of hardly playing at all. Next, I'd like to thank the stalwarts of BT6, especially Chris Z., for inviting me to explore some excellent breweries. Finally, I'd like to thank the Thursday night group—Steve, Milton, Jesse, Nathan, Steve W., and Chris—for some great gaming over the years. It's good to set down the (metaphorical) pen for a few hours a week!